TALON &

ARRABELLA

ORBUS IGNOTUM

The Greymage

"There is no light so bright
as that which rises from shadow."
— *Elarien Canticle, Verse IV*

Cover art by Paul Lucas

Cover Design by Patrick Dandrea

Map by Patrick Dandrea (created with Campaign Cartographer 3+)

ISBN (Softcover): 978-1-970726-09-1

Printed in the United States of America

First edition, 2025

10 9 8 7 6 5 4 3 2 1

Publisher: Greymage Publishing

Horseheads, New York

✶

For my wife,
whose strength steadies the storm,
my daughters, whose hearts kindle the light,
and my grandchildren, the bright tomorrow.

✶

From the Codex of the Elder Bough
A recovered fragment translated from the Valeheart leafscript, dated two
centuries before the First Rift.

✳ ✳ ✳

"When light forgets its path, and flame wears shadow's crown,
The bond of leaf and storm shall rise, two hearts unbound.
Where eagle sleeps and seed remembers,
Their names shall stand where others fall."

"One walks with bow, with wind and thorn,
The other, fire kindled, from ash is born.
Together they shall thread the Veil,
And where it breaks—they mend, or fail."

"Yet beware the gaze that does not blink,
The hunger old as root and ink.
What watches waits, and what waits weaves—
And not all seeds grow into leaves."

✳ ✳ ✳

— Attributed to Whispers, Tree-Speaker of the Vale of Eagles
Found inscribed on a blood-oak leaf
pressed between two pages of ashbark vellum

ORBUS IGNOTUM

Volume IV

The Chronicles of Talon and Arrabella

Books One – Five

A tale of flame and shadow, memory and light

Table of Contents

Book One

Roots of the Storm

"A root does not know the tree it will become.
It only knows the soil, and the storm."

— *Druid's Proverb*

Prologue

Oscar's Roots

An interlude from the Skythread logs

— Years 347–348 of the Second Age

*(During the short trade voyages preceding
the Skythread refit and the Great Mission)*

***

The Skythread drifted low over a wooded valley, her cloud-hull pearled with late light. Below, green rolled in heaves and folds—pine and oak and ferny gullies, streams threading silver toward a wider river.

Riggers called and answered. Ropes paid out. The ship settled like a great bird to hover among treetops while the crew made ready to descend.

"Plenty to forage," Briar said, shouldering a satchel. Her eyes slid to the aft mast. "But not water. That's handled."

A rigger nearby laughed. "Cisterns are near brim, druid! Enough for barrels, enough for cooking, maybe even a few baths if the captain doesn't find out."

More laughter. Someone groaned in theatrical despair.

Oscar flushed and tried not to look like the sort who would enjoy a shower every single night if allowed.

Briar wasn't always aboard the Skythread. She came and went like a migrating bird: present when the season asked for her, gone when the woods called her elsewhere.
But for this run—the last quiet year before the refit—she'd come along to help teach the new apprentices the difference between hunger and noticing.

Oscar, trailing after her with his humble satchel and his anxious heartbeat, wondered if she had come for him.

He tugged the weathered travel book from his belt pouch, thumbed the familiar frayed edge, and felt the quiet hum in the quill Thay'sa had given him. The hum was a promise: the book wrote back.

Runners lowered the gangplank. Briar nodded for the younger hands to follow. Talon stayed at the rail a moment longer with Bella beside him, both of them watching the valley with that half-guarded look they wore whenever sky met forest—the look of people measuring distance they didn't quite trust.

Oscar pretended not to notice. He tucked the book away and hurried after the foragers into the trees.

***

The forest was a tangle of resin and sunlit dust. Briar moved like she'd planted every trunk herself, stopping here to snap a twig, there to kneel and pinch at moss, murmuring the names of things that would soothe a burn or draw the sting from nettle rash.

"It's a pantry," she told Oscar without looking back. "But a pantry is kin to a chapel if you're paying attention."

"Is a pantry ever not kin to a chapel?" he asked before he could stop himself.

A grin ghosted over her shoulder. "Depends who's hungry."

They spread out. The older hands harvested berries and bark. Oscar kept to the edges, half-proud he could spot yarrow now without pointing at every similar thing and begging forgiveness.

That was when the sparrow found him.

It wheeled around his head, then snapped to a halt on his boot, tiny claws careful against leather. A chattering burst, a bolt away, then back again, insistent as a child tugging a sleeve.

"Shoo," Oscar said, and immediately felt foolish for it.

"Not at you," Briar called from somewhere in the green. "At something else. Listen."

Oscar swallowed. He remembered Bella's patient voice during lessons: *You can listen without words.*

He crouched. He didn't know if he believed in what came next, but believing was sometimes less important than trying.

He whispered the little chant Bella had taught him and he'd mispronounced a dozen times. The words snagged on his tongue. He tried again, softer.

For a blink, the world thinned. Panic brushed his mind like a cold finger: hollow place, teeth, danger—

The sparrow shot between two birches. Oscar followed, skidding—and stopped with his toes hanging over darkness. A pit gaped beneath a lattice of brush, its sides stabbed full of sharpened stakes. Fresh boot-marks scuffed the lip.

He backed away, breathing hard, anger rising hot and pointless at no one. When he found the others and pointed them to it, Briar's only response was a short, certain nod. Talon appeared—Talon was always simply *there*—eyes flicking from Oscar to the pit and back again. He offered no praise. But something in his gaze changed, as if a weight he'd been carrying shifted a finger's width. Then he turned and began to brush away sign, destroying the trap as neatly as a careful storm.

That night, Oscar wrote it all down: the sparrow, the hollow, the fear that hadn't been his and yet had been inside him.
The quill warmed and stroked the page by itself, Briar's looping hand spilling out as if she leaned at his shoulder.

See? Even a sparrow sings truth if you stop long enough to hear. Keep listening, boy. — B.

He couldn't help grinning. He tried to school his face when he glanced up, because Bella was there a few bunks over—pretending not to watch, pretending not to be proud.

***

Fog swallowed the shoreline two weeks on.
The Skythread hung in a gray world where even the gulls were suggestions. Oscar had the second dog watch. He paced. He tried not to yawn. He failed.

"Moths used to guide me," said Thay'sa from the prow, not turning. Her voice carried as if the fog cradled it. "When I was young and the woods refused my eyes. They always found the flame, even when I could not."

Oscar's throat went dry. He hadn't meant to say anything. He hardly ever meant to say anything to Thay'sa; his words went wrong around her like socks that twisted inside boots. But he thought of the moths, and the fog, and the little chant Bella had drilled and sighed about in equal measure.

He cupped his hands around the lantern and whispered. The sound caught, stumbled, and then went true.

A pale wing brushed his knuckle. Another. Then a cloud—soft as breath—circled the light, turning its glare to a silvered hush.

Thay'sa didn't look at him. She simply allowed herself one small, unguarded smile that felt like sunrise sneaking over a sill.

When the watch turned, Oscar fled to his bunk and cracked his book with hands that shook.
Ink bloomed into an image: a woman younger by centuries, her hair unthreaded by grief, striding through fog with lantern-moths blooming around her like a blessing.

She didn't speak. She didn't need to. The illusion's eyes found his, and he knew—simply knew—that she had sent it not by accident or habit but because she meant him to see who she had been, and to feel that he had lit some old, quiet room in her.

He pressed his thumb to the page. The image trembled and went still, as if it had held his hand and let go.

***

Heat came hard a month into the run. They moored low in a gap where rock shouldered out of the woods like a knuckle.

The crew sprawled with berry-stained mouths and sticky fingers and the indolent air of people who'd worked until their backs ached and found the results sweet.

Briar rolled onto one elbow, squinting at the bare outcrop. "Stone's a miser," she said. "But even misers misplace a coin."

Oscar blinked. "Is that a proverb?"

"It is now." She made a show of looking away. "Next time you camp on stone, coax something green from it. No excuses."

By the time he tugged his book free, the challenge was already written, her script teasing itself into existence: *No excuses* underlined twice.

He set his palm to a hairline crack. He tried the little Druidcraft murmur she'd shown him once and he'd murdered half a dozen times since.

Nothing.

He swallowed, closed his eyes, let the heat wash through him, and stopped trying to *make* anything. He tried instead to notice the lean of the sun, the sliver of damp still held in the stone's throat, the patient itch of earth wanting what it always wants.

A prickle answered his palm. He opened his eyes in time to see a green spear nose up through the crack.

It was small. It was everything.

He wrote with a grin that felt dangerous. Briar's ink came laughing down the page.

Told you. Life doesn't ask permission. It finds a crack and grows. — B.

When he glanced up, Briar was watching him sidelong with a look that said two things at once: *don't puff yourself up* and *remember this feeling, because it's the right one.*

***

"Try not to breathe like a thunderer," Bella told him that evening, watching him stalk an entirely innocent cooking pot. "Some of us are trying to think."

"I was thinking," Oscar said. "About... growing things."

"Excellent," she said. "Grow your patience first." Then, softer—because she could be softer when the ship quieted— "You know I'm not hovering, yes? If I write, it's because the margins are safer than my mouth. And if I ever step through—"

He looked up sharply.

"—it will be because you're bleeding out or the ship is on fire. I prefer the book." A hint of a smile. "It smells less of smoke."

"I don't think you're nosy," he said. It came out truer than he expected.

"Good," Bella replied. "Because Talon doesn't care if he seems nosy, and we can't have two of him."

He laughed, startled. She looked pleased with herself and pretended not to be.

***

The river's song drew them three days later. They moored above a long run where water combed itself through roots and stones, white in places, black in others.

It was here the cry came: high, furious, and afraid. Oscar slid before he thought, slipping down the cut bank with his hands out and his heart hauling like a bellows.

In a tangle of roots, a bear cub thrashed, one foreleg caught hard in a steel snare. Its teeth clacked in terrified warning.

He knelt. He did not reach. He breathed once, twice, remembered Briar's lesson about putting his ears in his chest and his chest in the ground.

He whispered the halting charm he'd mangled into usefulness by stubbornness alone.

The cub froze, eyes rolling to him, panting. Panic dulled to something that wasn't trust and wasn't not-trust.

He inched his hands along the wire, found the twist, and unwound it. The snare gave like a bitter joke. The cub's leg came free.

The wood breathed differently.

He turned his head slowly and found the mother bear already there.

She filled the gap at the top of the bank.
She came down with her hackles up and her jaw open and the steam of her breath in the cool shade.
She was the shape anger takes when it belongs to something righteous.

Oscar didn't move. He had no time for a bow or a blade or a book. He had the echo of the cub's breath against his hands and the thread of the charm still humming in his ribcage, and he had the frantic wish not to die.

He tried—clumsily, earnestly—to offer the wish to the same place the sprout had come from.

The bear stopped so near his skin prickled with the heat of her. Her eyes were wells, and he fell in.

Something weighed him. Something smelled the river and the boy and the copper tang of old snare-blood and the faint green echo of a druid's laughing lesson.
She rumbled low. It wasn't threat. It wasn't praise.
It was a statement: *not mine, but not strange to the world, either.*

She touched the cub with her muzzle and they went, the river closing the space behind them as if nothing had been there at all.

He stayed kneeling until the ache in his legs outshouted the thunder in his chest. He laughed once, softly, because he was not dead. Then he laughed again at the absurdity of laughing about that. Then, because he could not stop himself, he cried two quick tears that startled him with how hot they were.

Back on deck, he wrote. He told the page everything and then apologized to it for telling too much.

Ink bit back in two hands—Bella's quick, impatient slant: *Idiot boy. Brave idiot. Don't ever do that alone again. …But well done.*

And beneath it, a steadier script, each letter laid as if it mattered: *What you gave me I cannot repay. But when the day comes, I will be there—one way or another.* — T.

He put his thumb to Thay'sa's name until the ink warmed his skin.

***

They camped by the riverbank that night.
The fire burned down to a low, licking sleep. The others drifted off one by one.

Oscar stayed beside the embers with his knife turning idly over and over in his hands.

"You think I'll ever stop fumbling?" he asked the coals.

Talon shifted with a stone at his back and the sky in his eyes. "Fumbling's still moving."

"Half ranger, half mage, half druid—"

"That's three halves," Talon said, unimpressed. "You'll tear the world's math apart."

Oscar groaned. "You know what I mean."

11

Silence stretched, comfortable as an old cloak. Frogs took up their evening argument.

The river made its reasonable case to the stones and won, as it always did.

"Grow where you want," Talon said finally. "Roots don't ask permission. They twist, split, go where the earth lets 'em. Long as you reach for the sky, you're doing right."

Oscar looked up because he couldn't not.
The words had weight he wasn't used to hearing said aloud.

Talon tilted his head, deadpan. "Just don't turn into a morning glory. Viney little flowers all over the place, choking the good wood. I'll cut you down myself if you do."

Oscar barked a laugh that startled a bird from the reeds. Talon let the sound stand. For once, he even let the corner of his mouth admit it knew what a smile was.

They watched the strip of stars trawl slowly over the black seam of trees until the fire failed and the cold nudged them toward blankets.

***

They made two more days in the valley, filling sacks and barrels until even the gnomes admitted the ship could hold no more.

Everyone pretended not to hear the laughter that sometimes hummed in the pipes when the Skythread drank deep.

On the last evening Briar stood at the gangplank with her staff in the crook of her arm, looking down at the path that would take her back into the long green.

"I don't always sail," she said, not to Oscar and entirely to him. "But when a new root touches a hull, it's polite to be there when it takes."

He swallowed. "Thank you."

"Don't thank me," she said cheerfully. "Grow. Then bring me something worth teasing you about next time."

She thumped his shoulder with the back of her hand and went down the plank, and the shadows ate her in a way that made him certain she was ruled by them and not the other way around.

That night, after the final checks and the list of lists and the pesterings that kept ships from breaking, Oscar lay along the warm curve of the hull and opened his book.

The margins were busy: Briar's loops, Bella's neat corrections, Thay'sa's sparing line. There was nothing of Talon, of course. He stored his words in different places. But Oscar felt them pressed between the leaves anyway, like flowers hung to dry.

He wrote one line and then another, and somewhere past the middle of the page he stopped describing and simply told the truth:

I am not a ranger. I am not a mage. I am not even a druid. Not yet.

He let the quill hover. The ship creaked like a content animal settling into sleep.

But I am something. I am growing.

The letters looked small, but they did not look uncertain.

He closed the book. The quill cooled in his fingers. Wind passed over the deck with a sound like a mother's hand smoothing a brow. The Skythread lifted, light drawing under her like breath, and the valley fell away in slow folds until it was only a memory—and the stars were all that was left to steer by.

Chapter One

Stormlight

"Never trust a clear horizon.
The sky hides cliffs the sea never knew."

— *Marissa Veyne, first mate of the Skythread*

***

Late Summer 348 of the Second Age

The sky narrowed to a valley of dark iron. Cloud-walls rose like black cliffs veined with light; wind shoved hard from the west, a bully with cold hands. The *Skythread* took it with stubborn grace—keel-song thrumming, mastheads humming as she threaded high passes through the cloud-sea.

"Starboard two!" Marissa's voice cut the gale. She stood braced at the forward binnacle, half-elf poise turning chaos into lines and angles. The gyro-compass tried to lie; she glared it honest.

"Holding!" Oscar's knuckles whitened on the wheel, cheeks raw from wind-driven rain. Captain Tirpik moved like a hinge behind him—quiet, present, one hand on the taffrail, the other ready to steady the helm if the next gust tried to make poetry out of them.

A bosun's bellow rolled across the deck. Ballast shifted; water casks lurched. Lightning wrote bones in the belly of the storm, then rubbed them out with thunder.

"Main's talking," Marissa warned.

Tirpik turned to the mast. A wrong note lived in the timbers, a high keening under the honest creak.

"Corwin—"

"I hear it," Corwin snapped, hair plastered to his skull, quill still tucked behind his ear as if the storm would sign for receipt. He chalked a ward-circle on the slick deck—last resort, a minute's favor from indifferent gods.

The air prickled. Hair rose on wrists and napes. Lightning chose for them.

It came down like a verdict, found the main at mid-height, and rang it like a city-sized bell. Heat flashed cold; every line thrummed. Splinters spat. The *Skythread* sagged on her right shoulder with a sudden looseness that made stomachs go light.

"Topmast's sheared!" someone screamed.

"Hands aloft—Jil, take Hela's post! Knife that canvas before it clubs us dead!"

Tirpik's blade flashed. Sail went from plan to salvage in two strokes. The ship steadied a breath. Corwin's ward flared and guttered—good now only for keeping tools aboard. Oscar blinked through smoke and salt, knuckles bone-white on the wheel. The storm tested them again, less from malice than habit. The *Skythread* lived through out of habit, too.

When morning came, the world hung gray and hollow. The *Skythread* sagged in the wind's slack belly, her main still smoldering where lightning had carved its scar. Crew coughed smoke and soot, their movements slow, the sharp edge of panic dulled to exhaustion. The deck smelled of fire and wet oak; every groan of her hull sounded like pain.

Tirpik gripped the wheel, shoulders set. "We'll not limp home like a crippled gull," he growled. "She'll have a mast within two days."

Marissa was already at her slate, ticking down inventory. "We've spare spars—pine, not oak. They'll hold her rig for a while."

Corwin crouched beside the mast-root, fingers tracing the blackened grain. "The burn runs deeper than the wood," he murmured. "Lightning marked her keel through the join."

Oscar knelt nearby, Skyroot across his knees. "I can ease the splintering," he said, pulling a small pouch of herbs from his belt. "Same trick Briar taught me for bone fractures. Won't mend her, but it'll keep her from bleeding apart till we replace her."

Corwin looked up at him, rain streaking his face. "Since when do you patch ships like bones?"

"Since I started listening to the right teachers."

He pressed the poultice into the cracked join. A faint hum answered, the ship's groan softening by a measure. Marissa clapped his shoulder. "Good enough to keep her alive. But we'll need more than poultices—we need a mast."

Tirpik turned his gaze east toward the dark smudge of hills under clearing sky. "There—oak by the look. Straight, tall, and close enough to reach before dusk."

The crew followed his stare. Among skyfarers, any tree that grew in open air and weather like this earned the name *cloudwood*. It was only good hill oak, but sailors swore such timber carried luck if treated right.

"Axes and ropes," Tirpik ordered. "Corwin, you'll mind the lift. Oscar, you're with me."

They brought the *Skythread* down over the ridge and anchored above a clearing slick with rain. The smell of sap and soil rose through the wet air as the work party climbed down with saws and axes, boots sinking into loam. Tirpik laid a hand on one of the trunks—a proud oak with straight grain and steady heartwood. "This one," he said. "She'll carry us home."

Marissa's voice drifted faintly from the deck above through the speaking tube. "Don't take more than we need."

"Aye. One's enough."

The first swing bit deep. Erek and Jil followed, their strokes ringing in time until the tree shuddered, leaned, and fell soft into the clearing. They trimmed and bound it, ropes running up the ridge to the *Skythread's* winch lines. By the time they hauled it aboard, sweat had cut tracks through the grime on every face.

At dawn the next day, the work began in earnest. Corwin stood amidships, tracing sigils of levitation through the damp air. The charred mainmast lifted from its scarred socket, rising clean before tumbling into the valley below. "Clear!" he called.

The new oak came next, bound in guide-ropes. Acolytes along the rail whispered strength cantrips that lent muscle to every pull. Levers bit, pulleys groaned, and Tirpik's voice carried the rhythm:

"One—brace! Two—hold! Easy now!"

When the mast seated into its place, carpenters swarmed the deck. Wedges drove deep, pins hammered home, seams sealed with pitch and prayer. The oak settled like it had always belonged there.

Sailmakers salvaged what canvas they could from the ruined main, patching with spare cloth from the stores. The rest they'd replace once they reached Soahc. Yardarms went up, rigging re-run, blocks tested until the lines sang in the morning wind. Even after they set sail, the carpenters stayed aloft, truing the spar, tightening braces, and sealing seams while the *Skythread* glided through calm air. The smell of resin and oak replaced smoke and ruin.

By the seventh dawn, the sails filled again. The ship found her rhythm; the crew found their breath.

It was on the fourteenth night, when the stars crowded close and the wind forgot to misbehave, that the new mast sighed. Not a creak—a sigh.

Bark rippled across a handspan of the main where there should have been polish. Tiny leaves unfurled along the yardarm like green tongues tasting the night air. Oscar dropped his spyglass; it bounced off his boot and thought better of breaking.

Chapter Two

Season of Storms

"Storms test more than sails. They test the timber of the crew."

— *Fragment of the Mariners' Annals*

***

The storms had not relented since the lightning strike that marked the Skythread's mast.

A week on, the crew still swore the ship carried the memory of that blow—some claimed they heard a faint hum in the timbers when the wind shifted. Whatever truth lived in that tale, the storm season had only deepened. Each pass through the mountain cloud-sea felt narrower, darker, as if the sky itself remembered the strike and meant to test them for surviving it.

The sky had tightened to a keyhole in a mountain pass.

Storm-walls pressed in from both sides, tall as fortress ramparts, their bellies flickering with trapped lightning. A hard west wind slammed the Skythread broadside—flattening the sails one heartbeat and ballooning them the next, each gust trying to wrench the canvas clean off the masts. Yet she took it with stubborn grace: keel-song thrumming, mastheads humming as she forced her way through the highest corridors of the cloud-sea.

Tirpik braced at the wheel, jaw tight beneath his storm hood. Lightning skated along the nearest wall of cloud, too close for comfort, and thunder rolled hard enough to make the decking shiver.

"Lash it down!" Marissa's voice cut sharp above the gale. She was already halfway up the ratlines, silver hair plastered dark with rain, arms moving quick as knives as she tied off a shuddering spar.

Corwin leaned on the rail, robes whipped flat against him, muttering calculations under his breath. His fingers traced glowing runes in the air, measuring the storm's pulse and tilt.

"Not natural," he called over his shoulder. "The crosswinds are shearing against themselves. If we don't stay true on this line, the mast will—"

"—snap," Oscar finished, both hands gripping Skyroot like a staff to steady himself. He had Briar's old healer's pouch slung tight across his chest, crushed herbs filling the air with their sharp, bitter scent.

The ship pitched hard. Two deckhands lost their footing; Oscar dropped to a knee and caught one by the collar before the boy slid, shoving him back toward the ropes.

"Tie in!" he barked. "Don't make me drag you!"

The boy's wide eyes flashed gratitude before he obeyed.

Another fork of lightning burned the world white. This one struck true, slamming into the mainmast with a crack that deafened. The air filled with ozone, scorched timber, and a sound like glass screaming.

"Down!" Tirpik roared. Crew ducked instinctively as splinters flew. The mast split but did not fall; the druids' bindings and Marissa's knots held it upright—blackened, humming with a strange new energy.

Corwin's hands froze mid-rune. "That… shouldn't have held."

Oscar glanced at him, chest heaving from hauling lines. "You complaining it did?"

"No." Corwin's voice was hushed now, nearly lost in the storm's tantrum. "I'm saying something chose to hold it."

The mast trembled again, but not from the wind. A low groan ran through the deckboards—timber speaking in a voice none of them recognized. Marissa froze halfway down the rigging, eyes widening.

"Captain," she said softly, "that wasn't the ship."

Tirpik's knuckles tightened white on the wheel. "Whatever it was, it bought us time. Hold steady!"

The Skythread surged forward, storm roaring on all sides—but the crew felt something else in their bones now, as if another will had joined the fight, unseen but not absent, choosing in that instant to stand with them.

Chapter Three

Letter from Home

"Not every storm leaves wreckage. Some leave questions."

— *Mariners' Annals, addendum*

***

The storm passed as storms do—sudden in its fury, abrupt in its leaving. By dawn the sky had wrung itself dry, and the Skythread drifted in clean air. Her sails were patched, her lines checked, her crew bruised but standing.

Tirpik stood at the wheel, cloak stiff with dried salt, watching the first pale gleam of sun edge over the horizon. Marissa was beside him, compass steady in her hands, eyes sharp despite the sleepless night.

The mainmast still bore the scar where lightning had struck: blackened wood, char running like veins. Yet the mast stood solid, even proud, as though defying the storm that had tried to break it.

Oscar walked slow circles around it, palm brushing the grain, brow furrowed.

"Shouldn't be standing," he murmured.

"Don't start," a deckhand muttered nervously. "Ship's got enough ghosts without you calling more."

Corwin joined him, rubbing his wrist sore from too much rune-work during the gale. His gaze tracked the charred wood.

"It isn't just standing," he said. "It's… mending."

Oscar blinked. "Mending?"

Corwin rapped the mast with his knuckles. It returned a low, whole tone—not hollow, not split.

"Living things heal when they're cut," he murmured. "This feels the same. The grain's knitting back together."

Oscar's jaw tightened. "Trees don't grow on skyships."

"Not unless they want to," Corwin said quietly.

Tirpik's voice carried across the deck.

"Leave off poking it. We'll have druids look it over in port. Until then, we sail as she stands."

"Aye, Captain," both said, though their eyes lingered longer than they should have.

Later, as the crew broke bread on the morning watch, a strange quiet threaded the deck. Not unease—attention. The hush before a story begins. The mast groaned once in the new light, a sound deeper than timber ought to make. Every head turned.

Oscar lowered his cup.

"That wasn't wind."

Marissa scanned the rigging. "Then what was it?"

Corwin didn't answer. His mind was already racing, cataloguing every hum and tremor.

The Skythread carried on, sails full, mast silent once more. But each of them knew—without saying—that something had changed. The storm had left them with more than scars. It had left them with a presence, still hidden, but very much awake.

The ship found her rhythm again, creaks and hums settling into a kind of contented breathing. The crew went about their tasks with the brisk silence of folk who had been frightened and didn't want to say so.

Oscar lingered by the rail, Skyroot slung across his back, still feeling as if the storm had taken half of him with it.

A flutter startled him—not bird, not leaf.

Parchment spun down out of the empty sky and landed squarely in his hands. The seal was Arrabella's: a star circled by ivy. The ink shimmered faintly, as if resisting the long journey it had just made.

He blinked. "Uh... Captain?"

Tirpik squinted from the quarterdeck, then barked a laugh.

"Magic post. Looks like you've been found, lad."

Marissa leaned on the rail, grin tugging.

"Open it before the crew eats you alive wondering."

Oscar broke the seal. Arrabella's careful hand unfurled across the page.

***

Oscar,

These weeks you have been gone are not so long—unless you are the one counting each day. Then it feels like a season. Talon says you are learning more than you think. He remembers when the deck felt taller than his boots and the bowstring heavier than his will. If he found his footing, you will too.

The cabin is quiet. Balok's axe has been silent on the hearth—good news, we think. A little rain, but my garden is holding its own. Dug tramped through and scared the hens half to death, but they are laying again. Small mercies keep the days steady.

Briar insists I add something practical: drink the willow-bark tea if your head aches, and don't argue with the ship's cook no matter what stew he calls it. She says homesickness is like rain—it soaks, then passes, and the ground holds firmer for it. She's right, as usual.

We miss you, but more than that, we are proud of you. Write when you can. Magic travels faster than sails, after all.

   — Bella

***

He read it once, then again—slower this time. Crew sidled closer, pretending to mend rope or coil lines but fooling no one. When he finally looked up, the mainmast hummed softly behind him, as if the wood itself had strained to listen.

Marissa cleared her throat, voice gentler than usual.

"Well then, archer. Read it out proper. We're short on news from home."

Oscar hesitated, cheeks warming, then lifted the page.

Laughter landed in all the right places. Murmurs of agreement filled the quiet ones. When he reached *"a little rain,"* he stopped short and snorted.

"A little rain? Jeesh—if storms had mothers, the one we just sailed through was the great-granddam of the lot."

Laughter shook the deck, the kind that loosens fear and leaves only strength behind. Someone clapped him on the back; another muttered, "Rain passes," and meant it.

Oscar folded the page and tucked it to his chest. The shimmer of magic faded—the words were his now. For the first time since stepping aboard, the Skythread felt less like exile and more like a road.

***

The deck still smelled of pitch and new spar, the scars of the earlier storm not yet smoothed. Men tightened lines and caulked seams while the mainmast hummed faintly, mending itself in ways none of them understood.

Tirpik stood at the rail, arms folded, eyes narrowed at the bruised horizon.

"Storm season's worse than I've seen in twenty years. First takes a mast, second near splits another. Sky's got a temper this year."

Marissa, perched on the sterncastle with her logbook open, snorted.

"Not just temper. Feels like a siege. Clouds laying ambushes instead of passing like they ought."

Oscar, rubbing a sore shoulder, added, "Bella says we should drink willow-bark tea if our heads ache. And not argue with the cook, no matter what he's calling the stew."

He winced. "Probably shouldn't have said that out loud."

From the galley hatch came the cook's triumphant roar:

"Aye—smart lass, our Bella! Smarter than you lot, that's certain!"

The deck fell silent for a heartbeat—then burst into laughter again, bright and cleansing. The sound ran up the rigging and along the new mast like sunlight after storm.

Chapter Four

The Song in the Mast

"A ship remembers every hand that tends her,
and every hand that does not."

—*Dockside Saying, Port Ravenglass*

***

By the second day after the storm, the Skythread had found her rhythm again. Lines sang under tension, sails filled with honest wind, and crew voices rose in half-songs as they worked. To an untrained eye, everything looked ordinary.

But those who lived by decks and masts knew better.

The mainmast had taken to humming.

Not a constant sound, not loud—just enough to prickle ears on the night watch. A low tone, almost tuneful, rising and falling as though the ship herself were testing her voice.

Marissa paused in her rounds, palm pressed to the rail. "She isn't creaking," she said to Corwin, who was scratching notes into his weather-stained book. "She's… singing."

Corwin's quill froze mid-stroke. His lips tightened as he listened.

"Not singing," he murmured. "Speaking. We just don't know the tongue yet."

Oscar joined them, binding a deckhand's rope-burned knuckles. He frowned toward the mast.

"Trees don't speak."

"They do," Corwin countered, quiet and certain, "if they were born to."

His eyes narrowed. "This isn't lumber. It's listening."

Tirpik's gravelly voice ended the debate.

"Whatever it is, it's holding sail. That's enough. If it wants to chatter, let it chatter."

"Until it wants more than chatter," Oscar muttered.

That night, the voice came clearer—not words, not yet, but resonance. A vibration that made cups tremble on tables and lanterns sway though no wind stirred. Some of the younger crew whispered of spirits. Others prayed under their breath.

Oscar lay awake in his hammock, listening, trying to shape the sound. It reminded him of roots pressing through soil, of the hush in a glade where no axe had ever fallen. It wasn't cruel. But it wasn't silent either.

And though the Skythread cut through cloud with her usual grace, every soul aboard felt the truth settle deep:

The ship carried a new passenger now—one whose home was the mast itself.

***

The dreams began three nights later.

Soft rain pattered in every sleeping mind—not the pounding kind that drives sailors below, but a warm drizzle scented with spring leaves and clean earth. Each dream ended with the same feeling:

Wash the salt away.

When the message went ignored, the tone changed.

32

Crew woke with hair damp, blankets cool, and the scent of wet oak lingering in the air. Corwin admitted he'd seen green branches in his dreams—leaves trembling as if impatient.

By the fourth night, the rain stopped being polite.

It slipped through closed hatches, found hammocks and bunk-boards, and drenched every blanket aboard.

Oscar woke choking on a mouthful of water, sputtering and half-dreaming. The words echoed through him like distant thunder:

Wash up.

He bolted onto the deck, wild-eyed.

"Blast it all—she's leaking through the planks!"

Marissa stood in the rain, laughing despite herself.

"Leaking? Then why's it only you that's soaked, Oscar?"

The mast's hum deepened—amused, unmistakably alive. The drizzle turned playful, pattering over shoulders and hats, soaking even Tirpik where he stood at the helm.

"All right!" the captain barked, water streaming off his coat. "We hear you!"

Cursing gave way to laughter as the rain eased. It gentled into something softer—a baptism more than a scolding. Salt rinsed from skin, tar from rope, sweat from long days spent fighting storm and fear. The deck gleamed; the air smelled of sap and sky. The hum beneath their feet steadied into a slow, contented purr.

No one spoke of spirits after that.

They didn't need to.

The Skythread had chosen to remind them:

She was alive.

She was listening.

And she expected her crew to be clean.

Chapter Five

The Hums and the Hands

"Between one creak and the next,
a ship decides who she will trust."

—*Portside saying, scratched into a Grayhook railing*

***

The *Skythread* carried herself with an ease that belied the violence she'd just survived. Patchwork sails bellied cleanly; lines thrummed honest; the new main rose straight and pale, the lightning-scar a black vein running down its heart. To a passerby above the cloud-lanes, she looked only mended. To those who lived on her skin, she felt… attentive.

It began with the hum.

Not the old songs of strain and relief that any sailor could name in his bones, but a tone that lived in the grain itself. Low at first, like a kettle considering a boil. Then higher, just under hearing, the way a thought presses at the edge of speech. At night it laid a thread through the hammocks of the mid-deck; by day it trembled in the soles of boots when the watch crossed the shadow of the main.

"Ships talk," someone muttered, setting a coil true. "Always have."

"Aye," another answered, eyes sliding to the pale spar. "Just never heard one *listen*."

Marissa kept the log herself. She recorded wind and course, trim and temperature, cloud-pressure and drift. She did not ink the part where the night watch leaned their spines against the mast and swore they felt their pulse echoed back. Nor did she set down that Kit—fifteen, fixed on proving he belonged—woke from a doze swearing he'd dreamt of roots nosing through dark, gentle and inexorable. A captain didn't need madness in the book. But she walked the length of the deck between bells, palm to the rail, and she noticed where the wood warmed to her hand.

Oscar, binding a rope-burn that had kissed a knuckle raw, sniffed, frowning. "It smells green."

His patient made the sign against weather-charms. "It smells like *wood*, Oss."

Oscar shook his head, fingers steady as he tied. "Not tar. Not sunbaked. Green. Like sap." He tucked a smear of salve across the burn and patted it once. "Don't pick. I'll know."

He said nothing about the way the mast had thrummed against his palm two days prior—warm as a living wrist. He didn't know how to say it without sounding like he'd gone soft in the head. Briar would have teased him and then told him to trust the body of things. He trusted; he kept his mouth shut.

Corwin said less than usual, which worried everyone. He spent hours by the main, not chalking glyphs—that had felt wrong the moment he'd started—but listening. He pressed a knuckle to the scar and counted heartbeats. He held a tuning fork to the grain and watched the tines blur without his touching them. Once, he whispered a simple diagnostic charm that would have made rot blush out of lumber; the mast answered with a faint glow that moved like sap, not guilt.

"Not malicious," he said at last, to no one in particular. "Restless."

"Like you when ink runs low," Marissa said, passing.

He almost smiled. "Worse."

By second watch on the third day, the hum turned to something perilously close to language. Lanterns swayed though the air lay still. Cups quivered on tables. A deckhand with a voice like a rusty hinge hummed along without noticing. The pitch changed when the crew laughed; it steadied when Tirpik set a hand to the taffrail and took the helm through a crosscurrent with the gentleness he saved for bad nights.

"Captain," Marissa said quietly, watching the spar-lines stir without wind. "The crew's spooked."

Tirpik's eyes tracked the horizon, then the mast, then the horizon again. "Are they working?"

"Yes."

"Then let them be spooked on schedule." He shifted his grip, voice mild enough that only she heard the iron. "And if anyone says 'cut her free,' I'll hear it first."

He didn't have to wait long.

It came after noon, when labor makes courage foolish. Hest, who'd buried a brother in a storm five years back and had never forgiven weather for existing, spat through his teeth and jerked his chin at the pale spar. "We got a ghost in the timber. Don't care what your books say, wizard. I say rip her out before she rips us down."

Silence rolled like a wave across the foredeck. Corwin's mouth opened. Marissa's hand flicked a warning at him without looking. Tirpik turned slowly until the full weight of him faced Hest.

"What did she do?" Tirpik asked, and the pronoun wasn't lost on anyone.

Hest's jaw worked. "She hums. She… *answers* when you touch her."

"Like a good line does when it's taking your weight," Oscar said, voice even. He was coiling, not looking up.

"Like a friend does when you ask a thing hard," Marissa added, mild as summer.

Hest flushed brick-red. "It isn't right."

"Maybe not," Tirpik said. "But it saved your life when the lightning came. It holds our sail now. You want to gut your savior because the miracle offends your map?"

That wasn't fair; it was true anyway. Hest looked at his boots. Tirpik let him. "If harm comes, I'll answer for it," the captain went on. "Until then, we keep our rites. We keep our promises. We keep our heads. Understood?"

Murmurs. Aye. Aye. Hest nodded once, hard, and went back to work with rope that suddenly needed a great deal of attention.

That evening Oscar brewed willow-bark in a dented pot on the galley stove for wrists abused by line and weather. He dropped a thumb-sized piece of honeycomb in when no one was looking. Briar had said sweetness helped the body remember mercy. He poured three tin cups, left one on the capstan where the hum was strongest, and pretended he hadn't.

The cup went empty without a mouth touching it. No one remarked on that either.

Near midnight, Corwin found Marissa at the forward rail, chart tied down with a string of small stones against a breeze that didn't exist.

"You didn't write it," he said, nodding toward the log closed under her hand.

"No." She glanced sideways. "Do you want me to?"

He thought about words as tools: how the wrong ones bruise, how the right ones change the shape of a thing. "Not yet."

They stood and listened. The hum slipped up a shade, like a breath drawn before speech.

"Who are you?" Corwin asked the mast softly, scholarly mischief shut away for once. "What do you want of us?"

Marissa snorted. "Careful. If she's listening, she'll answer."

"If," Corwin said, because hope prefers grammar.

The answer came in morning's blue hour, the hush between watches when the deck is more thought than footfall. It was not a full word, not then. A syllable, lifted and left, like the first pluck on a string testing pitch.

Gr—

Marissa's head snapped up. She'd been cat-napping on a coil, one boot hooked through a rung so she wouldn't slide if a gust misbehaved. Her eyes found Corwin's in the half-light. He'd heard it too. So had Oscar, who surfaced from sleep like a man coming up from a deep pool, breath held without knowing.

—een—

The timber shivered, a ripple chased down its length, and knots that had been tied with miser's meanness eased a hair, as if someone had slipped a finger in to make room for breath.

"Saints," Oscar whispered. His hands were open and empty at his sides, the way you make yourself when approaching something that spooks easy. "She's… helping."

"That's what terrifies them," Corwin said, and then, gentler, to the mast, "We hear you."

Silence. The kind that isn't empty, just full of a choice being made. Then, lighter, almost shy:

—*bough*.

Marissa exhaled the laugh she hadn't meant to keep. "Greenbough," she said, tasting it, like a captain tastes a new wind for honesty. "All right, lady. We've a name for you."

The tone settled into something like satisfaction. A few of the crew who'd claimed they slept through storms dreamed of dappled shade and woke with the taste of rain on their tongue.

The day stretched clean. Work found its reasonable rhythms again. Men and women climbed, tied, sang. The hum answered when hands were kind and fell dull when tempers sharpened, which meant tempers didn't sharpen as often. Corwin, in a fit of either madness or genius, chalked a single glyph not for binding but for *thank you* near the mast-foot. It smudged in the very next hour as if licked away by sap.

"Rude," he said, offended.

"Hungry," Marissa corrected, amused.

By second bell, the *Skythread* met a thin band of contrary wind—one of those petty, stubborn things that pushes not hard but wrong. Sails shook; a top line snarled around a cleat with malice and history. Kit, eager to earn more than his fifteen years, darted toward it without a second pair of eyes on him.

"Leave it," the bosun barked—too late.

40

The snarl seized, bit deep. Kit yelped as the line taughtened and jerked, his palm skin left on hemp. He stumbled; the coil at his feet slithered like something that had learned to hunt.

Oscar was already moving. He dove, a hand to Kit's collar, the other catching the bitter rope. It burned. He grunted and didn't let go.

The mast *thrummed*. Not loud. Not flashy. The knot that should have tightened like a noose... loosened. Not on its own. With a very particular wiggle that sailors use when lines are old and jaws are tired and you need to talk a mouth into letting go.

The coil sighed. The snarl slipped. Oscar and Kit fell backward into a safer heap. Three different curses rose and failed to launch.

"Who did that?" the bosun snarled on reflex, eyes hunting for a hero to punish.

A dozen glances hit the mast at once. No one spoke. Then Tirpik's voice cut through, steady as a plumbline. "Thank you."

The hum answered with a note that could only be called pleased.

"Go wash that," Oscar said to Kit, showing him a palm striped red. "Cold water first. Then salve. Don't be brave. It'll scar if you lie to me."

Kit nodded, breathing fast, eyes flicking between his rescuer and the pale spar. "Was that—did she—"

Oscar didn't glance at the mast. "A line that's been at sea knows when to give instead of fight."

Kit swallowed and tried on a grin. It fit poorly. "Aye."

By dusk, resistance had found smaller, safer forms. Hest muttered softer. Others muttered at Hest. Someone hung a sprig of green at the foot of the main—a weed from a barrel of freshwater, haphazard and earnest. Oscar added a small dish of honey, set without ceremony, then pretended to be surprised when it was empty at bell's end.

"Corwin," Marissa said, watching him not-write in his book, "if you set down 'the mast drank the honey,' I'll make you scrub decks with your quill."

"Scientific observation," he sniffed.

"Superstitious crew," she returned.

They met in the middle, as sensible people do.

That night the hum changed again. Not louder—deeper. A chord under the ship's ordinary business. It smoothed the jumpy parts of people; it roughed the smooth parts where they needed grit. A pair of old enemies found themselves sharing tool oil without snarling. A song rose from the galley that had more harmony than usual. Someone—not Corwin, though he smiled and pretended offense at the theft—nudged their awkward, earnest chant into something like a hymn:

> Hold fast, hold true,
> Wood and sky and crew,
> Storm may split the dark in two,
> But heart will see us through.

They tried it twice, then a third time, sheepishness peeling away. The hum caught it, underlay it, and when the last line fell into the air it hung a heartbeat longer than physics would have liked.

Tirpik stood in the shadow of the quarterdeck, hat in hand, listening to his ship. He'd sailed sky since his chin could hold a blade. He'd heard hulls keen, keels argue, lines lie. He had never heard a spar sing back *with* his crew.

Marissa came to his shoulder, voice low. "We're past spooked."

"Aye," Tirpik said.

"What do we do with that?"

He considered, eyes on the pale main, on the places where the scar looked less angry today than it had yesterday. "We make room. We keep to our jobs. We learn her weather."

"And if someone asks again to cut her free?"

Tirpik slid his hat back on, the brim shadowing a smile that almost reached his eyes. "I tell them to go below and count soap."

Marissa huffed a laugh. "Aye, Captain."

Just before first light, when the eastern cloud-band bruised pink, the mast gave one more gift. A fine mist gathered above the deck and fell—not rain, not quite—just enough to lift soot from rope and sweat from skin. The crew woke to a ship that smelled faintly of needles and new bread.

Marissa, who did not go in for omens unless they paid rent, tipped a dipper of the clean water into the scupper and said, not looking up, "Good morning, Greenbough."

The hum answered—a small, pleased *yes* tucked inside a note.

And somewhere below the knotholes and the scar, below iron hoops and sailor's knots, a choice kept ripening: a voice in wood deciding how to be among them.

By noon, even Hest had stopped glaring at the main. He still glared at Corwin because it was a hobby.

"Two more days to Grayhook if the wind minds itself," Marissa said, compass steady, hand light. "We can dock, show her to the druids, let them berate us for crimes we didn't mean."

Tirpik grunted. "We'll hear them. Then we'll do what's right by *our* rites."

"And if she… asks for more?" Corwin ventured.

Tirpik didn't answer immediately. He looked at the mast instead, at the faint glimmer of green that moved in the grain when the light struck true. "Then we listen."

The hum purred, as if the timber approved of being consulted.

The *Skythread* trimmed her sails and took the westward current with the confidence of a creature who had found, at last, the beginning of a new kind of balance. The crew worked. The captain watched. The mast watched back. And in the narrow space between one creak and the next, trust began to splice itself into something that might hold in a gale.

Tomorrow, or the day after, someone or something would step out of that wood and take a first careful breath of the upper air. But for now—just now—she stayed within her bark and bone, a presence in grain, a syllable learning its own name.

The ship didn't mind. She had always loved a good story told slow.

Chapter Six

Greenbough Steps Aboard

'It's one thing when the mast groans in a gale.
Another when it tells you to wash behind your ears."

— *Captain Tirpik, logbook margin note*

***

The Skythread sailed in a hush that morning, not the silence of calm skies but of a crew listening for something they could not name. The cloud-keel thrummed softly, the sails whispered in a fair wind, yet every sailor kept half an ear turned toward the mast.

Corwin stood at the navigation table near the base of the mainmast, a chart spread beneath his hands. Candleflame hovered above it, not flickering, held steady by his will. Chalk lines crossed the vellum in arcs that matched stars overhead, and a compass-rose glowed faintly blue with magelight. His hair had gone more silver than black these days, and his shoulders bent not from weakness but from long nights bent over ink and runes. The crew knew him not just as a scribe but as the Skythread's wizard—reader of skies, master of bearings, a man whose words could stitch wind into order.

He frowned over his markings. "Another quarter-point north and we'll ride the lee longer. Another south, and we lose her gift."

He reached to adjust the line—and felt a distinct *tap* on his shoulder. Warm. Human.

He straightened at once. Behind him stood no one. Only the polished oak of the mast.

From within the grain came a laugh, low and delighted. "Still hunched. Still muttering. A spine is meant to stand, wizard, not curl like rope left in rain."

Corwin's lips twitched despite himself. He set his shoulders square, voice wry. "I was told masts were for bearing sails, not opinions."

"You nail tar and rope through my flesh. You drag me through cloud and cold. And you all stink."

Corwin stood up and faced the mast.

"And you were told true," the wood answered, prim and amused. "Yet here I am."

Across the deck, Tirpik, the gnome captain, cocked his head, feathered hat tilting back as he caught the sound. "What's she complaining about today?"

"Posture," Corwin said, dry as salt.

"Posture!" Tirpik spread his hands. "If she starts grading our handwriting. Saints save me, I barely passed my letters."

The crew chuckled, their unease easing for a heartbeat. For weeks Greenbough had been no more than a voice in the mast—nagging them into bathing, raining on hammocks that stank, praising only when things were properly done. She was half mother, half storm, and no one yet agreed if she was blessing or curse.

Marissa came up from belowdecks then, boots ringing steady on the planks. Half-elven grace lent length to her

46

stride, but her voice carried the firmness of a woman long at sea. First mate, navigator, and keel of the ship when Tirpik was at his most mercurial—she wasted no time on courtesies.

"What's her mood?" she asked Corwin, eyes flicking to the mast.

"Considering her appearance," Corwin replied, folding his arms.

Marissa arched a brow. "Her what?"

"Presentation," the mast confirmed, her voice as crisp as ever. "Of me. Now."

The deck froze. Sailors glanced sidelong, pretending to coil rope or check knots while their hands stilled. Oscar leaned out from the rail, shading his eyes as though sight would sharpen hearing. Even he—one of the younger sailors aboard but no boy anymore—felt the weight of the moment settle.

The grain of the mast rippled. Lines deepened into the clear suggestion of a face: cheek, brow, lips faintly pursed in disapproval. Sailors who had scoffed before found themselves staring now, hearts caught in their throats.

Then the timber softened, polished oak taking on the sheen of something pliant. The grain bowed outward like cloth pushed from behind, and the mast opened without seam or hinge—as though a doorway in the world itself remembered how to breathe.

From that living aperture, she stepped through.

Greenbough emerged with deliberate poise, as though she had rehearsed each motion before daring to show herself. Her form was elven in stature—tall, slender—but her skin gleamed like burnished bark, pale as driftwood along her arms, dusk-dark across her shoulders, veined faintly with sap-light that pulsed green and gold. Her hair fell in ordered braids of vine and fiber, each strand combed into perfection, blossoms bright at the braid-ends like jewels in a crown.

But it was her eyes that undid them all. Not mortal eyes. Not even elven. Amber at the core, green at the edge, ringed like the years of a tree, catching lantern-flame and giving it back as living fire. Eyes that declared she was spirit and mast both, and no disguise could change that truth.

The men stumbled, muttering oaths, some half turning away in awe. But the women moved first, quick and practical. Towels were produced, shoulders draped, dignity given without asking.

Marissa stood firm, hands on her hips, gaze leveled on the newcomer. "So. You're aboard now in truth."

Greenbough inclined her head, accepting the towel as though it were a mantle. "It seemed time."

"Then hear the rule that matters above all," Marissa said, voice steady, carrying to every ear. "This crew is family. That means no games with the men. No charms, no songs, no fogging of hearts. Whatever nymph-juice you carry, cork it. We'll not have strife here."

A hush fell. All eyes went to Greenbough.

Her smile curved slow, eyes bright with humor and understanding. "In the wild, such charms are shields. Men are teeth—eager, dangerous, and sometimes useful when given purpose. But…" She looked across the deck, at Tirpik with his feathered hat, at Corwin with his candlelit chart, at Oscar leaning forward with breath held, at human, dwarf, elf, and gnome alike waiting for her answer. "But here? Teeth would find me poor meat. You bite back for your own. I have learned this."

Her head dipped in a nod, not huffy but intelligent, accepting. "You needn't fear. I'll not waste myself meddling in hearts that already beat as one."

Marissa studied her a moment longer, then clapped her shoulder. "Good. That makes you crew."

A cheer went up—ragged but real, fists thumping rails, laughter breaking nerves. Tirpik doffed his hat, bowing low. "Welcome aboard, Greenbough. Officially. Unofficially, you've been cleaning us up for weeks."

"Not clean enough," Greenbough said serenely. "Nog still hides soap like treasure. I'll have cleaned by nightfall."

Laughter roared, and the Skythread breathed easier.

***

By dusk the wind returned, filling the high, pale sails. Corwin stood again with his map, this time not leaning, posture proper, because some lessons take the first time. The smell of soap and resin mingled under the usual salt. The Skythread slipped along her path, and on her deck stood a new kind of crew: the kind that had been listening for a change and was ready when it came.

When the stars came out—a sparse sprinkle first, then a river—Greenbough lifted her face to them. She could wear a shirt now, and she could keep her sap in a bottle, and perhaps in time she would learn the trick of looking mortal to eyes that needed it. But her eyes themselves would always tell what she was. They held the memory of rings and rain, of timbers that sing when the keel hums right, of a mast that is a spine for a hundred lives. And when she looked along the deck, what she saw there made those ring-lights warm: men and women, dwarf and gnome, elf and human, a family in all but name.

49

She had not come out of the wood to be alone. She had stepped aboard.

Chapter Seven

Market Errands

"The sky does not forgive the careless, nor does coin.
Both must be counted with clear eyes."

— *Saying of the Cloud-Fleet*

***

The Skythread made landfall at a modest port town clinging stubbornly to the low cliffside, its buildings huddled like wind-worn stones. Half the harbor was carved from rock; the other half was a ramshackle quilt of piers held together by rope, brine, and the good graces of whatever minor god oversaw **Patches and Prayer**. Still, gull-cries braided with the ring of ship's bells, and even here—far from the great ports—tradition traveled farther than any one vessel.

Before the crew went ashore, Corwin set a glamour across Greenbough. Nothing extravagant: a shimmer of light that softened bark-flecked arms into sun-browned skin, and her hair into a fall of dark, human-black curls. But her eyes—the green-gold rings, the leaf-veined irises—he left untouched.

"You could hide them too," Oscar murmured while cinching the coin purse Marissa had pressed into his belt.

Corwin shook his head. "The eyes are hers. Best the world learn to live with them, same as we do."

Greenbough tilted her head, pleased, posture lifting as though sunlight touched her spine.

*****

The market pressed around them in a crush of bodies and clamor: smoke from fish-sellers' braziers, spices sharp as flint, the clatter of cart wheels, the bark of merchants bluffing coin from sailors they assumed too tired or too new to haggle well. Marissa's list was long—grain, lamp oil, salted pork, fruit if it could be had—but she had sent Oscar with the purse, Corwin with his staff, and Greenbough with nothing but presence. It proved more than enough.

At first Greenbough moved quietly, observing with the calm of deep glades. But when a flour-seller tallied sacks at twice fair cost, something sharpened behind her leaf-ringed eyes.

"You charge them double," she said, voice soft, precise, and somehow more dangerous than a shout.

The man spread his hands. "Supply's thin, lady. Times hard."

She stepped closer—close enough for the scent of sap and rain-soaked leaf to reach him. Her gaze narrowed like a hawk choosing where to strike.

"Times are not so hard," she murmured, "that you came in new boots. Not so hard that your wife wears gold, not tin. You drank sweet wine this morning. You cheat my family."

Oscar stiffened. "Green—"

She raised a hand, palm gentle but absolute. It wasn't threat. It wasn't spellcraft. It was presence—the sort that made men rethink their sins and straighten their posture.

The merchant sagged under it.

"Twenty-five percent," she said. "For all sacks. You will still profit."

He nodded before his breath returned, hands fumbling over numbers. Only when the deal was struck did he realize he'd agreed.

Oscar blinked, half in awe, half in alarm. He'd seen glamours, truth-charms, even healers coax stubborn hearts—but this… this was different.

"That," he said as they hauled the grain toward the docks, "was reading a man like a ledger."

Greenbough's lips curled. "Men are easier than trees. Trees do not lie. And he smelled of greed the moment we stepped close."

Oscar laughed despite himself. "Remind me never to play cards with you."

Her answering laugh was bright as wind-chimes. "Remind me to teach you how to win."

Behind them, a pair of sailors whispered:

"Quartermistress Sapling, more like."

"Hells, she just saved us a week's coin!"

***

Back aboard Skythread, the mood shifted like a clean wind through stale sails. Men who had whispered curses under their breath now clapped Greenbough on the shoulder. Some brought her small offerings—an apple not yet bruised, a braid of rope, a cup of strong tea—as if she were a friendly spirit needing tribute. Even Tirpik allowed the corner of his mouth to twitch upward.

Marissa watched from the helm, logbook under her arm, expression softening as the crew stowed their supplies.

"We've gained more than a mast," she said quietly to Oscar.

Oscar followed her gaze. Greenbough stood at the center of the deck, lantern-light catching her glamour and the faint green sheen beneath it. She looked radiant—not polished like a noblewoman, but rooted. Certain.

"Aye," Oscar said. "She's one of us now."

They watched her a moment longer as she teased Nog about hiding soap again, earning a round of laughter that rolled across the deck like warm surf.

"And gods help anyone," Oscar added, "who tries to cheat her family again."

***

Harbor bells tolled eight strokes—clean, resonant, echoing through the harbor and up the cliffs. The sound rolled across the Skythread's timbers like a pulse.

Greenbough tilted her head.

"Your ship has a heartbeat," she murmured.

Oscar grinned. "Aye. And if you stay long enough, you'll hear it in your bones."

She smiled—slow, sure, and deeply at home.

And perhaps for the first time since stepping from timber into flesh, she looked not like a visitor aboard a ship...

...but like a woman who belonged.

Chapter Eight

Watches and Water

*"A ship keeps two ledgers: the one in ink
and the one in hearts that strike to her bells."*

— *Grayhook Dockside Proverb*

***

Evening slid down the cliff in thin blue sheets. The harbor settled; gulls traded insults for sleep; the cliff-steps grew their own weather of lantern-glow and tired laughter. The *Skythread* took it all in with the patience of old timbers and new luck.

They came aboard to four bells—oo oo—struck clean and even by Marissa's hand. The note walked the deck twice before fading, as if making certain it had been heard.

"Provisions aboard," she called. "First Dog Watch end—Second Dog Watch begin. Jerrik, secure the casks. Hest, mind that cleat or I'll make you apologize to it in writing. Greenbough—" She paused, surprised to hear her own mouth give the name so naturally. "You'll stand with me while I mark the log."

Greenbough drifted to the helm, bare feet whispering over plank. She glanced at the logbook like it was a creature that might bite.

"It only bites the careless," Marissa said, quill poised. "Time, course, wind, and what we put in the galley." Her mouth tilted. "Your discount can have its own line."

Greenbough's eyes warmed. "Write: 'Stolen back from a thief.'"

"'Negotiated,'" Marissa amended, the quill scratching. "We're respectable skyfolk."

By the main, Corwin set his palm to the pale spar and listened. The hum that lived in the grain—the one that had once unsettled the crew—sounded now like the ship had learned to purr. "She's content," he murmured.

"Because she ate," Oscar said, passing with an armful of salted pork.

"Because she was useful," Corwin corrected. He glanced after Greenbough at the helm. "That helps folk eat, too."

Supper was a clean, ordinary miracle: stew thick enough to keep a spoon upright, bread still warm from the galley stone, pears traded cheap for rumor and a favor owed. The mess filled with the scrape of bowls and the music of relief. Greenbough sat cross-legged on the deck with a wooden bowl balanced on her knee, inhaled the steam with wonder, and ate as if learning a new language one bite at a time.

"You taste like stories," she told the stew solemnly.

"Careful," muttered the cook, who had sworn never to trust sorcery before noon and had been converted entirely by midafternoon. "You praise a stew like that and I'll start charging."

"Feed her twice," a sailor said. "She earns."

Laughter moved along the benches. It didn't have the brittle edge it had borne after the storm. Something in it had loosened, like a knot shown mercy.

"Bells in twenty," Marissa called over the good noise. "Shift your bones, not the buckets."

Greenbough looked up. "You ring to mark the sun?"

"We ring to mark ourselves," Marissa said. She tapped the rim of her bowl with the end of the quill. "Eight bells ends a watch: midnight, four, eight, noon. Dog watches split the evening so no one grows old in one slot." She pointed toward Corwin's cabin, where a faint, smug *plink... plink... plink* kept time. "If cloud eats the stars, we ask the nagging bucket."

"The nagging—?"

"Wizard's water-clock," Corwin said from the hatch, appearing with a cup and the offended dignity of a man whose contraptions are loved for the wrong reasons. "Gnomish valves. Shock rings. Keeps true when you don't." He lifted the cup by way of truce. "You'll learn the rhythm. Most do—some in spite of themselves."

Greenbough set her empty bowl aside and tilted her head, listening down into the planks. "I can hear it now." She smiled. "Your ship has a patient pulse."

"Ship has ours," Hest muttered, not quite ready to concede he'd softened. He yanked at a knot with more gentleness than yesterday.

Oscar finished eating and carried bowls to the galley hatch, stacking them with the hush of someone who had once learned to make himself useful in a house that needed quiet hands. On his way back, Greenbough fell into step beside him.

"You were afraid," she said.

57

"Not of you," he answered without flinch.

"Of the part of me that could make a man forget his price," she said, not unkind. "That's sensible."

He blew out a breath that wasn't quite a laugh. "I've seen what happens when folk use an edge just because they can."

"And I have seen what happens when cheaters prosper," she returned. Then, softer, measuring where the words would strike, "If I press too far, you'll say. I'd rather be told 'enough' than become something I don't recognize."

"Deal," Oscar said. His mouth pulled crooked. "For the record, the stew did taste like stories."

***

At eight bells—oo oo oo oo—they changed the watch. The cloud-lanes were kind; a faint river of stars showed through the gaps. Marissa set the sextant to her eye, one hip to the rail, face all angles and focus. Greenbough leaned to watch, fascination bright as a lamp.

"You pinch light," the nymph murmured, "and the sky answers with numbers."

"Angles," Marissa said, aligning a brass arc to the horizon. "But yes. Then we reset the clock's pride, and the bells' habit keeps us honest."

"The sky would be offended," Greenbough said thoughtfully, "if you gave it too much pride."

"Which is why I prefer bells," Marissa said. "They don't gossip."

From below came the faint *plink... plink* of Corwin's clock, smug as a cat that has never once fallen off a shelf.

"Tell me about the stars," Greenbough asked. "Not their names. Their tempers."

Marissa hesitated. Then, because there are some questions you only get asked once and should answer fully when you do, she did. She spoke of a steady south lantern and a trickster in the east that always ran before storms. Of the thin winter cat's-back that pretended to be a road but turned smugglers around. Of the summer fox whose tail brushed a sailor's dreams if he slept on his back beneath open sky.

Greenbough listened as if to a story of kin she'd never met. Twice she laughed—once at the fox, once at the first mate's quiet confession that even she sometimes argued with stars and lost.

Night deepened. Watches rolled. The ship breathed in her sleep.

Oscar walked the Morning Watch from four to eight, boots whispering on plank, breath clouding, hands wrapped around a mug that steamed humbly of willow-bark. He let his mind go slack the way Briar had taught him—nothing mystical, just a kindness to thought. It drifted anyway to the market: the shift in the trader's face, the tilt of Greenbough's tone when she said family. He felt where unease and respect tangled inside his ribs and didn't hurry to untie them.

Close to the end of the watch, the world thinned to the blue that is not night and not day. He yawned, set the mug by the mast, and leaned his shoulders against the pale grain. The hum inside the wood stepped closer, matched him, slowed him, smoothed him. He closed his eyes and let the rhythm find him.

Sleep took him in one greedy swallow.

***

He dreamt of birch and bee and old laughter that rumbled like low thunder. Dug shouldered the dream aside as easily as a bear shouldered through brush, all gravity and gentleness, fur rimed with dawn light.

Stand, young archer, the thought came—affection lodged deep in it like a burr that says "home." Stand where you choose to, and no farther than that.

I am standing, Oscar thought, embarrassed to be caught napping in his own head.

Good. Dug's warmth pressed against the part of him that always expected a blow and found a shoulder instead. Do not let any friend—no matter how green—pull you off your root.

The bear's vast head tipped, a sneeze like a muffled avalanche startled him, and sap-sweet pollen glittered for a heartbeat before the dream shrugged it off. Dug's mouth did something like a smile. He smelled of honey and old forests. Then he stepped back into the quiet. The grove went with him.

Oscar woke wet.

Not soaked by rain—he would have forgiven rain. A single tidy cloud hung over his hammock like a pitcher held by an invisible hand, pouring precisely on his face and nowhere else. It had the nerve to drip with deliberation.

He sputtered and sat bolt upright. The cloud obligingly rose and poured at a slightly different angle, polite as a butler.

A laugh—soft, delighted—came from the doorway. Greenbough leaned there, arms folded, lanternlight snagging green in her eyes.

"Dreaming loudly," she said. "The bear sneezed."

Oscar wiped water from his nose with the back of his wrist. "If he sneezed here, you'd be mopping."

"He would never," she said gravely. Then, the corner of her mouth tugging up, "I will not rain on you again without invitation."

"Invitation?" he echoed, appalled and amused, swinging his legs to the floor. The cloud tilted to keep him honest; he stepped aside and it missed, offended, and sulked itself into vapor.

"You're trouble," he informed her.

"And you," she said, unbothered, "are the only one aboard who calls me that without trying to make a sermon of it." She dipped her head, a promise in the angle. "I will learn your edges. If I cross them, you'll tell me."

"I will," he said, and meant it. He squeezed water from his shirt, shook his head, and grinned despite himself. "And for the record—thanks for the market."

"You're my family's buyer of bread," she said simply. "He tried to steal from my family. It will not do."

Four bells struck—oo oo—and the note climbed the ladder of the day, crisp and right. The crew stirred. Marissa's voice went out across the deck with the morning: "Forenoon Watch muster! Hest, you and Jerrik see that barrel lashed proper before it walks itself off. Oscar, log and rounds. Corwin, stop arguing with your bucket and come take a sight while the sky pretends to be honest."

The *Skythread* shifted her weight and found it again. Lines thrummed. The mast answered with a contented whisper only those who had learned to listen could hear. Greenbough tipped her face into the light like a sapling testing sun.

"Your ship has a good day in her," she said.

"Then let's not waste it," Marissa answered, already raising the sextant.

And the bells—stubborn, human, beloved—kept time with a life that had decided to keep theirs.

Chapter Nine

Homebound

"The sky teaches by repetition;
a ship learns by remembering who repeated with her."

— *Margin note from a Nandanoléme apprentice's slate*

***

They made good miles after the market—clean wind, honest lanes, and a crew that finally pulled like one rope. The ache that had hung over Skythread after the storm eased into routine, then into laughter. That's the way of ships: danger shapes the first edge of camaraderie, but it's the days after that file it smooth.

The apprentices from Nandanoléme settled into the rhythm as if they'd been born from bell-metal and rope. They learned to take sights without arguing with the horizon, to coil lines without leaving snarls malicious enough to trip the next poor fool, and to write clean figures even when the deck rolled just enough to betray a sloppy quill. One apprentice—Lira—practiced her knots until her fingertips blistered, then kept practicing anyway. Another, Pellen, timed his turns with Corwin's water-clock until he could predict the **plink… plink… plink** with his eyes closed.

Marissa's quill prowled the log like a patient cat. Corwin's clock nagged smugly. Tirpik's voice kept the hours honest.

Greenbough learned, too. She walked her watches barefoot, not for effect, but because the grain spoke truer skin to wood than to leather. She could hear a drying pin before a bosun smelled it, could sense a hairline shift in the mast's hum when the wind prepared to yaw. She ate in the mess without being coaxed, praising stew until the cook turned pink with the fragile pride of a man whose craft was finally recognized as the magic it was. When a bell struck, she came to the rail instinctively—not in obedience, but because the sound told her where her family stood.

"First Watch—eight bells!" someone would call, and Skythread herself seemed to tuck the moment away in her memory.

Oscar kept his distance at first, the way a man stands one pace back from a fire he respects. He did rounds, wrote neat notes in his ledger—a habit Briar had wedged firmly into him—and watched. The grain-market moment had shifted something inside him: it wasn't only that the nymph could out-bargain thieves; it was that she had done it *for them*.

He tested the word *family* silently, rolling it under his ribs. It fit with quiet certainty, like discovering a bow had always been fitted to your hand.

***

On the third week, they dodged weather by inches. A fist-punch of bruise-colored cloud marched down from the north, tearing itself on the cliff-line. Marissa took a slant through a canyon of air so narrow it made the riggers curse her by name and then bless her in the same breath.

64

Greenbough leaned into the wind, the mast leaned with her, and the ship cut through the gap like a thread through a tight eye.

The apprentices cheered after because they were still young enough to celebrate what hadn't killed them. Tirpik spat, grunted, and pretended his heart hadn't just visited his throat.

They traded at two cliff-towns. In the first, a salt broker tried soft lies and harder prices. Greenbough leveled a look at him that would have unmanned a statue, and he discovered a sudden, lifelong devotion to fairness. In the second town, a cooper delivered barrels that didn't leak. Not every tale needed drama; a promise kept was sometimes miracle enough.

Night after night, bells struck; stars whispered their thin, old promises; and Skythread breathed like a creature sleeping lightly.

Oscar came to love the hour before dawn. The blue that wasn't quite night and not yet morning. The time when the ship felt most like a thought someone had decided to keep.

More than once he woke in that blue to Greenbough and Marissa talking low at the helm—not of constellations, but their *tempers*.

A steady lantern to the south.

A fox that ran before bad weather.

A winter cat's-back that tricked smugglers into sailing in circles.

Greenbough lapped up the lore like rainwater on roots.

"Trees keep stories," she murmured one morning, palm resting on the rail. "But they do not travel with them. Ships do."

"Ships carry what they must," Marissa said. Then, quieter, honest: "And sometimes what they want."

***

Corwin once caught Greenbough tilting her head toward the water-clock, listening as if it were a very small oracle. He cleared his throat with the dignity of a man determined not to scold.

"Lessons are by request. The clock is *never* touched uninvited."

Greenbough bowed her head—not quite chastened. "Then I request. Teach me why drops march."

Corwin tried to refuse. He did. But then he heard the apprentices in the hall holding their breath, rooting for the nymph to win. Vanity doomed him.

He set the oil and shock ring on the table and began with the line all teachers use when forgiveness has already been granted:

"We start at the beginning."

"Roots first," she said.

"Valves first," he corrected—and, for once, they were speaking the same language.

***

On the last long leg home, Marissa eased the sails until they sang a note you felt in your ribs. The crew moved through chores with that rare grace that looks like fortune from the outside and discipline from within.

Oscar walked his round with Skyroot on his shoulder. At the mast he paused, set his palm to the grain, and breathed with the ship until his heartbeat matched the hum within.

Briar would have told him it counted as prayer—even for cynics.

He didn't disagree.

***

Two months softened into habit, then into story.

Soahc revealed itself slowly—first as a shift in the light, then in the taste of the air, then in gulls who carried a louder, ruder confidence.

The apprentices sensed it before naming it. Bells far inland struck a pattern older than any sailor's oath. The city's gravity pulled on them before they saw a single roof.

And then—

Walls climbed out of the haze.

Stone tiers banded like a cliff choosing to be inhabited. Copper domes sweating noonlight.

Harbor chains ratcheting.

Signal flags blinking commands like impatient birds. Somewhere in the lower wards, a baker overproofed a loaf and every gull in Soahc judged him loudly.

"Lines ready," Marissa said, not raising her voice—so everyone heard her more clearly. "Hands to stations. Hest, if you kiss that cleat with a sloppy hitch, you *will* apologize to it."

"In writing?" Hest squeaked.

"In writing," she confirmed. Even Greenbough smothered a smile.

Skythread slid into her berth with the confidence of a dancer returning to a familiar stage. Sails exhaled their wind. Lines snaked. Cleats groaned contentedly. When her keel touched cradle timbers, the ship gave a long, relieved breath—as if she had been holding it since Soarwind.

67

"Eight bells—noon!" came the call. **oo oo oo oo**

The notes bounced off stone and water and back again. Soahc answered with its own chorus of shouts, carts, gulls, and children who saw their first griffon and immediately wanted one.

The apprentices lined the rail and waved to absolutely no one. Two wept, denying it passionately.

Tirpik scolded a stevedore for looking at a crate too aggressively.

Corwin hugged his water-clock case like a beloved, argumentative pet.

Oscar leaned on the rail and felt the knot behind his ribs—tightened by watch lists and old scoldings—begin to unspool.

Home, for now, he thought.

No teacher alive could shame him out of that truth.

Beside him, Greenbough placed her palm against the timber and closed her eyes. The city's noise was the opposite of grove-quiet, yet she met it the way trees meet wind—by listening to the pattern under the chaos.

"Your city breathes fast," she observed.

"It does," Oscar said. "You'll get used to it. Or it'll get used to you."

"Both," she decided. "Better."

Marissa shut the logbook, letting her hand rest on it a heartbeat longer than habit allowed. The final line she'd written wasn't meant for the Admiralty, but for the next crew who'd read it years hence:

"Apprentices trained; crew sound; storm behind; a mast with a voice keeps us steady."

"Dock leave by the roster," she called. "No fights I haven't scheduled. Pay in the morning. And if anyone sells their boots for a story, it had better be worth retelling."

Laughter chased the order down the gangplank. The first coil struck the stone. The city embraced the ship, and the ship gave back what she could: a tidy deck, a promise of return, a new story budding in every scuff waiting to be mended.

Greenbough lingered. Her roots—whatever shape they now took—ran through timber and bell and habit. She would wander Soahc soon, listening to courtyard trees and alley-grown saplings, deciding which forgave the city and which merely endured it.

But not yet.

"Come on," Oscar said, adjusting his satchel. "There's a man in the gnomish quarter who thinks clocks can shame wizards. You'll like him."

"I like clocks that keep time," she replied.

"You'll still like him," he said, grinning.

The bells of Soahc carried another pattern down the tiers.
Skythread answered with a small, contented creak that only those who had learned to listen would ever hear.

Oscar stepped off the gangplank—three strides into heat and noise and stone—before he looked back. Greenbough still stood at the rail, palm on the wood, eyes on the harbor. She nodded once.

I know your name now.

The ship—being wood and wind and stubbornness—pretended not to preen.

"Voyage complete," Marissa murmured, not for the log but for the part of herself that only loosened when lines were made fast and the wind's hand finally left her shoulder.

Soahc breathed.

The crew answered.

And Skythread—old timbers, new luck—rested only as long as a ship ever does between journeys:

A minute.

A month.

Or a single bell—whichever measure felt most like home.

Chapter Ten

Stones and Stories

"Every city is a loom: it weaves you tighter if you linger, frays you thinner if you try to leave too quickly."

— *Fragment of the Journeyman's Scrolls, Nandanoléme*

***

Soahc did not sleep—*not even at dawn.*

The sky-harbor tier breathed in tides of noise and color: hot bread and saltfish, tar-warm rope and cold seawind, ferrymen who knew fifty curses and fifty more clever uses for knots. Skythread lay moored and dignified amid it all, lines taut to stone bollards, sails furled neat as a folded shirt, her timbers humming faintly with relief after so many days aloft.

The crew scattered like sparks hitting dry tinder. Marissa oversaw the apprentices first, her voice crisp enough to cut through the din.

"Two hours ashore before the bell," she warned. "One bell late, and you'll pray for gnomes to drill numbers into your skulls instead of me."

The younger sailors laughed—some bravely, some nervously—and hurried down the gangplank clutching their purses like fragile eggs.

Oscar lingered at the rail until Greenbough's shadow joined his. She wore a cloak Corwin had cast with careful glamour, muting the soft glow of her skin and smoothing the unnatural stillness of her movements. For the casual glance it was convincing. For anyone who looked twice… her eyes gave everything away. Green-gold. Restless. Sentient as wind in leaves.

"You're coming with me," Oscar said. It wasn't a command—not even quite a question.

"I will."

Her fingers trailed along the railboard, reading the grain as if reassuring Skythread. "This place smells of stones trying to be trees," she murmured. "I want to hear them complain."

Oscar snorted. "Stones don't usually complain in words. Mostly groans. And dust."

"I've learned to listen where words aren't," she said. Then, with a mischievous tilt of her head: "Besides, someone must keep the coin safe."

***

The market tiers of Soahc curled uphill in a great helix, each level louder, brighter, and more eager to part sailors from coin than the last. Awnings painted with birds, beasts, and star-maps hung like banners over stalls where traders barked prices with theatrical despair. Gnome-run shops rattled and chimed with impossible devices behind iron-grated windows. Smiths hammered in dueling rhythms, daring each other louder and truer.

Oscar, Corwin, Greenbough, and half the watch wound upward through the chaos.

Jerrik bore Marissa's shopping list as if it were a holy writ; Hest shouldered an empty pack with the dread of a man who already felt its future weight.

Corwin peeled away first. "Calibration," he muttered. "Valves. Insolent gnome apprentices. I'll be in the clock quarter."

He pointed his staff vaguely toward the grain market. "Don't let him charge more than thrice fair," he warned Oscar. Then, flicking his eyes toward Greenbough: "And do *not* let her buy a whole stall because it smells honest."

Greenbough arched a brow. "I would never."

Corwin snorted. "You would *always.*"

Then he vanished into the hiss and clatter of the gnomish lanes.

***

The market ribboned along the cliffside in a river of color and sound—spices rising like sparks on the saltwind, glass beads winking bright, vendors calling from deep-shadowed booths. Oscar drifted while the others haggled, his hands tucked in his pockets, his thoughts pleasantly unmoored.

A shimmer caught his eye.

A small table was tucked between a potter's bench and a tinker's cart, its wares arranged on a faded cloth: shells, river stones, bits of polished glass—simple things shaped by careful hands. The woman behind the table wore a wide straw hat and eyes that sparkled with the mischief of someone who had seen too many sailors to be impressed by any.

"Looking for luck, boy?" she asked. "Sailors always are."

"Something like that," Oscar admitted. "Something small. For a friend."

She nudged a tray forward. Charms clinked together—brass leaves, blue glass droplets, polished stones wrapped in wire.

Oscar paused over one: a smooth river pebble carved into the shape of a single unfolding leaf, its etched veins catching the light as if alive. The cord was plain hemp.

"That one," the woman said knowingly. "For someone who hears more than most folk say."

Oscar smiled. "That'd be her."

He paid with two coins—more than she expected—and her eyebrows lifted in gratitude rather than protest.

When he found Greenbough again at the quay, sunlight caught in her hair like threads of gold caught in bark.

He hesitated—but only for a breath.

"Here." He held out the charm. "It's not much. But I thought… maybe the ship ought to have a bit of land with her."

Greenbough studied it as if reading memory carved into its surface. Then she smiled—slow, warm, and wholly genuine.

"Then it will be the first stone I've carried that wasn't part of a root… or a burden."

Oscar tied it around her wrist. The carved leaf gleamed, and for a moment the rigging above them shivered with a faint, approving hum—as if Skythread herself had noticed.

***

They reached the harbor tier just as the bells rang eight—oo oo oo oo—Second Dog Watch ending, First Watch beginning. Lanterns bloomed across the piers. Skythread waited in quiet pride, her cloudy timbers alive with evening breath.

Corwin rejoined them at the gangplank, arms full of brass fittings and diagrams that rustled like offended birds. His usual irritation was firmly in place—tempered only slightly by the glint of a puzzle half-mastered.

"Arm recalibrated," he said. "Clock recalibrated. My patience remains uncalibrated, but one must suffer something."

Oscar snorted. "Let me guess—the gnome outmaneuvered you?"

"No," Corwin said sharply, which meant yes.

Greenbough brushed a finger across a rolled blueprint. "The clock—does it truly nag you?"

"It educates," he snapped. Then softer: "And you will not step into my cabin to prod at it."

"Innocent" mischief flickered across her eyes. "Of course not, elder wizard."

He sighed. Dignity was all he had left, and even that wobbled.

***

Night settled its warm weight across Soahc. The crew stowed provisions, tightened lines, scribbled into the log, and chased each other's laughter across the deck. Lanterns shivered in the breeze. Pulleys squeaked like gossiping birds.

Marissa stood at the helm, logbook under her arm. She watched Oscar watching Greenbough, and Greenbough watching the water.

"She's crew now," Marissa murmured. "Not just timber we found in the wilds."

Oscar nodded, a soft smile caught at one corner of his mouth. "Aye. And gods help anyone who tries to cheat her family again."

Supper came late—stew thick enough to anchor a spoon, pears bought cheap, hard cheese sliced against a belt knife. Greenbough sat cross-legged on the planks, eating with an earnest delight that softened the roughest sailors. Someone joked about adopting her officially; Tirpik raised a mug in gruff approval.

She leaned close to Oscar. "This… is what roots feel like. Not soil. The circle it makes."

Oscar thought of Dug's rumbling voice, of standing firm and no farther.

"Then keep them," he said quietly.

***

The bells of Soahc tolled eight again—oo oo oo oo— and the watch changed. Skythread shifted on her moorings as if stretching after a long run. The city noise dimmed, folding into taverns and alleyways.

Greenbough remained at the rail, palm pressed to the timber.

She whispered, almost too soft for speech:
"I know your name now."

Skythread, stubborn as any old soul of wood and cloud, said nothing.

But the timbers purred under her hand.

And that was answer enough.

Book Two

Voyage to Safe Harbor

"Safe harbors are not found; they are made
—one rope, one hand, one heart at a time."

— *Dockside saying, Guardian Islands*

Chapter One

The New Mission

"Maps are promises inked on paper;
the world itself never signed them."

— *Saying among the cartographers of Ravenglass*

***

Early Winter, 348 of the Second Age

They boarded just after she had docked, the fog still clinging to the ribs of Soahc like a hesitant guest that didn't want to leave.

Talon stood at the sterncastle rail, cloak stirring like a living thing in the harbor wind. Bella joined him a moment later, drawing close enough that their shoulders nearly brushed. Her eyes tracked the crooked chimneys rising through the mist—chimneys she had known as a girl, chimneys whose soot had once marked her own cheeks.

Neither spoke. The weight they carried did not welcome small talk.

When the crew was dismissed to their duties, Talon and Bella descended into the officers' hall. Tirpik and Marissa were already there, maps unfurled across a table gouged with decades of decisions—victories, mistakes, hastily carved warnings no one bothered to sand smooth.

"You made good time," Marissa said. Her voice held a note that wasn't quite suspicion and wasn't quite welcome. It was the tone of someone who expected a truth and was bracing for its shape.

Tirpik peered over his beard. "And you're not here to deliver ledgers."

Bella placed two parchments on the table: the brittle, flaking map from Nandanoléme and the newer copy from Runedragon.

Side by side, the differences were almost violent.

Mountains rounded or vanished. Rivers had wandered like drunken serpents. Coastlines bulged where none existed today, while whole islands—present reality—were absent from both.

Talon lowered his voice.
"These maps weren't wrong. They were true in their time. But the world has outpaced them. Storms, rifts, quakes—the land moves. And if we trust these as gospel, we're sailing half-blind into an age that no longer resembles its records."

Marissa leaned over the mismatched coastlines. "You want to redraw the world."

"Not want," Bella said steadily. "Need."

Tirpik snorted. "So we embarrass every cartographer breathing?"

"Only the ones who refuse to learn," Talon said, soft but firm. "The Skythread was built to go where no ink has gone in a century. Let her chart what *is*, not what *was*."

Marissa's storm-lit eyes narrowed. "What you're asking is years. Unknown lands. Uncharted skies. A gamble."

Bella didn't blink. "We've all gambled more for less."

"And the coin?" Tirpik pressed.

"It will be there," Bella said. "Quietly."

Tirpik studied them for a long moment. Then he sighed—the slow, reluctant exhale of a man realizing he had already lost this argument hours before it was spoken.

"Then so be it. The Grey Ghost will map what the old charts can't."

A pause.

"And gods forgive us our ambition."

Talon allowed the faintest smile. "Ink dries. Truth doesn't."

***

Soahc's shipyard woke like a storm forging itself. Hammers rang. Sparks flew. Wizards barked incantations over scaffolds. Apprentices ran messages between forges, breathless and half-panicked.

The Grey Ghost—still whispered by her old name: the Skythread—stood in the middle of it all like a giant admitting she needed new bones.

Her cloud-forged boards were peeled back, strengthened, blessed, and re-sealed. Gnomes crawled through her ribs like industrious insects, bracketing new support beams in place. Wizards carved runes deep into her spine to house the fifth clouder stone.

That stone hummed differently from the others—lower, heavier, steadier.

A second heartbeat.

Decks widened until the ship seemed to inhale and stand taller. New cabins were added on the sterncastle: one for Talon, one for Bella, one for Corwin (who immediately complained that sailors stomped too loudly above "a mind as delicate as mine").

Belowdecks, marines now had sleeping quarters with footlockers, and the mess hall doubled in size. Lantern hooks increased threefold—Oscar counted them himself—because "a ship mapping the dark needs to see her own hands at night."

The workshops were expanded until they resembled a small town:

- smithy
- carpentry
- ropewalk
- storm-coil station
- gnomish tinkering den (the loudest)

Everything buzzed with purpose. Everything smelled of hot iron, pitch, steam, and hope.

Along her flanks, new thunder bumpers and lightning coils gleamed—a whisper of stormcraft so potent even the apprentices fell quiet around them. Sailors weren't sure if she was becoming a warship, a diplomat, or something stranger.

Oscar whispered to Jerrik, "Feels more like she's waking up."

Jerrik whispered back, "Aye. And I'm not sure she likes being watched."

***

Oscar's promotion to logkeeper's apprentice came with little ceremony, except for Talon's hand on his shoulder.

"Words carry our story," Talon said. "But when the marines take the rails, your arrows matter more than ink."

Oscar nodded, though he wasn't sure which frightened him more.

That night, Bella gave him the Traveler's Book.

Bound in silvered leather. Warm to the touch. Runes pulsing faintly like a sleeping creature.

"It's yours," she said.

He almost dropped it. "Mine?"

"To carry. To protect. To open only when needed. And if danger presses too close, the Book will stir. Thay'sa and I will feel it."

He swallowed. "So it… won't read everything?"

Bella's smile was kind. "We aren't tyrants."

Thay'sa's voice rose gently but firmly from the Book's memory-web:

Your joys, doubts, and small fears are yours alone. We honor your privacy.

Oscar exhaled in relief.

But then—during a weapons drill—he panicked for a heartbeat.

Just a heartbeat.

That was all it took.

Bella's handwriting had appeared instantly across a page:

We feel your fear. Speak to us.

Oscar groaned into his pillow for hours.

***

Greenbough found him on deck later, the Book clutched tight against his ribs.

"The roots run both ways," she murmured. "You worry, they feel it. They worry, you feel it. Do not be ashamed of being known."

Oscar breathed out. "Then I'd better give them something worth reading."

She smiled—slow, luminous, approving.

It made him stand straighter without realizing it.

***

By the second month, the shipyard worked under two suns.

The real sun, pale in winter haze.

And Anna's sun.

Anna's gift—the captured lamp once raised above Trechellus—now hung suspended over the shipyard in a reinforced cradle of ironwood and spellmetal. Its radiance washed over the ship so profoundly that even shadows seemed unwilling to form unless politely invited.

Some whispered Anna had died for that light.

Others whispered she lived inside it.

Everyone worked faster beneath it.

Oscar wandered the half-finished decks in awe, scribbling uneven notes into the Book:

"new keel plating... wizard fell into a coil bucket... Marissa and Tirpik arguing about tallow again..."

Bella wrote teasing corrections two days later:

You missed the part where the coil bucket exploded.

He groaned.

Greenbough wove vines through unused beams, coaxed herbs along outer planks, and tended saplings meant for the upper deck. Sailors whispered that boards hummed when she brushed them with her fingers.

By month four, "Skythread" became a whispered name again—not for secrecy, but reverence.

She stood taller. Broader. A storm-shaped creature of timber, cloudstone, lightning craft, and living will.

She was no longer just a ship.

She was the beginning of a promise: that the world would no longer be drawn by guesswork or memory, but by truth.

And she was ready—finally ready—to give the world its shape once more.

Chapter Two

Moments of Apotheosis

"Wisdom is not seized; it settles, like dew upon the patient."

— *Fragment from the Annals of Nandanoléme*

***

Spring, 349 of the Second Age

The Skythread was no longer merely a skyship.
In four relentless months beneath Anna's gifted Light—
moved from its tower and hung over the shipyard so day and
night blurred into a single golden dawn—she had been
reborn.

Her cloud-boards were resealed until they gleamed like
softened moonstone. Her timbers were braced and
reinforced, hardened to survive storms, sea-water, and the
unknown edges of maps. A fifth clouder stone thrummed
deep in her hull, slow and powerful as a new heart learning its
first rhythms.

Along her flanks, fresh thunder bumpers gleamed with
storm-hungry intention, and the lightning coils—silver-spined
and waiting—made the sailors mutter that she was no longer
a courier at all, but something sharper.

"The Grey Ghost," they whispered, half in awe, half in fear, as though naming her risked waking her early.

At the sterncastle, six staterooms lined a central passage polished to a dark shine. The captain's quarters—broad windows, steady compass, the smell of ink and salt—had become the de facto charting room. Maps lay everywhere: pinned to walls, rolled in racks, weighed down by dividers and stones. The eastward mission demanded not only skill, but ambition.

It demanded belief.

***

The Officers

Skythread carried ten officers, each sworn to Captain Tirpik's command:

Captain Tirpik — a gnome of iron will and older storms, stubborn as oak roots gripping cliffstone.

First Mate Marissa — storm-blooded; discipline made flesh, boots striking deckboards like the tick of a stern clock.

The Navigator — steward of charts, custodian of courses, keeper of the sky's moods.

Master of Sails — sovereign of rigging and clouder stones, whose hands danced rope and storm alike.

Master of Arms — commander of marines, voice of iron, authority of steel.

Chief Wizard — one of Corwin's senior apprentices, responsible for enchantments, wards, and the quiet safety no one thanked them for.

Quartermaster — overseer of larders, smithy, repairs, and the economy of survival.

Boatswain — hammer and lash, architect of every repair, judge of every plank.

Priest-Surgeon Elenn — half-elf healer of wounds, disease, despair, and occasionally pride.

Master of the Watch — keeper of bells, time, and discipline when all else frayed.

Through them, the Skythread's **200 sailors** and **150 marines** found rhythm.

Roles eclipsed names at sea; duty outweighed ego. Titles were not ornaments—they were the bones that let the ship stand upright in storms.

***

The Crew

Sailors were divided into **four watch regiments of fifty**, each keeping six hours of the day and night. Marines stood four to a watch alongside them, bows and mithril blades ready for sky-raiders, storm-wyrms, or the shadowed dangers east of any chart.

Every sailor wore a dagger—tool first, weapon second. Every marine wore elven steel and a bow fletched with bright feathers from the Vale.

Skythread was not preparing merely for distance. She was preparing for consequence.

***

Oscar's Three Callings

Oscar had expected to be one thing aboard the ship—archer, maybe. Or logkeeper. Something simple. Something clear.

Instead, he found himself straddling three roles:
logkeeper's apprentice,
archer,

assistant to the ship's healer,

…none of which he felt remotely ready for.

Elenn assured him that readiness was overrated.

"Hold it steady," she murmured, guiding his clumsy hands around a practice bandage. Her voice was calm, but her gray-green eyes glittered with patient amusement.

Oscar frowned at the linen. "Feels like I'm tying a roast, not… saving a life."

"Better a roast that holds together," she replied dryly, "than a man who doesn't."

She was half-elf, her hair caught between gold and shadow, her presence quiet as harbor fog. The sigil of Paladin rested at her throat, polished by countless hours of tending the wounded.

Oscar wrapped another bandage—slower, more careful. The knot held true.

Elenn nodded. "Good. Again. And next time, less commentary about roasting."

A few marines watching nearby snickered.

Oscar flushed. "This is going to take work."

Later that day, on the training deck, he drilled younger recruits. One boy—barely old enough to bend a shortbow—struggled, his arrow wobbling in the wind. Oscar's temper sparked, but he caught it.

"This one's going to take work," he murmured again, softer, echoing Elenn without meaning to.

The boy steadied. His next arrow struck the target's edge.

From the rail above, Marissa's voice cracked like a taut rope:

"Ink and arrow, Oscar. Both matter. Don't forget one for the other."

Oscar groaned under his breath. "Everybody on this ship hears everything."

"Only the important things," Marissa said, turning away.

***

The Moment of Apotheosis

Dawn rose with the tolling of Soahc's sky-harbor bells. One by one, the moorings fell away. The Skythread shuddered—not in fear, but in anticipation. Her sails snapped taut. Masts thrummed. The clouder stones roared awake, lifting her free of the docks like a creature shaking off sleep.

Dockhands shaded their eyes, watching her ascend. Some whispered blessings. Some whispered omens. Some whispered her many names:

Skythread.

Grey Ghost.

The ship that courts the uncharted.

On the quarterdeck, Tirpik's voice rang bright:

"Officers to stations!

The Watch is set!

Raise her proud—east we go!"

Skythread leaned into the cloudstream, her shadow shrinking across the harbor cliffs. Soahc dwindled behind them: lanterns, rooftops, gulls, the faint chaos of shore.

Ahead lay only horizon.

Only wonder.

Only danger.

Only the shape the world had yet to reveal.

Oscar gripped the rail, Skyroot bow slung across his back, the Traveler's Book warm in his hand. Elenn stood near him, binding a fresh roll of linen, her eyes on the brightening sky.

He was logkeeper.

He was archer.

He was apprentice healer.

And something more he could feel growing inside him—something unnamed, unvoiced, but real.

The Skythread climbed clean into the rising sun.

The voyage had begun.

***

Chapter Three

The Eastern Edge

"The map is never finished; the world is always rewriting itself."

— *Cartographer's Proverb of Ravenglass*

***

The Skythread pressed eastward, her cloud-keel whispering as it carved through the high winds. Days folded into weeks; weeks unspooled into two long months. Each dawn carried them farther from the world they knew and deeper into a coastline that felt younger, angrier, and ill at ease with its own shape.

Goblins massed in soot-black coves, bold enough to raise signal fires at approaching sails. Ogres prowled cliff roads where no ogre had business walking. Twice the crew sighted new volcanic isles still bleeding heat — raw stone steaming as seawater hissed across it. Beaches blistered to glass. Flocks of ash-gulls wheeled overhead, screaming warnings no one aboard could translate.

And still the crew charted.

They mapped volcanic ridges. Sketched reef knives beneath the breakers. Measured the ash in the air and the strange metallic taste creeping into the winds. Every mark

Oscar set down stitched one more uncertain thread into a world that no longer resembled any map in the Admiralty archives.

Oscar wrote faithfully.

Not always elegantly. Not always calmly.

But faithfully.

Under Elenn's quiet shaping hand, his logs shifted from stiff, clipped ledgers to something closer to observation — the fevered glow of night magma, the unease of silent harbors, the way morale bent and straightened depending on whether the crew saw gulls or storm-bats that morning.

He began to capture not just distances, but truths.

***

Practice in the Infirmary

On the fifty-eighth night, lanternlight swayed like tired breath along the infirmary's low beams. Elenn had laid out a neat array: a roll of linen, a birch splint, a jar of honey-salve, and three needles gleaming like stern warnings.

"Again," she said, her tone the soft, immovable kind that had ended many arguments before they began.

Oscar rubbed his face with both hands. "Did you take lessons from an elf ranger? Any word but *again*. You must know other words. A whole language of them, even."

Elenn simply waited, arms folded, patient as winter and twice as steady.

Oscar surrendered with a groan and set his hands to the linen. The bandage wrapped crookedly around the practice arm — one of the carved wooden models she called "my very quiet patients." He frowned at the knot.

"Feels like I'm gift-wrapping a log," he muttered.

"You'd better hope the man you're wrapping never hears you say that," she said dryly.

Her hair caught the lanternlight in a warm haze — not quite gold, not quite brown, an indecisive color that suited her. Oscar caught himself staring too long. Elenn caught him catching himself and smiled — a small, knowing curl of the lips that unstrung him faster than any bow.

He fumbled the knot. Again.

"Slower," she murmured, unwrapping it with careful fingers. "A good healer makes haste in his judgment, not his hands."

He muttered something about arrows being simpler. Elenn swatted him lightly on the arm.

"Arrows end lives," she said. "This saves them. Learn both, and Paladin will be pleased."

The rebuke should have stung. Instead, Oscar felt the knot in his shoulders loosen just enough to try again. The next wrap landed cleaner. Straighter. Elenn nodded.

"Better. Now do it without glaring at me."

He did. Barely.

***

Ink and Honesty

Later, on the quarterdeck, Oscar cracked open the Traveler's Book. The ink pooled on the page, a patient mirror waiting to be sworn into truth. He chewed the inside of his cheek, then scribbled quickly:

Learned bandaging tonight. From Elenn — our priestess-surgeon. She's a friend. A good one. A girl, yes, but—
Easy, Bella. Calm down.
It's not like that.
(...Yet? No. No, stop it. Focus.)

95

He stared at the words, horrified at himself, half-expecting Bella's handwriting to blaze judgment across the page.

But the ink stayed still.

Oscar exhaled, spine softening, and snapped the clasp shut. Enough vulnerability for one night.

***

Lanterns on the Horizon

On the fifty-ninth night, the lookout's cry carved the quiet:

"Lanterns! South by east!"

People ran for the rails. Rigging groaned as bodies leaned. Across a jagged volcanic ridge, pinpricks of light flickered — not random like goblin fire, but patterned. Deliberate. Civilized.

Below, a harbor glimmered with silhouettes of ships. Sleek hulls. Tall masts. A fleet — their rigging glinting silver under moonwash.

Captain Tirpik lifted his spyglass, beard bristling. "That's no raider camp," he muttered. "A city."

Marissa folded her arms, gaze narrowing. "And someone wealthy enough to light the whole coast."

The order was crisp, decisive.

"Set her down."

Skythread's cloud-keel groaned as she dipped from the windstream. Her hum deepened, pitch shifting into a low, ocean-born rumble. Mist curled along her hull like breath in cold air.

She descended.

Lower.

Lower still.

The ocean rose to meet her — an ink-dark plane rippling with moonlight.

Then—

Contact.

A hiss.

A shudder.

A roll that sent every stomach lurching into someone else's boots.

The hull steadied. The water embraced her. The Skythread floated.

A cheer exploded from the decks — raw, breathless, almost disbelieving. The Grey Ghost had survived the trial every shipwright whispered about: **she could fly and she could sail.**

Oscar clutched the rail, breath sharp with exhilaration. His bow dug into his back. The Traveler's Book pressed warm against his ribs, as if recognizing a moment history might envy.

Beside him, Elenn touched the sigil at her throat and whispered a prayer for safe approach.

Her fingers trembled — just slightly. Oscar almost reached out. Almost.

He didn't.

The city's lanterns burned brighter, clearer, closer.

Unmarked by any map.

Claimed by no known kingdom.

Alive with a people they had never seen.

For the first time since their departure, the eastern horizon burned with the unmistakable glow of civilization.

A new city.

A new danger.

A new chapter.

The Skythread sailed toward it, her prow cutting across waters no cartographer had ever dared name.

Chapter Four

First Contact

"Caution is the wiser half of courage."

— *Seafarer's Proverb*

***

The Skythread rode at anchor like a held breath—sails furled, cloud-keel humming a low, patient note under the tide. A new coast stretched before her: green hills rising like sleeping beasts, pale cliffs striated with mineral light, and—most surprising of all—a harbor shaped like an open hand.

Not a village. Not a hidden cove.

A city.

Its ships were too many, too disciplined, too sharply rigged to be anything but organized strength.

Oscar stood beside Captain Tirpik at the rail. The gnome's beard was plaited against the wind, his dark eyes narrowed to hard points. His fingers tapped the carved railing in a quick, irritated rhythm, as though counting out all the reasons this discovery should not exist.

"Not on our charts," Tirpik muttered. "Not on *any* charts. And yet… look."

Down in the harbor, ships pivoted with purpose. Long, sleek hulls cut arcs across the water, forming a half-circle facing them. Lanterns flashed in patterns Oscar did not know.

Someone was speaking to them in a language of light.

Oscar's gut cinched tight. He glanced toward Marissa at the companionway—arms folded, jaw set, stormlight threading through her hair like a warning.

The weight of the Traveler's Book burned against his hip.

He unbuckled it, stepped quietly toward her, and pressed it into her hands.

"Keep this," he said, voice low enough that only she could hear. "Don't let it out of your sight. If things go wrong—"

Marissa's grip firmed immediately. No fear. No protest. "So I'll know what to do," she finished for him.

He nodded once, gratitude thick in his throat.

Tirpik's voice cracked like a whip. "Lower the pinnace!"

Lines flew. Pulleys groaned. The small boat dropped cleanly into the water, rocking like a heartbeat waiting for its next command.

Tirpik gestured sharply. "Oscar. With me."

Oscar climbed down the rope ladder into the pinnace. Greenbough followed, her form subtly shifting—softer at the edges, barklight subdued—as if the very air here required gentler company. A young wizard apprentice clambered in next, clutching his satchel of charms like a fragile truth. Last came Elenn, her lantern steady in her hand, the sigil of Paladin glinting in the light.

The pinnace rocked once, then steadied.

Oars dipped in unison.

The Skythread loomed behind them, lanterns mist-blurred, a quiet titan letting her envoy go.

Ahead: unknown shore. Unknown people. Unknown rules.

Oscar rested his bow across his knees. His fingers tightened around the grip until his knuckles paled. He told himself it was caution. His pulse told another story.

"First mate wants to know our plan," Tirpik said with bone-dry humor, "since this isn't a port of call and those ships clearly marked us."

Greenbough tilted her head, listening to the water lapping the hull, the rhythm of oars, the distant clang of harbor bells.

Tirpik let the silence stretch, then grinned. "SAME plan as always: we make it up as we go."

Oscar groaned. "That fills me with so much confidence."

"Good. Confidence is lighter than armor."

The oars dipped again. The pinnace slid toward the waiting city.

The first contact had begun.

***

The pinnace glided beneath high stone walls, each block pale as old bone. Lanterns cast long teeth of shadow across the water. Soldiers lined the battlements—helms bright, bows half-drawn, pikes angled downward in perfect, lethal geometry.

These walls had seen assaults.

And survived them.

No cheering.

No murmuring.

Not even a hostile roar.

Just silence, taut as a drawn bowstring.

The escorting warship cut across their bow once more, guiding them with unmistakable clarity toward a narrow quay. Oscar counted pikes—thirty? Forty?—their polished heads gleaming like winter sun on ice.

"Easy," Tirpik murmured. "They'll take us for spies, raiders, or fools until we prove otherwise."

Oscar's hand tightened involuntarily around Skyroot. The bow throbbed once—soft, warning—like a pulse beneath skin.

Greenbough touched his shoulder with a hand cool and bark-smooth.
"Roots don't panic," she whispered. "They hold."

Oscar breathed out, long and steady. The bow quieted. He nodded. She nodded back.

The pinnace bumped gently against the pier.

They stepped ashore beneath a canopy of spears. Boots rang against stone.
Greenbough's form chimed faintly with the memory of the ship, her presence a quiet reminder of wind and wood in a place that smelled of iron and old battles.

A figure strode out to meet them.

Broad-shouldered. Mail shirt polished with care but not ornament. His helm bore a storm-wolf crest. His eyes, sharp as flint, appraised each of them in turn—not curious, not hostile. Calculating.

He raised a hand, palm outward.

Not greeting.

Command.

"You will come," he said in the common tongue, each word clipped and precise. "You will answer."

Tirpik bowed just enough to be polite, not enough to bend.

"We'll answer. But we didn't come as raiders, and we won't be treated as such."

The man's gaze shifted—slowly—to Oscar's bow.

Then to Greenbough's leaf-shadowed face.

Then to the wizard apprentice's trembling satchel.

His jaw tightened.

"Open hands," he repeated flatly. "We will see."

He turned sharply, striding up the quay.

Soldiers closed around the Skythread's landing party with the smoothness of a trap snapping shut.

Oscar's pulse hammered. Every step was a test. Every shadow a question.

Greenbough leaned close, voice low enough for him alone.

"They want to see if you flinch," she murmured. "Don't. Even reeds stand straight in the flood."

He lifted his chin, spine straightening.

"Right," he whispered. "Right."

They passed the first line of Guardians—and Oscar nearly stumbled.

A woman stood among them, cloaked in deep sea-green, her lantern raised high. Bronze eyes glimmered beneath her hood, studying him with an intensity that was too long to be chance.

Greenbough noticed instantly.

Her whisper slid into his ear like wicked leaf-humor.

"Ah. That explains the twitching bowstring."

He almost choked. "I wasn't—!"

"Of course you weren't," she said, smirking. "Roots don't panic. They… notice."

Oscar glared at her. She grinned wider.

Ahead, the gates of the city opened with a grinding rumble.

The Guardians waited.

Their judgment waited.

And Oscar—bow in hand, heart on edge—walked forward to meet them.

Chapter Five

The Council of the Guardians

"A city that survived did so by suspecting everyone."

— *Saying of the Watchtowers*

***

The chamber of the Guardians was carved from stone that had known both flame and flood. The walls bore soot-scars that no scrubbing had erased; the air carried the twin scents of smoke and salt. Hooded torches hissed softly, throwing long shadows that prowled like restless sentries across a table etched with ancient coastlines.

The landing party was ushered inside beneath the watchful eyes of armored soldiers. Greenbough ducked beneath the stone lintel—not out of necessity, but respect. She laid a palm lightly against the rock. Beneath its cold surface she felt starborn echo, old magic sunk deep into the city's bones. Not alive, but remembering.

Oscar followed, Skyroot against his back, the tension between his ribs wound tight as rigging in a storm. Ten figures awaited them—captains, elders, a robed priest, a woman with a lantern-lens braided into her cloak. Their armor was practical, scarred from real battles; their robes patched where fire had bitten through. These were not ceremonial Guardians. These were survivors.

At the center stood the storm-wolf captain. His helm lay on the table, its metal dented and beautifully maintained all at once. His hair was silver-shot, his expression honed to something sharp enough to cut rope.

Tirpik walked forward, the smallest among them yet somehow commanding more space than his height should allow. Oscar took his place just behind. Elenn stood at Tirpik's right—human now, not half-elven, her youth sharpened rather than dimmed by the lamplight. Her hair caught golden in the firelight, her presence a quiet steadiness that anchored Oscar's frayed nerves.

In the Skythread's sickbay, she was soft instruction and gentle hands. Here, in the city's seat of judgment, she seemed something else entirely: unshaken, unafraid. A healer who had long accepted the weight of life and death.

Oscar looked away before Greenbough elbowed him and grinned like a tree catching a breeze made of secrets.

The storm-wolf captain's voice broke the silence.

"You arrive in a vessel neither of sky nor sea alone. You come from no harbor known to us. You carry arms fit for conquest." His gaze swept slowly across them. "Speak plain. Who are you? Why do you come to our shores?"

Tirpik stepped forward without hesitation.

"We are explorers. Traders. Seekers of truth, not territory. The coastlines our maps show are a century old. The world has shifted under our feet. We came east to learn what has changed."

A ripple of skepticism moved through the hall.

An elder leaned forward, shadows sharpening the lines of his face.

"And your armaments? Your enchanted coils, your soldiers, your steel? Do explorers require a fortress on their deck?"

Tirpik kept his face serene.

"When ogres stalk the cliffs and goblins swarm the shoals, a ship with no teeth dies before dawn. We defend because the world demanded it—not because we seek a fight."

The cloaked woman beside the captain lifted her lantern slightly, the lens reflecting bronze light into Oscar's face. Her eyes were unreadable, but her voice was smooth as worn stone.

"And you?" Her gaze held Oscar's like a pin. "Do you speak with your words... or with your bow?"

Oscar froze. Heat crept up the back of his neck. The entire chamber seemed to lean toward him.

He cleared his throat.
"I keep the log," he said, voice steadier than he felt. "I draw the coastlines we find. And the bow..." He hesitated. "The bow is for when the maps won't save us."

Something almost-soft flickered in her eyes. Approval? Recognition?

"Then you understand that a map holds more than lines. It holds lives."

The captain cut her off with a sharp gesture. "Enough riddles. You've given us claims. Now we will see if they stand."

***

The Trial of Truth

Instead of cells, they were led into an infirmary hollowed deep into the stone. Lamps burned steady. The air was heavy with salves, ash, and fever-sweat. Rows of wounded lay on pallets—soldiers with bandaged burns, villagers with blade cuts, others pale with infection.

The cloaked woman addressed them plainly.

"Words deceive. Healing does not.

Show us you are what you claim to be."

Elenn turned to Tirpik. He gave a single, deliberate nod. "Do what you can. Do no more."

The wizard apprentice knelt beside a man whose breath rattled like failing bellows. He murmured cleansing spells, fingers tracing sigils of gentle blue. Greenbough moved to a soldier burned along one side, her touch coaxing cool green shoots that eased the heat without piercing flesh.

Oscar was directed to a boy only a few years older than himself, trembling under a blood-soaked bandage. Elenn knelt beside him.

"Here," she said softly, placing Oscar's hands atop the wound. "Steady pressure. Not too hard. Think of easing fear as much as stopping blood."

Oscar pressed down, heart pounding. The boy's breath hitched—then eased. Elenn worked with practiced calm, replacing the old bandage, cleaning the wound, and laying linen fresh as snow.

When they finished, she looked at Oscar with that same steady presence that had become anchor and compass all at once.

"You have a healer's patience," she murmured. "If you choose it."

Oscar gave a weak laugh. "Most days I can barely write in a straight line."

Across the infirmary, Greenbough's voice carried, wicked and clear: "And yet he looks at *you* straighter than any page."

Oscar nearly dropped the roll of linen. Elenn blinked, lips curving—barely but unmistakably—before she returned to her patient.

When the Guardians finally escorted them back toward the quay, suspicion had loosened, the silence no longer a blade at their throats. The wounded slept easier. Magic and medicine had spoken louder than any claim.

The first thread of trust had been spun.

***

Departure

Moonlight glittered across the water as the pinnace rocked gently beneath their feet. The Guardians watched from the quay—no longer poised to strike, yet far from welcoming.

As Oscar stepped in, Greenbough leaned close, voice like leaves brushing humor into his ear.

"Careful, little sapling. You're learning more than knots and maps on this voyage."

Oscar groaned into his hands.

Elenn settled across from him, lamp glowing faint in her lap. Her smile—quiet, warm, unshaken—met his for a heartbeat.

Above them, the Skythread's lanterns burned bright in the mist, waiting to reclaim her crew.

Waiting to hear what new world they had just stepped into.

Chapter Six

Fallen Illusion

"Truth never breaks; it simply waits for the lies to fall away."

— *Saying among the Oathbearers*

***

Morning unfurled gold along the water, bright and sharp as hammered coin. Gulls wheeled over the harbor mouth, their cries scattering across the decks like thrown pebbles. The Skythread breathed in rhythm with the tide, her hull groaning softly as marines drilled on the forward deck, bows singing in short, clean arcs. Ballista crews practiced their reloads. Sailors ran rigging drills until the lines hummed like taut harpstrings.

Oscar sat at the sterncastle rail beside Elenn. Her lamp rested between them, warm against the morning breeze. She guided his fingers along his wrist, shaping his hand with careful patience.

"Don't chase the pulse," she said. "Let it rise into your touch. A healer doesn't hunt a heartbeat—he listens for it."

Oscar snorted. "Listening's hard when my hand's convinced it's holding a slippery trout."

Elenn's smile curved gently. "Then stop squeezing it like one."

He laughed under his breath. It felt good—too ordinary, too human for what the next heartbeat would bring.

Because the air changed.

It wasn't sound. It wasn't light. It was *pressure*—a hush sweeping across the deck like the pause before lightning strikes. The boards shivered beneath them, a ripple traveling the length of the ship. Oscar's fingers curled reflexively around Skyroot.

A shimmer rose at the sterncastle's center—heat mirage curling over stone—then collapsed inward.

A woman stood there.

Tall. Bronze-armored. Sea-green sigils etched along her gauntlets. Her eyes gleamed storm-dark, too bright to belong to any mortal. Her presence bent the air around her.

Then the Skythread reacted.

Runes along the cloud-keel flared. Wards snapped awake—sharp, defensive, instinctive. A humming grew, low and thrumming like a plucked thunderstring.

The woman's form fractured.

Armor blistered into scales. Bronze light cracked through her skin. Wings tore outward in a flash of dusk-metal, their spread blotting out the sun. The air filled with the scent of ozone and deep stone caverns.

A dragon.

The Guardian—**not illusion, not glamor, but her true, ancient shape**—towered above the sterncastle, bronze wings spanning the rigging, her storm-lit eyes pinning every soul in place.

And the fear came.

Older than language. Older than fire. The instinct carved into mortals when the first dragons first shook the newborn world.

Men dropped lines and wept openly. A hardened marine fell to his knees, trembling. Ballista crews clutched rails with white knuckles. Even the storm-blooded Marissa staggered, breath leaving her in a sharp, shocked gasp.

Elenn collapsed beside Oscar, her lamp guttering, face pale.

Greenbough's leafy hair rattled violently, her hands gripping the mast as if the wind sought to tear her free. The Skythread herself groaned—timbers quivering in fear.

For a heartbeat, the world bowed.

But Oscar didn't fall.

He shook. His chest tightened. Fear dug cold fingers behind his sternum. But his boots held the deck. His spine locked straight. He remembered the rift's breath on his neck in Archeron. He remembered shadow claws scraping at his mind. He remembered Dug's voice—*Stand, cub.*

Compared to those terrors, this aura was terror—but terror he could survive.

He knocked an arrow without thinking. Skyroot thrummed hot against his palm.

And Oscar lifted his chin.

"I've been yelled at by Talon," he muttered hoarsely. "You'll have to try harder."

The words were small, defiant, and ridiculous. But they were his. And they were steady.

The dragon's golden eyes snapped to him—surprised, then sorrowful, then soft with something like regret.

She hadn't meant to break them.

"Forgive me," she thundered, her voice shaking the masts.

Bronze wings swept once, twice—air cracking like thunder. In a burst of stormlight she vanished upward, her shadow ripping across the harbor and fading into the bright morning sky.

Silence crashed down.

Sailors gasped like drowning men breaking the surface. Marines stumbled to their feet. Greenbough sagged against the mast, hands trembling. Elenn clutched her lamp tight to her chest, breath shuddering.

Oscar remained standing—arrow lowered now, gaze still searching the sky even long after she disappeared.

No one spoke of what they had seen. Not because it was forbidden—because their voices hadn't yet found their way back.

***

By evening, whispers had thinned into uneasy quiet. Captain Tirpik ordered the pinnace lowered again, though half the crew begged him not to return to the city. He ignored them all.

The landing party assembled:

Oscar—still pale, still steady.

Greenbough—leaves dimmed, but resolute.

Elenn—lamp restored, eyes fire-steady.

Castor—a veteran dwarven marine, jaw set like hammered granite.

The pinnace dipped into the darkening water. Lanterns from the Guardian city glimmered like waiting eyes.

The council greeted them in silence so tight it felt like a held breath. The storm-wolf captain watched for any tremor

114

in their steps. The elder priest traced silent patterns in the air, measuring truth. The bronze-eyed woman who had mocked Oscar the day before studied him with something new— wariness, perhaps, or respect.

Oscar felt the Traveler's Book heavy at his hip. He resisted the urge to touch it. He did not want to see what it might write of the fear still coiled behind his ribs.

***

Back aboard the Skythread, the crew whispered their own stories. Some swore the Guardian had tested them. Others believed she had come to warn them. A few feared she would return, this time without apology.

But deep beyond harbors and mapped coasts, beyond the edge of any chart—

three figures stirred.

They felt the dragon's fear-spill like a bell struck in the deep. They turned their faces toward the east.

Their path realigned.

They were coming.

Not for the dragon.

Not for the Guardians.

For the ones who had stood through the fear.

For Oscar.

For the Skythread.

And for what moved behind them in the darkening world.

The map ahead was no longer merely uncharted.

It was hunted.

Chapter Seven

The City of the Exiles

*"A tongue bends like a branch in the wind—strange at first,
but steady once you learn its sway."*

— *Saying among the Far Coast sailors*

***

The spears lowered, and the gates creaked open.
Beyond them lay a young city—hurried, scarred, and already
bowed beneath the weight of survival.

The first wall was not stone but timber: thick palisades
driven into raised earthen bulwarks, still damp with sea wind.
Ditches ran at their base, half-filled with brackish water
reflecting the gray sky. Wooden towers flanked the entrance
like clenched fists. Archers atop them watched every step the
Skythread's landing party took.

Oscar's boots sank into packed clay as they entered.
Smoke, tar, and hot iron filled the air.

Inside, the city unfolded like a tapestry woven from
desperation. Huts of thatch and rough-planked halls huddled
together. A handful of stone dwellings—blocks hauled from
cliff quarries—stood anchored among them. Fresh brickwork

and sun-baked earthen blocks formed tight alleys where people moved with wary purpose.

Near the center, a foundry roared. Sparks spat skyward as men hammered glowing metal. Apprentices carted slag to a steaming pit.

"They have smelting," Greenbough murmured, leaves brushing her shoulders. "Ore beneath the roots… and fire above. This place is not temporary."

Oscar swallowed.

A foundry meant permanence.

These weren't fugitives anymore. They were building a future with their own hands.

The streets brimmed with faces—drawn, patched, exhausted. Children clung to their mothers' skirts. Fishermen with net-rough palms hurried past soldiers whose armor bore layers of repair. Every gaze weighed the Skythread's party: suspicion first, then hope, thin and trembling.

At the front of the crowd, the robed leader raised his staff. His Common was rough but steadier than before.

"You see our hearth," he said. "Built fast. Built hard. We fled fire… claw… hunger without end. Here—we make stand."

Elenn murmured beside Oscar, "That explains the foundry. Desperation builds faster than kings."

Greenbough placed a quiet hand on his arm. "Listen."

The leader spoke again, voice dipping into something like prayer.

"We had ships. We had seas. We had… her. Without— we die. With her—we live."

A murmur swelled around them—part reverence, part fear.

One whispered word reached Oscar's ear in the old tongue:

Guardian.

The silence that followed hung like a held breath.

Oscar exhaled. "Well," he muttered, "seems we've walked straight into someone else's legend."

Greenbough's leaves rustled faintly, though her gaze drifted beyond the crowd, toward the city's heart—where smoke blurred into bronze-tinted haze.

"No," she said softly. "Not someone else's. Ours, too."

The foundry hissed. The palisades groaned in the wind. And somewhere deeper in the settlement, something ancient waited—watching with a patience older than the city itself.

The Guardian's shadow lay over this place.

And now the Skythread walked in it.

***

Aboard the Skythread lanterns burned low across the sterncastle as Tirpik and Marissa argued in clipped, quiet tones. Crewmen scrubbed decks just to keep their hands busy. Some clutched charms; others whispered into cupped palms. Fear still clung to the rails.

Then the air shimmered—
light folding inward like parchment burning without flame—
and three figures appeared beside the chart table:

Talon. Bella. Thay'sa.

Marissa gasped. Tirpik only sighed. "Figured you might come."

Bella's gaze locked on him, sharp as stormlight.
"A bronze dragon on your deck, Tirpik. When were you planning to tell us? After she swallowed the aftmast?"

Marissa stepped quickly between them. "She didn't mean to reveal herself. The ship's wards forced it."

Thay'sa's expression hardened. "And the panic that nearly broke your crew?"

Tirpik gestured toward the stern windows. "Not malice. Reflex. Dragons carry their aura like breath. She realized it—and vanished before it did worse."

Talon crossed his arms. "Reflex or not, she chose to show truth. Dragons do not appear in their fullness without intent. If she walked your deck, she judged you—your hearts and your purpose. Do not forget that."

Bella nodded, steady and clear. "She will return. Not as a threat, but as a test. So be ready for her—not with steel, but with calm."

Shadows flickered across the maps.
The room felt smaller now.
The world felt larger.

For the first time, the name Guardian was no longer rumor echoed on wind-scoured shores.

She lived.

She watched.

And the next step of the Skythread would take them straight into the hold of her city—where truth waited.

And where lies—ancient, heavy, half-buried—would not survive her gaze.

Chapter Eight

The Tell of Bronze

"A single truth, spoken without fear,
can open more doors than a thousand blades."

— *Saying from the Sailor's Catechism*

***

The hall breathed salt and smoke, its rafters thick with the hush of a hundred watching eyes. Oscar stood at the center, Skyroot slung over his shoulder, Greenbough beside him steady as the deep roots she always claimed to embody. Castor's beard twitched with restrained commentary—his version of silence.

The hush deepened when the Guardian rose. Even those who didn't understand her language felt the shift, as though a keel had settled deep into water. Elenn straightened. Oscar's ears burned. He had not asked for awe, but it pressed on him all the same.

The Guardian leaned forward, bronze eyes half-lidded. "You crossed the sea not to trade. Why come here?"

Elenn stepped forward, voice smooth from a lifetime of tending sickbeds and negotiating with stubborn sailors twice her size. "Maps," she said. "Coasts change. Storms carve new bones from the world. We chart so others can follow safely."

A murmur broke—skeptical, sharp at the edges.

The Guardian's head tilted. "And what do you see when you chart *us*?"

Elenn didn't flinch. "A people strong enough to build a future where others would have seen only danger. Strong enough to carve life from the sea's discarded bones. That is what I see."

The words stopped the murmurs. Strength named as praise, not threat.

She let the quiet settle, then added, gentler, "Guardian—your people have endured. But you do not always have to run. In the west, in the Vale of Eagles, there is room. Skyfallen Lake may be too shallow for your hulls, but the Vale itself—fields, timber, fresh water—is a haven. Should you ever seek it, there is land to till, and a place to stand without fleeing."

A ripple crossed the hall—fear and hope twisting together. Old men frowned into beards. Mothers held their children closer.

The Guardian's bronze eyes narrowed. "Is this promise?" she asked quietly. "Or lure?"

Silence fell again—thick, bracing, like the air before a storm breaks.

***

The long tables filled slowly, as if every soul waited to see where the strangers would sit before daring to claim their own benches. Platters appeared—smoked fish with charred edges, flatbread baked dark and crisp, bowls of thick root stew. Humble food, but warm, fragrant, alive with the taste of survival.

Oscar sat awkwardly among them all, bow set against the wall like a sleeping wolf. Every bite tasted of scrutiny. Men whispered behind callused hands. Children peeked from folds of cloth with wide, unblinking eyes. Even laughter sounded nervous, like a blade half-drawn.

Elenn broke the tension with gentle conversation— weather, tides, fishing seasons—topics any sailor recognized. Her calm wore down suspicion as patiently as surf wears stone.

Greenbough helped without trying: wherever she leaned, leaves stirred and the air seemed to breathe deeper, as if the hall found a little more room around her.

Castor took a far more direct approach to diplomacy. He swallowed a mouthful of mead, thumped his cup down, and declared, "Say what you want about your storms, but your mead hits like a forge hammer—and I like it."

Laughter rippled—small at first, then genuine. A young sailor refilled his cup with a grin.

Even the Guardian's gaze softened for a heartbeat before returning to its steady watchfulness—always drifting back to Oscar.

She sat at the high seat, speaking when addressed, but never losing sight of him. Her expression unreadable, measuring him against a memory he could not see.

Then she rose.

The hall quieted. She paced around the long table with the easy prowl of someone used to command. When she reached Oscar's bench, she slipped into the empty seat beside him.

Her robes—patched linen and bronze plates stitched with silver runes—whispered as she leaned close. A strand of hair fell loose across her cheek.

"You're holding the spoon like a dagger," she murmured. "Ease your grip. Root stew doesn't fight back."

Oscar nearly inhaled his own mouthful. "I—I wasn't—"

Her laugh warmed the air. Not mocking—just humanizing. "Half the hall expects you to sprout wings or breathe fire. Better they see you trip over stew than glower like a stormcloud."

She pressed another piece of flatbread into his hand, fingers brushing his for a heartbeat longer than courtesy required. His pulse jumped. He set the bread down like it was fresh from the forge.

Questions soon followed—directed at him more than anyone else.

A youth with windburned cheeks cleared his throat. "Your bow... what is it you carry?"

Oscar touched Skyroot's stave where it rested against the wall. He almost answered with bravado. Then something steadier rose in him.

"It's not for here," he said quietly. "I carry it for my crew. Pointing it in this hall would betray that trust."

The room held its breath. Honesty can be sharper than steel.

The Guardian's lips curved—faint, small, but unmistakable. Not approval, not fully... but respect's beginning.

Castor, ever the iron wedge between heavy moods, slapped the table. "Aye, and he's deadlier with that bow than he lets on. Lucky for us he's chasing stew tonight, not glory."

Laughter rose again—louder now, the edge gone.

Elenn watched Oscar with something like recognition. "Duty and mercy," she murmured. "Both parts of the oath."

As the meal wore on, suspicion thinned. Laughter grew steady. Children drew closer. Stories were traded—broken ones, hopeful ones. For the first time since landfall, the hall felt like a place where strangers might become something else.

Oscar tried to focus on his stew. But the Guardian kept drawing him out—asking of the Skythread, of the stars over Archeron, of herbs used by Vale healers and the storms that shaped distant coasts. Her questions were probing, curious, almost gentle.

Greenbough caught his eye across the table and tilted her head with a knowing look:

You've been seen.

And heard.

Oscar's ears burned again. He sank deeper over his bowl.

Yet when Elenn laughed at something Castor said, he found himself smiling—and didn't notice until far too late that his hand still rested close enough to hers that their fingers nearly touched.

Chapter Nine

The Weight of Secrets

*"The eyes of dragons are windows
—what they show is never all they see."*

— *Fragment from the Silver Oath*

***

The meal ended in an unexpected hush—voices folding
into a steady chant, the rhythm shaped less by melody than by
memory. The Guardians sang like people who had once
known a homeland and had built a new one from grief.
Greenbough swayed with the cadence, leaves shimmering like
soft applause. Oscar clapped roughly in time, but the notes
twisted past him—strange, mournful, uncomfortably familiar
in ways he could not name.

When the last verse faded, the Guardian rose.

"Walk with me," she said.

Not request. Command.

Oscar swallowed and rose, Skyroot brushing his shoulder
as he followed her through a narrow archway and into a small
courtyard carved from cliffstone. A brazier burned low,
tossing copper sparks into the wind. The noise of the hall fell
away until only the sea's whisper remained.

"You carry more than a bow," she said without turning. Oscar stiffened.

The Guardian faced him—bronze eyes luminous in the firelight, her expression unreadable. "When the Veil tore at Archeron, the scream reached us across the deep. My priests saw its shadow echo—bright silver, bright gold, then fractured into night."

Oscar's breath hitched.

She continued, voice softer. "We saw a shape in the rift. Wings… the edge of a star. And a boy. Standing. Wounded. Alone."

Oscar closed his eyes as heat surged up his throat. "I didn't ask for any of that."

"No one asks for the shadow's notice," she murmured.

He opened his eyes. Her gaze held neither accusation nor pity—only truth.

"I walked into that place with Talon and Arrabella," he said quietly. "But I walked out alone."

The memory pressed against him—the way the world had cracked, the scream of tearing light, Isa's fall echoing across time. The shadows beneath Archeron had clawed at his thoughts, whispering names not his own. Sometimes he still heard the scrape of them when the wind shifted wrong.

"I survived," Oscar said. "But that doesn't mean I understand it."

The Guardian stepped closer. Not threatening— assessing. "Few mortals stand before dragonlight and shadow both and come away whole."

"I'm not whole."

"No," she said gently. "But you are standing."

The brazier flared as a gust of wind rolled through the court. The Guardian's bronze eyes reflected the fire in twin rings, ancient and sorrowed.

"You speak Isa's name without speaking it," she said. "Most cannot. Her fall carried weight across the world. Some would call it omen."

Oscar swallowed. "She wasn't an omen. She was... kind. Brave. She gave up everything."

"And now her memory hangs around you like a cloak," the Guardian said. "Not as burden, but as bond."

Oscar felt Skyroot vibrate faintly against his back, as though remembering silver wings.

The Guardian's voice shifted—quieter now, but edged with purpose.

"My people did not flee here blindly," she said. "We followed signs. Currents. Rifts not of the sea. Something in the deep pushes against the world's bones. Your arrival— your scars—these are not accidents."

Oscar frowned. "Are you saying I'm part of whatever you're trying to escape?"

"No," she said. Her bronze eyes narrowed, as if weighing the shape of his soul.

"I am saying you are tied to what hunts us."

Silence hit him like cold water.

Oscar suddenly felt small, almost weightless. "I'm not a threat."

"You are not," the Guardian said gently. "But the one who drove us from our home—she knows your scent."

Oscar blinked. "Who?"

The Guardian exhaled, the sound like waves breaking against distant cliffs.

"A shadow wearing a name we only half understood in our flight.

Keera.

Or something like it. A word said wrong in fear."

Oscar frowned, confused. The name meant nothing to him.

The Guardian continued, "She tore through our streets with claw and storm. She led beasts twisted by anger, and the sky itself burned at her passing. We fled because to stay was to feed her fury."

Oscar's breath hitched. "I'm… sorry. I don't know who that is."

"Good," she said softly. "Then carry that ignorance while you still can."

A flicker of grief crossed her features—ancient, restrained, unmistakably real.

"She will not follow us here," the Guardian whispered. "Not yet. The sea confuses her. But the tide is shifting."

Oscar tightened his grip on Skyroot's hilt. He didn't understand the name, or the threat.

Not now.

He would.

He just didn't know it yet.

"I know," she said softly. "But the thing that marked you—that tore Isa from the sky—*is*. And if it felt you once, it may feel you again."

His pulse hammered. "Then what do I do?"

She stepped back, the fire glowing off the bronze runes at her wrists.

"You speak truth," she said. "You survive shadow. You carry dragon memory without breaking. Those are rare gifts, Oscar of the Skythread."

Her voice lowered.

"And tomorrow, you will need them."

The brazier crackled. Somewhere beyond the wall, a wave struck rock—hard, warning.

Oscar bowed stiffly, throat tight. "What happens tomorrow?"

The Guardian's gaze lifted toward the dark horizon.

"Tomorrow," she said, "the truth comes to weigh us both."

And before he could ask more, she turned and vanished into the shadows of her city—leaving Oscar alone with only the echo of Isa's wings in the wind.

Chapter Ten

The Return

*"Sometimes the truest weight we carry is not the blade,
but the faces we return to."*

— *Saying among the Oathbearers*

***

The pinnace struck the Skythread's hull with a soft thud, oars dripping, ropes tossed and caught by sure hands above. Six weeks away from the ship had felt like six seasons. When Oscar climbed the rope ladder, boots scraping wood, the familiar deck planks felt both foreign and achingly like home.

He swung one leg over the rail, dropped lightly to the deck—

—and froze.

Bella and Thay'sa stood at the stern rail like two stormfronts that had agreed, briefly, to share the same sky. Bella's arms were crossed, jaw clenched; Thay'sa's expression was carved from polished ice. Between them stood Marissa, the white quill tucked guiltily into her belt, teeth worrying her lower lip.

For one doomed heartbeat, Oscar heard Talon's voice in his head—dry, wry, and entirely imagined:

You asked for trouble. Trouble said, "Sure, why not."

Oscar swallowed and kept walking.

"Six weeks," Bella said. Calm. Too calm—the kind of calm one used right before casting a lightning bolt. "Six weeks of nothing but wind speeds, compass headings, morning meals… and silence bleeding through that book. And you thought that was fine?"

Marissa's hands shot up immediately. "I told them you were probably fine! I mean—I said you were *mostly* fine. I was very clear about the 'probably.'"

Bella gave her a look sharp enough to trim sails. Marissa winced, stepped sideways, and whispered, "He's yours. I'll be over there. Out of spell range."

Crewmen suddenly discovered urgent tasks to perform. Ropes were coiled with unnecessary vigor. Someone began scrubbing a clean plank purely for cover. The entire deck thrummed with the collective decision: *Nope. Not getting involved in this.*

Oscar tipped his chin up, though his heartbeat hammered.

Thay'sa spoke next, voice clipped as a snapped twig. "You let us feel every fear that touched you. Yet wrote nothing to ease it. Why?"

Oscar rubbed the back of his neck, caught between guilt and stubbornness. "If they'd seized the Traveler's Book," he said quietly, "it wouldn't just have been me in danger. They could have read more than my notes. They could have found you. The library. The Vale. I wasn't going to hand them a map of the world I love."

Silence. Sharp. Heavy.

He forced a grin anyway—crooked, helpless. "Besides… what sane man risks making two wizards he love—" He

134

stumbled, cheeks flushing. "—two wizards he cares about—furious because he lost their book?"

It cracked the storm.

Bella let out a sound halfway between a laugh and a sob, arms wrapping around him before he could finish bracing for it. She squeezed tight enough to drive the air from his lungs.

"You reckless boy," she whispered into his hair. "Don't ever do that again."

He hugged her back, eyes stinging. "No promises."

Thay'sa's muttered Elvish translated roughly—if Oscar caught the tone correctly—to *idiot child but thank every star you're alive.* When she drew back, she touched his shoulder with a quiet, trembling exhale before recomposing herself in a flawless sweep of robes.

Even the sailors—pretending not to stare—felt the shift. Later, in the mess, they would rib him mercilessly. Someone would call him "the captain's wayward son." Someone else would wager how long it would be before the wizards fitted him with a leash. But here, now, the deck belonged to family.

It might have ended there.

But Thay'sa's sharp gaze drifted upward, past Oscar's shoulder. She stiffened.

Bella followed her look.

And stopped.

Atop the sterncastle sat a massive grizzly bear.

He was perched precariously behind the aft mast like an enormous, fluffy gargoyle attempting stealth. Each time he peeked around the mast, his gold eyes radiated the unmistakable guilt of a child hiding behind a curtain with their feet still showing.

"...Oscar," Bella said slowly, "how long has *he* been here?"

Oscar blinked, then shrugged with saintly innocence. "Who?"

Dug snorted—deep, offended, entirely unimpressed with the denial. He lowered his head like a disgruntled mountain. The ship creaked slightly beneath his weight.

Talon's remembered voice echoed in Oscar's mind, a dry breeze of humor:

Secret fort mission. Keep an eye on things.

Oscar bit back a grin. "Long enough, I guess."

The bear huffed, rose with ponderous dignity, and padded down the stairs, pretending—as only a bear could—that he had *absolutely* intended to be discovered at that moment. Sailors stepped aside reverently. More than one whispered a quick blessing.

And just like that, the storm on deck eased.

The Skythread had all her guardians again.

But the calm that settled was not simple relief. Bella and Thay'sa exchanged a look—one Oscar almost missed. A look threaded with worry. Recognition. And the faintest flicker of fear.

Something was coming.

And now that he had returned, the Skythread would face it together.

***

Chapter Eleven

Safe Harbor

"The sea keeps no secrets, save those it swallows.
To walk away is to be remembered, not forgotten."

— *Dockside Saying, Port Ravenglass*

***

The mess hall buzzed with warmth and clatter, bowls scraped clean, mugs sloshed with ale. The *Skythread's* crew ate like wolves after a long watch, and tonight they had more than stew to chew on.

Oscar tried to keep his head down, but the first jibe landed before he'd even lifted his spoon.

"Careful there," one sailor called, loud enough for the whole hall. "Best not spill your soup, lad. Might be both your mums come down here and scold you proper."

The room erupted in laughter, hard and sharp as rigging in a storm.

Another chimed in, "Two mages for mothers! What chance does the lad have? One frown and the young man looks like he's swallowed an anchor!"

Oscar groaned, burying his face in his hands. "You're never letting this go, are you?"

"Not a chance," Tirpik said from his seat, beard wet with ale. His grin was merciless. "We'll carve it on your bunk if need be. Mammas' boy—all the way to the Vale and back."

Greenbough leaned forward, leaves brushing the lanternlight, and smiled sly as spring. "At least you're loved. Some would trade for half so much." Her tone was softer, meant for him more than the crowd, but her twinkling eyes betrayed she was enjoying the sport too.

"Even Dug saw it," another sailor heckled from the back. "Bear's been sitting on the sterncastle like a nursemaid! Whole ship knew, only you pretended not to."

The hall roared again.

Oscar shook his head, cheeks red but lips tugging upward despite himself. He lifted his mug, met their jeers with a toast. "Fine. To mothers. May we all have two angry ones waiting when we come home."

That earned a cheer loud enough to rattle the beams. The laughter rolled on, good-natured and merciless. Oscar sat among them, red-eared and grinning, knowing he'd never live it down. And that, perhaps, was the point.

***

The next morning, laughter gave way to solemnity. A single pinnace rode the waves alongside the *Skythread*, her hull dark and polished, ropes drawn taut between the two vessels. The oarsmen waited in silence, and an officer in a sea-blue cloak hailed the deck.

"Orders from the Guardian of the Isle," she called. "Only Oscar of the *Skythread* is to come aboard."

The crew exchanged wary glances. Oscar looked to Bella and Thay'sa, who stood near the rail with the morning light haloing their hair.

Bella frowned. "Only you?"

"Seems that way." Oscar rubbed his neck, trying for a crooked grin. "Guess I made an impression."

Thay'sa folded her arms. "Dragons rarely summon mortals without reason." Her gaze softened a little. "Be careful what truths you give them—they have a way of turning honesty into oaths."

Oscar gave a small nod. "I'll keep my mouth mostly shut, then."

Bella stepped forward, pressing the *Traveler's Book* into his hands. "If she tests you, remember who you are," she said quietly.

He slid it into his tunic, over his heart. "I'll be fine."

"Fine," Bella echoed. "That's sailor-speak for *in over my head.*"

He grinned, a little sheepishly. "You know me too well."

"Someone has to," she said, her smile softening the edge of her worry.

Thay'sa touched his arm briefly. "Go, then. Speak truly, but remember: even dragons listen for what isn't said."

Oscar nodded and swung himself over the side, climbing down the rope ladder into the waiting boat. The officer gestured sharply, and the lines were cast off. The pinnace drifted clear, then turned toward the mist-shrouded harbor, the city's walls rising ahead like a memory out of legend.

The hall was quiet after the assembly, braziers low, smoke curling toward beams blackened by years of salt and fire. At the high seat sat the woman they called Guardian, bronze-eyed, bronze-souled, scales hidden beneath the glamour of skin. Her people filled the benches with reverence; none questioned, none guessed.

Oscar stood awkwardly on the rushes before her seat, bow unstrung, posture caught between soldier and uncertain guest. He bowed—too shallow for a court, too deep for a casual hall—then straightened, cheeks warm.

"You asked for me," he said, voice respectful, if wary.

The Guardian studied him, her gaze leaving him bare against the air. "You are marked. My seers confirm what I saw with my own eyes. You walked where no mortal should, and returned. Such a thread must not be cut."

Oscar shifted. "I'm a sailor. A mapmaker's guard. Nothing more."

She leaned forward, eyes like molten coins. "You are more. And because you are more, I must keep you safe."

The words landed like a snare.

"What do you mean by 'keep'?" Oscar asked slowly.

"You will have quarters. Food. Comfort. You will not want for care," she said, each syllable heavy with the finality of judgment. "But you will not walk beyond these walls. The world is cruel and careless. I will not see fate's sign squandered on its teeth."

Oscar's mouth went dry. "So… a tower. Fed well. And never see the sun again."

The Guardian tilted her head, calm and inexorable. "If that is the price of your safety, yes."

Oscar opened his mouth, closed it. Somewhere in his skull, Talon's remembered voice muttered: *Uh, wait—what?*

Then the air shifted.

A presence filled the hall, heavy as earth, vast as mountains. The Guardian's words faltered as the shimmer of fur and golden eyes bloomed at the edge of her vision. Dug stood there—no, not stood: manifested—a shape of Elysium, half in this world, half in the eternal green. His gaze bore no anger, only certainty.

Her counselors gasped, the sound thin against the weight of his arrival. The Guardian did not move. Dug's eyes swept past them, locking only with hers. No growl, no roar—just presence.

A reminder that some lives were not hers to bind.

Between them, no words were spoken aloud, yet meaning passed as surely as breath.

You've judged too quickly, his thought carried, not as sound but as memory of wind through trees.

Her mind answered without intention—*This one trespasses beyond his place. I must—*

—*must nothing,* the echo came, steady and vast. *Some burdens are chosen, not chained.*

The Guardian flinched, faintly, her scales tightening across her shoulders. That voice, that weight—she remembered it from older days.

An Oathbearer.

***

Oscar heard none of it.

All he felt was the pressure—the air thickening until it pressed like water against his chest. He tried to speak, thought better of it, and stood very still. The silence stretched until it hurt. The Guardian's eyes no longer seemed fixed on him but on something behind or beyond. He dared not turn.

Gods, they're deciding my sentence, he thought. *This is it. I'm done.*

***

The Guardian inhaled, a slow, shuddering breath. Then, at last, she lowered her gaze. Her voice, when it came, was quieter, humbled by something unseen.

"Perhaps… confinement is not the way. If such guardians stand for you, then my hand need not close so tightly."

Oscar blinked, thrown off-balance. "Wait—what? I mean… glad to hear it. No offense, but I'm not much for gilded cages."

Something almost like a smile ghosted her lips. "Then we agree. Go, young one. I will summon your friends from the ship."

***

As he bowed awkwardly and turned to leave, Dug's form began to fade—fur to light, light to memory. The Guardian did not look up; she simply inclined her head in reverence, eyes reflecting gold where no lantern burned.

So it is true, she thought. *Elysium still watches.*

And the air, now lighter, carried only the whisper of leaves in reply.

***

After his meeting with the Guardian, Oscar wandered the great hall, tracing its worn stones and high arches. Bronze lamps burned low along the walls, their light catching on banners faded by salt and years. Within a few hours, the quiet was broken by the sound of oars and voices—a small host of the Skythread's company had come ashore, nearly fifty in all. Each bore the faint mark of Archeron, the unseen scar left by that distant darkness.

Thay'sa remained aboard with Dug, her watchful presence steady as the tide, while Talon, Arrabella, Tirpik, Marissa, Elenn, and the rest of the sailors made their way into the city. Among them stood one who had died and returned—Oscar alone carried that burden.

That evening, when the hall gathered once more, the Guardian rose before them all. Her scaled robes shimmered like deepwater bronze, every motion drawing light and silence in equal measure.

"You died," she said, her voice ringing not as accusation but as certainty. "You fell with the Hollow when its mouth closed. And yet you returned—first feathered, winged as an owl, and then judged by the **Archons** themselves. Few mortals bear such a passage and walk again as man. You are marked, boy returned, and even I must honor that mark."

A rustle moved through the benches—part awe, part unease—the weight of words too heavy to ignore. Elenn stiffened among them, her breath catching. The rumor she'd dismissed as sailors' talk now stood proven before her eyes. *He died,* she thought, pulse quickening. *And came back.*

Her gaze found Oscar across the hall, and for the first time she saw not the boy with a crooked grin and ink-stained hands, but someone carrying something far older.

Later, she told herself. *When this is done—I'll ask him.*

Oscar bowed his head, ears burning, but said nothing. He could feel her eyes on him, though he didn't dare meet them.

The Guardian's decree followed, calm and solemn. "By your scars and your silence, you may rest here. My harbor will not turn you away. But you will not carry my name eastward, nor speak of these islands to the nations that hunger beyond the horizon. Swear it, and you will have safe harbor."

One by one, the crew of the Skythread spoke their oaths. Tirpik's was rough but steady, his hand pressed to his beard as he swore. Marissa followed, her voice low but clear, the sea's cadence still in her tone.

Then Talon stepped forward, his shadow long across the firelight. "By the wind and the wild that guide my kind," he said, "I give my word. No map I make nor tale I tell will name these shores without your leave." His voice carried the calm of forests and stormbreaks, a ranger's truth given freely.

Arrabella followed, her hand brushing the ring at her finger, eyes bright with quiet resolve. "And I swear," she said, "by the flame that guards memory, by compassion and by craft, that no harm shall come from what we have seen here. Not by my tongue, nor by my magic."

The Guardian's gaze lingered on them both, something ancient stirring behind her bronze eyes—perhaps recognition, perhaps sorrow.

Oscar hesitated then, memory heavy in his chest—until Greenbough's quiet rustle steadied him. He gave his word, and the hall exhaled as though a tide had turned.

The Guardian inclined her head, bronze eyes glinting like deepwater fire. "Then rest, and take what you need. The sea remembers," she said, "but so do I."

It was Tirpik who stepped forward next, his voice carrying over the quiet.
"Fleetmother," he said, bowing low, "let me offer what I can. I'll not take passage myself, but I can share what we've charted—our courses westward, the safe lanes and soundings, the distances to Ravenglass and Runedragon. If you wish it, send a small expedition. The routes are true."

The Guardian regarded him for a long moment, weighing his words as if testing their sound against the sea itself. Then she inclined her head. "So it shall be," she said. "Knowledge for safe passage—direction given, and distance shared. A bond sealed in silence, and in goodwill."

As the hall bowed and the torches dimmed to embers, Elenn's eyes found Oscar again. He looked exhausted, bewildered—still trying to make sense of it all.

You died, she thought once more, shivering despite the warmth of the fire. *And somehow, you came back.*

She said nothing then. But the question—*how?*—would not leave her.

***

That night, Oscar slipped out onto the deck. The air was cool, the sea below dark and restless.

Dug sat where he always seemed to—on the sterncastle, broad shoulders hulking against the stars.

Oscar leaned against the rail. "You saw her too."

The bear rumbled, low and steady.

"That dragon… when she looked at me, it was like she could see straight through. Like I was—bare, against the sky. Not just flesh, but all the mistakes, all the doubts. She could've ended me in a breath, Dug. Smashed me flat without trying."

The bear's head turned, eyes catching starlight.

"I don't know if I said the right things," Oscar admitted. "I did my duty, kept the crew safe. But what if duty wasn't enough? What if I should've bowed lower, or… or stood taller?"

A thought brushed his mind, warm as fur and heavy as stone.

The right thing is not the easy thing. You stood. You did not aim. That is enough.

Oscar swallowed. "Talon would've known how to act. And Bella... she always knows what to say."

Dug huffed—a sound somewhere between a chuckle and a snort.

And yet, came the gentle thought, *it was you who stood today.*

For a long moment, there was only the night wind and the quiet rise and fall of the bear's breath beside him. Then:

Their hearts were tempered by time, came the thought, low and sure. *Yours is human—and burns bright. Sometimes the hardest thing is not knowing the way, but choosing one. You did. That light is enough to blind the dark, if you let it.*

Oscar let out a long breath, eyes lifting to the constellations wheeling above. "Then maybe... maybe she saw that too."

***

When the *Skythread* put out to sea again, she did not rise alone. For two days' sail, a pair of island ships ran beside her, bright sails catching the wind, their crews shouting greetings over the spray. Only when the coast bent westward did they part company, raising oars and horns in farewell.

Oscar stood at the rail, watching their sails fade. For the first time since the trial, he let out a long breath. Marissa touched his shoulder lightly.

"Safe harbor," she said, almost to herself. "And a road ahead."

The *Skythread* sailed on, her mast humming low, as though the ship herself remembered.

Book Three

The Skies of Fate

"Every storm bears two gifts: the wave that threatens, and the wind that carries you home."

— *Old sailor's toast*, Ravenglass Harbor

***

Chapter One

Westward into Fate

"A ship may follow her captain, but the sea follows only itself."

— *Old Sailor's Saying, Port Runedragon*

***

The Guardian's isle faded into the western sky, bronze-lit and dwindling. For a time the Skythread sailed in company, two island ships pacing her like kin. Their sails flashed bright against the horizon until, with a final cry of horns and the lift of oars, they turned back. Alone again, the Skythread pressed on.

Arrabella lingered at the quarterdeck rail beside Tirpik and Marissa. Sea-spray shone like glass on her sleeves.

"Your charts are the best gift we could've asked for," she told the gnome. "I'll take copies to Nandanoléme and Runedragon so they can begin updating their records. The world should see what you've mapped here."

Tirpik's grin was all mustache and twinkle. "Then you'd better come back soon to make sure the librarians don't change the coastlines on us."

Marissa folded her arms, a flash of lightning-blue tattoo visible on her wrist. "And next time," she added, "try to

149

arrive *before* a dragon does the boarding. My crew still twitches at shadows."

Bella smiled. "I'll do my best."

A low sound drew their attention — a huff, half growl, half sigh. Dug stood half-hidden behind the mainmast, pretending not to listen, ears flicking in embarrassment.

"So," Bella said softly, "you were staying quiet after all."

The bear rumbled, deep and weary. "Oscar will be fine," he said, giving a sideways glance — half snort, half grin — toward Elenn. "He's getting better at seeing dangers... well, sometimes, if it doesn't have a wry smile attached." He turned his heavy gaze directly on Oscar. "Might as well get a sun tan for the shades of red you've turned lately."

Laughter rippled across the deck.

Talon laid a hand on his thick fur. "Rest well, my friend."

Dug's form shimmered, light breaking through mist, and then he was gone — leaving only the scent of pine and rain.

Arrabella exhaled. "I'll miss him every time I turn around."

"Then we'll know he's watching," Talon said. He offered his hand. "Ready?"

"One more ship, one more sunrise," she murmured — then traced the circle of the spell. Light folded over them like a curtain of silver, and in a breath, the Skythread's deck was empty.

***

They reappeared in the cool hush of twilight, on the hill overlooking the Vale of Eagles. Wind moved through the grass like a sigh.

Talon looked across the valley — the lights of Dragonfall faint in the distance, the Silver Ring glimmering beyond. "She wasn't just a guardian," he said at last. "You saw it too."

Arrabella nodded. "A being that old… she remembered the world before it cracked. She *was* part of it. I think she's one of the ancient dragonkind that never chose sides when the rifts opened."

"Neutral," Talon murmured. "Or waiting."

"She made us swear to keep the skies whole," Bella said. "That wasn't for her—it was for what's still coming."

They stood a while longer, watching swans glide across the far lake. The air was sweet with frost and peat smoke from distant hearths.

Talon turned to her. "Let's check the cottages tomorrow. Make sure the path's still clear. Then we'll go see the Collegium."

She smiled faintly. "You just want to delay the paperwork."

"Maybe," he admitted. "But tonight, let's just breathe."

***

Back aboard the **Skythread**, dawn crept rose-gold across the sea. The light spilled over the deck in long, slow ribbons, catching in the rigging and the mist still clinging to the rails. **Elenn** found **Oscar** sitting cross-legged on the main deck, scribbling in his journal, hair unkempt from sleep.

"You think they'll be back soon?" she asked.

He shrugged without looking up. "No way to tell. They vanish like wind and reappear with twice the trouble."

She laughed quietly, leaning on the rail beside him. "When everyone spoke those oaths… I felt something. Heavy. As if it tied itself to my ribs."

151

Oscar set the quill down, considering. "It was heavy. Oaths sworn before something as old as that dragon aren't just words. Break them, and the world listens."

Elenn hesitated. "You think something bad would happen?"

He reached into his vest and drew out a small skeleton key of pale, bluish steel. The bow of the key was wrought in the likeness of an owl's wings. "**Thay'sa** wrote about that once," he said. "Said that when an oath is bound by an ancient soul, it becomes a thread through time. Pull the wrong end…"

He turned the key in his fingers, its metal catching the light. "…and what's bound unravels."

Elenn studied it, brow furrowing. "That key—**Archeron**?"

"Part of what's left of it," Oscar said. "And of me."

A silence settled between them, filled by the sound of the sails filling and the low hum of the Skythread's heart. The morning light glimmered on the key like a heartbeat.

Then, softer, almost to herself, Elenn asked, "So… it's true, then. You really died?"

Oscar froze. The question hung between them, fragile as glass. He stared out toward the horizon where the sea met the clouds, letting the light wash over his face.

He didn't answer right away.
The Skythread breathed around them—the faint creak of timbers, the whisper of wind through the sails—like the world was waiting to hear if he remembered.

Finally, he spoke. "Yeah," he said quietly. "For a while."

Elenn waited, but he didn't look at her.

Then he sighed, and something in his shoulders loosened. "Truth is, I don't even know what that means. I remember… *not being*. Like a thought left unfinished. Then light—too much light—and voices that didn't use words." He hesitated, searching for the shape of what couldn't be spoken. "And when I woke, I was… different. Not worse, not better. Just… less certain I came back as the same person."

He gave a half-smile, a tired one. "Talon and Bella would probably know what to make of it. But they're still with the Guardian, sorting the politics of dragons and promises. So maybe I'll ask **Greenbough**."

Elenn tilted her head. "Greenbough? About dying?"

"She understands things in ways the rest of us don't," Oscar said. "Roots, death, memory—they all mean the same thing to her. Maybe she can tell me if I'm missing something… or if I just need to stop thinking like a man who ever left the ground."

For a moment, neither spoke. The sea whispered against the hull, and the first bell of morning tolled faintly from below deck.

Elenn smiled, small and real. "When you do ask her, tell me what she says. I'd like to know which parts of you made the trip back."

Oscar's eyes flicked toward her, surprised—and then, despite himself, he laughed softly. "If she says any of them are missing, I'll send you a map."

"Good," Elenn said, brushing wind-blown hair from her face. "Just make sure you mark the dangerous parts."

Oscar pocketed the key, still smiling. "A good rule," he said, "for sea and sky both."

***

The *Skythread* drifted steady in the morning calm, her sails turned toward the slow light. Below deck, near the heartwood garden where the ship's living roots climbed the walls, **Oscar** found **Greenbough** tending to the saplings she'd coaxed from seed during the long voyage. The air smelled of soil and salt and the faint sweetness of new leaves.

She looked up before he spoke. "You walk heavy this morning," she said, her voice soft and creaking like old wood in the wind. "Not in your steps—your thoughts."

Oscar managed a half-smile. "Guess I'm not good at hiding it."

"You never are," she said, straightening. The small vines around her wrists shifted lazily, like pets stirring from a nap. "That's what makes you easy to like and impossible to ignore."

He leaned against the bulkhead, arms crossed. "Elenn asked me if I really died. I told her yes. But I don't know if that's the truth or just the best word I've got for what happened."

Greenbough tilted her head, studying him with eyes that carried both leaf and storm. "Death is not an ending, little wanderer. It's the part of the song where the melody bends before finding its way again." She brushed a hand along the nearest sapling. "The leaf falls, feeds the root, and the root remembers. That's the way of things."

He nodded, looking down. "Yeah, I've heard that. But what happened to me... it didn't feel like part of that song. It was like someone stopped the music altogether. And then started it again because they changed their mind."

A quiet rustle passed through the branches. "Then you've walked somewhere even I cannot see," Greenbough said, almost reverently. "But if the powers that keep the stars turning—Archons, Eternity, whatever names you mortals

154

give them—chose to send you back, it was not by accident. No wind bends without a reason."

Oscar frowned slightly. "So you think there's a reason I'm here?"

She smiled—a slow, knowing thing, kind but weighty. "There's *more* to you than I think you've let yourself believe. The world doesn't waste its miracles." She turned, plucking a fallen leaf from the soil and letting it rest on her palm. "You are surrounded by people who care, Oscar. Some more loudly than others. And Thay'sa—" she laughed softly, the sound like branches brushing glass—"well, sometimes so much it frightens even me."

That earned a laugh from him, genuine this time. "Yeah. She doesn't do halfway."

"No," Greenbough said. "None of you do. That's why you keep finding your way into stories." She looked up toward the filtered sunlight above deck. "So when the next storm comes—and it will—don't waste time wondering *why* you came back. Live like the world had a reason."

Oscar nodded slowly. "I can try that."

"Good." Her tone softened again. "Now go above. The air will clear that knot in your chest. And take the long way up—I've set the moss to listening. It enjoys your voice."

He blinked, half smiling. "You've got plants spying on me?"

She arched an eyebrow. "Listening, not spying. There's a difference."

He chuckled and turned toward the ladder. "Guess I'll keep the singing polite then."

The vines shifted as he left, and Greenbough murmured, half to the trees, half to herself,

"He walks between life and what comes after… and still looks for the sun. The Archons chose well."

***

By dawn the next day, the haze was gone, and the truth stood clear.

The mountains did not roll gently inland like the familiar ridges of home. They rose sheer from the sea itself—walls of black and gray that plunged straight into the depths. Waves broke against cliffs that offered no beach, no harbor, no mercy. From crest to foam the stone fell unbroken, as if the bones of the world had been hammered upward by some titanic forge.

The Skythread kept her distance, sails trimmed wide as she ran parallel to the cliffs. From the deck the crew stared, silence broken only by the gulls. Even Marissa had no orders to bark.

"Mountains that go into the sea," Tirpik muttered, tugging his beard. "No wonder the Guardian's borders never stretched beyond this coast. There's no place to land, no path to climb."

He was right. For hours they sailed, and the Spine never bent, never lowered. It marched westward without pause, jagged peaks catching the sun like teeth. Clouds clung to the summits, their edges lit in molten gold. The scale of it dwarfed even the Skythread's courage.

By midmorning, the shadows shifted. To the south, beyond a long cape where the cliffs softened, smoke drifted faintly through the air — not from battle, but from hearths long cooled. Villages dotted the shoreline, their roofs intact, their fields neatly divided, and groves heavy with fruit.

Marissa narrowed her eyes. "Those trees are tended. Look at the rows — that's cultivation, not wild growth."

"And yet no one's there," Tirpik murmured. "No boats at the piers. No livestock moving. It's like they walked away mid-harvest."

Greenbough leaned over the rail, her leaves rustling uneasily. "No — not walked. Whatever took them, it came quickly. The ground still holds their footprints."

Elenn folded her arms. "Could be plague. Or something worse."

Oscar shaded his eyes with a hand, watching the abandoned groves. "They were alive not long ago," he said quietly. "You can still see the color in the fruit."

Marissa spat into the wind. "I don't like it. Empty towns make for haunted seas."

Tirpik gave a grim nod. "Then let's keep to the windward side and hope the mountain gods are content to keep their secrets."

The Skythread pressed on, her sails glinting under the sun. Below them the silent villages faded into mist, their smoke trailing thin as memory. The cliffs loomed ever higher, and somewhere beyond those stone walls, a narrow pass waited unseen.

Oscar set his pen again to the page, words coming slow.

The sky carries us where it will. But fate... fate places the roads we cannot ignore.

Chapter Two

The Pass of Stone and Smoke

"Every horizon begins as someone's doubt."

— *Sailor's Proverb of Soahc*

***

The mountains rose like broken teeth, their peaks chewing at the haze. The pass itself was a wound—narrow, red-veined stone running north into a blur of heat.

Marissa held the *Skythread* close to the cliffs, trimming canvas until the sails sang. The air burned dry and metallic, as though the gorge still remembered old fires.

"Currents are wrong," Callen muttered at the helm, his knuckles white on the spokes.

"They're not wrong," Greenbough murmured, eyelids half-closed to the wind. "They're angry."

Ahead, thunder rolled without rain—four heavy beats, then two—as if giants were drumming in the deep. The sound crawled through the hull. The crew's laughter died.

"Up two points," Marissa ordered. "We take the inside bend and see who's making that noise."

Oscar shaded his eyes. The ridge swung away—and the valley opened.

159

Terraces climbed the mountainside like stacked stone waves, each crowded with carved dwellings. Banners hung limp in the hot wind. Smoke coiled from broken roofs.

"Tortosians," Greenbough whispered. "And they are not alone."

Two vast shapes prowled the sky above the terraces—dirigibles, their stretched canvas bellies stitched to iron ribs. One spat a tongue of fire that crawled across a parapet; another dropped a bundle that burst into hungry orange, clinging wherever it struck.

"Napalm," Marissa said flatly. "We're late."
She didn't sound surprised. Only tired.

Men who had sung through storms now stood silent. The scale of it was obscene—ships as large as their own, cruel and deliberate, raining fire on homes that could not answer.

"Beat to quarters," Marissa called. "Coils warming—ballista crews stand by."

The *Skythread* came alive. Rope hissed through blocks, boots thudded along planks, powder kegs rolled to their cradles. Below decks, a bell struck three slow notes. The gorge threw the sound back at them like a warning.

The *Skythread* began to climb.

***

Below, Tortosian defenders raised shields against another volley. Napalm hissed as it clung, burning through bronze and bone alike. Men and women beat at flames with cloaks, dragging the wounded toward stairwells.

A child crouched behind a rail, eyes wide, watching the fire-cannons swivel. Then she saw it—a shadow cutting through the smoke, sails flaring white, hull gleaming where the sun caught bronze inlay.

Another ship.

A murmur spread through the terraces, half despair, half disbelief. In all their long memory, cloudships never came this far. And if they did, they never came to save.

***

Marissa leaned into the wheel. "They've got reach with those cannons. We'll only get one pass before they range us."

"They're bigger," Callen said quietly. "Heavier guns."

"Not heavier," Danner growled while locking the rigging on his ballista. "Just dirtier."

Oscar felt the coils humming through his bones, the vibration pressing against his teeth. He drew a long breath, steadying himself. He remembered the Rift, the Hollow's black mouth closing; this—fire and iron—almost seemed merciful. At least here the enemy bled.

"Greenbough," Marissa said. "What does the mountain say?"

The nymph's leaves trembled though no wind touched them. "It says the stone has had enough. One more spark and it will fall."

Marissa's eyes hardened. "Then let's give it spark enough."

The dirigibles turned together, massive bellies shifting with the updrafts. One leveled its cannons on the terraces; the other wheeled toward the *Skythread* head-on.

"Here they come," Callen said.

"Steady," Marissa ordered. "Ballista crews—pick your targets. Oscar, coil on my mark. No wasted charge."

The first volley screamed through the haze—iron bolts wrapped in firecloth, striking the cliffside in explosions of light. Rock cracked; smoke belched outward in choking waves.

The *Skythread* burst through that cloud like a blade, sails blazing white against the black. Men coughed, spat grit, but held their lines.

"There!" Danner shouted. A boarding skiff dropped from the nearest dirigible, goblins clinging to its ropes, teeth bared.

"Range it!" Marissa barked.

Ballistae thumped. Two bolts whistled wide, but the third caught true, skewering the skiff's prow. It spun away, spilling its passengers into the abyss. Their screams vanished beneath the roar of wind and flame.

"Good," Marissa said, voice calm as cut stone. "Now let's teach them fear."

***

On the terraces, the Tortosians saw everything—the smaller vessel daring to knife between giants. A ragged cheer broke loose. Hope tasted foreign on their tongues, like wine long forgotten.

An elder gripped the parapet until his knuckles cracked. "If they can fell one…" He left the rest to the fire and the wind.

But for the first time in weeks, Tortosian eyes turned skyward not in despair, but in awe.

***

The *Skythread* crested the inner bend, sails taut, coils blazing with blue light. Ahead, the gorge opened into chaos: goblin ranks swarming the lower valley, Tortosians fighting on their walls, and two monstrous dirigibles circling like wolves over a wounded prey.

"Helm steady," Marissa said. "We've got one chance to cut their teeth."

Oscar braced the coil housings. Callen's hands found hers on the wheel. Greenbough whispered to the buried roots in the cliff, begging them to hold a little longer.

The gorge thundered again—stone answering fire, mountain answering man—until the sound became a heartbeat.

And the *Skythread* climbed into flame.

***

Chapter Three

The City Besieged

"Cities do not fall in a day—they fall in the heartbeat when watchmen stop believing dawn will come."

— *From the **Annals of Ravenglass**, Siege Cycle I*

***

The nearer dirigible swung to meet them, ugly and purposeful, its canvas bellies swollen like diseased lungs. Goblins lined the rails—faces blackened with soot, crossbows ready, their laughter swallowed by the wind.

From the second airship, another gout of fire crawled across the terraces below. A dozen rooftops flared. Tortosian defenders answered with stones, spears, and the few arrows left to them—brave, futile gestures against iron and flame.

"Range in two hundred," Danner called from the forward nest. "Wind favors them."

Marissa's hand tightened on the wheel. "Then we'll take what the wind refuses."

Her voice was flint; her eyes, wildfire.

"Oscar—coil signal."

Oscar pressed his palm to the bronze plate. The lightning coil awoke with a low growl, deep as an animal rousing from sleep. The air around the foremast crackled—sharp, dry, electric. Tiny hairs lifted on arms and necks.

"Ballista, left side!" Tirpik barked. "Aim for the rigging—cut them loose! Don't waste a shot on armor unless you can taste it!"

***

A black jar arced from the enemy gondola, trailing rope like a burning tail. It shattered against *Skythread's* starboard lines and burst into liquid fire that moved like thought. Sailcloth caught. Rope screamed. Men swore and ran.

"Douse!" Greenbough shouted. She hurled a clay stopper the size of an apple. It shattered midair and spilled a tangle of vines that crawled over the flames. Leaves blackened; sap hissed; but the fire died.

The ship gasped—a living thing burned and healed—and steadied itself against the cliff wind.

Across the gap, goblins laughed. Their teeth gleamed in the soot, eyes bright with the cruelty of creatures who had never learned fear. A trumpet split the noise. Crossbows leveled.

"Brace!" Tirpik roared.

The volley came in a hiss of black-feathered bolts. Two sailors dropped without a sound. Another screamed, clutching his thigh as blood spread across the deck.

***

A skiff unlatched from the enemy gondola—its belly glowing with bottled fire. It swung down toward *Skythread* like a thrown axe, trailing smoke and sparks.

"Hold your line," Marissa said, steady as granite. "Callen—keep her level. We don't blink first."

The skiff struck the rail with a bone-splitting shriek. Grapnels bit deep. Goblins poured over the sides, howling—three missed, spinning into the abyss; five landed hard, blades between their teeth.

"Marines!" Tirpik bellowed.

Steel answered steel. The deck became chaos—iron ringing, wood splintering, the smell of pitch and blood thick in the air.

Tirpik moved like an avalanche. His sword carved one raider clean from shoulder to hip. "Push them back!" he roared. "Deck's ours!"

Oscar tried to draw, too slow. A goblin lunged at him—wild-eyed, blade high—only to be cut down mid-leap by Tirpik's sword.

"Stay on your coil, lad!" the captain barked. "That's your fight!"

Oscar swallowed hard and obeyed, hands trembling as he clamped the coil. Sparks licked his palms, eager. The copper stank of ozone and fear.

***

Below, Tortosian defenders waged their own desperate war. On the lower terraces, shield-bearers braced against ogres pressing up the causeways. Stones rained from the walls above, smashing into goblin ranks that surged again and again like a tide. The air reeked of pitch, smoke, and burning hair.

A young archer stood on a mid-terrace, loosing until his fingers bled. Between volleys he looked skyward.

"What is it?" his sergeant shouted, shoving another quiver into his hands.

"The sky," the boy whispered.

High above, through the curtain of smoke, a smaller ship carved a path of lightning through the clouds. He saw the strike—white fire lancing from hull to hull, goblins thrown like rag dolls. Canvas tore; thunder rolled. His bowstring trembled in his grasp.

***

Another jar smashed against *Skythread's* forward railing. Fire spilled and crawled toward powder.

Greenbough sprinted, dropping to her knees, palms flat. Roots erupted through the planking, twisting and hissing, swallowing the fire into black soil that hadn't existed a moment earlier. Smoke rose in damp curls and vanished.

A goblin lunged for her, blade raised. Callen met it halfway. His axe rose, fell, split skull from jaw. He kicked the body clear.

"Not her," he spat.

***

"Now, Oscar!" Marissa's voice cut through the din.

He loosed the coil. The world went white.

Lightning speared from the bow like a living thing, ripping through smoke and iron. The bolt struck the enemy gondola dead-center. Iron screamed. Canvas ignited. Goblins flailed, their howls lost in thunder. One of the engine spars exploded outward, trailing molten debris into the gorge.

Skythread's crew roared. Tirpik grinned through soot and blood, raising his sword high.

"That's it, lads! That's how a real ship bites!"

For a heartbeat, hope returned.

168

***

Down on the terraces, defenders froze mid-swing. Even ogres halted, staring upward as thunder walked across the sky.

An elder clutched the wall with both hands, his voice breaking. "Stone remembers. Stone remembers!"

The words caught like wildfire. The chant spread—hoarse, uncertain, growing louder with every voice:

Stone remembers! Stone remembers!

For the first time in weeks, the Tortosians dared believe the siege could break.

***

The damaged dirigible bucked but held, leaking flame. Another skiff swung loose, more goblins dropping like locusts toward the *Skythread*. Across the gorge, a fresh jar streaked toward the terraces below, bursting into a fireball that devoured three homes at once.

The second dirigible wheeled wide, catapults cranking back toward the city. Its engines howled; its shadow rolled over the terraces like an eclipse.

Marissa turned the *Skythread's* prow into the wind. "Again!" she shouted. "Coils hot! Ballista, ready!"

The sky thundered. The gorge roared. Flames leapt higher than the walls.

And the *Skythread* climbed straight into the heart of fire.

***

Chapter Four

Fire in the Gorge

"Some battles are fought for victory.
Others are fought simply because turning back is death."

— **Balok Ironforge**, *personal log, Skythread Campaign*

***

Battle narrowed to breaths and inches. The deck tilted; smoke stung; everything became blue spark and red heat and the ugly, wet sounds of work no one wanted to name. *Fire in the gorge*—that's what they'd call it later. In the moment, it was only survival.

Oscar anchored the coil in his hands, sighted, and loosed. Lightning leapt like a hunting cat, tearing through the dirigible's forward lines. Canvas sagged; the ship yawed; a goblin pinwheeled into the chasm, mouth open on a scream the wind swallowed.

Ballista bolts thudded against iron ribs and glanced away in showers of sparks. One lucky shaft skipped through a gap and shattered a fire jar mid-flight; burning jelly rained into the gorge, hissing where it splattered bare rock.

"Keep them off the coil!" Danner shouted.

Two goblins bounded for Oscar; Elenn met them first, staff snapping a knee, then a jaw. "Mind your feet," she said, almost conversational, and shouldered the second into the scuppers.

Across the deck, Tirpik met the boarders in the old way: shield forward, short cuts, no nonsense. He moved like a gate on good hinges—open, close, open—and goblins crumpled wherever he set them down.

The second dirigible banked toward the terraces again. Tortosian shields lifted like a field of scaled shells. Fire crawled and clung; men beat at it with cloaks and bare hands until the air stank of scorched wool.

"Marissa!" Callen shouted through the din. "We can't split the ballista and win both ways!"

"We don't split," she said. "We end one."

"Which?"

"The one trying to kill my ship."

She pointed, and the *Skythread* lunged.

***

Oscar felt the surge before the order. The coil thrummed against his palms, begging release. He loosed again.

Lightning tore the gulf, punched through canvas, split a spar in two. The dirigible staggered as its gondola swung wide. Goblins shrieked, some leaping into emptiness rather than burn.

"Press it!" Tirpik roared. Marines drove the last boarders back over the rail. Callen leaned on the wheel, teeth clenched; the ship groaned but obeyed.

Greenbough flung a clay stopper into smoldering sail— vines burst outward, sucking fire to wet black soil that hadn't existed a heartbeat before. Dew beaded the planks.

For a breath, the tide seemed to turn.

***

On the terraces, Tortosians raised their heads through smoke. They saw a sky-monster slump and spit sparks; they saw goblins fall like ash.

"The storm fights for us," rasped an elder.

But the young heard something else in the thunder, something they had never dared to hope—*not storm, allies.* A boy dropped his spear, pointing upward with a cry that cracked his voice: "They bleed too!"

"Stone remembers!" the chant rose, half battle cry, half prayer.

***

The wounded dirigible struck back—catapult and ballista firing in savage rhythm. A jar smashed across *Skythread's* bow, splattering flame. Marines screamed as pitch chewed through leather. Elenn thrust her staff; wind spiraled, snapping the fire clear.

"More powder to the coil!" Marissa barked.

Oscar's hands were raw, but he forced another surge. Lightning cracked so close it salted his vision with white ghosts.

The gondola's forward chamber blew apart. Iron ribs tore loose; cables snapped like bowstrings. The dirigible sagged toward the cliff, trailing flame.

The crew howled triumph. Even Tirpik threw back his head and bellowed, grin black with soot.

But the second dirigible wheeled over the terraces again, ballistae coughing. Homes popped into orange blossoms. Screams echoed up the gorge.

***

Callen's eyes tracked both ships, sweat carving pale lines through ash. "Cap'n—we can't guard both! The city or us—choose!"

Marissa never looked away from the wounded brute. Her hands were steady on the wheel; her gaze was iron.

"We don't split," she said again. "We end one."

Her finger cut the air. "The one trying to kill my ship."

And the *Skythread* dove—thunder gathering in her bones.

***

From the terraces, defenders watched in disbelief. The cloudship turned not toward their burning city but toward its own enemy. Fire still rained. Men burned. Children screamed.

"Why?" a soldier cried, bitterness raw. "Why do they leave us?"

"Stone chooses," an elder answered, eyes on the sky. "We do not question."

Grief mixed with awe. The strangers had saved themselves. Perhaps tomorrow they would save others.

***

Skythread closed the gap. Goblins shrieked; crossbows rattled.

"Coil—again!" Marissa snapped.

174

Oscar loosed everything left in him. Lightning hammered the gondola head-on. The explosion rolled across the gorge like the gods beating a drum.

Iron screamed. Canvas collapsed. The dirigible spun broadside into the cliff.

When it struck, the world broke.

The blast ripped night apart, shrapnel hissing like razors. Screams tore through *Skythread's* deck as fragments ripped rigging and men. Heat hit like a single devouring hand.

Oscar felt impact before sound—a hammer to shoulder and chest. Metal burned through coat and skin; another shard scored his forearm; fire kissed his neck. The coil slipped as his knees failed.

Elenn was there in a breath, hands staunching blood, voice stitching silver words. Light pulsed under her palms, knitting just enough to hold him here. "Stay with me," she whispered, face sharp with fear.

Through pain and smoke, Oscar saw the battle still clawing at the gorge—flame coiling up stone, wind howling through the wound.

And then he saw it—

A single crossbow bolt, spinning end-over-end through firelight.

The bolt struck Tirpik square in the chest.

He rocked once, sword lifted, mouth opening—not for a cry, but for a breath he would never finish. Coil-light flickered across his armor as he fell, one hand still reaching for the rail.

Marines shouted his name. Callen lunged, a fraction late. The captain hit the deck hard, eyes wide to the storm above.

Oscar's vision blurred. Beyond heat and tears he saw more than men: Dug loomed—massive, grave—with another at his side, the faceless shield-bearer of Elysium, radiant and still. Together they lifted Tirpik, bearing him down a path of green and gold that opened across burning air.

Time stretched—one heartbeat containing all sorrow and grace—then snapped back.

Smoke. Fire. The fight far from done.

***

Chapter Five

Stormforged

"Some ships are built. Others are born—carved from thunder and nailed together with will."

— *Flyer's Cant, common among early skysailors*

***

The wheel spun free. For a heartbeat, the *Skythread* herself seemed to stagger. Men cried out—some in rage, some in disbelief.

Marissa caught the spokes, blood wet against her palms, and dragged the ship back into line. The wheel shuddered—wood slick, iron pegs hot—as if the vessel had tried to veer away from the moment and been forced to look it in the eye.

Silence swallowed two heartbeats—impossible, bottomless. Then the ship screamed back to life.

"Tirpik!" Callen cried—and stopped at the empty space where a grin and a curse should have been.

Marissa's face was marble; only the tremor in her jaw betrayed the human beneath the helm. "Callen—the line. Oscar, I need the coil hot as the sun. Danner, forget armor—give me rigging, gondola struts, pilots if you can see their eyes."

"Cap'n—" Greenbough began.

"Not now."

The enemy swung wide to rake them. Marissa knifed *Skythread* under its belly instead, so close Oscar saw patchwork stitches in the canvas—tar-black scars, hand-sewn seams, a painted jaw of white teeth grinning false courage.

"Now," she said.

Oscar loosed.

Lightning tore the air in hungry sheets. Iron screamed. For a breath the dirigible held—its bones glowing from within—then the forward chamber let go and the ship caved like a lung punched empty. It folded into the cliff, bled fire, and slid down the rock in a river of sparks.

A cheer rose and died as eyes turned back to the helm. Elenn knelt there, hands already red. She looked up, met no one's gaze, and shook her head once.

Marissa swallowed. "He'll have his rites," she said. "But the living are not done." She lifted her chin toward the gorge where the second dirigible savaged the terraces. "Ready the bumpers," she said. "All of them."

"Cap'n…" Callen's voice was small. "That'll bring the mountain down."

"Yes," she said. "On them."

***

Crew scrambled. Men and women whose hands still shook with Tirpik's blood wiped them on their trousers and went back to stations. Bad knots were retied; powder passed hand to hand with the ferocity of prayer. The *Skythread* groaned as coils recharged and the thunder bumpers—great storm-loaded spheres slung along her flanks—were armed for the first time in months.

Oscar staggered to his post. His ears rang from the blast that had swallowed the first airship, but his fingers moved by instinct, tightening copper housings until the threads sang. Metal tasted like pennies on his tongue. Hairline cracks along the coil pulsed white-blue, little rivers of light hunting an ocean.

Danner and Callen worked in brutal rhythm at starboard midships, levering the first bumper along its track. The sphere—bronze-banded glass with stormlight trapped inside—shivered with its own heartbeat.

"Mind the lash," Danner warned. "She bites if you look at her wrong."

"Everything bites today," Callen muttered, gray beneath the soot.

The second dirigible loomed, fat-bellied, its gondola bristling with goblin engines. Fire cannons boomed; arcs of burning pitch cascaded onto Tortosian terraces. Through the rails, the crew saw defenders on the walls, shells blackened, shields locked, voices raised in ragged chants. Every blast broke their line; every prayer blew back with the smoke.

"They won't hold another volley," Elenn said, voice flat, hands red to the wrists; beneath the blood, her fingertips flickered with a tired blue.

Marissa's knuckles whitened on the wheel. "Then they won't need to."

She breathed once—slow through her nose—and tilted the ship by a degree only helmsmen notice. The *Skythread* answered like a spent horse answering a trusted rider: grudgingly, completely.

"On my mark," she said. "Hold."

The gorge took her word and threw it back thinner. *Hold. Hold.*

179

From the terraces, a Tortosian archer squinted through smoke. For days they had fought hopelessly—shields buckling, stone cracking. He had burned his hands on a spear that had been his father's. He had counted their gaps by the faces that never came back.

Then the cloudship came—a thunderbeast veined with lightning.

It dove beneath the goblin dirigible; light split the sky; the enemy's belly tore and slid down the cliff in sparks. His mouth fell open, a silent O he could not close.

Beside him, a woman old enough to be his grandmother pressed river-pebble charms to her lips. "We will owe for this," she whispered. "All gifts carry weight."

"The mountain has remembered us," an elder breathed. Others crossed their arms against smoke, not daring to name it miracle.

When the first thunder bumper cracked the air, the Tortosians dropped their bows, clutching ears, thinking the mountain itself had split. A child screamed—and then laughed, too young to know the difference. When the echoes cleared, goblins lay shattered, and the cloudship still flew.

"Storm-born," someone said. The word spread without permission, as awe does. Storm-born. Not a ship's name—a moment's.

***

The price came due in thunder.

Callen and Danner wrestled the first bumper into firing position, the storm-sphere creaking in its cradle. The enchantments within thrummed like a held breath. Bronze banding hummed in sympathy with the coils—two beasts, one lightning and one thunder, straining at their leashes.

"Never thought I'd live to see these loosed," Callen grunted. "Tirpik always said they were for the Last Fight."

"This is it," Danner said through his teeth. "Feels like the Last to me."

Below the quarterdeck, Greenbough braced both palms to timber, whispering to wood that had carried them through kinder years. "Hold," she told the planks. "Do this, and I'll ask nothing of you for a long time." The ship creaked— answer or complaint, none could tell.

Oscar steadied the coil. On Marissa's signal, he flared lightning through the bumper's binding. The sphere dropped from the hull with a hollow boom—then split midair, a blossom of storm. White shock rippled outward, turning air into a fist.

Thunder cracked between cliff walls, shaking marrow. The dirigible reeled under the shockwave, ropes snapping, goblins flung shrieking into the void. Their cries trailed down the rock like torn banners.

"Again!" Marissa shouted. "Load the next!"

"Cap—" Callen bit off the rest and bent to the work. There was no room left in the day for doubt.

Two more bumpers went. The enemy ship staggered. The gorge itself shuddered; boulders sheared loose; avalanches rolled, grinding goblin ranks to paste on the valley floor. Tortosians cheered from their walls—half triumph, half terror—because all victory in a pass is purchased with stone and bone.

Elenn, panting, swept her staff; the last licks of pitch in *Skythread's* rigging curled back into themselves and died as if ashamed to burn where they had no leave.

181

Greenbough reeled against the rail, leaves at her temples singed. "No more from me," she told Marissa frankly. "I've borrowed too much."

"Then we pay it back with steel," Marissa said. "And with speed."

***

The dirigible tried to climb, pilots wrestling burning canvas. *Skythread* pursued—bumpers hammering, coils sparking. The hull hummed so hard the nails in her seams walked a fraction toward daylight; masts sang like bowstrings strained past sense.

Oscar glimpsed the enemy captain for a heartbeat: a massive goblin in brass goggles, screaming orders from the gondola. Their gazes met across the gulf, and for that instant there was no malice—only two men who knew this was the end. A choice made, a cost owed, a ledger balanced.

Oscar loosed. The bolt punched through the gondola. The captain convulsed and vanished in smoke.

The dirigible sagged. Its belly split, venting fire. It crumpled into the cliff. A second river of sparks poured down the gorge, lighting night like noon.

For a breath, sound failed. The gorge held its breath too, deciding whether to keep standing after such insult. Then the hiss of fire crept back, thin and wicked; the far crack of falling stone picked up the rhythm; a broken skiff pinwheeled until it shattered on rock too far below to see.

No cheer rose this time. Men stared at their hands as if surprised by the blood. A sailor retched quietly over the scuppers and wiped his mouth, ashamed of the human noise his body made.

Marissa bowed her head a fraction. The lines around her mouth deepened—and eased. Only a breath. Then she straightened.

"Report," she said.

"Rigging scorched but holding," Callen managed. "Three spars sprung—we can splint. Coils… angry." He tried a grin that made him look younger and breakable. "But alive, Cap'n."

"Wounded?"

"Many," Elenn answered from the helm. Her voice faltered, then steadied. "And… one we will not mend."

Marissa let the truth pass through her like wind through rigging. There would be a time. Not now.

***

On the highest terrace, shield-bearers rose behind blackened merlons. Ash lay on their shoulders like gray snow. They watched goblin ranks break and run, watched ogres turn, confused, as the last dirigible fell like a dying sun.

"Is it done?" the young archer asked.

"Nothing is done that cost this much," the elder said, lowering his bow with swollen fingers. "But we may see another morning."

They watched the cloudship steady itself in smoke—not banking or strutting like a victorious hawk. It only moved on, slow and deliberate, ashamed of its strength and sure of its necessity.

"Storm-born," the archer whispered again, softer now, as if the word might offend.

***

Elenn covered Tirpik's body with canvas. Her hands did not shake—not because she felt no grief, but because the work demanded steadiness, and she would not fail him in that. His proud beard was matted with blood. One hand still clutched the wheel, as if even in death he meant to hold the ship steady. She loosened his fingers one by one, murmuring to them like a friend to a stubborn child. When the last finger let go, the wheel creaked and turned a quarter, as if exhaling.

Callen wiped his face with a soot-black sleeve. His eyes were wide and hollow. "Cap'n... we'll never replace him."

"No," Marissa said softly, laying one palm on the wheel, still sticky with his blood. "We won't."

Beyond the rail, Tortosians gathered and raised spears in salute. The mountain smoked, but the city still stood. The sight made something complicated move in her throat— gratitude, shame, relief braided too tight to name.

"He'll have his rites," Marissa said, voice steadier. "Stone remembers. So will we."

She did not add the other truth priests would dislike and the young would fear: some stones remember too well, and some captains are remembered for what they broke to save what they could.

Oscar leaned on the rail, exhausted. Smoke and unasked tears blurred the world. His hands shook in waves he could not master. He thought of Dug, of the Elysium Fields, of Tirpik walking a green path no goblin fire could scorch. In his mind the bear turned once over a shag of golden shoulder, as if to tell Oscar he wasn't late—only early to grief.

Greenbough eased beside him, smelling of wet earth and cinder. "He liked you," she said, almost apologetic.

"I know," Oscar answered. He didn't, not truly, but he wanted it so fiercely that truth bent toward it.

The *Skythread* creaked underfoot, alive still though something in her heart had cracked. Nails ticked as the hull cooled. Sails sighed as they were eased a hand's breadth to rest aching cloth. Men stepped softer, as if the planks were sleeping children.

And the gorge went quiet. Too quiet.

The kind of silence that comes when a storm has left but not finished speaking—a silence that weighs the dead and the living at once and finds both wanting, both beautiful.

Marissa released the wheel and flexed blood-slick hands. "We're not done," she said to no one and everyone. "Make fast. Gather our wounded. We'll speak when we have breath."

She did not look back at the terraces, at the people whose morning they had purchased with thunder, whose names she did not yet know. She did not look at the canvas-wrapped body at her feet.

She looked only forward—to the bend where smoke thinned to gray and wind found its voice again—and set the *Skythread* to follow.

***

"The sea buries its dead in silence.
But a ship carries them still,
in every nail and every rope that outlives their hands."
— Sailors' saying of the Skyreach Coast

***

Later, when fires guttered low and the gorge gave back only the hiss of cooling stone, the crew gathered by the berth where Tirpik's hammock still swayed. His pipe was tucked into the ropes, soot darkening the bowl. No one touched it.

Marissa stood apart, one hand on the beam. She did not speak; words could not carry the weight of his absence. She let silence stretch, and the silence said enough.

Danner tied off the empty hammock as if it still bore weight. "Told me once these bumpers were for the Last Fight," he muttered, a laugh catching and failing.

"Then I reckon we've had it," Callen said without looking up. "Only thing is—we're still breathing."

They both knew what they didn't say: the Last Fight never comes all at once. It comes piece by piece, with every loss that leaves a ship smaller than she was.

Oscar lingered at the doorway. In the lantern's dim, he thought he saw Tirpik's shadow resting there still—broad-shouldered, bearded, grinning. Hope twisted—maybe the bear of Elysium had already found him, and the captain was only waiting for the rest to catch up.

The lantern guttered. The shadow was only cloth.

The ship sighed around them, timbers easing like tired lungs. And the crew kept vigil, knowing stone remembers—but so does the skies above.

Chapter Six

The Choice

"Courage is never the first step. It is the one taken after the last rational argument fails."

— *Briarwood Saying, author unknown*

***

The crew gathered below the quarterdeck—soot-black, bandaged, breathing hard. The gorge stank of pitch and hot stone. Far below, the goblin horde swelled and moved north through the narrow pass like a tide, banners snapping, siege engines dragging on chains. Their war-horns rolled through the cliffs like the call of something ancient and hungry.

The men and women of the *Skythread* stood close, drawn together by exhaustion and instinct, every face lit harsh in the lantern glow. Some clutched blood-spotted bandages to their ribs; others still held their cutlasses unsheathed, too weary to clean them. Above, Tirpik's absence was a hole no rope could mend.

Marissa stepped forward. She stood where all could see her, and none could mistake her meaning. Her coat was torn at the sleeve; her hands were still streaked with Tirpik's blood. She didn't wipe them clean. She let them see.

"You've seen what waits," she said, her voice raw with smoke and grief. "You know what it means if we turn away. I'll speak the truth once and only once: the thing I am about to order will stain us. It will save a city. It may damn me."

The words fell like stones into the gorge. No wind moved. Even the sails seemed to hold their breath.

"If any of you cannot bear this," she went on, steady and merciless, "you'll go below decks now, and I'll set no blame on you. There's no shame in refusing. There is only truth. Choose."

She looked from face to face—the old salts, hard-eyed but trembling in their beards; the boys who hadn't yet learned how to hide their fear; Greenbough with grief in her gaze and iron in her spine. Elenn's hands twitched once, red to the wrists, but she held them still.

For a long heartbeat, no one breathed.

Then Danner lifted his chin. "With you, Cap'n."

Oscar found his voice next, rough but certain. "With you."

One by one, the words came. Quiet at first, then stronger. Hoarse, cracked, unshakable: *With you. With you. With you.*

From the back of the lantern circle, a sailor rose— wrapped in bandages, face gray with pain, one arm bound tight against his ribs. He swayed once, found his balance, and met Marissa's eyes.

"Still in the fight, Cap'n," he said. The words were soft, but they carried through the hold like a bell in fog.

No one laughed. No one cheered. They just stood a little straighter, each hearing their own voice in his.

Greenbough spoke last. She didn't raise her voice; she only said it once, her tone like roots gripping stone. "With you."

Marissa's shoulders eased a fraction. She bowed her head, then lifted it again, hard as steel. "Then hear me. We take the pass. We drive them north. We do not stop— because we cannot stop. Coils, charge. Thunder bumpers, all stations. On my mark."

She set her hand to the wheel, and the ship leaned into her touch like a tired animal asked for one more mile. Every timber hummed, every spar groaned, as though *Skythread* herself had heard the choice and bowed to it.

Marissa closed her eyes, breathed once, and spoke the word that would set the gorge on fire.

"Mark."

***

On the terraces of the mountain city, the Tortosians steadied their shields and stared into the gorge. Smoke veiled the cliffs, red as a forge. Through it came the cloudship— scarred, trailing sparks, sails torn and soot-stained—yet unbroken.

An elder captain of the shell-guard leaned on his spear, breath rattling in his throat. "Storm-born," he whispered. "But not born for us. Born against them."

Below, children too young to fight pressed their foreheads to the stones and prayed. Mothers dragged buckets of ash-water to douse the flames and paused to watch lightning crawl along the *Skythread's* masts. They had lived long enough to know that salvation often wore the same face as destruction.

The goblins massed in the gorge, confident in their numbers. They did not yet understand. The Tortosians saw it first, dread and awe tangled in their bellies.

One warrior murmured, "If this is rescue, it will scar us all."

Another, younger, gripped his bow tighter. "Then let us be scarred—and alive."

When Marissa's command rang out—*Mark!*—the mountain itself seemed to shudder in anticipation.

And so they chose—not for glory, nor for orders, but for the promise that no city would fall while breath remained aboard.

When the mark was given, the storm itself bore witness. The Tortosians, who had guarded these stones for centuries, bowed their heads. Not in surrender, but in reverence for the storm about to be unchained.

***

The crew heaved the first bumper into its cradle, stormlight bleeding through its bronze bands. Danner steadied the coil, mouth dry, lungs raw with smoke. Callen locked the safety clamps and met Danner's eyes.

"No turning back now," he said.

"There never was," Danner answered.

Oscar loosed. Lightning surged into the bumper, and the sphere dropped away with a hollow boom.

For a breath, the gorge itself went still, as if afraid of what came next.

Then the storm bloomed.

Thunder cracked the cliffs. Avalanches tore loose. Goblin ranks shattered like surf against stone.

The Last Fight had begun.

Chapter Seven

Stone Remembers

"We mend what the wind teaches us to break."

— *Guild Saying*

***

Skythread plunged. Thunder bumpers struck the cliff in staggered cadence—left, right, fore, aft—each blow a hammer that turned rock into roar. The gorge itself became a drum of ruin. Shockwaves rolled down the crevice like invisible surf, shaking loose centuries of stone in a single night.

Packed ranks became meat for stone. Bridges of rope and bone snapped; ladders flailed into emptiness, carrying screaming goblins with them. Ogres bellowed, their voices breaking like splintered horns, before avalanches swallowed them whole.

The dirigible that hunted the terraces tried to rise, canvas bulging, rudders fighting for height. But the gorge betrayed it: currents twisted, updrafts died, air itself turned hostile. Marissa cut across its tail, coil-fire blistering the canvas. The ship wobbled, clipped a spur of black rock, and tore open like a seam. Burning jelly rained, sticking to armor and flesh alike. Screams climbed the gorge and broke against the sky.

"Drive them!" Marissa shouted, not to the crew but to the pass itself—as if the mountain were her weapon and her enemy both.

The coils sang until teeth ached and hair lifted and every nail on deck rang with heat. But the coil kept hungering for more.

Every ounce of energy finally left Oscar's wounded body. He drifted in and out, the world shrinking to Elenn's hands pressing light into torn flesh. Over her shoulder he caught flashes—the coil screaming, thunder blooming, Marissa braced at the wheel like stone against a tide. He tried once to lift his arm, but fire lanced down his side and the darkness pulled harder. He let it, trusting the ship to the living.

Marines dropped goblins from the rails with relentless arrow barrages. Greenbough hurled water that became strangling vines the instant it touched flame, binding shrieking shapes until the gorge swallowed them.

Callen and Danner manned the bumpers until their shoulders tore and their palms bled, shoving storm-spheres down their tracks with curses that sounded like prayers.

And still *Skythread* did not stop.

They drove the goblin horde until formation vanished and cruelty became panic, until even ogres ran blind with fear, until the goblin mass fled north as a single animal with no mind left in it. The gorge drank their fear and gave it back in echoes, a tide of broken voices fleeing into darkness. They ran but they were still in massive numbers

Skythread did not rest.

The first night bled into day with fire still in the gorge. Coils spat in endless arcs, each strike burning goblins from the field like weeds under a storm. Marines leaned over rails to hurl oil jars, their fuses spitting flame as they fell. When they shattered, whole swathes of the valley blazed, screams rising like incense.

The horde ran north, but the cloudship shadowed them step for step, her sails stretched wide like the wings of a hawk stooping for the kill. The crew worked until hands blistered and eyes wept from smoke, but none dared stop. Marissa's hands never left the wheel.

At night the fire made its own daylight, rivers of flame painting the cliffs in cruel orange. The goblins tried to scatter, but avalanches herded them back into the choke. Every path became a trap, every rise another place for thunder to fall.

By dawn of the second day, their numbers had halved. Still Marissa pressed them.

***

They reached the encampment by mid-afternoon, a sprawl of tents and crude fortifications that had fed the siege. Goblin banners drooped, skulls nailed to pikes glaring at the sky.

"Drop everything," Marissa said. Her voice was sanded flat, nothing left of mercy in it.

They dumped oil casks in waves, the decks tilting as sailors strained to roll them over the rails. Thunder bumpers followed, their bindings glowing as coils flared. When the first hit, the encampment folded like parchment, canvas and timber erupting into a single sheet of flame.

Screams vanished beneath the roar. The air turned black and then red. Men on deck spat bile into their hands, kept loading, kept throwing. Some wept while they worked, their tears as much smoke as salt.

By the time the last bumper struck, the camp was ash. Only a ragged company of goblins and ogres broke free, fleeing north in panic. From the deck, they looked less like soldiers than shadows trying to outrun the sun.

***

Marissa finally lifted her hands from the wheel. Blood cracked at her knuckles, but she did not flinch. "Enough," she said, and the ship seemed to sag in relief.

The chase was over. The gorge was empty.

Two days later, *Skythread* came south again, her hull scorched, her crew gaunt-eyed and hollow. They sailed over a land remade: black scars across terraces, forests stripped to kindling, rivers clogged with ash. No sound rose from the north but the hiss of fire eating itself.

When the terraces of the Tortosian city came into sight, the crew held their breath. Would the stonefolk curse them for what they had done? Or bow for having survived because of it?

***

On the highest terrace, the Tortosians staggered to their walls, ears ringing, and eyes wide. They had braced for death. Instead, they had watched annihilation.

A young archer dropped his bow, too dazed to notice. "They are... gone."

An elder clutched the stone with both hands, nails tearing against it. "Not gone," he said. "Driven. The stone will remember."

All around him, men and women wept without shame. Children stared at the sky where the cloudship prowled, its belly glowing with coils like the ribs of a storm made flesh. They would tell stories of that night—the night thunder itself took sides—and they would tell them with awe and with fear.

When *Skythread* turned south again, injured but alive, the terraces raised no jeers, no chants of victory. Only a heavy, terrible silence—the silence that comes when the price of survival is counted in ash.

From the cliffside city, the elders began their descent— slow, deliberate, as if stone itself had chosen their pace. They carried no banners, only their years, and they came with empty hands. The crowd parted to let them pass.

At the base of the terraces, they stood waiting, their eyes on the scorched cloudship that had damned itself to save them.

And above the ash, the wind whispered what the stone would never forget.

Chapter Eight

After and Always

"The deepest gratitude is spoken without a voice."

— Tortoise-Folk Reflection, attributed to Elder Shell-Gray

***

They limped to the valley shelf below the terraces, sails patched with whatever cloth could be spared. The timbers creaked as though the ship herself mourned.

The tortoise people came down in a gray line, faces carved from long memory. They did not cheer. They bowed—slow, deliberate, as if to stone.

An elder stepped forward, a wool cap like frost, skin the color of old granite. He took Marissa's forearm in both his hands. His grip was firm, not as soldier or supplicant, but as one who understood burdens.

"You have repeated our defense," he said. "Stone remembers. So will we."

Marissa held his gaze. Her throat caught before she found words. "We'll need time. For repairs. For rites."

"You shall have both," the elder answered. "And hands to spare."

In the days that followed, *Skythread* became a small village of grief and work. Bodies were washed and wrapped, bellies of sailcloth turned to shrouds.

A chest of flagstones took new etchings for the memorial at Soahc. Sailors bent over them with hands that shook, carving clumsy but honest lines: Tirpik's name among them, cut deep and unornamented.

Oscar dragged himself topside despite Elenn's protests. His shoulder was bound, his breath ragged, but he would not be absent. Greenbough steadied his hand as the knife touched stone. Together they pressed the line. No words were needed; the mountain wind scattered ash and prayers alike, carrying the names into stone's keeping.

When the carving was done, *Skythread* turned south, slipping out of the pass and into the wide sea.

The crew gathered on deck. Some stood straight with hands on the rail, others knelt with heads bowed, a few folded their arms across their chests in the way of their homelands. Each gave the dead what honor they knew.

Shrouds slid one by one into the deep. Canvas bellies, heavy with their last weight, struck the water and were gone. The tide took them without struggle without favor.

No words were spoken. Only the creak of timber, the slap of waves, and the hush of wind bore witness.

Stone had taken their names. The sea now held their bodies. Between them, memory was complete.

***

Twenty Tortosians joined the ship—riggers with valley-calluses, carpenters who read grain like script, and a dozen marines who fought like metered verse. They moved with a grave precision, like stone taught to walk, and their presence filled the empty hammocks with new weight.

One elder, ink-stained and spare, asked for a hammock by the coil-room and a small desk beside it. His eyes had the calm of someone who had measured centuries against ledgers.

"I will be your historian," he told Marissa, "and your stubborn tongue when you need one." He looked toward the pass, and the smoke still drifting there. "If this is a one-way road, then it is the right one. My name is Augustine."

Marissa inclined her head. "Then let it be so."

***

On the morning they rose again, the new hands stood abeam while the old salts thudded fists on wood. A Tortosian proverb moved through the ranks like a tide:

"Stone does not move, but it remembers."

Marissa's voice came back low. "So will *Skythread*."

They set their course through the last of the heat and into wind that smelled like far hills. Behind them, stone held the silence they left. Ahead, the world shifted—maps waiting to be wrong, stars waiting to be true.

Oscar stood at the rail until the terraces shrank to lines and shadows. His chest ached with everything lost and everything still carried.

"Safe harbor?" he asked no one, remembering a dragon's gaze, a bear's certainty, a promise spoken under another roof.

The historian beside him answered anyway. "Not always," he said. "But a true one today."

The ship took the breath of the pass and turned it into forward motion. When the gorge at last released them, the sky opened wide and *Skythread* climbed as if a weight had fallen away.

The sea beyond did not keep their secret. It only carried it.

And stone, as ever, remembered.

***

Chapter Nine

The Sky Returns

"No ship ever sails alone;
the hands that built her are never far behind."

— *Old Gnomish Saying of Soahc*

***

The air aboard *Skythread* was quiet in that heavy way grief leaves behind—like a song remembered but no longer sung. The rigging creaked softly, the sails shifting with the slow rhythm of morning wind.

The ship herself seemed to breathe again, patched and mended, but her heart—her captain—was gone. Tirpik had been a sailor of the skies for one hundred and thirty-seven years, a gnome who had crossed more horizons than most mortals had dreamed of. He had fallen doing the only thing he had ever truly loved: standing the deck, hand on the rail, eyes on the storm.

A makeshift shrine stood beneath the foremast: his old spyglass, a half-burned lantern, and a strip of his chart folded beneath glass. Someone had placed a corked bottle beside it, sealed with wax and a coin pressed into its top—an old Soahcian flyer's token, *fare for the wind beyond.*

Marissa stood before it now, head bowed. Her hand rested lightly on the railing, thumb tracing the grain as if the ship could still answer her. The Tortosian historian stood nearby, ink-stained fingers clasped, eyes reflecting the dim blue light that lingers just before dawn.

Oscar lingered a few paces back, Elenn at his side. His shoulder was nearly healed, but the ache ran deeper. Greenbough moved quietly among the crew, brushing fingertips across shoulders and arms, murmuring small comforts that sounded like wind through leaves.

The bell tolled once—clear and steady. It was not a call to work but a signal for remembrance.

And then the world changed.

A shimmer rippled through the thinning starlight above the sterncastle, a sound like distant thunder and wings unfurling all at once. The air bent, gold over blue, and three figures stepped through as if the dawn itself had opened: **Talon**, **Arrabella**, and **Faloswansei**.

For a heartbeat, no one moved. Then the crew dropped their tools, their lines, their silence.

Talon's eyes swept the deck, the rigging, the faces—until they found the shrine. He said nothing, but his jaw tightened, and his hand pressed to the railing as if steadying himself against an old wound.

Marissa stepped forward, her composure a fragile thing held together by duty. "Captain Tirpik," she said softly, "was lost at the ridge pass. He saved half the valley before the mountains gave way."

Talon bowed his head, the motion slow and deliberate. "He always said he wanted to go with his boots wet and his beard full of wind," he murmured. "Seems he got both."

Bella touched the spyglass on the shrine, her fingertips glowing faintly with the light of remembrance. "He was never meant for still skies," she said. "Now he has every horizon."

The griffon gave a low, throaty trill—half grief, half blessing. His wings folded, feathers brushing the deck like benediction.

The crew gathered closer, quiet as prayer. Elenn's eyes shimmered, hands clasped before her as she whispered something too soft for mortal hearing. Oscar stood beside her, bow slung, gaze fixed on the endless expanse above.

Talon looked to Marissa. "He'd have wanted you to keep her flying," he said.

Marissa nodded once, steady. "We will. For him. For all of us."

Falos stepped closer to the shrine, his voice a deep rumble. "He rides the bright currents now," he said. "The winds remember their own."

For a long moment, no one spoke. Only the hum of the ship answered, the soft stretch of canvas and the whisper of the morning breeze through the rigging. Then Talon reached up and unpinned the old captain's badge—a small, round piece of bronze etched with the sigil of Soahc. He pressed it into Marissa's palm.

"Keep it close," he said quietly. "It's not just his mark— it's the weight of every soul that trusts the sky to hold them."

Marissa closed her fingers around it. "Aye," she whispered. "And the sky will."

***

That night, the stars burned clear above *Skythread*. The winds rose gentle and sure, as if something vast had turned its gaze upon them once more.

Talon stood alone at the rail, Falos silent beside him, both watching as the horizon brightened from indigo to gold. No words passed between them—none were needed.

Tomorrow, they would chart a new course. But tonight, even the heavens seemed to hold still, listening.

***

The last of the repair crews came aboard with the dawn tide. Frost still glazed the rigging, but the air smelled faintly of thawing pine and iron. The *Skythread* sat ready—patched, provisioned, her new hands signed to the log and the ship's cat already asleep on a coil of line as if it had never known another home.

On the quarterdeck, Marissa ran her fingers along the polished rail, still streaked with the scars of the storm that had taken Tirpik. "She's sound again," she said quietly. "Stubborn as her crew."

Bella joined her, cloak drawn close against the mountain wind. "He'd say the same of you," she said. Then, softly but clear enough for the nearest hands to hear, "You kept her steady when no one else could. It's time you took the helm proper, Captain."

The word hung in the air for a heartbeat—and then someone near the mizzen called, "Aye, Captain!"
Another voice echoed it. Then a dozen. Within moments the deck thundered with the sound of boots and cheers, not loud but full of promise.

Marissa bowed her head once, humbled. "All right then," she said. "We've a course to chart and the world waiting to be mended. Let's make ready."

The crew answered as one—
"We're with you, Cap'n!"

The sound rolled through the sails like a gust of wind, and for the first time since the storm, the *Skythread* truly felt alive again.

Talon turned to Bella, a faint smile in his beard. "Seems the sea's chosen its captain."

"No," Bella said, eyes on Marissa at the helm. "She earned it."

***

By noon, the winds had steadied from the east, and *Skythread* rose through the thinning clouds like a wounded bird testing its wings. Her patched sails caught the new light, and the fresh crew from the valley fell into rhythm under Marissa's clear orders.

Talon stood at her side at the helm, lending quiet strength rather than command. Bella watched from the charting table, eyes tracing the new route drawn in silver ink—west by northwest, following the cold band of the northern continent's edge.

Beyond those coasts lay rumor and danger both—lands scarred by the march of goblin legions and peaks that gleamed like tempered crystal. Whatever waited there would test both their maps and their courage.

"Set your course for the rimwinds," Marissa called, her voice cutting clean through the hum of ropes and canvas.

"Aye, helm to windward!" came the reply.

The ship tilted gently, and the horizon turned.

Talon rested a hand on the rail. "She's still got her spirit," he said.

Bella smiled faintly. "So do her people."

Above them, Falos stretched his wings and leapt from the deck, rising into the light. His call rang clear against the morning sky—half cry, half promise—and *Skythread* answered, her sails swelling with wind that smelled of stars and stormlight.

They turned westward into the sun, carrying memory and hope alike—toward whatever waited beyond the veil of cloud.

Book Four

Dirgewood

*"In the deep wood, every step is heard, every breath weighed.
Walk not as a thief of silence, but as a guest of roots and stone."*

— *Saying of the Troll Guardians*

Chapter One

Ash Upon the Sea

"The earth forgets nothing—it only waits for someone to listen."

— *Tortosian Proverb*

***

Captain's Log — Entry 14, Month 15 of Voyage
Two months since leaving the Tortosian city.
Two since setting our prow west along the northern coast.
The land bears no welcome.
Our maps name cities where there are only bones, and fields where only ash remains.
We chart anyway—because someone must remember.
— *Marissa Veyne, Acting Captain of the Skythread*

***

The first three weeks west were quiet—almost deceptively so. The winds held steady, sharp with salt and high cold. The sea shimmered like tarnished glass beneath a veiled sun.

Below, the coastline unspooled like an old scar—dark cliffs, gullies drowned in mist, plains gone fallow from fire and neglect. Every horizon looked washed clean of color, as though the world had exhaled its last warmth and grown tired of being looked upon.

On the twenty-first day, they saw the first ruin.

A city once white against the sea now lay broken.

Docks burned to blackened teeth.

Towers collapsed into heaps of pale rubble.

Even from miles offshore, the stench of char and salt carried on the wind.

Marissa lowered her spyglass slowly.

"By the tides… it's leveled."

Talon stood beside her, eyes narrowed, the lines of his face older than the years he carried. Bella's hand found the rail beside him.

"The Guardian's people must have fled from here," she murmured.

Oscar joined them, shoulders drawn tight beneath his cloak.

"It looks salted. Nothing could grow in that soil again."

The Tortosian historian, shell-gray skin glinting in weak daylight, folded his hands behind his back.

"They did not conquer," he said softly. "They consumed. Even the earth grieves."

Marissa passed him the spyglass. "How far inland?"

"Farther than sight allows," he said. "This was no siege—it was an erasure."

Silence took the deck. Even the gulls avoided the air.

Only the Skythread's cloud-keel hummed beneath their feet, steady as a heartbeat. Falos circled overhead once before settling atop the sterncastle, feathers dim against the ash-colored horizon.

That night, whispers rode the wind—dry, brittle, like voices trying to speak through distance and dust. Elenn lit the watch lanterns herself and whispered a prayer for "those who built before the burning."

Oscar wasn't sure if she prayed for the living or the ruins below.

Each dawn brought more silence.

Villages collapsed into ember mounds.

Forests shorn by fire.

Rivers running red with rust.

By the third week, even speech grew brittle. The crew charted ruined coastlines without words. Sometimes the quills faltered mid-letter, as if the names themselves resisted being remembered.

One morning, Oscar tried to sketch a coastline once bright with fields. The ink bled outward.

"It doesn't hold the line," he muttered. "Like the world's bleeding through."

Bella laid a hand on his shoulder.

"Then let it bleed," she said gently. "It means it can still heal."

***

The City That Refused to Kneel

The morning after the lookouts cried from the mast, a ruined city appeared in a coastal valley—vast, ash-gray, silent as a forgotten tomb.

The Skythread slipped closer to shore, her sails glinting like a lone spark beneath the gloom. As the shattered skyline widened, the deck fell utterly still.

At first the ruins looked only like bones and shadow.

Then Oscar breathed, "There…"

Bella followed his gaze—and froze.

One structure remained upright at the valley's heart.

Not untouched.

Not whole.

But standing.

A temple of pale granite rose amid the devastation. White columns scorched black.

Roof split.

Doors battered and gouged.

Bodies littered the steps—twisted goblins, broken ogres, ash-covered war-beasts. The remnants of a siege so furious it had devoured the rest of the city.

Marissa lowered her spyglass. "By the tides... they threw everything they had at it."

"Not just them," Tirpik said. "Trebuchet stones. Pitch cauldrons. Fire pits. They attacked for days."

The historian drew a long breath.
"They wanted it erased."

"No," Talon murmured. "They wanted it **first**."

Bella's eyes narrowed. "Because the temple meant something."

"The Hall of the Paladin," the historian said. "If it fell, the civilians' spirits would break."

He gestured at the carpet of enemy dead.

"But it didn't fall. These attackers died here trying. And because they failed... the people escaped."

Greenbough brushed the railing with her fingertips. "The temple did not defend itself," she whispered. "Someone defended it."

Oscar swallowed. The bodies were arranged in clear waves of assault, not retreat.

"They made a last stand."

"One hundred twenty-seven Oathbearers," the historian said. "The Guardian believed they fell early—before the ships cleared the horizon."

Talon shook his head. "She couldn't bear to look back."

The Skythread drifted closer.

The temple doors hung crooked but unfallen.

A faint brittle glow—oathlight stretched thin by time—clung to the arch above.

Tirpik wiped his eyes. "Captain… the temple is still watching the road."

Marissa nodded. "Lower the pinnace."

Oscar felt the owl-key of Archeron stir faintly against his ribs—like a heartbeat.

Bella whispered, "Whatever happened here… the Dirgewood won't speak until we do."

Above them, Falos circled once and released a low, broken cry—

the sound a griffon makes when honoring the fallen.

***

Inside the Ruins

The pinnace cut through gray water, oars dipping silently as the ruined city rose before them. Smoke curled from broken stones like the last breath of a long-dead forge.

The city was nothing but ruin—

except the temple.

Columns cracked.

Windows shattered.

Doors forced inward.

But it stood.

And the bodies strewn across the steps told the story of why.

Ogres in crude armor.

Goblins with rust-flaked blades.

War-beasts bristling with soot.

"Someone held this place," Talon murmured. "Held it with everything they had."

"One hundred twenty-seven Oathbearers," Bella whispered.

The pinnace scraped the stone pier. The air here was colder—colder than ruin should be. Elenn touched two fingers to her heart.

"This place remembers," Greenbough said softly.

They climbed the long stairs. Scars marked each step—dried blood, spiderweb cracks, blackened stone.

The fallen thickened near the top: waves that had shattered again and again and failed.

"They didn't just hold," Tirpik breathed. "They broke everything sent against them."

"And paid the price," Talon murmured.

Bella knelt beside a crouched skeleton wrapped in faded blue.

"They died on their feet," she whispered. "All of them."

Then Oscar's breath caught.

"Look."

***

The Banner

Talon pushed the temple doors open. Hinges groaned. Fractured sunlight spilled across cracked tiles and ash.

And there—

in the sanctuary's center—

hanging from a bent pole—

a banner remained.

214

Blue and white.

The sigil of the Paladin-Oath.

Burned. Torn.

But whole enough to be seen.

Whole enough to mean something.

Bella covered her mouth. "It shouldn't be standing."

"Someone placed it here after the fall," Talon said.

Oscar frowned. "How do you know?"

Talon lifted the bottom edge.

A single dried handprint marked the cloth—dark, deliberate, final.

"They carried it inside," Talon whispered. "After the gates broke. After the Guardian fled with her people. They planted it here... and held until the last heartbeat."

Bodies leaned against pillars.

Some sat with backs to the wall, weapons still in hand. Others formed a circle around the banner—shields raised, locked together.

"A sanctuary within a sanctuary," Greenbough murmured.

"They knew no one would see this," Elenn said softly.

"No," Bella whispered. "They hoped someone would."

Oscar reached out.

The banner brushed his knuckles—warm as memory.

"We're taking this home," he said. "The Guardian deserves to know what was bought for her."

Talon nodded. "We will. And speak every name."

Together, they lowered the banner with the reverence of kin.

***

The Hallowed Ground

Before they left, Bella paused, looking back over the rows of fallen Oathbearers.

"They should rest here," she whispered. "Not in some far grave. Here, where their vow held."

Greenbough stepped into the sanctuary's center, palms over cracked stone.

"Let this ground become theirs," she murmured. "Let sorrow become soil."

A tremor pulsed beneath them.
Ash shifted.
Stone softened.

From a single fissure, a faint green bud emerged— glowing not with drained oathlight, but with **welcomed** oathlight.

Dug rumbled from the doorway, voice low and certain:

"Not a cairn. Not a monument. A hill. A living one. Let one tree remember them."

Greenbough nodded.
"A sentinel of roots and quiet honor."

Bella exhaled shakily.
"Then let this place be hallowed."

And it was.

***

A Promise for the Dead
Outside, the wind shifted.
Falos cried from the rooftop—
a long, keening salute—
and the Skythread's sails answered.

Oscar wiped his eyes. "Captain… let's bring them home."

Marissa straightened.

"We carry the last oath of this city."

The ruined temple watched them go—its vigil finally fulfilled.

And for the first time since the flames consumed its streets, the wind carried something other than ash.

It carried memory.

***

As they pushed further west, the sky dimmed.

The fifth week brought quieter ruin—gray silence instead of scorched bone.

The land softened into misted valleys. The air grew damp—smelling faintly of pine and something older... something listening.

Bella stood beside Oscar at the rail.

"This aligns," she murmured. "With what the Guardian dreamed."

Oscar glanced over. "The dream of the shadow leading the horde?"

Bella nodded.

"Yes. She called it *Kiera*. But she said the name troubled her—it never felt right on her tongue. A mis-heard word. A warning twisted by fear."

The historian nodded slowly.

"In the old tongue, *Kiera* is derived from *ky'reth*—'mistaken,' 'twisted from its intended form.' And deeper still, the root echoes a far older name."

Talon exhaled.

"Mystyx."

The historian bowed his head.

"Whatever destroyed that city... whatever scattered its people... it was not a goblin shadow-demon."

Bella whispered, "The Guardian has no idea."

"And she must not know," Talon said. "Not until we understand more."

Ahead, the horizon shimmered with a deeper haze—moving like breath.

"Once," the historian murmured, "this was the cradle of the northern lands. Groves full of rivers and rain. Now... we call it the Wood of Sorrow."

"In our tongue?" Talon asked quietly.

"Perhaps... Dirgewood."

Greenbough traced the rail with her fingers. "A dirge may yet end in dawn, if someone dares to sing the last verse."

"Then let us be its echo," the historian said.

The Skythread pressed onward, sails pale against the dimming sun.

Behind her, the land still smoldered in the long light of evening.

Ahead, shadows gathered—tall, ancient, patient.

The Dirgewood waited.

***

Chapter Two

Roots Beneath the Ash

"When the oldest roots are cut, the world does not bleed—it remembers."

— *Saying among the Elders of Nandanoléme*

***

That night before putting wind to sail and flying over the Dirgewood, the Skythread anchored above black water that smelled of iron and rain. No stars pierced the haze. The horizon pulsed faintly—an unseen glow breathing just beneath the cloud line. Lanterns were shuttered. The crew spoke little. Even Falos kept to the rigging, feathers slick with mist.

Bella woke near midnight, her journal open to a page half-filled with sketches of trees. The ink shimmered faintly in the lamplight—lines that should have been still seemed to waver, as though caught in some unseen current. She frowned, dipped her quill, and wrote a single line in the margin:

The forest dreams, even when it sleeps beneath the sea.

When she closed the book, she realized the sound that had woken her wasn't wind.

It was deeper—a slow, rhythmic thrum, rising through the

deck. It reminded her of the Cála-nírë's heartbeat back in Nandanoléme, though fainter, older, lonelier.

She stepped onto the deck. Mist curled along the planks, glowing faintly where Greenbough knelt by the fore rail. The druid's palms were pressed flat against the wood, eyes unfocused, lips moving in silence.

"Do you hear it too?" Bella whispered.

Greenbough nodded. "Not hearing—remembering. The roots beneath the ash are calling. Something stirs… something vast. The world is turning in its sleep."

The wind shifted, carrying the faint scent of pine and deep water. Somewhere far below, the sea—or what had once been forest—sighed like breath drawn inward.

Bella turned her gaze toward the unseen shore. "Then tomorrow," she said, "we'll see what it dreams of."

Greenbough smiled faintly, her eyes reflecting ghost-light. "If it wakes gently," she murmured, "we may yet call it by name."

Behind them, the Skythread drifted in the breathless dark, her cloud-keel glowing with pale heartlight. Above, the last star winked out, as though the heavens themselves were holding their breath.

And beneath, the world waited.

***

The first days within the Dirgewood were like stepping into a cathedral half-buried in shadow.

The trees towered higher than any mast, their trunks wider than cottages, bark furrowed with age and grief. Light filtered through their crowns in slow, copper shafts. The air tasted of damp soil and secrets.

The Skythread glided low, sails whispering against the canopy. Even her cloud-keel dimmed its hum, as though unwilling to disturb the silence. Crewmen spoke in hushed tones. Tools were muffled with cloth. Greenbough kept to the forecastle, eyes closed, palms on the railing.

"They're listening," she murmured once. "Not to us—to each other. They remember something terrible."

No one asked what.

At night, Marissa forbade fires. Lanterns were hooded. The crew took to speaking softly or not at all. Oscar noticed that even Falos moved differently—slow wingbeats, head turning as though reading words only he could see in the dark.

Bella sat near the prow one evening, sketching the towering trunks. "These trees… they look grown from grief."

Talon nodded. "The roots of the world always remember what was buried in them."

She smiled faintly. "You sound like Dug."

"Then I'm finally learning," he said.

They charted carefully, tracing broken ridges and black rivers that twisted through the green haze. The deeper they went, the stranger the air became—sweet and sharp, threaded with a resonance that made teeth ache and compasses tremble. The stars above blurred each night behind luminous mist that pulsed like a living heartbeat.

Bella called it residual aether, fallout from the old thinning of the Veil. "It seeps into everything," she said. "Even the roots here drink it."

By the third week, the forest began to change. The ground below fractured into wide sinkholes. Mist poured upward from glowing cracks that ran like veins of molten silver. Quakes rolled through the earth—slow, rhythmic, like the breathing of something vast beneath the world.

Then came the sound.

At first it was distant thunder—slow, rolling, endless. But it did not fade. It grew. The trees trembled, birds scattered, and the air thickened with dust.

"Starboard helm!" Marissa shouted. "Take her high!"

The Skythread surged upward on a burst of cloudlight as the horizon split apart. Below, the forest caved in on itself—thousands of trees, whole ridgelines collapsing into a widening gulf. Roots thicker than towers tore free, curling skyward before vanishing into boiling water and steam.

"The land's falling!" cried one of the Tortosian marines. "The forest is dying!"

"No," Greenbough said softly, eyes reflecting the abyss. "It's... changing."

The collapse continued for hours. What had been woodland became a vast inner sea—its waters glowing faintly with the heat of the world's heart.

When the roar finally died, steam hung like ghosts between the cliffs. The Skythread hovered over the newborn gulf, her crew struck silent.

Oscar stood at the rail, throat tight. "We just watched a forest die."

Talon rested a hand on his shoulder. "No. We watched the world shift its weight. Sometimes that's how it survives."

Bella's eyes gleamed with pale reflection. "Then this sea has no name yet."

Marissa drew a long breath. "Then we'll give it one. The Sea of Roots."

Greenbough bowed her head. "And may it remember what it once was."

The Skythread drifted forward again, cloud-keel gleaming against the dawn of a newborn sea. Behind her, the smoke of centuries curled upward from the drowned trees—an elegy and a beginning.

***

Mist clung to the valley below, the trees shifting like slow breath under the fading light. The air carried the smell of pine and salt—and the faint metallic tang left behind by battle.

The deck was subdued now, the kind of quiet that follows chaos. Crew moved softly about their duties, still tending to repairs, still catching their breath. Even Faloswansei perched silent atop the aft rigging, feathers stirred by the wind.

Oscar stood near the starboard rail, staring down into the cloudbreak where the forest canopy met the fog. He didn't notice Arrabella approach until her reflection joined his in the glass of the observation lantern.

"Couldn't sleep?" she asked gently.

He shook his head. "No. Tried, but every time I close my eyes, it's just... noise."

She nodded. "It takes time. The mind keeps fighting when the heart's already tired."

Oscar hesitated, fingers drumming the rail. "Bella... can I ask you something? Something about... dying?"

Her expression softened, but she said nothing. The wind filled the pause, brushing her hair across her face.

He exhaled slowly. "Greenbough talked to me before the fight. She said death isn't an end—it's just the melody bending before it finds its way again. That I wasn't sent back by accident." He swallowed, voice low. "She thinks I came back for a reason."

Arrabella studied him in silence for a long moment. The *Skythread* creaked beneath them, timbers whispering with the wind. "She's not wrong," she said finally. "You carry something the rest of us don't. You've walked a path even the elves can't see."

Oscar frowned slightly. "I don't *feel* special. I just feel… unfinished. Like I got stitched back together wrong."

Bella smiled faintly. "We all do, after coming that close. The world changes shape when you see both sides of it. But you came back because something—or someone—believed you still had work to do."

He looked at her, eyes uncertain. "You really think it wasn't just luck?"

Her gaze turned east, toward the horizon where sunlight broke faintly through the mist. "Luck is the name mortals give to what they don't understand. I call it design. Or mercy."

He nodded quietly. "Greenbough said almost the same thing. She told me the Archons don't waste miracles. Said I'm surrounded by people who care." He smiled faintly. "Even mentioned Thay'sa—'sometimes scarily so.'"

That drew a small laugh from Bella—soft, genuine. "That sounds exactly like her."

Oscar smiled too, though the question still lingered behind his eyes. "Guess I'm just trying to make sense of it all before the next storm hits."

Bella turned toward him, her hand brushing his arm. "You don't have to make sense of it," she said gently. "Just live it. That's what the living are for."

He met her gaze and, for the first time since Archeron, felt something like peace. The hum of the *Skythread* rose beneath their feet, steady and sure—as if the ship herself agreed.

Above them, Faloswansei gave a low, rumbling note, deep as distant thunder. It rolled through the air and down into the mist, the first whisper of the sky stirring again.

Chapter Three

The Forest That Waits

"Even the oldest trees bow when the world changes its song."

— Elven Saying of the First Age

***

The forest had been uneasy for days.

The hum beneath its soil—soft at first, almost melodic—had shifted into something deeper. A rhythm that felt like breath.

The Skythread drifted low through the giant trunks, her cloud-keel parting fog that glowed faintly green. Each pulse of light felt like a heartbeat rising from the roots below.

Here, the world felt older than memory.

The trees rose like pillars of a forgotten temple, their crowns lost in darkness, their roots coiled around ancient bones and stone veins. The air was thick with elder enchantment; every gust carried the trace of voices half-remembered. Moss rippled over the bark in luminous waves, tinged with the last remnants of the First Songs—magic older than language, older than war, older than grief.

Oscar crossed the forward deck slowly—boots soft, breaths softer. "It feels like they're listening," he whispered.

"They are," Greenbough murmured. She rested her fingers gently on the lichen-soft rail, as though afraid to disturb it. "They've sung through every age. They know every sorrow. Now something calls to them again."

Falos shifted on the rigging above, feathers rustling like leaves in rain. "Then it isn't just the wind," he said. "The air smells like… change."

Bella raised her staff. A faint shimmer of blue ran down its runes—then dimmed. "No leyline map records power like this," she said. "It's not wild aether. It's focused. Breathing. The Veil's pulse is gathering."

Talon watched the horizon where shadow met cloud. "Or something beneath it," he said, voice low.

The Skythread creaked once—soft, questioning—then fell silent again.

***

On the fourth night, the winds vanished.

The sails drooped like veils, and the cloud-keel dimmed to a dull ember-pulse.

Then—without helm, without hand—the Skythread began to move.

"Hands off the wheel," Marissa ordered. "Let her choose."

No one argued.

Her movements were slow, deliberate—like a memory traced in the air. The forest parted for her as she drifted, branches bending back in silent recognition.

Fog rolled like surf between the trunks. Then the mist thinned, and they saw it:

A living mountain of wood rose from the forest floor. A single tree—if "tree" was still the word—its bark laced

228

with pale, pulsing veins of light. Its crown vanished into darkness. Birds spiraled above it in slow circles, their calls muted and strange, echoing an ancient melody.

The Skythread glided closer. Her sails folded without command. When her hull touched the massive trunk, the air trembled—not collision, but recognition.

Light rippled outward from the point of contact, like breath drawn and released by the world itself.

"She's docking," whispered a Tortosian marine. "As if she remembers."

"Maybe she does," Marissa whispered.

The bark exhaled.

Light deepened.

And three figures stepped forth.

Tall. Ageless. Cloaked in moss and starlight.

Eyes faint as dawn through leaves.

Ancient elves.

Wardens of the Rootsong.

***

The tallest bowed—not to Talon or Bella, but to the Skythread.

"You return, child of cloud and craft," he said in Elvish older than the First Age. Forged by the Free Peoples, sealed in promise. Your coming was foretold—when the first roots stirred toward waking."

Bella stepped forward, staff lowered. "You know this vessel?"

The second warden bowed lightly. "We helped weave her heart before your wars of rift and flame. Her clouder-stones breathe the same song that guards this forest."

Greenbough's reverence dimmed into fear. "Then what stirs now? Why here?"

The smallest—oldest—placed his palm on the trunk. The bark rippled beneath his touch like skin over a sleeping giant.

"What you feel is not death," he said softly. "It is memory. The forest has held its vigil for an age and a half. But now the oaths of the First Roots stir again. When roots move… the sky soon follows."

Talon's hand settled on his hilt. "A warning, then?"

The warden smiled faintly, like moonlight slipping through branches. "Both warning and welcome. A song buried ten thousand years must rise again. Your ship will hear it first. Her heart will pulse with the rhythm of the world's renewal. Do not resist it."

Bella's brow furrowed. "Renewal through destruction?"

"Sometimes," he said gently. "A seed cannot grow while clinging to its shell."

Leaves sighed overhead—an echo of ancient truth.

***

As the wardens stepped back toward the bark, the eldest paused.
His hand brushed the Skythread's hull, tracing runes worn nearly smooth by time.

"Tell your kin in Nandanoléme," he whispered,
"that the promise of the Skythread endures.
She was not built merely to ride the wind.
She was born to remember what the world forgets."
Talon bowed. "We'll see that she does."
The warden nodded.
The bark swallowed him.

Light faded to a pulse… then stillness.
Even the forest bowed.

***

For a long moment, no one spoke.
The only sound was the slow beat of the cloud-heart, now pulsing in rhythm with the earth beneath.

Marissa laid a hand on the wheel. "She's humming stronger."

Talon nodded. "Then the roots are waking."

Bella stared into the glowing mist where unseen ridges steamed like breath. "And soon," she whispered, "the sky will be."

The Skythread drifted upward, bow slicing through silvered fog.
Behind her, the Dirgewood whispered farewell through a thousand leaves.

And far beneath the soil—where roots touched stone and memory dreamed—something vast stirred.

Not beast. Not god.

But the heartbeat of a world remembering its name.

Captain's Log

The Dirgewood

The forest moves beneath us. Not with wind or tide, but with memory.

For days now, the ship's heart has pulsed in rhythm with the soil below. The crew feels it even in sleep—dreams touched by voices we cannot name. I believe the Skythread remembers this place. Perhaps she was built from its timber, or from something older still—root and storm and promise woven together.

The wardens spoke of renewal. They said the world must shed its bark before it can grow again. I do not know whether that means rebirth or ruin. But the forest seems content with either, and perhaps that is its wisdom.

We drift above a living sea of roots, its veins glowing with light drawn from the deep places of the earth. Falos circles overhead, uneasy. Greenbough keeps vigil at the prow. Even Bella—who trusts in maps more than omens—walks the deck as if listening for a heartbeat not her own.

If these are the first stirrings of the world's renewal, then I pray we have the courage to sail through it. If not, then let this entry stand witness.

The forest remembers us. May we prove worthy of being remembered.

— *Marissa Veyne, Acting Captain of the Skythread*

Chapter Four

The Sea That Dreamed

"The world below is never only water."

—*Saying among the Tortosian mariners*

***

Dawn found the Skythread hanging over a sea no map had ever named. The air tasted of resin and salt and something metallic at the back of the tongue, as if a forge had cooled beneath the world and the steam of it still climbed. Halo light made soft rings around the rigging. Where the forest had stood, a basin of pale water stretched in a vast, breathing curve, its surface steaming in quiet veils.

No one spoke at first. The ship seemed to listen—her cloud-keel dimmed to a low, sympathetic hum, sails furled to keep from disturbing the newborn calm. The smell of scorched wood drifted up from the drowned trunks along the rim—the last incense of an age collapsed.

"Slow circuit," Talon said at last, voice low, hands easy on the rail. "Keep her steady."

Marissa lifted a hand; the helmsman bowed his head and eased the wheel. The Skythread responded like a patient creature learning its strength again, turning on currents that

233

weren't quite wind. Bella stood at the chart table beneath the sterncastle lanterns, silver ink catching the dawn. Oscar braced the parchment with his wrist to keep his lines from shaking; even his careful script quivered, as if the world refused to hold still long enough to be measured.

The Tortosian historian took his place beside the coil-room door with a small desk and a jar of ink that glimmered faintly green in the light. He recorded time, temperature, direction, the look of the sky—a ledger for a sea that had been born yesterday.

Greenbough leaned on the forecastle rail, eyes half-lidded, the leaves woven through her hair awake and listening. "It's quiet," she murmured, "not empty."

Falos circled once above the mainmast, feathers gilded, then alighted on the yard with a muted trill. "The sky smells wrong," he said. "Wrong like thunder that forgot where to go."

Marissa nodded without looking up. "Log it: odor metallic; atmosphere charged. Begin east-to-west transect. Depth soundings by echo-stone, every five furlongs."

"Aye," came the reply from belowdecks where the drum of the echo-stone began to throb—a thump that ran outward and returned thin—and strange—from beneath the water, as though it had traveled farther than the basin should allow.

Oscar glanced over the rail and swallowed. Something about the surface unsettled the eye. It glittered, yes, but not like sun on waves. The light seemed to run across it as if across glass, then under it, then back again, like breath beneath skin.

He sketched what he could—shoreline, drift, the half-drowned buttresses of trees the size of towers—and forced himself not to draw what his mind kept offering up: a slow spiral, widening, widening, toward a heart he couldn't see.

***

The first two hours passed with work to fill them. Bella called for ley-line readings, sent two apprentices to the aft gallery with crystal loops to listen for the hum of the world beneath; she set her staff against the table and traced the faintest runes—a mesh of sight and silence she said would keep their instruments from lying outright.

"Compasses?" Talon asked.

"Sleepwalking," Bella answered. She laid the off-kilter needles beside the chart, where they twitched and spun as if dreaming of north rather than pointing it. "The Veil's thin in patches. The lines don't agree on what's real."

Marissa didn't curse. She only tightened the strap on her slate and spoke so the crew could hear. "We chart anyway."

A few voices answered—quiet, fervent, almost liturgical: "Chart anyway."

Greenbough's voice drifted back from the bow. "There's a rhythm under us," she said. "Not waves. A pulse. Lean your cheek to the rail—you'll feel it in your teeth."

Oscar tried. The wood was warm, the hum soft. It climbed into his jaw and settled there, not sound exactly, but the memory of it.

He lifted his head, a little dizzy, and blinked hard to clear the haze from his eyes. "I don't like it," he confessed.

"That makes two of us," Falos said.

***

They had almost completed their first long pass when the vertigo arrived in earnest.

It began as a shiver in the hands. Sailors paused mid-knot, staring at their fingers as if the rope had flickered to smoke. Then the deck seemed to tilt—not to port or starboard, but downward, as though the sky itself were a slope and the ship had begun to slide toward something waiting below.

"Steady," Marissa called. "Keep your eyes on the horizon."

But the horizon wasn't there. It was there and not; it bent inward, then out again, as if someone had cupped the world and was testing its shape.

"Captain," the navigator said through clenched teeth, slate tucked hard under his arm, "request permission to—"

He didn't finish.

At the starboard shrouds, a young rigger named Kethan—all elbows and good intentions—went white as chalk and dropped the coil in his hands. The coil snaked over the rail. He reached for it, misjudged his own arm, and stumbled. For an instant he hung, fingers clawed on the rail cap; then the world tipped further inside his skull and he tumbled, graceless, into the bright steam below.

"Man overboard!" someone shouted—Oscar, he thought distantly; he heard his own voice and didn't feel his lips move.

The deck exploded into motion. Marissa's orders cut clean through the surge. "Belay starboard! Anchor drift! Claycap, with me!"

A gnome in a patched dive harness—Perrin Claycap—whose laugh carried across three decks and who claimed to know the name of every river in the eastern hemisphere, was already slinging the buoyant stone-pack over his shoulders. A human mate, broad as a door and quick on his feet, knotted a rescue line to his belt and clipped Perrin's line to his own. Two more sailors braced at the cleats.

"On the count—" Marissa began.

"—We jump on 'two,'" Perrin said, and leaped on 'one.'

They struck the surface like stones onto a drum. The water wasn't cold. It wasn't anything a man could name. It flexed around them—skin thick as glass, thin as breath; it pushed at their ears with a pressure that hummed with the same soft tone that lived in the ship's bones.

The human mate—Roul to those who knew his quiet—went straight for the last ripple. The steam blinded him; he felt more than saw Kethan, a limp shape drifting down through light like pollen in a sunbeam.

"Pull!" someone bellowed from the rail above, and the lines went taut.

Perrin wrapped his legs around Kethan's waist and hooked his forearm under the boy's chin, the way a man hauls a half-drowned dog out of a spring flood. Roul kicked hard, boots churning, eyes on the bright smear that was the ship's shadow.

For three impossible heartbeats, the sea took them sideways instead of up.

Then the Skythread answered herself. The clouder-stones brightened—no one touched the helm; the ship simply chose—and she sank low until her belly almost kissed the shimmering skin of the water. Hands reached. Lines bit. The world lurched.

They came up in a tangle of rope and coughs and curses. Kethan retched sea and light and a little shame onto the deck and lay gasping against the scuppers, eyes wild, skin flushed as if with fever.

"You're all right," Oscar told him, though he wasn't sure he believed it. "You're all right."

Perrin flopped onto his back and stared at the waking sky with an expression that wasn't far from reverence. "Cap," he said, voice hoarse, "that isn't water. Not all the way. Feels like falling through a song."

Roul pushed hair from his eyes, spat once, and nodded grimly. "There are depths that look back at you."

Marissa knelt, pressed fingers to Kethan's throat, then lifted her head. "He's breathing. Elenn—"

"I have him," Elenn said, already at Kethan's other side. Her hands were steady; the small blessing she spoke smelled faintly of wild thyme and candle smoke. Color returned to Kethan's lips by degrees. He blinked to focus, flinched from the sky, and clamped his eyes shut.

"Don't look down just yet," she said gently. "Look at me."

He did, and the panic receded a finger's width.

Bella stood very still at the rail, eyes narrowed as if reading something written only in light. "The surface tension behaves as if it were more than matter," she said softly. "As if thought had weight."

Talon met her eyes and did not ask her to explain what she already knew could not be explained. "Log it," he said. "In the language we have."

The historian's quill scratched: *A fall into shining; retrieval successful; pressure not wholly physical; water behaves as a mirror of mind.* He looked up only once, and when he did, his eyes shone like a man who has heard distant music he cannot forget.

The vertigo didn't leave when the rescue ended. If anything, it grew more particular, choosing its moments with a mind of its own. A sailor would lean to coil a line and find his hand pulling toward the sea as if the water had hooked it. An officer would glance at the horizon and see it arcing toward her like the inside of a bowl. The cup of the world seemed to tilt whenever anyone tried to pin it to the page.

"Eyes on the line, not the drop," Marissa called every watch. "And if the drop looks back at you, take a breath and blink. It isn't you. It's the sea."

Oscar tried to laugh the first time he felt it pull at him; the sound came out thin. He forced his gaze to the chart, to the safe insistence of ink and margin, and wrote without looking over the rail.

***

Captain's Log — Survey of the Sea of Roots, Day One

Wind: light and fickle. Clouds: high, veiled.

Compasses: untrustworthy.

Echo-stone: returns from below inconsistent with basin depth; suggests cavernous structure or—

He lifted the quill, stared at the word he had almost written, and did not write it.

Greenbough came down from the bow with a stillness that quieted the deck around her. She set her palm flat on the rail; the leaves in her hair shivered as if to a breeze no one else felt. "The roots that fell still remember standing," she said. "They pull. It's not malice. It's... homesickness."

239

"Everything does," Greenbough said kindly. "Even stone. It pretends it doesn't."

Falos mantled his wings and settled closer to Oscar than usual, big head low, eyes narrowed at the open water. "You'll stay away from the rail today," the griffon said. It wasn't a suggestion.

"I will," Oscar said, and meant it.

***

They laid their second transect in the afternoon, this time running north to south to cut the basin into knowable quarters. The light changed while they worked, brightening rather than dimming as the sun angled west—as if some other hidden sun beneath the sea were refusing to set.

Bella sent a runner to fetch her crystal loops; she held them before her face, listening with her eyes closed. They quivered in her hands, sang a high, thin chord, then fell silent in a way that was not silence. She opened her eyes and looked older by a breath. "The lines are braided," she said. "Not only in earth—in air. We are sailing across a place where the Veil has slept against the world so long it learned our names in its sleep."

"And now?" Talon asked.

"It is stirring," she said. "And I don't know if it is waking to comfort or to change."

Falos tilted his head, listening to nothing the human ear could keep. "Then mind your footing," he said. "Songs choose their dancers."

Marissa's mouth quirked. "Both, if the world is itself. We keep working."

"Captain," the navigator said from the quarter, swallowing as he stared into the white-lipped light,

240

"respectfully request permission not to throw up on your boots."

"Permission granted," she said without turning.

He went to the lee-rail and was quietly sick in a manner that offended no one and upset only the gull that had chosen that moment to sail alongside and consider them. Someone clapped his shoulder. The ship adjusted her height on her own, as if taking pity on all their stomachs.

By last bell, the deck had gone soft-footed, the way a crew moves when they've learned that loudness is a kind of rudeness. The hum beneath the boards deepened in the night watch, and sleep came in shallow pools. Those who dreamed woke with a taste of pine on the back of their tongues, or with the feeling they had stepped off a high branch and were still waiting to land.

Oscar didn't write about the dream he couldn't quite catch. He drew instead—the curve of the basin's northwest rim, the way the drowned trunks looked like pillars in a ruin-temple, the small, odd rings that appeared and widened without ripple and faded as if embarrassed to be seen.

He added a note in the margin, small and cramped: *The sea is not empty. It knows we are here.*

***

The second day began with a false dawn. Light rose from the basin before the sky had earned it. It crept up the hull in pale fingers and made the ropes glow. Elenn called the midwatch to drink; half of them sipped without tasting, eyes fixed on the water as if looking too long would make it reach for them.

The echo-stone's drum called and returned and called again. Its pulse came back slower than the strike—lagged in a

241

way no basin its size should. Bella wrote a string of numbers that meant nothing to Oscar; when she set the chalk down, she stared at her own hand like it had told her a secret she was not ready to keep.

"What is it?" he asked.

"If the returns are right," she said, "we are not sounding a bowl. We're sounding a throat."

He blinked. "Like a... like a—"

"A place made to sing," she said, and wouldn't say more.

Perrin laughed then, just once, small and wild. He slapped Roul's shoulder and tilted his head at the water the way men look at an old enemy who might yet be a friend. "If you're going to spit me back out, do it gentle," he told it. The sea did not answer except to lay flatter than a mirror.

Talon had the look he wore when he set his stance before a storm: weight balanced, hand light, eyes on everything at once. He walked the line between main and mizzen and stopped above the chart table to read what Bella had refused to say out loud.

"We keep to the plan," he said. "Finish the east-west grid. If the ship hums, we hum with her. If she lifts, we let her. She knows this better than any of us."

Marissa dipped her head in assent. The crew repeated the plan back in crisp fragments, as sailors do when the work is hard and the fear is worse.

"Finish the grid."

"If she hums, we hum."

"If she lifts, we let her."

"Chart anyway."

Greenbough smiled without her mouth moving. "Good," she said. "Now be kind with your feet."

They were.

The accident at third bell might have become a story if there had been appetite for stories left in anyone. A coil-half froze in winter. A cook dropped a ladle the size of a child and swore in a whisper almost reverent. A lantern flared and then dimmed without going out, its wick refusing to burn too brightly as if brightness would be rude in a place like this.

By late afternoon the vertigo had become an accepted guest. The crew adjusted their stance and kept their eyes flicking to lines, to cleats, to the safe rattle of blocks and tackle. Oscar learned to steady himself with the set of his jaw, a sailor's trick he'd watched Talon use: teeth not clenched, just placed, as if holding a word gently between them.

He managed a sketch that might not embarrass him later. In the corner of the page he drew a series of faint, translucent shapes beneath the water and wrote beneath them, *Not fish. Not shadow.* He did not show anyone that part.

At last light, the basin took on a color that had no name—not blue, not green, not the gold of evening. It was the color of a thought you can almost catch. The air tasted like the seconds before rain. Falos left the yard and moved to the mainmast cap where he could see everything without seeing too much.

"Report," Marissa said—the word softer than it would be on any other day.
"Lines hold," came the answer. "Grid: half-complete. Echo-stone returns inconsistent. Crew… quiet."

"Quiet" was generous. They were reverent and tired and frightened like men and women are when they know they are standing near a thing bigger than the names for it.

Bella set down her chalk. "That's enough for today," she said. "The world is in no hurry. We don't need to be either."

Marissa nodded. "Strike to night sail. Half-height."

"Aye, Captain."

The Skythread rose a shade, sails easing until they gathered only enough wind to keep her trimmed. Her cloud-heart thrummed once, deep and contented, like a creature settling its bones.

Talon glanced toward the historian, who had not once looked up from his desk since noon. "Add this to your ledger," he said. "Chart incomplete. Waters unstable. Beneath lies something alive, or longing to be."

The historian paused, quill above the page, then wrote Talon's words exactly. He underlined *longing to be* and did not ask permission.

Oscar closed his journal, laid the quill across its spine, and let his feet feel the music in the boards. It rose and fell, not like tide, not like storm, but like breath. He looked over the rail despite himself and saw only his—his own face—then something behind it, moving, slow as continents.

Greenbough came to stand beside him and did not speak. After a while she placed her palm lightly over the curve of his knuckles where they gripped the rail.

"Do you hear it?" he asked.

"Yes," she said.

"What is it?"

She tilted her head as if listening to a note almost out of range. "A promise. Or the memory of one."

Falos' voice drifted down from above, low and sure. "Keep your balance, little archer. The sky will shift before the sea does."

Oscar huffed a laugh he hadn't planned and found, to his surprise, that it steadied him.

Night lifted out of the basin the way mist lifts from a field after harvest. The *Skythread* drifted through it like a ghost. Far below, faint circles of light appeared, widened, and faded without sending even a ripple toward the rim. No one named them. Some things lose their power if you say them too soon.

On the last watch, when the crew had learned how to breathe again without tasting metal, the ship's heartstone pulsed once—steady, resonant, alive. Men and women looked up, then at each other, and smiled small and honest in the dark.

The charts were half-finished. The names had not yet been written. But they all understood the truth without saying it:

They were sailing across the skin of something waking.

***

Below deck, the world felt smaller. The hum of the **Skythread's** heart was a steady, patient sound, like the pulse of something ancient dreaming. **Oscar** lay in his bunk, one arm over his eyes, the other resting across his chest where the ache never quite went away.

Sleep wouldn't come. His thoughts spun like the gears in the navigation room—turning, aligning, never stopping.

Greenbough's voice whispered through memory: *"The world doesn't waste its miracles."*

Bella's echoed after: *"You came back because something—or someone—believed you still had work to do."*

He turned onto his side, staring at the faint silver line of lanternlight tracing the wall. "Work to do," he murmured. "Or debts to pay."

The ship creaked around him, alive and listening. Somewhere above, a rope shifted in its pulley.

"Maybe it was luck," he said to no one. "Maybe it was just… the wrong soul in the right place."

The air changed.

A soft, familiar warmth pressed against his thoughts— half growl, half heartbeat.

"Dug," he breathed.

The huff came first—low and heavy, the kind that always smelled faintly of rain and earth. It ruffled his hair.

Oscar smiled despite himself. "You always show up when I'm overthinking."

A pause. Then the slow weight of meaning—not words, but certainty.

Stop chasing the why. You're here. That's enough.

Oscar swallowed. "Was it you?" he whispered. "Did you—?"

The bunk's timbers gave a soft creak, like laughter through old wood. The warmth deepened, filling the space around him.

They took too much from too many.

A pause, heavier.

They would've left you there to keep their balance sheet clean. I disagreed.

Oscar blinked at the dark. "You mean the Archons? The universe?"

The presence rumbled, neither denial nor confirmation.

Names don't matter. Intent does. You sealed what they wanted sealed. That was enough for them. But not for me.

The words—or the feeling of them—hung in the still air. Oscar's throat tightened. "You pulled me back."

Some debts aren't meant to be collected.

The warmth eased, the air cooling again. The smell of rain faded, leaving only the steady pulse of the ship's heart.

He let out a slow breath. "Guess that's one reason not to question miracles."

The answer came softer now, like fur brushing through fog:

Miracles aren't reasons. They're reminders.

Then it was gone.

Oscar stared up at the curved ceiling of the bunk, eyes stinging but calm. For the first time since Archeron, he didn't feel lost—just small, and somehow that was enough.

Above deck, the wind began to shift. The ship stirred. And the first threads of light from the coming Ascension reached the Skythread's hull.

Above deck, the wind changed—not with force, but with purpose. A gentle lift, like a hand beneath the hull, raised the Skythread into a slow, graceful drift. Her lanterns glowed brighter without flame catching them; her rigging sighed as if waking from a long, patient sleep.

The world below responded.

Light gathered beneath the basin, faint at first—then blooming upward like dawn rising from *beneath* the sea. Rings of radiance unfurled across the water in perfect circles, touching the drowned treetops with soft gold until they shone like lanterns hung in some forgotten sanctuary. Each pulse carried warmth, not heat; memory, not warning.

The pullback widened.

From high above, the basin looked less like a wound and more like a cradle. The bright water curved in a vast, luminous bowl, every ripple answering a song older than sky or stone. Threads of light traveled outward from its center— thin, silver pathways sinking into the earth, linking root to root, valley to valley, as though re-stitching something the ages had frayed.

The Skythread drifted upward with them, not resisting, her cloud-keel shimmering in agreement. Her heartstone thrummed in harmony—steady, gentle, alive.

Creatures in the forest remnants stirred. Birds lifted their heads. Even distant stones seemed to breathe easier.

On the far shore, where mist parted in slow curtains, the faint shape of an older world shimmered—something watching, not with envy, but with ancient yearning. A presence that had waited lifetimes to witness this rising.

The wind rose again—soft, warm, carrying the scent of rain, pine, and the promise of renewal.

And in that moment, as the basin shone like a newborn star cradled in the world's hands, every soul aboard the Skythread felt the truth:

Some miracles do not arrive to change the world.
They arrive to remind it how to begin again.

Chapter Five

When the Sky Trembles

"Before the first dawn there was the breath between
— the hush when the heavens waited to begin again."

— Fragment from The Songs of the First Sky, *preserved in Nandanoléme*

***

The first sign was the color. Long before the sun cleared the rim of the world, the Sea of Roots turned white—pure, living, and wrong in the way a heartbeat would be if it started outside the body. It was not reflected light but light becoming. The glow rose from below, staining the undersides of the mist and laying pale fire along the ship's hull. Sailors froze at their posts. Breath steamed into the half-dark and hung there, as if the air had thickened. Even the gull that had followed them for three days went silent, wings arrested above the mainmast like a blessing that had forgotten to fall.

The Skythread began to hum.

It started as a murmur underfoot, a thrumming that traveled the length of her cloud-keel and kissed every plank. The deckboards picked it up and sang back—a quiet, thrice-folded harmony like an old lullaby the ship suddenly remembered. Hands went to rails. Eyes went to sky. For a heartbeat the crew stood as one creature—listening.

Marissa reached for her compass. The needle spun in lazy abandon, then bucked hard and rattled itself flat against the glass. She steadied the chart table with her hip, set the useless thing down, and lifted her head to the wind.

Bella's staff answered the hum with a pale, sympathetic light, filaments winking between rune and wood. She spread a hand against the rail and closed her eyes. "The Veil's tension is breaking," she said—not loudly and not for effect. "It's drawing in everything. Magic, memory... even thought." She opened her eyes and looked east. "Hold the ship easy."

"Easy," Marissa echoed. "Half-sail. No sudden changes."

Oscar squinted into the glare, shading his eyes. "Drawing in for what?"

Greenbough didn't look away from the water. Her voice rode the hum. "Birth," she whispered. "The forest prays still."

The word moved across the deck and settled in the hollows of the crew like a stone placed upon a cairn—not an ending, an answer.

***

By midmorning the air forgot how to be mere weather. Wind didn't blow; it circulated, climbing in polished spirals that caught the light and turned it to dust motes of gold. Filaments of raw aether drifted across the deck, kissing bare skin and dissolving with the sensation of snowflakes that warmed instead of chilled. Every rope hair seemed to stand on end.

Falos crouched on the starboard rig, claws whisper-soft on the spar, wings half-open to balance what could not be

250

balanced. His eyes narrowed against the brightness.
A thought brushed the minds of those nearest—rough as stone, edged with stormlight.

The sky smells wrong.

His nostrils flared, tasting the unseen. *Ozone. Iron. And—*

His head tilted, beak on the last word as though even thought itself must bow before it.

—and birth.

Above them, the cloud bank gathered with a purpose no wind-map had ever dared explain. It tightened into a gyre the size of a small country, the center black as an eye without iris. It did not spin so much as *turn*—slow, deliberate—as though the universe were a wheel and they stood at its rim.

From the hollow's heart fell a tone too low for the ear, too true for the bones to ignore. The world sang a note it had learned before there were ears to hear it.

Talon's palms found the rail. The hum ran through him—from finger to shoulder to spine—almost, almost pain.

"Same resonance as the Sea," he murmured. "Sky and water are speaking the same tongue."

Bella had already set her crystals—three small loops, each no wider than a teacup, suspended from the sterncastle canopy. They spun of their own accord, then slowed as the chord found them.

"The song of creation," she whispered, voice trembling not with fear but recognition. "And it's waking again."

Falos's mind-voice deepened, threading through both their thoughts like thunder rolling under calm water.

The Veil thins. What sleeps beyond it dreams of light again.

Below, the historian braced his little desk with both elbows as the ink jar danced circles upon the wood. Still he wrote—curt, dense lines meant for readers who would never stand on a deck that *sang*.

The sky shook, and the water answered. Between them our ship held her breath.

Then, without willing it, he underlined *held her breath*— and felt his eyes sting.

***

Marissa moved as a captain does when awe threatens competence—down the ladder, along the lane, up past the coil-room to the forward beam. She touched shoulder to shoulder, spoke names where names steadied hands, and checked the lashings on anything that could betray them if the ship leapt. "Lash spare blocks. Secure the kitchen chest. Helm—two points' leeway either way, no correction unless we drift more than a line's width off course."

"Aye."

"Riggers, lash yourselves."

"Aye."

"Eyes up, not down."

The word *down* made the air tilt. Several men swallowed hard.

"Breathe," Elenn said from the midships ladder, where she had set a basin, a small cup, and the clean rag she kept with her as carefully as any blade. "In through the nose. Out through the mouth. Let the ship do the steadying."

They did. It helped.

***

It began without warning.

A single straight fracture of light cut the horizon—thin as a drawn blade, bright as new snow under noon sun. Another followed, then another, until the west became a pane of luminous glass broken by the hand of a god. The sound that came with it wasn't wind. It was voices—not words, not meaning, but the truth of voices, thousands layered: joy, grief, goodbye, hello.

A sailor stumbled to his knees and began to laugh through tears. Another clutched his amulet and held it against his mouth without quite knowing why. Falos flared his wings as if to leap, then stilled, head bowed—as if even air should kneel.

The Skythread lifted.

No hand touched the helm. The cloud-keel surged until the basin below lay out like a perfect, shifting chart—the drowned buttresses of the ancient forest drawn in silver, the rim a bright ring, the center a pale wound. The ship found the balance she needed and held it—a living thing poised upon the smallest bones of the wind.

Then came the column.

It erupted from the heart of the Sea, a spiral of radiance more felt than seen, and lanced the belly of the gyre above. Water rose in silken curtains around it, sheets of vapor catching the light and breaking it into a thousand living ribbons that ran over the ship's hull like the hands of saints.

"Brace!" Marissa cried. The word went out and was eaten by the roar. It didn't matter. The crew had braced already—feet wide, knees soft, hands where they needed to be.

The wave of light struck them.

It wasn't heat. It wasn't force. It was memory, layered and layered again until even the air sagged under it. It moved through them without asking permission. It showed them themselves.

Talon saw Isa's scales—a dark mirror in firelight; Garick, standing in the door of a green place that no longer existed, a hand lifted in a goodbye that had been a beginning; Genni's laugh, a thrown coin that had bought someone's life when none of them knew that was the price.

Bella tasted the first spell she had ever spoken that had not belonged to anyone else.

Marissa heard a bell toll in a fog-hung harbor in another country and realized, with a quiet, wrenching certainty, that it had been the moment she chose the sea and everything after.

Oscar felt a small hand clutch his—his own, years younger—felt the hungry wind of Archeron, the warmth of a tavern that no longer stood, and the bow in his hands become not wood but promise.

Then it passed.

The roar fell away all at once, as if a great lung had emptied. The sky's gyre turned three more slow degrees— then came apart into nothing at all. The light collected itself.

***

From the unstitched sky rose a shape.

Not yet flesh. Not yet bound to any law but its own. Light gathered itself into wings—vast, deliberate—whose edges darkened the horizon as a mountain would. The neck followed, long and clean as a river. Atop it, a brow and a crown formed where gold and silver met in a flame that consumed no fuel.

A dragon. But not of this world.

"The Celestial," Bella said. Tears ran clean tracks through the dust on her face, and she did nothing to stop them.

The being's gaze lifted. The ship stilled. Every knot, every nail, every feather and strand of hair felt the moment stop—as if a hand had pressed gently on the world and said *rest*.

Its eyes opened.

Twin orbs—not color, not shape, but knowing—turned upon the Skythread. Each soul aboard felt itself picked up and weighed in a palm that neither condemned nor excused. Kindnesses they had not named for fear of pride stood beside cruelties they had not admitted for fear of truth. None were thrown away. None were kept as weapons. All were seen.

When the dragon exhaled, the world remembered how to move.

Clouds burned without flame and were gone. Sound returned—not the roar, but the creak of rope, the faint slap of a loose line, a cough, a prayer whispered into a sleeve. The dragon's outline grew less fixed, then less, then became a field of stars rising in slow arc until the firmament took it back and made it pattern and story.

The Sea of Roots stilled. Its light quieted to a sheen that was not daylight and not dream.

No one spoke. Not for a long time.

***

The afterglow came on soft feet.

Heat lived in the planks in the way boards hold winter long after the fire in the grate has gone out. The sails kept a faint luster as if someone had rubbed them with the milk of moons. Men and women whose hands had bled for less

255

worthy moments found those same hands steadying strangers without being asked. Even the gull, forgotten and forgetting nothing, rode the ship's slipstream with the gravity of a priest at festival.

Talon stood at the sterncastle rail and looked not at anything in particular but at everything—as if it might become particular if he stared long enough. "Every world is born twice," he said softly, like a man waking into the sentence he had dreamed. "Once in darkness, once in memory."

Bella rested her fingers against his shoulder. "And both," she said, "are light."

Falos' head came up, feathers walking a ripple outward. "The sky no longer trembles," he said, satisfied—almost playful for the first time in days. "It sings."

From the helm came Marissa's voice, steady, reverent, practical. "Then we'll follow that song. West, until the stars tell us to stop." Her hands moved—tiny corrections, a lover's touch on an instrument she knew by breath alone. The Skythread turned toward a horizon that looked newly washed. Her cloud-keel left soft silver wakes in the morning air.

Behind them, the newborn constellations burned as if they had always been there and the crew had simply forgotten how to see.

***

They tried to rouse him at first bell.

Oscar carried the mug because Miles of Bywater liked his tea the way he liked his decks—unadorned, hot, and honest. He nudged the old salt's boot with the toe of his own and grinned in anticipation of the ritual grumble. "Up you get,

256

Miles. You can yell at the new hands for calling the Skythread a 'she' instead of 'the lady.' "

No grumble came.

Miles lay with one arm resting across his blanket, his other hand loose near his knife as it always had been—even asleep, even old. His eyes were open, not staring, but fixed on the seam of light that lay along the planks above. His face wore the expression of a man listening for a bell far away, one he knew would sound when it was ready and not before.

Oscar set the mug down carefully on the little shelf above Miles hammock and reached to feel for breath. None came. There was no struggle in the body. No plea. Only the kind of quiet that comes when a wave finds its own shore.

"Miles?" he said, though the ship had already answered with a single low creak that carried through the beams like a mother's hum.

Then the air changed.

It thickened—not to weight, but to meaning. The bunkroom's timbers softened to shadow. Light pooled where shadow had been. Oscar blinked, and the angle of the world lifted as if a door had opened in a wall no one had noticed before.

Miles stood on a shore. The old coat—patched, salt-stiff, beloved—hung new upon his shoulders. The lines the sea had carved into his face remained, made beautiful by time instead of tired by it. Before him arched a bridge of light, its far end swallowed in radiance too generous for eyes to hoard.

Two figures waited upon the bridge.

Dug, broad as an oath kept, eyes warm with the patience of mountains. Falos, wings half-furled, golden feathers catching wind that Oscar could not feel and still recognized. They bowed to the sailor without theater. Miles smiled the small, lopsided smile that had ended a hundred deckside stories and wiped more tears than he'd ever admitted to. He offered no words. Dug rumbled a greeting that meant *you did well.* Falos lowered his head, and the three of them turned and began to walk.

They crossed into the light and were gone.

The bunkroom returned: wood, nail, lantern, the faint clink of the forgotten mug settling on its shelf. Oscar breathed in and out. A tear—just one—escaped and cut a clean path along his cheek. He wiped it away with the back of his wrist because it felt right to keep the moment small.

"Safe voyage, old friend," he whispered.

When they bore Miles topside, the dawn had found its courage and bled gold through the rigging. It fell across the old sailor's face and made it fire and peace at once, as if he were still watching the sky and would correct anyone who claimed otherwise. No speeches were made. Someone straightened the blanket. Someone else set the knife upon it in a way that made it clear the blade would never be needed again and would always be ready.

They did not carve his name that morning. Names are for lists and the keeping of records. Legends need only breath to live.

From that day forward the crew—quietly, in the way men who have known both hunger and holiness are quiet—said that Miles of Bywater saw the Celestial Dragon rise and went home in her light, escorted by bear and griffon both.

And if, on certain mornings, when the sails caught the first clean light of the new sky, a soft humming seemed to walk the rigging like a man on his rounds—well, the crew knew better than to put that in a log. Some songs belong to the ship alone.

Chapter Six

The Bridge Between

"The veil remembers every footstep that crosses it;
the world remembers who returned."

— *Saying among the Oathbearers*

***

The light of the newborn constellations still lingered when the Skythread steadied her course. Her sails glowed faintly, imbued with the breath of what had been born from the Sea of Roots. The world beneath them shimmered like a painting redrawn in living light—mountains reflecting the glow, the new inner sea gleaming like a mirror for heaven.

No one spoke much that evening. Even laughter—when it came—was hushed, reverent, like song in a temple.

Marissa kept the helm steady, her hands light on the wheel. "She knows her way," she said softly, and no one argued. The Skythread's cloud-keel hummed in low, soothing tones, as though the ship herself dreamed.

Bella and Greenbough had withdrawn to the forecastle, tending to readings and sketches, measuring how far the sea had stretched since dawn. Falos rested near the bow, half-sleeping, half-watching the constellations above. His feathers shimmered faintly with lingering starlight.

And below, in the quiet of the middeck, Oscar wrote.

He tried to capture it—the birth, the silence, the feeling that for a moment all creation had looked back at them and chosen to remember their names. But every word felt smaller than what his heart held. His journal stayed open, ink still wet, when his eyelids finally gave up their vigil.

***

Talon dreamed of light and sound and silence.

The Veil was open before him—no longer a wound, but a window to something endless. He stood at the bridge of worlds, where once he had fallen and been returned. Now it was whole again, gleaming with threads of silver that stretched beyond sight.

He could see the shimmer of souls crossing: the lost, the old, and the remembered. Dug's deep presence rumbled somewhere beyond the horizon of light. Isa's song echoed faintly in the distance, folded into Eternity's hum.

This time, Talon did not fall. He simply *was*.

And in that stillness, he remembered everything that mattered—not knowledge, but truth. That light was meant to be shared, not owned. That those who guard the world do so not as masters, but as keepers of its fragile fire.

A soft voice touched the edge of the dream, familiar as home.

"Wake, Oathbearer."

***

The Mending of the Veil

Talon's eyes opened to dawn. He was back at the sterncastle rail. Falos had not moved, though his head was turned slightly, one golden eye fixed on him.

"You walked the Bridge again," the griffon said, voice low and knowing. "Did you find it quieter this time?"

Talon drew a slow breath, the air still shimmering faintly with the Celestial's afterlight.

"Not quieter," he said. "Just... healed."

Falos tilted his head, beak clicking softly. "Healed things hum different. The broken ones scream. This morning I hear humming."

Talon's mouth curved faintly. "Then the world's learning to sing again."

A deep sound rolled in Falos's chest, half purr, half thunder. "A good sound for dawn."

He spread his wings, feathers gilded by the newborn light. The air bent around him—soft, shimmering, alive. Threads of gold drifted through the brightened sky, answering his breath like reeds to wind. The shimmer traced the heavens where the Celestial Dragon's light had passed, still mending what time had frayed. Falos watched it in silence, eyes reflecting dawn.

"The work's hers," he murmured at last. "I only feel the echo."

Talon nodded. "And even an echo can remind the world it's whole."

Falos gave a low trill—the sound of contentment, of faith rewarded. "Then let it breathe easy again," he said. "The song's found its rhythm."

"You always know when to trust the wind," Talon said.

"Instinct," Falos replied, folding his wings. "Or maybe the wind trusts me. Hard to say anymore."

Talon smiled. "Either way, I'm grateful."

The griffon snorted softly. "Then don't ruin it with speeches." He flicked his feathers once—half amusement, half dignity—and returned to his perch at the bow.

***

As dawn arrived over the Sea of Roots, the Skythread drifted onward, her sails bright with morning. Below, the water glimmered with quiet luminescence, mist rising in slender columns that caught the newborn light like incense.

Bella emerged from belowdecks, hair unbound, eyes bright with sleepless wonder. She carried her crystal loops and a sheet of readings pressed to her chest, the paper still warm. "She's done it," she whispered. "The ley-lines have aligned again—no fracture echoes, no distortion. The resonance has gone still."

She looked to Talon, her expression full of awe. "The Veil's steady. It's whole."

Talon nodded. "We didn't mend it," he said softly. "We just listened, and the world remembered the rest."

Oscar climbed up from the ladderwell, still clutching his journal. "Then the world's quiet again?"

Falos turned his head, one golden eye catching the sun. "For now," he said, his tone dry, feather-tips twitching. "Don't get used to it. The Veil likes to breathe—it'll stir when it's ready."

Oscar smiled faintly. "I'll write that down."

"You'd better," Falos said. "Someone has to remind the future we did more than just float."

Falos clicked his beak—openly amused and not dignified in the least for an Oathbound griffon—and returned to his musings as though nothing at all had changed.

Oscar blinked, lowering his journal. "Wait," he said slowly. "You're not in my head this time. I can actually *hear* you."

Falos turned that golden eye toward him, something between mischief and wisdom in the gleam. "Maybe the world wanted you to listen," he rumbled.

Talon's smile deepened. "Then the song's louder than we thought."

And as the Skythread rose above the shining mist, her hull glowing faintly from within, the crew looked to the horizon. The world no longer trembled. It breathed—whole, luminous, alive.

Above them, the newly formed constellations shimmered in slow rhythm, as if the heavens themselves were exhaling. The Sea of Roots reflected every light, every memory.

Between them sailed the Skythread—child of wind and cloud, keeper of what the world forgets.

***

The Skythread drifted steady above the Sea of Roots, her lanterns dimmed to a soft, living glow. Mist curled off her rails in thin ribbons that caught the starlight and vanished. The air was calm—*earned* calm—the kind that comes only after too many nights of storm.

Oscar and Elenn stood near the bow, shoulders almost touching, the world stretched open before them. The stars above were different now—new constellations written by the Ascension's light. They shimmered slow and uncertain, like names still learning how to be spoken.

Neither of them spoke for a while. The wind, the hum of the ship, the faint whisper of waves far below—those were enough.

Oscar finally broke the quiet. "He said the world doesn't waste its miracles," he murmured. "Maybe this is one of them."

Elenn smiled, not looking away from the horizon. "Then we'd better make it count."

He nodded. "We will."

Behind them, unseen, Talon leaned against the rigging on the upper deck. Arrabella stood beside him, her cloak drawn close against the high air. They watched the two figures by the rail without speaking.

"Reminds me of another pair who couldn't stop talking under strange stars," Talon said softly.

Bella smiled, a glint of warmth in her eyes. "History has a way of rhyming."

Talon smirked. "You think it'll last?"

Arrabella tilted her head, watching the two at the bow. "If he's smart enough not to overthink it."
She stepped away from the rail, cloak catching the wind. "And if he isn't…"

Talon arched an eyebrow. "You'll have words?"

Bella smiled sweetly, the kind of smile that once made ogres rethink their life choices. She lifted one gloved finger and pointed toward the distant deck where **Oscar** stood.

"Not *words*," she said, tapping the air as if aiming for his nose. "A reminder. A very clear one. Because if he hurts her—*emotionally, spiritually, dimensionally*—I will invent a new school of magic just to make him regret it."

Talon laughed under his breath. "Remind me never to get on your bad side."

"You already did," she said. "And you're still here. So maybe there's hope for him, too."

Below, Oscar glanced toward Elenn, and for a fleeting moment she looked back. Neither smiled this time—but the understanding there was more than enough.

Above them, Faloswansei circled once, feathers catching the moonlight, a silent guardian tracing the edges of the new heavens. The world breathed with him—slow, contented, alive.

And on the wind, faint but certain, the Skythread's song carried forward—not mourning, not triumph, but the sound of beginnings.

Chapter Seven

Portals and Portents

"Ships remember the seas they have not yet sailed."

— *Inscription carved into the Skythread's keel*

"When a vessel remembers her name, the world should listen."

— *Fragment from Songs of the Cloudwrights*

***

The ship drifted through a pale, sleepless dawn.

No one had truly rested since the ascension. The world felt thinner now—quiet in a way that was not silence, but aftermath. Each breath carried weight. Each footstep echoed too long. Even the air seemed gentler, as though afraid to disturb the stillness left by the Celestial Dragon's birth.

Marissa walked the upper deck alone, boots hollow on the boards. Sails hung slack and shimmering, still touched with the newborn constellations' glow. The sea below lay mirror-flat, white mist curling at its edges where the drowned forest whispered in its dreaming. Every rope and spar hummed faintly—the same low, continuous tone that had begun the moment the Dragon's light touched the world.

She turned toward the sterncastle, meaning only to check her charts, to feel the familiar solidity of duty beneath her hands.

But when she stepped inside the captain's quarters, the light was wrong.

Morning usually came through the stern windows in a thin gold bar. Now the light was silver—fluid, rippling, as though the sun shone through water rather than air.

Marissa blinked.

Turned.

And froze.

There, where solid oak wall had stood since the day the Skythread was christened, now stood a door.

Tall. Narrow. Framed in pale metal that pulsed as if it had veins beneath its skin. The surrounding wood bore no seams, no joints, no tool marks. It didn't look **installed**. It looked **grown**.

As if the ship had decided it needed one.

Marissa stepped closer, breath unsteady. Her fingers brushed the frame—

Warm. Not like wood warmed by sun. Warm like *breathing flesh*.

She jerked her hand back.

The door's faint center seam glowed, a soft, silver heartbeat pulsing once.

Marissa didn't waste time. She sent for Bella, Talon, Oscar, and Falos.

***

Bella arrived first, lantern-blue runes glimmering along her staff. She crouched before the door as a healer might examine a wound in the world.

268

"Not elven craft," she murmured. "But near to it. The light flows through natural channels—like tree-sap carrying memory. No spell. No artifice."

Talon knelt beside her, running his hand along the frame without touching the light itself. "If it wasn't made…"

"It woke," Bella finished.

A soft rustle answered her words.

Greenbough had come—soundless, as always—her hair trailing dew and the scent of earth after rain. She studied the door with an expression of reverence edged with unease.

"This wasn't shaped by hands," she whispered. "The ship remembered it. Like a seed remembering it can bloom."

Marissa exhaled sharply. "You're telling me the Skythread created… a door?"

Greenbough nodded. "Not created. Revealed."

Oscar crossed his arms, staring at the seamless glow. "Revealed to what? There shouldn't be anything behind that wall but sky and wake."

Falos stepped forward at last, slow and deliberate. The silver glow rippled across his feathers, scattering gold shadows along the bulkhead. He lowered his head, studying the pulsing seam.

When he spoke, his voice was a deep, certain chord.

"The Skythread remembers what the world forgot."

Talon frowned. "Explain."

Falos kept his gaze on the door. "She was built to listen. To learn. She's heard the Veil's song since the moment it tore… and again when it healed. The world is dreaming, and she dreams with it."

A beat.

"She's answering something. Or calling something back."

No one moved. The ship's hum deepened beneath their feet—steady, patient, alive. Then the door's glow flared—bright as a held breath.

A soft pulse.

A second.

A third.

Then the light softened, leaving only a silver outline.

Marissa drew in a slow breath and stepped forward. "Open it," she said quietly. "We need to see what we're dealing with."

Talon pushed the latch—though none of them remembered a latch being there—and the silver seam parted soundlessly.

The space beyond was small, no larger than a storage nook, but it felt impossibly *still*, as though the air were holding its own heartbeat. At its center hovered a pale orb, bright as mist caught in sunlight. Its pulse quickened as they entered.

Once...

Twice...

A third time, brighter.

Bella's voice was barely above a whisper. "It's responding to us."

Corwin leaned in, eyes reflecting the soft glow. "No... not just responding. *Recognizing.*"

A faint tremor passed through the deck, more felt than heard.

Falos ruffled his feathers, solemn and unsure. "The ship will tell us when she's ready."

They stood in silence, gathered around the little chamber the ship had grown without permission, without warning, without error.

Below deck, whispers spread that the Skythread had begun to dream.

Above, dawn broke—pink into white, white into gold.

And in the captain's cabin, the newborn heart of the Skythread pulsed once more—as if greeting its crew for the very first time.

Chapter Eight

The Living Map

"Every voyage is a question the ship asks the souls aboard her."

— *From The Codex of Wind and Stone, preserved in Nandanoléme*

***

Few aboard the Skythread truly rested, but when they dreamed, they dreamed the same dream. Each soul carried it in fragments—flashes of stars, a whisper through fog, the touch of an unseen tide beneath the planks. And when they woke, they found those fragments waiting for them: sketches in the margins of the logbooks they hadn't written, phrases scrawled across the deck in chalk that no one remembered placing.

By morning, the ship's hum had deepened again. The tone was no longer the tremor of the wounded world—it was steadier now, harmonic, the quiet breathing of something newly born. Some of the crew swore they could feel it under their ribs, as though the Skythread were trying to match her pulse to theirs.

***

Oscar was the first to notice the pattern.

He had taken to rising before dawn, sitting near the bow with his journal open across his knees. It had become a ritual—part discipline, part refuge. But the words he found there one morning weren't his own. Three distinct scripts— his, Greenbough's looping hand, and Marissa's sharp angles—each described the same thing: a sea made of light, and a map drawn on the underside of the sky.

He blinked, once, twice, and ran his thumb over the ink. "This isn't possible."

Greenbough's soft voice came from behind him. "It's happening to all of us." Her expression was unreadable, but her eyes shone with quiet wonder. "The ship is weaving our thoughts together—not to control, but to remember."

Oscar turned. "To remember what?"

"The first voyage," she said simply. "The one before ours."

Before he could ask more, Marissa approached with the same hollow-eyed expression most of the crew wore now. She set a handful of small glass compasses on the rail. Each needle spun slow and steady, in perfect unison—not pointing north, but toward the ship's center.

"She's calling us inward," Marissa murmured. "Every time we sleep, the Cloudheart opens a little wider. I can hear it sometimes—like voices under the keel."

Talon joined them soon after, the fatigue around his eyes deepened by too many reveries stitched from someone else's memories. "Not voices," he said. "Memories. Balok once told me a ship holds every step her crew takes aboard her. Maybe this one's just learned how to speak."

From the rigging above, Falos tilted his head, eyes bright in the half-light. "Ships are stubborn that way," he murmured. "Give them too many souls, and they start collecting pieces of us like feathers in the wind." His beak curved faintly—half amusement, half warning.

"Just remember, Oathbearers—what you give a ship, she never gives back unchanged."

Oscar swallowed. He wasn't sure whether the griffon meant that as comfort or caution.

***

That afternoon, they opened the captain's chart table and found something none had drawn.

Across the vellum maps of the western coast, faint silver lines had appeared—not ink, but luminous threadwork that shimmered like starlight. The new lines extended into blank spaces beyond their knowledge, curving in elegant, shifting patterns.

Marissa leaned close, awe softening her voice. "These aren't coastlines. They're… lives. Every path we've taken aboard her. Every person who's set foot on this deck."

Bella touched the page lightly. The glow pulsed once beneath her fingertips, matching the rhythm of the Cloudheart. "She's charting memory," she whispered. "Mapping the history of every soul she's carried."

Oscar stared at the glowing threads, pulse quickening. "That means she's aware of us—all of us."

"She's more than aware," Greenbough said. "She's listening."

Talon exhaled slowly. "Balok always said a good ship knows when you're lying to yourself." His mouth twitched faintly. "Guess we've built a very good one."

Falos gave a low hum of approval. "Good. A ship that listens won't be lost for long."

That night, Oscar couldn't bring himself to sleep.

He sat alone in the coil-room with his journal open, the quills trembling as the ship's hum grew louder. Around him, the lanternlight flickered—dimmed—and then steadied again in a pulse that matched his heartbeat.

He whispered into the quiet. "If you can hear me… what are you?"

The air stirred, and the ink on the page rippled like disturbed water. Slowly, words formed—delicate, hesitant, as though remembering how to be written:

I am what remains of every voyage.

Of every question asked beneath a sky that forgets.

You are my breath.

Oscar's throat tightened. "We built you."

No, came the reply.

You remembered me.

His breath caught. The quill stilled. He stared at the page until the words faded, leaving only the faint scent of salt and starlight behind. A weight settled over him—not fear, but the fragile awe of someone realizing they'd awakened a story older than themselves.

***

By midmorning, the crew gathered again in the main hall. No one spoke at first; they didn't need to. The same realization hung in every mind like a low chord waiting to resolve.

Bella broke the silence, her voice quiet but steady. "The Skythread is not a vessel. She's a bridge—between memory and the world that keeps forgetting."

Talon nodded once. "And now she remembers us."

For a moment, no one breathed.

Falos shifted his wings where he perched above the helm, feathers catching the light like shaken gold. His gaze moved from one to the next—sharp, knowing, but not unkind. "Then hold your memories well," he said, "because from this moment, they are part of her forever."

A hush followed. Not fear—reverence, layered with a fragile kind of pride.

The kind that comes from realizing you are being written into something larger than yourself.

Marissa rested a hand on the wheel, and for the first time, it seemed to breathe beneath her touch. She closed her eyes briefly, as if listening to a voice only she could hear.

Greenbough whispered, "She's becoming whole."

Oscar whispered back, "So are we."

***

Outside, the sky was bright and newly blue. The sails shimmered with starlight even in daylight. And the Skythread—the ship that remembered—turned west again, following a song only she could hear, and carrying the souls who had finally learned that she was listening.

Chapter Nine

Where Roots Remember

"Some journeys end not in distance, but in depth."

—*Saying of the Dirgewood Waykeepers*

***

The morning after the last survey run, the Dirgewood breathed like a creature finally free of fever. Mist lifted in ribbons from the water-veined groves; each leaf wore a bead of light. The Skythread hung at idle above a clearing where the trees parted of their own accord, a hush expanding outward as if the forest had chosen to give the ship room for its goodbye. Even Falos moved quietly that morning, as if the air asked for gentleness.

They had mapped what they could: channels braided like veins, hill-islands crowned with root and moss, drowned stones where old roads vanished into green. Bella had spent half the night with charcoal smudged along her fingers, connecting lines no one had walked in a century. She kept pausing, fingers hovering above the parchment, as if listening for echoes only she could hear. Talon checked their bearings with a hunter's patience, small notches on the rail marking where the sun bled through fog at noon. Marissa paced the quarterdeck with a ledger tucked against her ribs, every new nickname for wind and current pressed into the margins.

Oscar knelt near the starboard shrouds, sketchbook open, tongue caught between his teeth in concentration. He drew a seed-pod the size of his palm, translucent as a lantern, tiny filaments inside trembling when he breathed on them. Elenn stood above him, steadying the page with a fingertip whenever the ship rocked.

"Hold," she murmured.

He smiled without looking up. "You say that like the wind listens to you."

"It does," she said, not quite teasing.

Oscar tried to decide whether she meant it—but with Elenn, the world seemed willing to listen to her in ways it denied others.

He glanced up and found her watching the forest instead of him, eyes soft as if seeing something he could not.

A bell tapped once—no alarm, just time reminding them it still moved. Below them, a ripple traveled across the clearing. Leaves turned their narrow faces as though following a thought.

Greenbough stood at the rail opposite Oscar, motionless enough to be mistaken for part of the ship. Dew had taken up residence in her braid like pearls from an old tale. Her palm lay flat on the timber; the knuckles darkened, lightened, darkened as if she were feeling for a pulse.

Bella crossed to her. "Well?"

Greenbough's mouth curved—more weather than smile. "They're awake."

"The roots?" Oscar asked before he could stop himself.

"The memory," she said.

They waited for more. Greenbough did not hurry words; she let them rise the way a spring rises from stone—first the damp, then the taste, then the water.

"Once," she went on, "these trees kept a ledger no one could read. Tonight the ink returned." She touched the rail again, fingertips lingering as if listening through bone. "They know the names of the rains again. They remember how to bend without breaking."

Bella's breath caught. Some part of her—some quiet, private place—had feared this forest might remain wounded forever.

Marissa made a mark in her ledger almost absently and closed it. "Then we've done what we came for."

Greenbough's gaze moved from the forest to the faces gathered beside her—Bella, Marissa, Talon, Elenn, Oscar. "You have," she said. "I have something else to do."

She said it gently, and the words landed gently. Even so, something in Oscar went tight at the hinge.

"Something else?" he asked. "On board, you mean? We'll need you when we turn west."

Greenbough smiled with actual warmth now. "You'll need me," she agreed, "in the way a seed needs a shadow."

Talon's brow lowered a fraction. Bella, who understood plain speech from a lifetime of ornate lies, heard what was inside the words first. "You're staying."

Greenbough looked past them toward the place where the clearing met a stand of elder-barked trees. They leaned into one another like old conspirators. "The Dirgewood is not a patient student," she said. "It will take the lesson and remake it in its own tongue. But for a while—while the new sea decides how to breathe—I am of more use with my feet in the loam than above it."

281

Talon exhaled slowly. Greenbough was the closest thing the Skythread had to a conscience; losing her felt like removing a keel and hoping the ship remembered its balance.

Marissa's grip on the ledger loosened. "This is your permission," she said softly. "Not your request."

Greenbough tipped her head in acknowledgment.

No one spoke, and for a long heartbeat the only sound was the slow chime of water as it fell from high leaves into hidden bowls.

Oscar shut his sketchbook too sharply; the seed-pod drawing blurred under his thumb. "We still don't know what waits along the Sea of Stars," he said. "We're short two hands already. We're—" Not ready, he almost said, and then swallowed it, embarrassed by how young it sounded.

Greenbough crossed to him in three unhurried steps and put a hand against his shoulder. Her palm was warm; the warmth traveled farther than it should have. "Readiness isn't the absence of fear," she said. "It's the habit of going on."

"I know," he muttered, though he did not, not entirely.

She glanced at Elenn, whose hand was still on the corner of Oscar's page. "Keep him from falling off the sky," she told her.

Elenn's mouth twitched. "I'll tie him on with something stronger than rope."

"That would be kindness," Greenbough said.

Talon came forward then, his boots silent on wet boards. He drew two fingers to his brow and then to his heart in the Vale's old farewell. "You'll have watchmen as long as I breathe," he said. "We'll make this forest part of the map again, not a scar people skirt."

"It already was never only a scar," Greenbough said. "But maps teach how to look."

"Will you be safe?" Bella asked, practical to the last.

Greenbough bared her teeth in something like a grin. "Bella. I am older than most storms."

"Storms change," Bella returned.

"So do I."

Somewhere in Bella's chest, something old and cautious whispered: storms return too. She did not say it aloud.

They made ready as if for any short landing. A ladder lowered. A sling of canvas lifted bundles lashed tight with hemp. Greenbough chose almost nothing: a satchel, the small copper knife she used to clean sap from edges, a length of cord knotted with beads like captured dawn. She left her bunk untouched—blanket folded, pillow smooth—as though the shape of her could linger there and talk to whoever needed listening.

When the sling swung out over the clearing, she did not take it. She set her hand instead to the ladder and went down into mist step by careful step, as if descending into a story.

At the bottom, she did not look back. She walked into the fold of elder-barked trunks, and the forest took her without pause, the forest accepting her the way water accepts a stone: without argument, with the understanding that both will be changed by it in time.

No one said anything for a while. The air above the clearing developed a brightness not of the sun, as if light had grown curious. A cluster of blue-winged insects stitched a wandering seam through it and vanished laughing into leaves.

Marissa cleared her throat gently. "We'll hold at height until third bell," she said. "Then we take our westing."

"Aye," Talon murmured. He took the watch half a step forward on the bow and did not bother to explain that he was looking for a sign that would not come. In another season, another life, Greenbough would have teased him for it.

Oscar remained where he was. The leaves below had begun moving in slow currents, a tide with no ocean. He tried to draw it and succeeded only in drawing the steadiness of Greenbough's hand.

Elenn touched his elbow. "Walk?"

He nodded, grateful for the excuse to move, and fell in beside her along the outer rail. The ship creaked contentment around them—the small noises of a hull cooling after work. Far off, a heron stepped from shadow into water and became part of both for a breath.

"She chose this," Elenn said.

"I know."

"Do you?"

Oscar's mouth tilted. "No."

They paused by the after winch. Someone had tucked a sprig of new-grown fern into a crack between boards— Greenbough's, no doubt, or one of her small pranks of blessing. He touched it and found moisture there, not dew— the plant's own drink handed back to his fingertip.

"I keep thinking of all the times she told me to 'let the world happen,'" he said. "As if that were easy."

"It is not," Elenn said. "That is why it is worth learning."

He stared at the clearing until the green blurred. "Bella will miss her weight on the decisions," he said. "Marissa will miss that extra steadiness when the wind says two things at once. Talon will miss someone to argue with when he's certain. And I—" He stopped before he confessed too much.

Elenn spared him the confession. "You will miss having someone who sees the shape of your thought before you draw it."

He huffed a laugh that tasted wet. "Yes."

"Then," she said, calm as the inner cabin bell, "become the person who can do that for yourself. And when you cannot, ask."

He looked sideways at her. "Ask whom?"

She raised one shoulder. "Whomever is near. Most of us want to be useful."

"Even you?"

"Especially me."

Oscar wanted to say something brave. Instead, he nodded—because courage sometimes looks like the smaller gesture.

The third bell sounded—one tone, lingering, the sound rounding the edges of the world. Across the deck, sailors knotted lines and checked buckles. Someone, unashamed, wiped both eyes on a sleeve and smiled like a person relieved their heart still worked.

Bella came to the quarterdeck rail and took a long breath through her nose. She did not cry. She had learned long ago to cry when it would change the outcome. This would not. Instead she opened the little tin she kept for charcoal and used her thumb to smear a shadow where the clearing met the river.

"There," she said. "If anyone asks where memory lives, we can point to it."

Talon murmured something in the Vale's tongue then— a traveler's benediction, too soft for anyone to catch fully.

Marissa set her hands to the wheel and coaxed the vessel a fraction higher; the ground fell away until the clearing turned to a coin balanced on velvet.

"Course?" Talon asked.

"North-by-east until the river shows its shoulder," Marissa said. "Then west for the long look." She glanced at Bella. "You'll have the signal ready?"

Bella tapped the tin. "Already imagined."

Oscar leaned on the rail and tried to match his breath to the slow swing of the hull. He thought of Greenbough's palm against his shoulder, of warmth moving farther than it should. He thought of seeds choosing dark to become more than they were.

Elenn's hand found his, unremarked, fingers lacing with a precision that felt older than practice. He did not startle; he had been expecting the world to take something. He had not been ready for it to give.

Below, a draft moved through the canopy, starting somewhere he could not see and traveling outward in a widening ring. Leaves flashed their pale undersides all at once like the turning of a thousand small coins. The ring expanded until it touched the edge of the clearing, then the forest released it like a held breath.

"Signal received," Talon said softly.

"From whom?" someone asked.

"From the one who just went to ground."

Oscar swallowed hard. He wondered if Greenbough felt the ship's answer in her bones the way they felt hers.

They put the Dirgewood behind them by inches, not leaps. No one was eager to invent distance faster than the heart could travel it. Elenn's hand remained in Oscar's until the first of the river's silver bends lifted from the trees, until the air took on the clean smell of stone rather than leaf. When she let go, his palm remembered.

By the time the sun tipped over the high branches, the forest's voice had softened into ordinary birds and the plop of hidden fish. The Skythread rose to cruise height, sails bellied by a wind that had been there all morning and had politely waited for them to notice.

"Mark the farewell," Marissa said.

Bella nodded. On the log she wrote a single line: Greenbough of the Dirgewood took root this day. She did not add a flourish. She did not need to. The hand that had not shaken at kings trembled once, almost invisibly, and then was still.

Oscar added a sketch below the line—a leaf seen from beneath, veins arrowing toward an unseen stem. He left it unfinished on purpose. Some shapes are truer when they are not closed.

Marissa set the heading and squared her shoulders in a way that had nothing to do with wind. Talon rolled his neck and smiled without showing teeth. On the lower deck, someone began a work song under their breath, a tune with too few notes and all of them right.

The ship eased forward into a sky that had waited for her, and the Dirgewood fell away, not as a place forgotten, but as a part of them like breath. When they thought of it in winters to come, they would remember that ring of turning leaves and know that for once, a goodbye had been answered.

From the stern, Oscar looked back until the green became distance, then story, then something he would someday read to a child without quite managing to hide his voice at the last line. Elenn stood with him and did not ask him to stop looking; when he was ready, he turned.

"Map?" she said.

"Map," he agreed.

They went forward where Marissa waited at the helm and Bella had cleared a space on the chart table. Talon set a finger down where the river lay like a blade and traced the line of their path. The ship's cat rose, stretched, turned a tight circle on the nearest coil of line, and slept exactly as if nothing in the world had altered.

"West," Marissa said, the word neither heavy nor light. "We'll write the edge of the continent with our wake."

The Skythread answered by doing what it was built to do—move. The crew found their stations. The clearing become a memory, then a promise, then simply part of the world again, which is the highest honor a place can earn.

Sometime before noon the wind carried a smell of the far sea—salt without shore. Oscar breathed it and thought, the way he always did when something ended cleanly, of how Greenbough had once defined hope: not a light at a tunnel's end, but the stubbornness to keep lighting matches.

He opened his sketchbook to a blank page and let his hand walk there without forcing it. Lines found one another until they were something like a ladder against something like a tree. He smiled at the almost of it and wrote in the margin, She stayed. We go.

He set his pencil down and looked up. Elenn caught his eye. For a heartbeat—no more—their expressions mirrored one another: gratitude shaped like ache, ache shaped like a beginning. Neither of them said it, because saying it would make it smaller. The wind said enough for them both.

They left the Dirgewood the way a boat leaves a harbor at dawn: without spectacle, with reverence, with the tide. And if the trees took note of a ship lifting away, if roots lifted rumors of sails through soil, nothing in the written world could prove it. Some ledgers are kept elsewhere.

By evening, the forest was a dark ribbon on the eastern horizon and the world ahead widened, unspooling into the

Sea of Stars like a thought the sky had been saving. Marissa held her heading; Bella drew the new line; Talon watched the weather without blinking; Elenn stood a shoulder's width from Oscar and did not measure it.

Oscar spoke first—not loudly, but in the way someone does when a thought has been circling too long.
"Do you ever feel like we're supposed to understand something," he said, "but the world only lets us see the edges?"

Elenn glanced at him, then back toward the dark line of forest fading behind them.

"That's the problem with edges," she said. "They're honest. They tell you where things end. They don't tell you why they began."

Oscar nodded, chewing on that for a moment.

"I thought the ascension would feel… louder," he admitted. "History changing, power shifting, the world moving under our feet. I thought it would explain something."

"Did it?" Elenn asked.

Oscar considered the question longer than she expected.

"No," he said at last. "But it made everything else matter more. The small stuff. Who we stand next to. Who we keep safe. What we choose when no one's watching."

He shrugged. "Maybe that's enough. Maybe that's the meaning."

Elenn looked at him fully then, her expression softening in a way she didn't yet have a name for.

"My mother used to say life isn't a test," she murmured. "It's a response. To what we're given. To what we lose. To what we choose to carry."

A faint smile tugged at her mouth. "I think you gave the better answer, though."

Oscar's ears flushed pink, though he pretended the wind deserved the blame.

"I'm just trying to keep up," he said.

"You are," Elenn replied. "More than you know."

They fell into a comfortable silence—not avoidance, not hesitation.

Just two people standing at the bow of a ship headed toward a widening world, each feeling a little less alone in it.

***

In the log that night, under Bella's line about roots, someone—no one ever admitted who—added a second sentence so small it could have been a smudge.

Where she stays, we grow.

Chapter Ten

Arrival in Arden

"Every paradise hums with the echo of its own undoing."

— Saying attributed to the Wanderer of Soahc

The days after the Celestial Dragon's ascent felt weightless.

No one aboard had slept easily, yet all spoke softly, as if the world itself might still be listening. The Skythread sailed west across calm skies, her sails faintly translucent, tracing the heavens with starlight that seemed her own. By night, the crew dreamt vivid, half-shared visions—fragments of oceans yet unseen, of forests singing in languages long forgotten.

Bella noted them all. "The Cloudheart remembers," she said quietly. "It's mapping through us."

The air itself carried a low resonance, the subtle harmony Falos had described when the Veil healed—a pulse threading sky, water, and soul back together again.

Talon said nothing. His eyes lingered on the horizon where the new sea gave way to open sky, and beyond that— smoke.

Oscar drifted to the rail near Elenn, notebook in hand. "Does the world always feel like this after something grand?" he murmured.

291

Elenn rested her hands beside his. "No. Sometimes it feels worse," she said. "But this… feels like we're holding our breath with the sky."

Oscar swallowed. "Then let's hope it exhales gently."

Her glance at him was small, warm. "Hope is quieter than fear. But stronger, if you let it be."

***

They found the coast at dusk, a thin silver line pulsing beneath a lid of cloud.

"City light on the horizon," Marissa called from the helm, though the word carried no cheer.

The Skythread descended on a breath of wind, her cloud-keel thrumming like a low bell. Ahead, a crescent bay opened in the dark—cliffs veined with light, water bright from within, as if the sea itself had learned to glow.

Oscar leaned over the rail, eyes wide. "It's… alive."

"Residual radiance," Bella murmured, knuckles whitening on her staff. "What the Celestial left behind when it rose. The world's marrow, still singing."

Falos shifted on the mainmast, feathers crackling faintly. "The Veil thins here," he said. "Something is taking more than it gives, Oathbearer."

Talon's jaw set. "Then we'll find who's doing the taking."

They eased into the bay, sails gliding like starlit cloth. The air tasted of iron and rain; every breath rasped as if they were standing near a storm that wouldn't break.

As the mists parted, a city stepped out of the glow.

Towers of white glass rose in courses like bone, their seams filigreed in bronze. Lattices of runes crawled along the spires in a slow, living script. At the harbor's heart, a single needle of stone stood hollow as a flute, its crown open to the sky; from it poured a steady column of blue-white fire.

Streets braided beneath in precise arcs, canals ran clear as crystal, and bridges shone like wet shell. Everywhere, light moved—not reflected, not lamp-lit—moving like the breath of some captured star.

"Arden," Marissa whispered.

"The last time this bright a city burned," Bella said quietly, "we called it noon."

Falos ruffled his wings once and muttered, "Let's hope this one remembers dusk."

Oscar felt Elenn shift beside him—minutely, but enough to feel her unease. "It's beautiful," he whispered.

"It is," she said. "But beauty with a cost always hides the bill."

***

The harbor—if it could be called that—was an immense platform of smooth white stone extending over the cliffs. No chains, no cranes, no docks. Only a ring of pylons that hummed with low, musical tones.

When the Skythread drew near, the tones changed pitch, harmonizing with her Cloudheart. A beam of pale light stretched outward like a bridge, solid enough for landing.

"They recognize the signature," Bella said softly. "They know what she is."

Talon nodded to Marissa. "Take her in easy. Let them see we mean peace."

As the Skythread settled toward the beam, her hum shifted—warmer, but wary. The Cloudheart pulsed twice in quick succession, as if bracing. Lines of soft radiance crept along her rails and vanished where the pylon-light touched them.

Marissa's fingers tightened on the wheel. "She doesn't like being anchored to something she didn't choose."

"Not anchored," Bella murmured. "Tuned. They're trying to bring her into the same chord."

Falos' feathers lifted along his neck. "A ship that stops singing her own song becomes someone else's instrument," he muttered. "Remember that."

They descended upon the beam. The Skythread touched down without a sound, but the tremor that passed through her planks felt, to those who knew her well, very close to a shiver.

Waiting for them were a hundred figures in silver-blue armor and flowing robes, their faces calm, their posture unbowed.

At their head stood a tall man with hair like spun metal and eyes the color of dawn over ice. Power radiated from him—not brutal, but absolute, like gravity.

"Welcome, travelers of the Cloud-Born," he said, voice a perfect blend of warmth and command. "You stand in Arden, the city of the everlasting light."

Oscar leaned slightly toward Elenn. "Everlasting light sounds… final."

She whispered back, "Or inescapable."

The man's gaze flicked toward them for the briefest moment—as if he had heard and chosen, politely, to pretend he had not.

***

The streets were wide, immaculate, and unnervingly quiet. Fountains shaped from living quartz spilled water that glowed faintly. Trees grew in ordered rows, each leaf identical to its neighbor. Every surface—walls, walkways, even the air itself—carried a hum, as though energy bled constantly from unseen veins.

The people of Arden walked gracefully, their garments pale and their faces luminous with health. Yet something in their eyes was off—not malice, not emptiness, but a serenity too practiced to be human. They smiled often, but rarely first.

Children were rare; Oscar counted only three among the crowds.

"They look immortal," he whispered.

Bella glanced sideways. "They may be. But that doesn't mean alive."

A woman at the market offered them fruit that shimmered faintly with captured light. When Bella touched it, she felt a faint pulse—the same resonance as the Dragon's breath, the same chord that had healed the Veil.

"It sustains them," she murmured. "They've woven the Celestial's gift into every meal, every breath. They thrive on borrowed dawn."

Talon's expression hardened. "Then let's find who taught them to do that."

Oscar turned the fruit over in his palm, frowning. "It's perfect," he murmured.

Elenn took it gently from him. "Perfection rarely tells the truth."

It should have been a harmless line.
Instead, something in Oscar shivered—an instinct he wouldn't understand until the Stone Giants confronted them and Elenn's words returned sharper than prophecy.

***

Their guides moved with effortless politeness and absolute certainty.

Whenever the crew tried to pause too long—to sketch a corner, ask a question of someone in the crowd, follow a side street—another robed functionary would appear with a smile already in place and a new path already chosen.

"This way, honored guests. The High Magistrate wishes you to see the upper gardens."

"Of course you may speak with our artisans—after you have been received in the Hall of Accord."

"I assure you, there will be time for maps. Arden has nothing to hide."

The phrase repeated often enough that it became its own warning.

Oscar fell into step beside Talon as they climbed a broad, gleaming stair. "Do you notice," he said quietly, "how every route brings us closer to the spire? No matter where we think we're going?"

Talon's mouth barely moved. "I notice. And I notice we haven't seen a single alley that isn't clean enough to eat off."

"Is that bad?" Oscar whispered.

"Any city that never looks tired," Talon said, "is lying about something."

Above them, Falos circled once and did not land—an unspoken refusal to be herded.

**

They were led through ascending terraces to the central spire—a hall of mirrors and cascading light where the ruler of Arden awaited.

He was both warrior and mage, his presence impossible to divide between the two. His cloak shimmered like forged starlight; a sword of pure flame hung at his hip, unburning. Runes moved slowly across its blade like thoughts in no hurry.

"I am Aurelian," he said. "High Magistrate of Arden, bearer of the Accord Flame. The dragon's breath touched our sea a millennium ago, and from it, we learned to perfect the balance between body and mind. You come from afar—yet your ship hums with that same harmony."

Bella stiffened almost imperceptibly. "You can hear her hum?"

Aurelian's smile deepened. "We hear all harmonies that touch our light. Your vessel is… unusual. Old song in a new chord. Arden is eager to learn."

He gestured for them to rise. "You are welcome here, Oathbearers of the old light. Rest, learn, and see what we have built."

Talon bowed, but his eyes never left the ruler's. "We've seen what perfection costs," he said. "But we'll look."

Aurelian's gaze flicked briefly to the small scars along Talon's knuckles, to the worn leather of his bow-grip, to the lines at the corners of Bella's eyes that no glamour could erase. His smile did not change, but something in it cooled.

"Every cost is weighed here," he said. "That is what separates us from the chaos beyond our walls. You will find that in Arden, nothing is wasted—not pain, not joy, not light."

His hand brushed the hilt of the Accord Flame with unconscious familiarity. The runes along its length shifted, just once, in a pattern Bella recognized from old Collegium diagrams.

Containment. Channeling. Yield.

Aurelian let his fingers fall away. "In time," he went on, "you will understand why we cannot fall."

Oscar felt Elenn's hand brush his briefly—an unconscious gesture, steadying them both.
He wasn't sure whether she was offering comfort… or asking for it.

Falos' feathers rustled faintly from the high beam he had claimed. "Things that say they cannot fall," he murmured under his breath, "usually forget how to land."

***

That night, from the Skythread's deck, Bella watched the city glow—not with torches, but with the steady heartbeat of the Dragon's fading power.

"They've made paradise," she said.

Talon joined her, silent for a long time. Then: "Paradise that forgot to sleep. Even gods rest, Bella. What happens when they can't?"

She considered that, eyes on the tower where the Accord Flame burned a little too steadily. "Then something else rests for them," she said. "Or breaks for them."

Falos turned one keen eye toward the shining spires. "Then the sky trembles again," he said.

Below, Oscar stood at the rail, Elenn at his side. The light of Arden reflected in their eyes—beautiful, yes, but unsettling, as if something inside the glow was looking back.

"This place feels like it knows us," Oscar whispered.

Elenn nodded slowly. "Or expects us," she said.

A faint vibration passed through the planks under their feet—the Skythread's hum, answering the city's pulse but not quite joining it. The two tones overlapped, then slid apart again like magnets refusing to fully touch.

Oscar laid a hand on the rail. "Easy, girl," he murmured. "We're only visiting."

The Cloudheart thrummed once, as if to say: *We'll see.*

And somewhere deep within her, the ship hummed softly—not in warning, but in remembrance.

Chapter Eleven

The Ruler's Temptation

*"Some doors open inward so slowly you swear
they are not opening at all."*

— *Scribe's proverb, Nandanoléme*

***

The night before they reached the mirrored shores of Arden, the Skythread sailed through stillness so profound it seemed the stars themselves had stopped breathing.

The sails hung in suspension, faintly luminous—not from moonlight, but from the quiet pulse of the ship's own heart. No wind pressed her masts; she moved because she remembered how.

Bella stood in the chart-room with the lamps trimmed low, fingers resting on a sheet of spider-silk vellum dusted with powdered moon-quartz. Each rune along its border caught light like frost on glass.

She had written and rewritten the letter three times before finding words she could live with.

***

Corwin,

The stars ahead are too perfect. Their light holds steady where it should flicker. I fear we are sailing toward harmony learned by rote—something that remembers the notes, not the song.

I trust your mind, and the questions it refuses to silence. Come quickly. Bring your quill, and your honesty. We may need both more than courage.

— A.

***

She hesitated, hearing again her mother's voice from the Collegium tower:

If you can name what you fear, it is not yet power over you.

Bella whispered the words, half-spell, half-prayer, and the ink steadied.

Lifting the page toward her staff's crystal, she breathed the activation rune. The words sank into the fibers and vanished, leaving only the faint scent of ozone and rain on stone. A thread of silver light leapt upward—thin as a hair, bright as memory—and disappeared into the constellations.

Marissa's reflection appeared in the glass before her voice did.

"You're calling him, aren't you?"

Bella didn't look away from the stars. "Corwin? Yes. The horizon feels wrong. Too quiet. Too measured."

"Quiet horizons don't bother you."

"They do when they look back," Bella murmured. "Whatever waits out there—it's listening. Not to learn. To decide."

Marissa folded her arms beside her. "Then call him. The stars are steady tonight; they'll carry your words fast."

"Faster than thought, if the Weavers are kind."

"Corwin will come," Marissa said, her tone a small act of faith. "He never could resist a mystery."

Bella smiled faintly. "Or an argument."

They watched the Sea of Stars mirror the heavens until sky and water became the same unbroken page—and the Skythread, a single ink-stroke drawn between them.

***

Later, with most of the crew asleep, Talon lingered on deck. Falos perched high on the rigging, gold feathers catching the starlight.

"She doesn't trust what's waiting," Talon said quietly.

"Nor do you," Falos replied—no judgment, only patience. "The air smells of stillness. Not peace. The kind that waits to choose who breathes next."

Talon nodded. "That's what she feels too."

"Then she's wise to call the scholar. Some riddles bite less when answered with ink instead of steel."

"I'll remind Corwin of that when he starts arguing with Bella."

"You won't need to," the griffon rumbled. "They argue because they trust each other to remember where the truth ends."

Talon chuckled. "So not us."

"Exactly."

They stood in silence while the night turned silver and the Sea of Stars thickened beneath them like polished glass.

***

Just before dawn, the air above the mid-deck shimmered. A spiral of motes turned like a page caught between unseen fingers. The crew gathered as the spiral expanded, folding inward and outward at once.

When the light collapsed, Corwin stood within it.

He looked worn, his cloak dusted with ash and chalk from the library fires of Nandanoléme, but his eyes were bright with the same restless curiosity that had once exasperated every elder in the Collegium.

"You might have warned me," Marissa said dryly from the helm, though relief softened her tone.

"If Bella's right," Corwin answered, brushing starlight from his sleeves, "then every moment matters."

"Always the dramatic entrance," Talon muttered.

"Always the necessary one." Corwin clasped Bella's arm. "Your letter was short. That means trouble."

Bella gestured toward the horizon. The first silver curve of Arden's coast gleamed through the haze, towers rising like glass spears piercing dawn.

"That's the trouble."

Corwin squinted. "Too perfect."

"That's what I said."

He inhaled, catching the air's faint metallic tang—the residue of something more ordered than weather. "This city wasn't built," he murmured. "It was solved."

Under the aft lanterns, Bella described what they had seen so far: the distant gleam along the western rim of the new sea, the symmetry of what little their spyglass could catch, the way the wind itself seemed to hum in even intervals. Corwin listened, eyes narrowing.

"A city that cages illumination," he said at last. "Yes... I see why you called."

Marissa joined them. "We'll reach the outer pylons within the hour. The harbor sings when we near it."

"That's no harbor," Corwin said. "That's a gate disguised as welcome."

Falos dropped from the rigging with a thump that rattled the deck. "Then best we mind which side it closes on."

***

By full dawn the Sea of Stars turned to molten pearl beneath them. The Skythread's sails glowed faintly, as if catching their reflection from below instead of the light above.

As they lowered toward the western shore, the coast resolved into a thin silver line pulsing beneath a lid of cloud. Cliffs ahead were veined with light; water below glowed as though the sea itself had learned to breathe.

"Residual radiance," Bella whispered. "What the Celestial left when it rose—the world's marrow, still singing."

Falos's crest lifted. "The Veil thins here. Too thin. Something is taking more than it gives."

Talon's jaw set. "Then we'll tread lightly."

The Skythread tilted into descent, sails sighing like a creature exhaling. Mist rose around her hull, white and soft as breath, and the crew watched the city of Arden appear—each tower aligned with uncanny precision, each bridge gleaming like a frozen song.

No gulls called. No bells rang. Only the hum of a civilization that had forgotten how to rest.

***

The Hall of Light
The audience hall was built of patience and light. Columns rose like frozen waves beneath a mirrored ceiling

305

that multiplied a single torch into a thousand stars. The air's tuned hum quieted even the pulse. Talon recognized the trick—a room designed to make agreement feel inevitable.

They were announced softly: Talon of the Vale. Arrabella's Bella. Marissa the Helm. Corwin of Nandanoléme. Oscar, bow-bearer.

At the dais stood the ruler of Arden. Aurelian wore no crown, only a collar of crystal frost at his throat. His silver hair framed a face carved from symmetry itself—beauty, as geometry.

"Travelers of the Skythread," he said. "You arrive at a hinge of our age. We honor hinges—without them, doors are only walls pretending to be kind."

Bella's mouth twitched. Corwin's quill lifted, hungering to keep pace.

"Sit," Aurelian said. "The Accord Flame warms even strangers."

They sat. Oscar's hands stayed near his bow. The hum underfoot was real, the warmth measured.

"We've seen your city," Bella said. "How long has Arden held such balance?"

"Eight generations since the first harnessing," Aurelian replied. "Two and a half centuries per generation, on average."

Corwin's head came up. "Two hundred and fifty years?"

"Two hundred to two hundred fifty. Longer, rarely. Shorter, only by violence. We are not immortal, scholar—merely unhurried."

"You live long," Talon said, "and well. But your streets are quiet with children."

"We do not squander lives we can barely fill," Aurelian said evenly. "When time stretches, birth need not."

306

Bella's eyes narrowed. "Or cannot."

"Choose either verb," he answered. It wasn't evasion—just arithmetic spoken by a man who had ruled too long to love uncertainty. "We measure what sustains us."

Oscar's fingers tightened on the bench. A city that counts lifespans like constellations: no need for new ones while the old still burn.

Aurelian's gaze turned to Bella. "Arrabella. Our Scriptorium keeps the complete *Codices of the Deep Vein*. The theories your Collegium knew only as rumor are solved here—elegantly."

He inclined his head. "They are yours."

"In exchange?" Bella asked.

"For nothing. Or everything. Knowledge changes the one who holds it—that is both cost and wage."

Corwin's quill betrayed him with a scratch of longing.

Then Aurelian turned to Talon. "Oathbearer—our Wardens of the Edge hunt storms as other men hunt boar. Out where the goblins test our walls, the wind itself is blade and companion. Ride with us at dawn. Feel what it is to move with an element that obeys."

"Storms that obey forget how to be storms," Talon said.

"Or learn to be better," Aurelian countered gently. Beneath the dais, the floor's hum climbed half a note—as if the city itself sought to persuade.

"There are no priests or druids here," Bella observed. "No dream-keepers."

"Our ancestors prayed until zeal burned hillsides," Aurelian said. "We found less ash when we set wisdom to the work. Druids tilt toward growth without cost; priests toward cost without growth. We keep balance."

"And like many old marriages," Corwin murmured, "the partners have stopped listening to keep the peace."

Aurelian only smiled. "The listening that mattered was to the heart below our city—the sea the Dragon breathed into being. It sustains us; we sustain what can be sustained."

Bella's staff rang softly against the floor. "How direct is the draw?"

"Direct enough your ship's heart sang near our pylons," Aurelian said. "Indirect enough no vessel need bleed. We are careful surgeons."

He let the silence stand, a mark of mastery.

"You must eat," he said at last. "Our table is yours."

***

They dined beneath a dome that held its own moving sky. The food was simple—bread faintly sweet, fish that tasted of leaves as much as salt. Even the knives felt biased toward mercy.

Bella watched the servants pour wine whose color shifted with temperature, the liquid refracting thin threads of light. She whispered, "Air lifting, water carrying, fire feeding, earth holding—it's a city of elements kept in leash."

Corwin answered under his breath, "Then we're dining in a leash's comfort."

"Two hundred and fifty years," Corwin repeated more loudly. "Do your oldest remember their first dawn?"

"Most," said a magistrate beside Aurelian. "We curate our lives. The mind need not hoard every winter to understand cold."

Oscar frowned. "Curate?"

She smiled. "We choose which years to carry forward with warmth."

"And children?" Bella asked quietly.

"When lives are long," Aurelian said, "desire widens. Fewer children, more consensus. Our forests once seeded lavishly because many trees died. We whisper the hymn more rarely now."

"The song becomes small," Bella said.

"Or pure."

They spoke of wars—three in the early centuries, none since. Their Wardens no longer tired, their light no longer dimmed.

"But when they leave the city?" Talon asked. "Do they carry their calm with them?"

"Calm is a discipline," Aurelian said. "We carry it because we choose it."

Oscar studied his wine. "It dims."

The magistrate's pride showed. "You see well. Farther from the pylons, the body remembers labor. We pay double for that burden."

"Tethered," Corwin wrote in his notebook. "A system that promises forever but weakens at distance."

Aurelian lifted his cup. "Write fairly of us."

"I'll write honestly."

"Honesty is a kind of fairness," Aurelian said, "if you don't wield it like a cudgel."

Halfway through the meal, the dome's light faltered—barely. Talon felt it first, a hunter's instinct: one string fraying. The hum underfoot slipped a note. Bread lost its sweetness. Oscar blinked; wine dulled.

Aurelian inclined his head to someone unseen. The floor's tone returned. The glow flowed back into the glass. Bella's eyes had not left him. He met her gaze without pretense—then set his cup down with care.

Talon did not flinch under Aurelian's gaze.

The hall's light caught in the ranger's eyes, turning them a shade Keening River blue—steady, unblinking, older than any city made of glass.

Aurelian smiled with the practiced ease of a man accustomed to sacred inevitabilities.

"You long for a world that listens," he said. "One where wind respects the worthy, where roots bow to understanding, where storms answer a righteous voice. The world could be that—if guided."

Bella's fingers tightened around her staff. "You mistake him," she said quietly.

Talon didn't move, didn't look at her—didn't need to.

Every word she spoke braided itself through him, grounding him in the truth neither of them ever needed to say aloud.

Aurelian tilted his head. "Do I?"

Bella stepped forward by half an inch, the smallest warning the hall had seen in a century.

"You think he wants dominion. He wants balance. Nature listening—to itself. Respect—for the world, not from it. Obedience—to natural law, not a man's voice. Wildness kept wild. Harmony that comes from choice, not design."

Talon's jaw flexed once, a subtle thank you.

And for the first time since they'd entered Arden, something behind Aurelian's perfect calm flickered—an almost-memory.

A sound.

Soft.

Light.

Wrong.

A laughter none of them heard… except him.

***

The sight of the ranger and the mage—two opposites in effortless accord—opened a door Aurelian had sealed so long that even time had stopped checking its hinges.

It was the twelfth dawn of Arden's founding.

The towers were scaffolds.

The sea still boiled with newborn light.

And she appeared.

Not emerging.

Not arriving.

Being.

A girl with no age and too much of it, bare feet on broken stone, eyes holding two colors that contradicted each other.

"Your city is beautiful," she had said, touching unfinished stone like blessing or farewell.

Aurelian had been young then—young enough to mistake gentleness for grace.

"We hope it will be," he'd said. "We hope to build something that lasts."

Her expression softened.

"Why hope, when certainty is so much kinder?"

He remembered how she circled him—curious as a stray thought, dangerous as a forgotten truth.

"The sea beneath you sings," she whispered. "It wants to be shaped. It wants to be held."

"We shape nothing we don't understand," he'd answered.

She had laughed.

Light, ringing, merciless.

"I can help you understand."

311

Her fingers had brushed his temple—

and suddenly the Dragon's Sea filled his mind, pure radiance humming like a caged cosmos.

A power no mortal should reach.

A gift no mortal should refuse.

"You will build towers of light," she said. "You will live long. You will learn to choose without fear. All you need—"

Her hand pressed lightly to his chest.

"—is to listen."

And then she vanished.

Like a breath withdrawn.

Like a promise unmade.

The grove where she'd stood never grew again.

He called her a messenger.

A teacher.

A beginning.

He never called her by name.

Not even to himself.

But now—

now, watching Bella's suspicion, Corwin's frown, Talon's honesty—

Aurelian recognized the echo in the hall's tuned hum:

a resonance like her laughter.

Fragile.

Cold.

Hungry.

And he understood, dimly, that the visitors aboard the Skythread had brought truth deeper than they knew—

For the first time in centuries, the certainty he'd built his city upon was… listening back.

***

Bella felt it before she could name it: a shift in Aurelian's posture, as if a shadow crossed the sun of his certainty.

Talon sensed it too—a hunter's instinct catching the scent of something ancient and wrong.

Corwin's quill hovered mid-note, reading the ruler's face with the precision of a man measuring the first crack in marble.

Falos's feathers bristled along his spine.

Oscar, from his place near the back, felt a thin shiver trail down his wrist—the same sensation that meant a page had turned somewhere he hadn't seen.

Aurelian's smile returned, serene.

Weightless.

Practiced.

"Arden offers much," he said, "to those who let themselves be perfected."

Bella inhaled sharply.

Perfected.

Not grown.

Not taught.

Perfected.

A word that wanted obedience dressed as enlightenment.

He rose from the table with unhurried grace. "After supper," he said, "let me show you a thing we do well."

A servant paused mid-pour, staring at the wine that no longer glowed. For a heartbeat the scent of ozone touched the air, faint and sharp. Then the light steadied again, as if nothing had happened.

***

As the company broke apart—some to observe, some to think, some simply to breathe air that wasn't tuned to

313

someone else's idea of harmony—Oscar drifted toward the outer gallery. The city's glow spilled up the walls in pale bands.

Elenn found him at the rail.

She bumped his shoulder lightly. "You're thinking hard again."

"I'm thinking," he said, "that perfection hums too loudly."

"And you're wondering what kind of hand first taught it the tune."

He blinked at her—surprised she caught the thought he hadn't spoken.

Elenn grinned, small and bright. "Ask me again after supper," she said. "I might have a better answer."

Oscar huffed a breath that wasn't quite a laugh. "Better than nothing."

"Better than perfect," she corrected softly.

They leaned on the rail, watching a city that shone like dawn and trembled like a chord stretched too tight.

***

Night in Arden never really goes dark.

Even aboard the Skythread, the air held a faint luminosity—light without warmth, a glow that never quite rested. Oscar sat on the forward deck with his back against the rail, bow laid across his knees. He wasn't keeping watch, not officially, but the stillness wouldn't let him sleep.

Elenn joined him without asking, her footsteps soft as falling ash.

"You're awake again," she said, tucking her legs beneath her. "I can tell because your shoulders do that thing."

Oscar blinked. "What thing?"

"That thing where you try to look calm and end up looking like someone stuffed too many truths in one small human."

Oscar huffed a quiet laugh. "You sound like Corwin."

"I sound like me," she said, nudging him with her knee. "Start talking."

He hesitated. Elenn waited. She always did—not pushing, just being, which was somehow worse.

"I think," Oscar began slowly, "that I understand Arden more than I want to."

"Oh?" Her eyebrow arched. "Do you also glow when you're judgmental? Because that could be helpful."

Oscar smiled, but only briefly.

"They choose what's easy," he said. "What keeps them orderly. What keeps things quiet. Even when quiet hides something wrong."

Elenn tilted her head. "Is that what's bothering you? That they want comfort too much?"

"No," Oscar said. "It's that I… get it."

A long breath left him, something almost like confession.

"I spent most of my life trying not to stand out. Trying not to make mistakes. Trying not to break anything I couldn't fix. I know what it is to want a world that doesn't surprise you. I know exactly why that kind of peace feels tempting."

Elenn looked at him sideways.

"Oscar," she said softly, "you break things constantly."

"Not on purpose."

"On what purpose, then?"

He swallowed. "Because I'm trying. And trying is messy."

She considered that, then nodded once.

"And you're afraid Arden got so good at avoiding mess that they stopped trying."

Oscar's breath hitched. "That's it."

They sat in silence while the Skythread rocked gently on its suspended beam. Far below, Arden's light washed the cliffs in pale gold. The whole city looked like a painting—perfect, unchanging, untouchable.

Elenn reached out and tapped the bow sitting across his knees.

"You know something, don't you?" she asked quietly. "About what's coming."

Oscar didn't answer at first. He watched the horizon where the towers stood like glass bones.

"I keep seeing… pieces," he admitted. "Flashes. Not visions, really. More like consequences waiting for a reason."

Elenn didn't flinch. She never did. "And you think they'll land on us."

"I think," Oscar said, voice low, "that something about Arden is already leaning the wrong way. And leaning can turn into falling fast."

Elenn leaned back on her hands. "Then we'll push the other way."

Oscar shook his head. "I don't want to be the reason something breaks."

She snorted. "Oscar, things break because they're fragile, not because you breathe near them. And sometimes breaking is the only honest thing they can do."

He turned to her. "And what if I'm the reason?"

Elenn shrugged lightly. "Then you fix it. Or you learn from it. Or someone else helps you fix it. That's how it works."

She nudged his shoulder again, gentler this time—more like reassurance than teasing.

"You carry so much that isn't yours," she said. "You always have. I saw it the first day you stepped on this ship. You said it was to be useful. I think it's because you're terrified of being the match in a room full of dry leaves."

Oscar stared at the deck. "Yeah," he whispered. "Exactly that."

"Good," Elenn said.

He blinked. "Good?"

"Better a match that knows it's fire than one pretending it's cold."

Oscar let that settle. Her words always landed like truths spoken sideways.

She stood and offered a hand. "Come on. Let's get some sleep before Bella drags us into another tower full of singing crystals."

Oscar hesitated—then took her hand.

As she pulled him to his feet, he felt something shift.

Not a prophecy, not a warning—just clarity.

Elenn wasn't unburdening him.

She was preparing him.

Because when the cliffs ahead tremble, when the giants wake, when the cost of Arden's design comes due—it will be Elenn who turns to him and says, *Oscar, what did you think would happen?*

And she'll be right.

But for now, she squeezed his hand once more and said:

"You're not a danger. You're a direction. Try leaning the right way."

For the first time since he saw Arden's glow, Oscar exhaled.

And in that small, fragile breath, something like courage began.

Chapter Twelve

The Weight of Light

"Every borrowed light carries the weight
of what could have grown in the dark."

—Thay'sa, *On the Veil and Its Fractures*

***

Morning came like polished glass—clear, bright, and strangely silent. Even the gulls glided without cry, their wings catching the reflection of a city that had long ago learned to shine without the sun.

From the Skythread's deck, the city of Arden looked like a perfect equation written across the land: every tower mirrored, every bridge exact, every street too smooth to have ever known rain. The hum of unseen power reached even to the harbor.

Marissa tightened the mooring lines herself.

"Feels like the wind's afraid to touch it," she muttered.

Talon's eyes followed a pair of wardens marching along a crystalline causeway. Their armor caught the light, but their steps made no sound.

"Maybe it's afraid to be changed by what it touches."

Corwin joined them, blinking against the glare.

"A civilization tuned to the edge of stasis. They've engineered serenity so complete it can't afford to move."

Falos spread his wings on the rigging, feathers flickering gold.

"Then movement will find them, whether they wish it or not."

***

They went ashore under escort—two wardens in silver-blue mail and a magistrate of Trade who moved like a man reciting lines rehearsed for centuries.

The harbor quarter shimmered with a faint haze. Cranes of articulated bronze swung without pulleys. Carts rolled uphill unaided, leaving cold trails where wheels kissed stone. Even the shadows obeyed, shifting softly to match the angle of the light.

Bella paused beside a fountain whose water rose in spiral threads before falling again as mist. She touched the vapor; it tingled against her skin.

"Dragonlight," she murmured. "Distilled and directed. Every street's drinking from the same vein."

Corwin traced a sigil on the marble lip.

"A harmonic lattice. They've built the entire city as a containment glyph—each tower a point of resonance. Beautiful," he said. "And impossible to sustain forever."

"Unless you redefine forever," Bella replied.

The magistrate smiled politely, overhearing without comment.

"Arden endures because its heart does. The beam beneath the city renews itself with each turning of the Veil."

"Self-renewal," Corwin said dryly. "You must teach me that trick before my next winter."

As they crossed into the first terrace, the streets widened, clean as mirrored glass. No soot, no cobwebs, no children shouting. A few citizens nodded in passing—serene, pale, and ageless. Their movements were unhurried, their eyes steady, as if each gesture had been practiced until no trace of impulse remained.

Oscar whispered, "They look carved, not born."

Bella's answer was quiet.

"They've traded life's noise for its silence."

***

The magistrate led them through the Hall of Harmonies—a vast open square where light danced between crystalline pylons. At the center, a single tower rose, its sides veined with flowing silver lines that pulsed in time with the city's heartbeat.

"This is our regulator," the magistrate said. "The Accord Flame flows through here to balance the outer wards. You may feel the pulse."

They felt it—through soles and skin alike. The air seemed alive, carrying a faint rhythm that made the lungs unconsciously match it.

Bella slowed as they entered the Hall of Harmonies. The air thrummed—soft, ordered, tuned to an emotion she could not name. Light rippled along the pylons like music played on glass.

Talon brushed his fingers along the nearest railing. "Feels… familiar."

Corwin's quill hovered above the page. "Not the architecture. The intent."

Bella nodded. "A place shaped to guide thought. To soften disagreement before it begins." She frowned, listening deeper. "Trechellus had chambers like this. Beneath Soahc. Rooms where the light and sound weren't decorations but… persuasion."

Talon's jaw tightened. "Those halls tried to tell you what to feel."

Corwin added, "This city does it gently. Elegantly. But it still nudges the mind toward a single harmony."

Bella glanced at a pair of citizens passing them—serene, untroubled, every movement measured. "Arden doesn't need sykshredders," she whispered. "It uses its own song."

Corwin spoke in earnest. "A cage that sings is still a cage."

Talon's hand tightened on the rail. "It's inside the breath," he said softly. "Like the air's teaching you how to breathe its way."

Corwin crouched to study a hairline crack spidering along the pylon's base.

"When a system hums perfectly, even small fractures echo."

He straightened. "You're bleeding resonance."

The magistrate looked pained. "Every lighted city has strain. But ours holds."

"For now," Corwin murmured.

They continued into the living quarters. Doors opened by thought, meals assembled themselves in quiet kitchens, and mirrors adjusted to complement their observers. Yet for all the wonder, there was an unease—a stillness between heartbeats.

A vendor pressed luminous fruit into Oscar's hands.

"Taste," she urged. "The light keeps it fresh."

He bit and winced.

"Sweet. Too sweet."

"It's meant to be," she said, and turned away before he could ask more.

Bella watched her go.

"No one lingers."

"Perhaps they've learned that conversation wastes light," Corwin answered.

***

By midday, they reached the elevated market district. The air buzzed faintly with rune-song, and channels of pale energy ran beneath the paving stones. A child rolled a silver hoop along the path; it glided far past his reach, circling him of its own accord.

Bella studied the pattern beneath their feet.

"The lattice extends under every street. They've turned their foundation into a conduit."

Marissa knelt beside a glowing seam.

"And if one line fails?"

Corwin's quill was already scratching notes.

"The harmony fractures. Energy finds the shortest path, and anything alive along that path—burns."

They passed through a plaza where three black towers stood dormant, their bronze filigree charred and warped. Citizens skirted them without a glance.

Oscar whispered, "What happened here?"

The magistrate's tone didn't change.

"Dead wards. The pylons there lost balance. We build anew, two streets over."

Bella frowned.

"And the people who lived here?"

"They were relocated."

"To where?"

He didn't answer.

When they moved on, Falos's wings rustled faintly. "A city that refuses shadow will always find a place to hide it."

***

At dusk, the group stood atop the fourth terrace. Below them the city spread in flawless order—veins of light, towers like blades, bridges spanning canyons of glass. Yet as the sun sank, the light faltered for the first time.

A heartbeat too long between pulses.
A hesitation.

Corwin's eyes caught it.

"There. The rhythm's slipping."

Bella felt it too—the same uneasy resonance she'd sensed before.

"Like breath held too long."

Their escort tensed, listening. The hum steadied again, but faintly out of tune.

"Minor oscillation," he said quickly. "The regulators will correct it."

Talon's gaze followed the glow running toward the outer pylons.

"Correction or denial?"

***

Later, they stood upon a narrow balcony overlooking the western wards. Beyond the terraces stretched the sea of light—fields of crystal vines and canals flowing with luminescent water.

Marissa leaned on the rail.

"Looks peaceful from here."

Bella shook her head.

"Peaceful the way a frozen lake is peaceful."

Corwin opened his journal again.

"They've perfected the illusion of equilibrium. Every imbalance is redistributed, not resolved. They 'move the line,' as their magistrate said. But you can only move a boundary so many times before the world runs out of edges."

Talon's gaze lingered on the horizon, where a thin thread of darker cloud gathered.

"Then we find the edge before they fall from it."

***

They left the central spire at nightfall, descending by open tram toward the outer wards. The conveyance drifted on unseen force, guided by robed tenders who balanced crystals in their palms. When a child reached for one, the tender smiled and let him touch the light.

"Borrowed radiance," Corwin murmured.

"Leased," Bella corrected.

The tram slid between towers, the hum softening to a lullaby. But as they neared the lower terraces, that harmony fractured again. The pylons below them flickered like fireflies in wind. A faint scent of ozone drifted through the open air.

"Something's failing," Oscar said.

"No," Bella whispered. "Something's remembering."

***

Their escort—a Custody captain named Kera—met them at the base of the lowest tier. She carried no weapon, only a staff capped with mirrored glass. Her armor's seams glowed faintly.

"You wished to see the edge," she said. "I'm authorized to show you the western trench before shift-change."

Talon nodded. "Lead on."

They passed through a gate of transparent bronze, beyond which the city's perfection began to fade. Here the light thinned, the hum weakening to a low tremor. Far fields glowed in uneven rows—barley, flax, and strange crystal growths that shimmered as though photosynthesizing memory. Between them ran narrow canals of liquid light.

Bella crouched beside one, dipping her fingers in. "It's warm."

"Runoff," Kera explained. "Residual energy from the central vein. It nourishes the outer fields."

"And if it cools?"

"Then the fields die."

Corwin's voice was low. "You're bleeding the dragon's marrow dry."

Kera's lips thinned.

"We survive. The inner wards demand draw; we give it. Balance requires cost."

Oscar gazed toward the dark ridge beyond. Shapes moved there—slow, heavy, indistinct.

"What's past that line?"

Kera followed his look.

"The wastes. Ogres in the hills, goblins in the trees. Without the beam, they'd have taken us centuries ago."

"And when the light fails?" Talon asked.

Her silence was answer enough.

***

They climbed a short rise to a scaffold of crystal and iron. Above it, mirrored prisms gathered and focused stray radiance into a single thread pointing back toward the city. Beneath the scaffold, the soil steamed faintly—too hot for life, too cold for ash.

Bella studied the light-line with narrowed eyes. "You're feeding the city backwards. It's not renewal—it's siphon."

Kera bristled. "You misunderstand our harmony."

Corwin's quill scratched. "Harmony without rest becomes tyranny. Even notes need silence between them."

Talon placed a hand against the ground. Heat pulsed beneath his palm, rhythmic and strained. "The earth's burning under your feet, Captain. You just haven't seen the smoke yet."

***

On their return, the tram passed a square where citizens gathered around a flickering pylon. A single warden knelt beside it, chanting a slow, resonant phrase. When the light flared and steadied, the crowd sighed as one.

"Ritual," Bella said softly.

"Maintenance," Kera corrected.

"Faith in another shape," Corwin added.

Falos's wings twitched.

"And faith, too long contained, becomes hunger."

***

By the time they reached the harbor again, the moon had risen—pale and perfect above a city that refused to darken. The Skythread floated on reflected glow, her sails dulled as if unwilling to outshine what she did not trust.

Marissa oversaw the night watch in silence. Oscar lingered by the gangway until Bella's voice found him.

"You're thinking loud."

He gave a small shrug.

"If we had their time… could we end up the same?"

Bella's gaze softened.

"It's not the length of time we have, Oscar. It's what we choose to do with it. They've had centuries—and somehow run out of living."

Talon stood at the rail, eyes on the shining spires.

"They've built paradise on borrowed breath. And the debt's coming due."

Corwin closed his notebook with a sigh.

"Then we'd best learn their numbers before the bill arrives."

In the margin of his notes, a faint line appeared—not written by Corwin's hand:

illusion ≠ balance

balance ≠ consent

Falos's feathers rippled once in the night breeze. "Light without shadow," he said, "is blindness given form."

And deep within the Skythread's Cloudheart, a low hum answered—not warning, not fear, but remembrance.

***

Long after the crew had settled into uneasy rest, the Skythread's Cloudheart pulsed once—a deep, resonant thrum that rippled through her timbers.

Not alarm.

Not warning.

Recognition.

As if she had heard this tune before, long ago, in a place where light learned how to lie.

Falos stirred on the perch above the helm, feathers rattling. Bella sat upright in her hammock, staff glowing faintly. Oscar jolted awake on the lower deck, breath sharp. Instinct made him check his hands—the bow at his side, the quiver strap, the deck beneath him.

"I didn't break anything," he whispered to the dark.

Then quieter: "...did I?"

No answer came.

The Cloudheart gave one last, soft pulse—almost apologetic—and fell silent.

But the silence felt different now.

As though somewhere deep beneath Arden, something listening had finally heard them back.

***

Night deepened, though Arden refused to dim. The towers gleamed with unwavering precision, each pulse of light asserting a perfection the world itself had never promised.

On the Skythread's deck, Bella stood beside Talon, neither speaking.

The city shone beneath them like a lantern held too close to parchment—brilliant, brittle, and one tremor away from flame.

Corwin joined them at last, journal under his arm, the ink on his fingers still warm.

"I used to envy cities like this," he said quietly. "Places that looked finished."

Talon didn't turn.

"Nothing living is ever finished."

Falos shifted on the rigging, golden feathers catching the unmoving glow of Arden's outer wards.

"The question," he murmured, "is whether Arden remembers it's alive at all."

Bella's fingers brushed the railing, the metal warm with borrowed radiance.

"No balance can stand forever on light alone," she whispered. "Something always grows in the dark. Even truth."

A breeze stirred then—thin, hesitant, almost ashamed of itself—as if the wind had finally remembered how to move.

Oscar stepped out from the companionway, rubbing sleep from his eyes. "Did something happen?"

Bella looked at him, saw the faint worry still clinging to the boy's shoulders.

"Yes," she said gently.

"And more is coming."

Oscar swallowed.

"I'll try not to break anything."

Talon almost smiled.

"That's not the danger."

"What is?"

"That we'll find something already broken," Bella answered, "and think we're the ones supposed to fix it."

The Skythread rocked once on her mooring beam, a motion like a heartbeat—or a warning.

Far below, a single pylon flickered. Just once.

Just long enough.

And the city of Arden, perfect to the eye and flawless to the touch, held its breath.

Waiting.

Chapter Thirteen

The Quiet Between Sparks

"Every borrowed light carries the weight
of what could have grown in the dark."

— *Thay'sa, On the Veil and Its Fractures*

***

Morning rose in a hush so complete even the tide forgot to lap. A faint shimmer clung to the air, like dust made of light. The Skythread floated steady in the inner bay, her reflection tremoring across the bright surface. From above, the city appeared unblemished—its runes alive, its pylons straight, its order absolute.

But from below came a sound that did not belong: a slow pulse… irregular as a heart learning to stutter.

Bella felt it before she heard it.

"The draw's slipping again." Her hand found her staff without thought.

Corwin appeared with his journal still open, quill tucked behind one ear like a man unwilling to pause mid-sentence. "Then we find its source before they bury it in ceremony."

Talon gave the order to make ready. "Marissa—keep the Skythread tethered and quiet. If we don't return by nightfall, take her out of range."

The helm saluted once. "Understood."

***

They crossed the causeway beneath a sky that refused to change color. At the spire's base, wardens barred their way until Aurelian arrived. The ruler looked immaculate as ever, though the light haloing his collar trembled with a flaw he could not hide.

"You should be resting," he said mildly.

Bella inclined her head. "Your city is breathing unevenly."

"Cities do that. They sigh."

"This one is choking."

For the first time, something human flickered behind his perfect composure.

"Then let me show you why," he said quietly, "we cannot afford to loosen its throat."

***

The descent wound through transparent stairs. Light bled through every surface until depth itself became uncertain. The hum thickened, becoming rhythm—becoming breath.

At the final landing, three women waited—braided copper crowns, pale crystal circlets. The Warders. Their faces serene. Their hands trembling.

"The balance shifts," said the eldest. "Outer wards lost tone on the midnight change. The beam compensated."

332

"Over-compensated," said the second.

The third did not look away from the column of light at the chamber's center. "And now it remembers being free."

Bella's pulse quickened.

Corwin's quill stilled.

Even Talon felt the wrongness ripple.

Aurelian gestured toward the beam. "This is what sustains us."

The beam did not shine—it seethed. Spiraling layers of living radiance twisted through one another like a storm given shape. Within its heart, something moved: a curve like scale, a ghost like wing.

Bella stepped closer until heat licked her skin.

"You're drawing directly from the dragon's breath."

Aurelian shook his head. "We borrow its echo."

"You consume its dying," she corrected.

Corwin's voice came soft, almost reverent. "Residual consciousness... the matrix still holds memory. You've built your eternity atop a corpse that refuses to rest."

Aurelian spread his hands. "And yet we live. We thrive. We—"

The floor shuddered.

A crack of light split the air above them—

—then sealed like a wound unsure whether to bleed or heal.

"It's thinning," whispered the eldest Warder.

Bella raised her staff. "Let me help you taper the draw."

Aurelian's tone hardened—not loud, but final. "Intervention collapses the system. Tens of thousands would die."

"Not intervention," she said. "Mercy."

He took a step toward her. "Do you think we have not prayed? We built this because the world beyond our walls burned. We took the dragon's breath so our children would never smell smoke again."

Corwin's eyes lifted to meet his. "And in saving them from fire, you taught them never to feel warmth."

Aurelian's shoulders flinched—the smallest fracture in a flawless mask.

"You speak," he said, "as those who will fly away. We must stay."

"And die slowly," Talon murmured. "You've turned survival into worship."

Silence settled—thick, vibrating with the beam's pulse.

Then—

"Another pylon!" the youngest Warder cried.

The hum leapt to a shriek. Light speared upward.

For the barest instant, the beam brightened enough to reveal the silhouette inside:

A dragon, coiled upon itself.

Mouth open in a roar the world could no longer hear.

Then the brilliance guttered.

The rhythm returned, ragged and weary.

Bella staggered back, tears burning hot.

"It's still aware."

Aurelian's voice cracked. "Then may it forgive us."

***

Hours later, they reached the open air.

The city still gleamed, unaware of its own fracture.

Children laughed in distant markets.

Fruit-vendors called soft greetings. Pylons glowed unevenly—but no one looked up.

Oscar rejoined them at the quay. "Two pylons dimmed while you were gone. People say it's the wind's fault."

334

Talon answered only: "It always is... until it isn't."

Bella turned to Aurelian. "You could taper the draw. Shift the lines. Teach your people to live with darkness again."

He did not meet her eyes. He looked toward the shining column crowning the horizon.

"Darkness is the one thing they will never forgive me for returning."

Corwin closed his journal. "Then the city will choose for you."

Aurelian's tired smile said everything.
"Perhaps that is mercy."

He bowed—not to them, but to the invisible shape within the light—and walked back toward the spire.

***

Night gathered like a deep breath. The Skythread rose on a whispering wind, her sails catching the faintest glimmer of Arden below. No bells rang. No torches burned. Only the hum of a civilization holding itself together by will alone.

Oscar leaned on the rail.

"Will they survive?"

Bella shook her head gently. "They'll endure. That's not the same thing."

Corwin watched the beam dwindle behind them. "Arden stands upon the breath of a god and mistakes the silence that follows for peace."

Talon placed a hand on the railing. The Skythread's Cloudheart pulsed beneath his palm—sure, living, honest.

"Then let's remember what peace really costs."

Falos looked back one last time.

"Light without shadow," he said, "is still blindness."

The griffon spread his wings. The ship climbed higher.

And the city of Arden shone on—perfect, fragile, paying its price in silence for a little while longer.

***

Chapter Fourteen

Whispers Beneath the Light

"When the stars go silent,
listen instead to the breath between them."

— *Saying of the Skyborn Mariners*

***

The *Skythread* drifted westward through a calm that felt too complete to be natural. Below them, the **Sea of Stars** shimmered faintly—an ocean vast and unbroken, its mirrored surface catching the heavens in endless reflection. Even the wind seemed reverent, as though unwilling to disturb the hush that followed Arden's light.

For days, the crew spoke little. Each had seen too much—perfection that hid decay, beauty that demanded obedience. The silence of the air was not peace; it was waiting.

Oscar sat near the forecastle rail, his journal open but his quill unmoving. The page stared back at him, accusingly blank.

Marissa crossed the deck, placing a steaming mug beside him. "Words won't come when you stare them down," she said.

He sighed. "What would I even write? That we left gods who forgot how to dream? That their paradise was just stillness pretending to be peace?"

Her smile was tired, but warm. "Then write that. Truth looks better when it's not polished."

Oscar nodded, though his eyes never left the horizon. "Maybe one day we'll go back—to see what changed when their light finally faded."

Marissa's gaze softened. "If the world lets us."

***

That night, the stars changed.

Bella was the first to notice. The constellations over this far western sea had always seemed sharper, colder—but now they pulsed faintly, as though breathing in rhythm with the ship's cloud-heart.

She called Talon to the deck. "Look there—Orath's Belt. The southernmost star is moving."

Talon squinted, brow furrowed. "Stars don't drift that fast."

Corwin joined them, his voice low. "They do if the Veil's currents are stirring beneath them. That's not motion in the heavens—it's reflection from the sea."

As one, they turned their gaze downward.

The water glowed with its own constellations, luminous but imperfect—stars below that didn't quite match those above. The longer they stared, the more it seemed that something *beneath* the reflection was moving, reshaping the light like a slow heartbeat.

Bella whispered, "The Sea of Stars remembers. The Veil's still thin here—the echoes bleed through."

Talon's jaw tightened. "Then something on the other side is remembering us."

***

Sleep came uneasily that night. Dreams blurred the line between sea and sky.

Marissa dreamed of Tirpik's laughter rolling across the wind. Greenbough saw roots that glowed like constellations, threading through the dark.

Oscar dreamed he was writing, but the ink flowed upward, forming not words but the shape of wings.

And Elenn dreamed beside him—of music under water, of voices that hummed in patterns older than speech. She woke with tears in her eyes and found Oscar standing at the rail.

"The sky's too quiet," he said softly.

She joined him. "No. It's just listening."

Their hands brushed. Neither drew away. Above them, the stars pulsed once—bright, brief, and whole—and the sea below answered with light.

***

By morning, the air had thickened to a subtle hum. The *Skythread's* sails glowed faintly even with the sun behind clouds.

Marissa checked her instruments. "Pressure's rising again. Not tide—something deeper."

Corwin frowned at the horizon. "Residual Veil current, maybe. The Dragon's ascension is still echoing through the world."

339

Bella nodded. "Then we're sailing over the heartbeat of what comes next."

Oscar closed his journal, at last writing one clean line across the page:

The stars are breathing again.

Talon stood at the helm, his voice steady. "Then we chart what breathes, and give it a name."

Marissa raised a brow. "You have one?"

He looked out over the silver horizon. "The Sea of Stars."

***

That night, Bella stood alone on the sterncastle. Falos perched above her—still as sculpture, save for the faint flick of his feathers in the starlit wind.

"They're still singing," she murmured. "The stars, the sea… even the ship. It's as if they're waiting for something."

Falos's gaze drifted skyward; the words drifted to Bella's mind. "Waiting for us to listen."

"And if we don't?"

His crest shifted with a soft click of beak. "Then they'll teach us again."

She smiled faintly. "You sound like Dug."

The griffon's eye glinted gold, with just the hint of mischief. "He listened too—though a touch more *bearitone*."

Below them, the Skythread's sails caught the mirrored starlight. For a heartbeat, they truly looked like wings.

The ship drifted on through the whispering dark, westward toward the Vale—and toward whatever awaited in the uncharted dawn.

***

Chapter Fifteen

The Language of Storms

"When thunder speaks, the wise do not hide.
They listen for the grammar."

— *Balok Ironforge,* Field Log 7: Mistmantle Trials

***

The storm ahead wasn't weather so much as an intent.

High clouds stacked in cathedral tiers, wind running along their faces in braided streams. Lightning webbed inside the vault like veins through marble, but when it struck it made no light—only sound: layered chords, too measured to be chaos.

Bella's staff tingled in her palm. "That's patterned."

Augustine tilted his beakish snout toward the roil, eyes half-lidded. "A metered pulse. The wind is counting."

Marissa, hands steady on the helm, squinted through the forward glass. "If that's counting, it's the loudest abacus I've ever sailed into."

Corwin leaned over the chart table, quill hovering. "Cloud Giant lore says they speak in thunder and read in gale… if the old notes aren't just poetry."

Falos banked low across the bow, gold feathers catching pale flickers, and gave a rising trill—the sound of agreement. Corwin glanced up, half smiling. "Not poetry," he murmured. "Memory."

Talon's gaze never left the storm. "Then we approach as if it remembers us."

The Skythread climbed, her Cloudheart thrumming with a low silver-blue pulse the crew felt in bone more than ear. Every plank breathed with the ship; every rope hummed in sympathy. Ahead, the cloud wall curved inward—an eye, a gate, a funnel. The sound deepened.

They gathered at the bridge rail: Talon, Bella, Marissa, Corwin, Augustine, Oscar, Elenn. The air smelled of iron and rain not yet fallen.

Bella tapped her quill against the map. "We need a reply they can hear."

"Words won't carry," Corwin said. "A sending that large risks igniting the entire field."

"So we need thunder that talks back," Marissa said, looking directly at Oscar, a half-smile under the concern. "Preferably without flattening the sky."

Everyone looked at Oscar.

He blinked. "What?"

Bella narrowed her eyes fondly. "Whatever it is you're about to suggest, say it out loud where we can stop you."

Oscar rubbed the back of his neck. "Balok's Thunder Bumpers can shape amplitude. If we quarter-load the coils—no boom, just a hum. A cone we can steer. A greeting."

Talon folded his arms, weighing the sky. "You're proposing we answer people who speak in storms with a weapon."

344

"With an instrument," Oscar said. "Balok built it to crack fortresses, but sound remembers intention. If we don't ask it to kill, maybe it won't."

Marissa exhaled through her nose, the faintest laugh in it. "Just don't teach it any swear words."

Augustine tapped a claw on the map's margin. "If thunder is grammar, cadence is courtesy. Begin with a greeting."

Elenn nodded once. "Fine. We'll do it. But on my count and under my hand."

Talon met her eyes. "Yours and Oscar's. If either of you says stop, we stop."

"Agreed." She gathered her gloves and lamp. "Let's see what Balok left us."

***

The crew called the spot The Thunder Bay. The chamber was a cathedral of pressure and brass. Coils veined the ceiling, pulsing with caged glow; the air shimmered with old charge. Along the port side crouched three Thunder Bumpers— bronze throats narrowing to crystal mouths, runes crawling their cones like frost-lit vines.

A plaque riveted to the bulkhead bore Balok's unmistakable hand:

⚠ WARNING: WHEN ACTIVE, NOT SAFE FOR MORTAL HABITATION.

Below it, in chalk—almost certainly Oscar:

But fun!

Elenn leaned to read it, brow arching. "Not safe for mortal habitation…"

She dropped Balok's logbook with a clatter. "You have got to be kidding me." Then, quieter, as she stooped to retrieve it: "If I could swear in this world, I would."

Oscar tightened the release valves. "We're not living in here—just borrowing an echo."

She flipped open the log. The smudged pages were warm.

***

Field Test 1:
Sounded like a bear's belly rumbled, then burped, then fell apart.
Result: Inconclusive but memorable.
    Field Test 2:
Flattened a ridge and a tower. Vaporized a passing wyvern.
Conclusion: Effective. Possibly too effective. Excellent.
— Balok

***

Elenn snorted. "Reassuring."

Oscar grinned. "If it can't terrify a mountain and traumatize a wyvern, why build it?"

She shot him a look somewhere between disbelief and fondness. "Try not doing either today."

He winked. "No promises."

She sighed, then softened. "Sometimes I think you measure bravery in decibels."

He tightened a coupling. "And you measure it in pulse rates. We balance."

That drew a quiet laugh. "Maybe." She bent toward the console. "Power?"

346

"Twenty percent. Quarter load. Wide cone. We're going to speak, not shout."

***

Up on the bridge, Marissa's voice came through the speaking tube. "Helm steady. First ring."

Bella's reply followed, calm and electric. "Begin on Augustine's count."

The tortosian loremaster inhaled. "Three short pulses. A bow before a name."

Elenn braced at the console. "Ready. And if your face melts off, I'm not healing that."

Oscar blinked. "Check—face melt—wait, *why is that even on the table*—"

"**Now!**" the loremaster barked.

Oscar jumped. Reflex took over. His hand slammed the lever down while his brain was still mid-complaint.

Sound erupted—pure, resonant, rolling through marrow and metal alike. The Skythread shivered as her timbers answered, every spar and sail humming in sympathy. The cloud wall rippled—not from force, but invitation.

Silence followed: one breath long.

A chord rose from within the storm, harmonic and questioning.

Falos's feathers rustled—approval.

Marissa smiled. "They heard."

Talon's grip eased. "Again. With courtesy."

"Shape to the Cloudheart," Elenn said. "Let it carry our rhythm."

Oscar feathered the wheel, bleeding power into the living core. The next pulse wasn't heat—it was identity.

The sails flared briefly with star-pricked light.

The storm answered in kind.

The wall parted.

Within the opened ring, vast shapes moved—shoulders like hills, brows like cliffs, eyes like cyclones rimmed in gold.

Bella whispered, "Cloud Giants."

Corwin didn't write. He only looked.

A giant leaned close, thunder rolling through its vaporous face:

—Who calls in the borrowed breath?—

Augustine's eyes gleamed. "They taste the Celestial in our wake."

Talon spoke into the tube. "Oscar, Elenn—give them truth."

"One long chord; two soft bows," Elenn said. "On my count."

Three. Two. One.

The Skythread's self—her true name—went out across the wind.

The giant's vast face softened.

—You carry a shard of the First Breath. And the will of those who sing to build. Why do you speak?—

Bella answered, though no mortal voice could form storm-speech. "Because we would listen. And we carry a message, if you'll trust us."

Lightning traced the giant's brow—curiosity.

***

Dozens more shapes stirred, their voices merging:

—Our histories are not ink.

They are wind.

Not parchment—cloud.

When the world forgot to read us, we drifted.

When the dragon's breath sang, we were anchored.
When it rose, we loosened again.—

***

Falos bowed his head, a cry escaping him—half lament, half reverence.

"They've been untethered since the Ascension," Augustine whispered.

"Then help us tether them again," Marissa said.

The giants considered the Thunder Bumpers, glowing and warm.

—You speak with a weapon's throat and a singer's heart.
Will you carry our voices to rain?—

"They ask us to let their stories fall," Augustine said. "Where people still listen."

Talon looked to his companions. They nodded.

"Yes," he said.

The wall shivered. Wind shifted. Pressure eased.

—We will guide.—

A corridor opened. New currents formed, thick as ropes. The Skythread slipped into them, her Cloudheart humming higher, as if recognizing an old trail.

"Hold her gentle," Marissa whispered.

***

Belowdecks, Elenn leaned back, laughing in disbelief. "We did it."

Oscar thumped his head lightly against the brass. "Told you it would talk."

She eyed him. "Still attached."

349

"My eyebrows?"

"Also attached," she said. "Infuriating."

He offered her a hand. "Come on. Let's watch the sky write."

***

They stood at the starboard rail as rain began—soft, musical. Each drop carried a whisper of giant song.
The water pooled and ran to the sea, a silver script the world would read when it touched fields and roofs and hands.

"They'll hear it in the Vale," Bella murmured. "On Soahc. In the Dirgewood."

Corwin lifted his quill at last, not to own it—only to witness. "Thunder to rain. Sky to soil. Story to memory."

Falos lifted his head and cried—clicks and whistles threading through the departing thunder until the sky seemed to answer.

Marissa smiled faintly. "Balok would've loved this."

Over the tube, Oscar's voice warmed. "He'd call it progress."

Talon's mouth tilted. "Fun."

"Both can be true," Augustine said.

The storm city drifted west—its bridges flashing like lanterns carried through mist. Far away, the Vale's peaks caught the new light and held it.

The Skythread eased over a rinsed sky. For a heartbeat, her sails looked like wings.

Talon breathed deep. "Log it. Thunder can be a weapon. Today it was a tongue."

Bella smiled. "Then let's become fluent."

Marissa turned the helm west. The ship hummed, pleased.

350

Behind them, the storm spoke in rain. Ahead, the map left room for a new line.

***

Elenn checked the gauges. "She's happier than most people after a conversation that loud."

Oscar watched her. "Still running smooth?"

"As smooth as you're reckless." She hesitated. "Tell me something. Are you doing all this to prove something?"

"Prove?"

"You know—flirting with disaster because the girl's watching." Her tone softened. "You don't need to be that guy."

Oscar opened his mouth, then closed it.

Elenn met his eyes. "I saw you stand to a dragon when we all wanted to flee. That wasn't luck or bravado. That was courage. You have nothing to prove to me."

For once, Oscar had no quip. His grin faltered into something gentler. "Then I'll settle for keeping the eyebrows."

She smiled. "Good plan. They suit you uncharred."

Just as the moment grew still, she jabbed a knuckle into the nerve cluster at his shoulder.

Oscar yelped. "Ow—what was that for?"

"Keeping you humble."

He rubbed the spot, laughing. "You've got a cruel sense of affection."

"Aren't you supposed to be a priest of Paladin—pious, not punchy?"

Elenn smirked. "I can be both."

Their laughter didn't echo.

It just settled into memory.

Chapter Sixteen

The Sky Remembers

"The wind forgets nothing; it only changes where it whispers."

— *Saying among the Cloud Giants*

***

The storm faded behind them like a cathedral closing its doors.

Rainlight—thin as silver ink—still clung to the rigging, each drop humming with the remnants of the giants' farewell. The Skythread glided smoother than she had in days, as if the storm had brushed her hull with purpose rather than wear.

Oscar emerged from the Thunder Bay rubbing his shoulder, muttering, "My face did not melt, for the record," while Elenn walked two steps ahead, entirely unrepentant.

Marissa snorted from the helm. "Give it an hour. The ego usually melts first."

Corwin, roller still drying on his page, didn't look up. "Technically, the waveform displaced enough ambient resonant pressure that—"

Bella raised a hand. "Corwin. Let him have this one."

Talon stepped past them onto the forward deck. He didn't smile, but something in his shoulders eased—like a

353

bow unstrung at last. He stared into the thinning clouds ahead, where faint breakers of sunlight were just beginning to bleed through.

Falos circled above, releasing a whistle-click that echoed like approval and warning in one breath.

Bella came to stand beside Talon. "You feel it too."

He nodded once. "Storms don't end. They choose where to go next."

She followed his gaze. Not toward Arden behind them— but toward the western horizon.

Something was waiting there.

Something old.

Something that knew their names.

Oscar joined them, still buzzing with adrenaline and the sheer joy of not being vaporized. "So. New heading? Or are we waiting for the giants to send a follow-up letter in cumulonimbus?"

Marissa tapped the helm's glass. "Skythread's reading a current. Not wind. Something... calling."

Augustine emerged slowly, leaning on the rail. His eyes had gone half-lidded in that *I know more than I want to say* way.

"A language far older than thunder," the tortosian murmured. "And harder to mistranslate."

Bella frowned gently. "Memory magic?"

"Worse," he said. "Truth."

The word sat there, heavy as iron and just as difficult to lift.

Corwin finally closed his journal. "Then whatever waits ahead isn't just another wonder. It's a reckoning."

Oscar swallowed. "Why do you say that like we don't already have five of those scheduled?"

Bella's hand brushed Talon's—just barely—but the gesture carried quiet certainty.

"We answer anyway."

Talon nodded.

Skythread's Cloudheart brightened in agreement, a pulse like a heartbeat that wasn't entirely the ship's.

Ahead, the western horizon rippled—light bending, colors sharpening, sea mist rising in shapes too deliberate to be mere weather.

Something was forming.

Something that remembered storms.

Something that remembered *them*.

Talon exhaled slowly.

"Helm," he said. "Carry us to whatever knows our names."

Marissa's voice dropped reverent. "Aye."

The Skythread turned toward the shimmer waiting beyond the cloud line.

A new path opened.

A new voice waited.

And the sky—quiet now, watching—remembered.

***

Dawn came slow and amber. The last of the rain still clung to the rigging, every droplet humming faintly with echoes of thunder long gone. The giants had withdrawn into the upper currents, their vast silhouettes dissolving into the brightness of morning—but their gift lingered. The new trade wind they'd woven followed like a vow, steady and sure.

Bella stood near the stern lantern, fingers brushing the rail. "The air feels different."

"Balanced," Talon said. "As if the world just exhaled."

Marissa smiled faintly. "Or sighed in relief that we didn't blow it up."

Oscar stretched, soot still dusting his sleeve. "I call that progress."

Elenn elbowed him lightly. "You call anything that doesn't explode progress."

Corwin was already sketching in his journal, lines crisp and sure. "We'll need to chart the new current. The Giants' tether changed the entire western corridor."

Augustine's slow voice rose behind them. "And so the maps must change, as all stories do when the world breathes again."

He tapped his stylus against the railing, the sound soft as rain. "What you did yesterday will live in cloud and tide alike. That's not conquest—that's conversation."

Talon's gaze swept the horizon. "Let's make it a lasting one."

***

Below deck, the Cloudheart pulsed with a soft silver rhythm, almost sleepy now. The crew moved quietly, as though afraid to disturb it. Falos rested near the mainmast, wings half-spread, feathers catching stray motes of light.

His mind brushed Bella's.

They listen still. Even sleeping, they dream of us.

She nodded. "Then we'll dream of them too."

***

That evening, Skythread sailed beneath a belt of high fire-clouds. Each spark of sunset shimmered like runes across their surface—letters written in air and light, vanishing even as they formed.

Augustine watched from the observation deck, ink drying on the page. "Once," he said, "the ancients thought the sky was a mirror of the soul. Now I think it's the other way around."

Bella tilted her head. "Meaning?"

"That the sky changes because we do," he replied. "And because we choose to."

No one answered. The wind did that for them, brushing past with the sound of distant laughter—Balok's, maybe, or something older still.

The Skythread leaned into the current, sails full and true, and the storm behind them whispered one final word that only the ship could hear:

Remember.

And she did.

Book Five

Voyages of the Skythread

"The sea does not choose who sails it,
but the stars remember every name that dares their mirror."

— *Mariners' Lament*

***

Chapter One

The Return to Soahc

"The leaving stretches the canvas,
the returning paints the picture."

— *Saying of the Vale*

***

The Spine of the World fell away at last.

For days they had followed its shadowed ridges westward, the mountains rising like titans at their side, until one by one the peaks dwindled and sank into rolling hills. The air grew warmer, gentler; the clouds took on the copper hue of late autumn. Below, the land unfurled in patchwork golds and reds, the trees of Soahc's borderlands dressing themselves for winter's first whisper.

The Skythread held her course southward, sails trimmed close, hull gleaming with the pale light of a long journey nearly done. Even the ropes seemed to hum softer, as though the ship herself could sense what waited beyond the horizon.

Each morning the hills looked more familiar. Creeks glimmered where Talon remembered them, cutting through meadows gone to seed. Old roads glinted in the sunlight, the same ones they had once walked on foot years before, when the world had felt impossibly wide.

It took several days, though the crew counted each one by heartbeats and bells rather than by the turning of the sun. Conversations grew quieter. Faces turned homeward. Even the air felt weighted by remembrance.

Then, one gray-gold afternoon, Soahc came into view.

At first it was only the familiar shimmer of the lake beyond the hills—then the rising arc of stone where the sky-dock met the city wall. What had once been a short defensive parapet now stretched for nearly a mile along the southern edge of Soahc, gleaming in new-cut granite. Fresh towers stood half-finished along its length, cranes and scaffolds swaying in the wind. From the completed watch-tower flew great banners: silver and blue, the mark of the Vale and the Skyguard both.

A murmur rippled across the deck. Men and women who had seen storm and shadow together now leaned against the rail like children returning from a long exile. Oscar wiped at his eyes and pretended it was the wind.

"Take the wind out of her," Captain Marissa ordered quietly.

The sails eased, white sheets spilling light like poured water. The Skythread slowed, her song softening into a low hum that trembled through the planks beneath their feet.

"Bring her in easy," Marissa called from the helm.

The ship answered. She drifted over the last rise, shadow crossing the rooftops of the outer quarter. Bells began to ring below—first one, then a dozen more, their echoes rising to meet the Skythread's approach.

Talon stood at the prow, watching the city spread beneath them: the terraces, the gardens, the white arc of the bridge over the river. Arrabella came to stand beside him, her hand brushing his. Neither spoke. They didn't need to.

The Skythread glided at last over the heart of Soahc, her cloud-keel whispering against the high wind, until the towers of the sky-dock rose before them. With a final breath of canvas she settled into her berth, ropes cast and caught, timbers sighing like a traveler setting down a long-carried pack.

Home.

***

The Skythread settled into her berth with the soft exhale of sails gone still. Lines tightened, gangplanks dropped, and the hum of the ship eased to a contented murmur beneath their boots. Around them, Soahc's sky-dock bustled like a hive newly awakened.

Yet one sight caught every eye at once.

Along the next slipway, beneath a canopy of canvas and light, a new hull gleamed pale against the stone. Workers swarmed her frame, hammering brass rivets into curved timbers that still smelled of sap. The ship was smaller than the Skythread—half her length and finer in the lines, her design meant for speed rather than reach. A narrow keel of cloud-wood ran the full length of her belly, still tethered by silver ropes to the shaping dais.

Oscar leaned over the rail, grinning. "She's barely born," he said. "Still drawing her first breath."

Marissa folded her arms, eyes sharp with appraisal. "Fast one, by the cut of her hull. Light cargo, short hops— messenger class, if I had to guess."

Arrabella smiled faintly. "Then the dream held. We left to see what lay beyond, and they built something to follow."

Below, masons and engineers moved with easy confidence, their orders carried by voice and spell alike. The banners overhead snapped bright in the breeze: the sigil of the Vale of Eagles entwined with Soahc's crest of the rising star.

Talon rested a hand against the rail, his gaze soft. "They learned," he said quietly. "They watched us go, and they learned how to fly."

A faint smile touched Oscar's lips. "Greenbough would have liked this," he said. "Roots and wings."

Arrabella nodded, her eyes reflecting the wind-silvered light. "She'd say the same. The forest keeps her, but her work still grows."

For a long moment, no one spoke. The bells of Soahc rang again—this time not for alarm, not for mourning, but for homecoming.

Then Marissa clapped her hands, breaking the spell. "All right, you sentimental lot. Let's tie her proper, before the dockmaster starts charging us rent by the heartbeat."

Laughter rippled through the crew, the kind that meant safety at last. Ropes flew, blocks creaked, and the Skythread came to rest beside her newborn sister, the elder ship's shadow falling gently across the fresh-laid keel.

From above it looked almost like a blessing.

***

The crew had just finished tying the last mooring line when a ripple of motion stirred the far end of the sky-dock. Heads turned. Even the workers paused mid-stride.

Something—someone—approached at a rhythmic, four-beat trot.

Bella blinked.

"Talon… is that—?"

The ranger's breath left him in something like a laugh. "Of course it is."

Briar appeared between two towering stacks of supply crates, mane of braids bouncing, charms chiming like soft wooden bells. Her hooves struck the stone with confident ease—she moved like someone who belonged everywhere, yet owed allegiance to nothing but the wind.

Her eyes swept the deck, bright with wisdom and mischief.

"You're late," she said with a grin large enough to warm half the city.

Oscar nearly dropped an entire coil of rope. "BRIAR!"

Elenn—caught between awe and confusion—whispered, "That's *the* Briar? Forest-circle Briar? The one from the Telmath Leaves commentary?"

She instantly regretted blurting it out, but Briar heard and beamed.

"I've been called worse," the centaur said. "Much worse, actually. And yes—hello, young priest. I know your temple's leaf-scribe. Terrible handwriting. Lovely tea blends."

Elenn looked starstruck and mortified at the same time.

Briar turned toward Bella and Talon, warmth overtaking the teasing.

"Stormspeakers," she said softly. "You answered the sky. And it answered you back."

Bella smiled. "We only listened."

"You listened well."

A thunderous huffing approached from behind Briar.

The dockmaster—puffed, flushed, and deeply offended by the laws of physics—stormed up the ramp like a man trying to reclaim authority that had fled at first sight of hooves.

"Captain Silverbow!" he bellowed. "You cannot simply land without—Briar!—without notice! Without protocol! Without ANY—would you please stop walking ahead of me!?"

Briar stepped slightly aside, letting him bluster past as though the entire dock belonged to him personally.

He planted himself before Talon, panting.

"This is—utter chaos! Bells ringing off-sequence! Ledger sheets thrown into disarray! A centaur arriving before me, the official welcoming officer—"

Briar patted his shoulder with serene condescension.

"They'll write ballads about your leadership."

He stopped sputtering. "...will they?"

"No," she added gently. "But it soothed your heart for half a moment, didn't it?"

Elenn snorted into her sleeve.

Oscar whispered, "Dockmaster one, ego zero."

Briar looked to Talon again, expression shifting to something deeper.

"The forest remembered your return," she said quietly. "The leaves trembled this morning. The Vale stirred. And Soahc has been... restless."

Bella felt it immediately—the tone, the truth beneath the words.

Talon's hand tightened on the rail. "Restless how?"

Briar's eyes drifted west, toward the distant treeline.

"Your story is reaching for you," she said. "And it won't wait long."

The wind shifted—carrying the smell of pine, hearthfire, and the first edge of winter.

366

Behind them, the Skythread hummed, recognizing the moment.

Home was no longer an ending.

It was the beginning of what came next.

Chapter Two

Echoes Along the Keel

"A ship is never finished, only paused between voyages."

— *Dockmaster's Proverb of Soahc*

***

The smell of stone and sky-oil hung over the docks. Hammers rang like bells in the morning air—bright and measured, each strike echoing against the carved walls of Soahc's sky harbor. The **Skythread** lay in her berth beside the southern wall, sails furled, her proud hull gleaming faintly with the polish of long travel and longer memory. She seemed content to rest at last—like an old wanderer setting down a pack heavy with stories.

Oscar leaned over the rail, watching the builders below. They worked in rhythm—lift, brace, strike, check—the wordless language of those who shape what will outlive them. The rhythm carried its own strange music, and even the gulls seemed to listen between the blows.

On the open slipway beside the dock, a new vessel was taking form. Her lines were sleek and daring, her hull only half-planked, ribs of pale cloudwood curved like the bones of a

369

bird. A nameplate already hung from the scaffolding: *The Morning Zephyr.*

Beneath the name, a small plaque had been affixed in gleaming brass:

In memory of the Skythread's fallen crew, whose courage carried the wind farther than fear.

Oscar read it twice before speaking, a half-smile in his voice. "He would've hated that plaque," he murmured.

Marissa stood a short distance away, arms folded, eyes tracing the rising frame of the new ship. "Aye," she said softly. "He'd have told them to put the coin into better timber. But he'd have smiled just the same."

Arrabella came up from below, her journal under one arm, hair lifted by the sea breeze. "They say she'll be Soahc's first courier ship—built for speed, light cargo, and word-carrying between the cities."

Talon's gaze stayed on the shining keel below. "Good," he said. "The world's learning to speak again."

A group of young mages in linen vests formed a circle at the keel's base, their voices rising in soft incantation. Light spread along the grain, silver and sky-blue, tracing the curve of the timber until it pulsed like a heartbeat. The crowd that had gathered—dockhands, apprentices, children balanced on crates—broke into applause that rolled across the harbor like surf.

Marissa's voice was almost lost in the sound. "We used to be the only song in the sky," she said. "Now listen to them."

Bella smiled faintly. "We were never meant to be the last."

A gull wheeled overhead, its cry sharp against the rising wind. The bells of Soahc answered—slow, solemn—the dockmasters' blessing for a new keel. The sound rolled outward across the lake and up through the **Skythread's** masts. Somewhere deep in her timbers, the old ship answered with a low, contented hum.

Oscar rested his hands on the rail, blinking against the brightness. "Feels strange," he said quietly. "Coming home and finding the world already moving on."

Talon's voice was steady. "That's what home's meant to do. Keep growing while we're gone."

For a moment, no one spoke. The sound of hammers filled the silence—the building of what would come next. Then Bella closed her book, pressing a hand to its worn cover.

"Roots and wings," she said softly, echoing an older friend's farewell. "That's how the world remembers."

The light climbed higher along the harbor wall. The new ship's keel glowed like a blade drawn for its first voyage. And the **Skythread**, moored beside her, seemed to smile in the creak of her rigging—as if whispering a blessing to the next to rise.

***

Elenn lingered at the rail long after the applause faded, her eyes following the glow along the Zephyr's keel. Oscar stood beside her, arms braced on the rail, chin tucked down as if committing the whole scene to memory.

She hesitated—just long enough for him to notice.

"What?" Oscar said, without looking up. "You're doing the thinking-face."

"I am not," she protested, then sighed. "All right, maybe a little."

A breath of laughter escaped him. "Go on then."

Elenn's voice softened. "Briar… you've known a lot of people. A lot of stories. Did you ever hear one about a boy from the mountain outskirts? A boy who—"
She caught herself, glancing at Oscar. "—who learned to build things because breaking them hurt too much?"

Oscar blinked hard and looked away, suddenly very interested in the gulls.

Briar stepped forward from behind them, her hooves whispering over the dock's stone. The scent of pine followed her like a cloak.

"I've heard many stories," she said gently. "Some written in ink, some written in scars, and some written in the way someone looks at a new keel and forgets they're breathing."

Oscar's shoulders stiffened, then loosened, like he wasn't sure whether the words comforted him or hit too close.

Elenn glanced between them. "So… is that a yes?"

Briar's eyes warmed with quiet humor. "It is a nothing," she said, "except that you care for him. And that is a story older than any hurt he carries."

Oscar made a sound somewhere between a scoff and a laugh.

"She does this," he muttered to Elenn. "Talks like I'm a tree with feelings."

"You *are* a tree with feelings," Elenn said brightly.

"That's not helping."

Briar smiled, tapping the rail with one finger. "When the time comes, he'll tell you the truth of his own roots. Until then... let him choose which branches to show."

Elenn opened her mouth to reply—but Oscar beat her to it.

"That," he said quietly, "was incredibly unhelpful."

But he wasn't smiling because it wasn't funny.

He was smiling because it was true.

Chapter Three

Bells of Home

"A city's bells do not ring for triumph alone.
They ring to remind the weary that they are still welcome."

— *From the* **Canticles of Soahc***, Verse of Homecoming*

***

The bells of Soahc were still ringing when the crew set foot ashore.

It began as a formal salute from the dockmasters—eight strokes, clear and measured—but it grew quickly into something else: a sound that rolled through the streets and rooftops until every tower seemed to answer. From the air above, the city looked alive with motion—people spilling from workshops and markets, banners unfurled, lights kindling in upper windows like the first stars of evening.

The **Skythread** had come home.

Marissa was the first down the gangplank, boots striking the stone with the steady rhythm of someone reacquainting herself with gravity. Her uniform was clean, her silver hair tied back with precision—but her eyes betrayed her: the shimmer of memory, the weight of ghosts.

"Dock records are current," called one of the harbor clerks as she approached, quill already poised over his ledger. "Permission to record your return, Captain Veyne?"

Marissa hesitated a heartbeat, then nodded. "Record it as safe passage," she said. "And add the names of those we lost. Let the ink remember them, even if the sea forgets."

The clerk bowed low. "So noted, ma'am."

Oscar followed, boots clattering down the ramp, a grin fighting its way past the exhaustion on his face. The smell of Soahc wrapped around him like a forgotten blanket—roasted grain from the merchant square, lake reeds and resin from the carpenters' quarter, the faint iron tang of autumn in the air. After months of salt and storm, it felt like breathing again.

Children pointed up at the **Skythread** still hovering above the dock, her mooring lights pulsing softly. "It's her!" one shouted. "The Skythread's back!"

Another, smaller voice chimed in: "And look—the *Morning Zephyr!* They're building her for the new couriers!"

Oscar turned at that, smiling. Beyond the harbor cranes, the skeleton of the new ship gleamed in the evening light— her half-finished hull catching the glow of the setting sun like a promise.

Bella followed his gaze. "They'll have her flying by spring," she said quietly. "The builders say she'll outrun the wind itself."

Talon rested a hand on the railing, eyes soft. "Good. The world's learning to move faster than fear."

The crowd pressed in as more citizens arrived from the upper tiers—merchants, dockhands, guildmasters, even scholars from the lower observatories. Soahc had been busy since their last departure: new arches spanned the waterfront, the harbor's wall now fortified with glimmering wards, and the great tower of the Skyguard rose higher than before.

At the base of the steps, a figure waited in gray-blue robes: Master Geren of the Cartographer's Guild, his map case slung over one shoulder.

"You took your time," he said, smiling as Bella approached.

She returned the smile despite the weight in her eyes. "You always said a proper map takes patience."

"And perspective," he added, tapping the case. "The east is full of half-truths and rumors. Now we'll replace them with your words."

"I've brought plenty," Bella said, holding up her journal. "Some of it even true."

"Good." His eyes softened. "Truth or not, it's the living kind of story. That's the one worth keeping."

Behind them, the **Skythread's** crew spilled into the streets—laughing, shouting greetings, embracing old friends. Someone produced a flute, then a drum, and soon a melody rose—the same song played when they'd launched years before. It carried through the harbor like the echo of a tide returning.

Talon lingered at the edge of the celebration, watching the glow on the lake. The city had grown brighter in their absence, but something in its light felt older, too—steadier, wiser. He looked toward the distant curve of the new ship's keel gleaming beyond the cranes. "She's smaller," he said. "But she'll fly farther than we ever did."

Bella joined him, her voice soft as the bells fading across the water. "She'll carry what we left behind."

A young courier ran up then, breathless and beaming, a polished brass tube clutched to her chest. "Message from

Nandanoléme!" she said, offering it with both hands. "Arrived two days ago—sealed with the Silver Star."

Bella accepted it carefully and broke the seal. The parchment within shimmered faintly with **Thay'sa's** handwriting—elegant, precise, and undeniably alive.

The Veil holds. The stars are calm. The library stands unshaken. When the time comes, send word—there are roots here waiting to receive you.

Bella closed her eyes for a moment. "She's safe," she whispered. "And still watching."

Talon nodded, his gaze still turned toward the horizon. "Then so are we."

The bells tolled one final time, softer now—a benediction, not a summons. Around them, Soahc glowed in the dusk, its towers alight, its harbor alive. The **Morning Zephyr** stood beside the **Skythread**, her half-born shape catching the fire of the setting sun like a torch passed from one age to the next.

Elenn lingered near Oscar as the celebration swirled around them—laughter, drums, the rush of familiar streets filling with life. Oscar stood a little apart, hands in his pockets, staring at the Morning Zephyr's half-born hull like it held a secret no one else could see.

"You're quiet," Elenn said gently.

"I'm always quiet," Oscar replied.

"That is a spectacular lie."

He huffed, corner of his mouth twitching. "Fine. I'm… medium-quiet."

Elenn stepped closer, voice dropping. "Seeing the Zephyr—does it make you think about…" She hesitated, searching for a word that wouldn't bruise. "…before all this?"

Oscar's eyes flickered—just once, just enough to betray the weight behind them.

Before he could answer, Briar approached, her hooves soft on the stone, her presence settling around them like pine-scented dusk.

Elenn glanced at her. "Briar... you're good at reading people. Leaves. Weather. All of it. You ever... get a sense of where someone comes from? Even if they don't say?"

Oscar's shoulders tensed. "Elenn—"

Briar raised a calming hand. "I read only what is offered," she said. "But some stories leave traces. The kind that cling to a person the way moss clings to northern stone—quiet, constant, never asking to be understood."

Elenn looked to Oscar again. "Is that you?"

Oscar swallowed. "...I don't know."

Briar's voice gentled. "Roots don't demand to be spoken aloud, Oscar. They reveal themselves when someone chooses to listen."

A flush rose in his cheeks. "I didn't say anything."

"You didn't need to." Briar smiled softly. "You have the look of someone who's been bracing against the wind for years, and only just realized it stopped blowing."

Oscar blinked hard and looked away, muttering, "Super great. Love that for me."

Elenn nudged him lightly. "Hey. For what it's worth... I like this version of you. The one who doesn't have to stand alone at the rail."

He tried for a smirk, failed halfway, and settled on something more honest.

"...Yeah. Me too."

Briar inclined her head. "Then let this place be your beginning, not your refuge."

Oscar exhaled—a laugh tangled with a breath he didn't know he'd been holding. "You druids," he said, "always know how to make a man feel like a complicated tree."

Elenn grinned. "You *are* a complicated tree."

Oscar groaned. "I really walked into that one."

***

And as twilight deepened, the **Skythread**'s shadow stretched long across the water—an old ship at peace beside her heir, the air between them trembling faintly with the sound of wind yet to come.

Chapter Four

Skyfallen Light

"Still water remembers storms better than sailors do."

— *Dug*

***

The sea around Soahc was calm that morning—**too** calm.

Mists drifted low over the lake, blurring the horizon and turning the sun into a dull bronze coin. Far out on the water, the Skythread hovered half a league from shore, her lines drawn taut as if she, too, were holding her breath.

Inside the harbor hall, the air smelled of slate dust and sky-oil. Charts hung from the rafters—new trade currents, revised storm lines, inked routes traced in gold thread. Soahc had changed since their last return: stronger docks, more airships, rising towers. Yet its heart remained the same— work, wind, and the stubborn belief that the world could be rebuilt plank by plank.

Marissa stood at the long table's head, her captain's coat neat but frayed at the cuffs. Across from her waited the Harbormaster—old Rendal, whose voice had weathered more storms than the hulls he tended. Between them lay a sealed ledger bound in blue leather.

"So," Rendal said, tapping the cover, "you brought her home."

Marissa nodded. "Not whole," she replied. "But true."

Rendal's eyes softened. "That's more than most can claim."

He opened the ledger and lifted his pen. "The Skythread of Soahc, returned after nearly two years abroad. Cargo: charts, reports, relics. Crew: diminished. Captain—"

A pause, heavy as surf.

"Tirpik Orem?"

Marissa did not flinch. "He fell in the eastern reach. The sea has him now."

Rendal bowed his head. "Then let the harbor remember him."

He wrote the line with deliberate care:

Tirpik Orem — Lost with Honor.

Ink whispered across paper. Outside, the fog thinned. The first clean bells of morning began to ring.

Oscar stood near the hall's back wall, hands shoved in his coat pockets. Ledgers of loss unsettled him; too neat, too final. He'd survived too much to be boxed into a column. Elenn stood beside him, her fingers worrying the grain of the table.

She didn't look at him when she spoke.

"What happened to you out there?" Elenn asked softly. "Not the part the crew talks about. The part you haven't told anyone."

Oscar drew in a slow breath, eyes fixed on the window where the morning mist curled like something remembering its shape.

"When it happened… when I fell," he said, "I remember seeing Dug."

His voice stayed low, steady only because it had to be.

"It was quiet. It didn't hurt. It felt like the world was letting go of me—or maybe I was letting go of it."

A faint tremor passed through his fingers.

"And then something pulled me back."

Elenn turned toward him, searching his face.

He didn't look at her; his gaze stayed on the mist.

"Back in the Dirgewood," he said quietly, "Bella told me something. She said I didn't have to make sense of it — just live it. That that's what the living are for."

He breathed out. "I've been trying to hold onto that."

He rubbed his thumb against the seam of his coat.

"I don't know what it was," he continued. "Or why. Dug said—"

He stopped, brow tightening. "I can't remember what he even said. I remember… Archons, and then I remember being alive in Archeron."

He shook his head, frustration catching in his voice. "It's like the middle pieces are missing. Or someone took them. And whatever I am now… it isn't who I was."

There was no fear in Elenn's expression — only the steadiness of someone choosing to stay beside a truth instead of running from it.

"You're still you," she said quietly.

"I hope so," he murmured. "Most of the time."

He managed a crooked smile that was half apology, half confession.

"Another tale," he said, "for calmer weather. Or when I finally understand why I'm still here."

From the front, Rendal closed the ledger with a soft thump.

"Captain Veyne," he said, rising, "the city owes you and yours a debt. Soahc is stronger because you returned."

Marissa inclined her head. "We only carried the wind," she said. "The builders and dreamers kept it."

Rendal extended his hand, palm down. "Then the old oath," he said. "For tradition's sake."

Marissa laid her hand atop his.

"By the water that bears us," he intoned,

"by the stones that hold us, we pledge to guard what is given, to mend what is broken, and to send forth what must sail again."

Marissa echoed it. "To guard, to mend, to send forth."

Rendal smiled. "Then go. The docks are yours."

A breath seemed to leave the hall — relief, release.

Outside, sunlight pierced the last veils of mist, catching the Skythread's masts. Her sails, still furled, glimmered faintly like wings remembering flight.

At the door, Elenn paused as Oscar stepped past.

"When you're ready," she said, "I'll want the whole of it. Not the easy version."

Oscar gave a small, honest nod.

"When I know it," he said. "And when I'm not afraid of the answer."

He hesitated, then added, almost to himself:

"Some stories don't start where you think they do."

And as the bells of Soahc rolled across the water, the crew of the Skythread stepped into the brightening day— ready to meet whatever horizon waited next.

Chapter Five

The Quiet Between Winds

"Between one storm and the next lies the truth of why we sail."

— Inscription found on the Skythread's mainmast

***

Morning found them aboard the **Skythread** once more.

The city below still dreamed, its rooftops pale with frost, chimneys sending up slow curls of smoke. The lake mirrored the first light of day—thin, silver, and trembling. From here, Soahc seemed peaceful in a way few places ever managed to be: not silent, but content.

Talon sat on the edge of the forecastle, his boots dangling above the empty air, a mug of cooling tea in one hand. Arrabella leaned against the railing beside him, a blanket draped across her shoulders. Neither spoke for a long while. The wind between them did the talking—soft and steady, humming through the rigging like an old song remembered.

"She sleeps easier than I expected," Bella said finally, meaning the ship.

"She's earned it," Talon replied. "So have we."

They watched as the sun cleared the far hills, spilling gold across the half-finished hull of the **Morning Zephyr**. Workers were already gathering at the docks below, their voices faint in the cold air. Even from this distance, they could hear the soft ring of hammers—the same rhythm that had followed them across continents.

"Soahc's changed," Bella murmured. "Grown in every direction at once. Walls where there were roads. Roads where there were rivers."

Talon nodded, eyes on the horizon. "And somewhere beyond all that, Tortosia's loremaster is trying to do the same."

She turned, surprised. "You heard from him?"

He held up a folded scrap of parchment, the seal marked with the sigil of a tortoise framed by script. "Delivered last night—before we reached the lake. He writes that he's found 'threads of old stone' in the ruins east of the Skyreach. Patterns in the glyphs that match Soahc's foundations. He thinks this place and his little city were once part of a single network—a line of light that stretched from one coast to the other."

Bella took the letter, reading the cramped lines with a scholar's fascination. "A ley channel?"

"Maybe. Or something older." He paused. "He says if we follow the symbols carved on the southern face of the docks here, they point east. Always east."

Her lips curved. "So even the world wants to stay connected."

"Seems so." He smiled faintly. "He asked if we'd come see for ourselves one day."

Bella looked out over the water, eyes bright in the morning light. "Someday," she said softly. "But not yet. The wind's still catching its breath."

A gull wheeled overhead, its shadow brushing the deck like a passing thought. Below, the sound of hammers built to a steady rhythm—hope made audible. The *Morning Zephyr*'s skeleton caught the rising sun, glowing white and gold, its timbers streaked with sky-oil and promise.

Bella closed the letter carefully and slipped it into her journal. "It feels strange," she said. "The way the world keeps moving even when we stop."

"That's how we know it's alive," Talon said. "And how we know we belong to it."

They sat together a while longer, listening to the wind, the hammers, the faint murmur of life below.

Then Bella turned to him. "Do you ever miss it? The danger? The not knowing?"

He smiled, just barely. "Sometimes. But I think I'm learning to love the quiet between winds."

The ship creaked beneath them, her timbers settling as though she'd heard.

Below, the bells of Soahc began to chime the hour—clear, bright, steady. Each note rang like a heartbeat across the harbor.

Bella reached for his hand. "Then maybe this is what we were meant to find," she said. "Not another storm to chase, but a place where the wind can rest."

Talon nodded. "And still remember how to fly."

They stayed there until the last of the mist burned away and the day came fully to life. Around them, Soahc breathed, rebuilding, renewing, remembering.

The **Skythread** swayed gently in her berth, sails furled, shadow touching the half-built hull of the **Morning Zephyr**—the old and the new joined by light and air, bound by everything they had carried home.

Chapter Six

The Weight of the Wind

"Some burdens can't be set down—only carried with greater grace."

— *Saying of the Skyguard*

***

Night thinned slowly over Soahc.

Below deck, the Skythread breathed in long, quiet creaks—old timbers settling, ropes sighing in their sleep. Oscar lay awake in his bunk, eyes following the slow ripple of lanternlight across the beams above. The ship's hum had softened since they returned, no longer a heartbeat, merely a memory trying to rest.

He rolled to his side. No matter how long he stared at the ceiling, he still felt the pull of that other place—the hollow between heartbeats where he'd died.

Bella's words from the evening lingered like an echo:

"You didn't come back by accident. The Archons don't deal in luck."

And Greenbough's voice drifted in behind it, soft as wind through cedars:

"Death isn't an ending, Oscar—it's the breath the world takes before it speaks again.

The circle turns because it must, not because it's fair. But if the Fates sent you back, then the circle wanted your voice in it still."

He'd nodded at the time, pretending to understand. He wasn't sure he ever would.

He pressed the heels of his hands against his eyes. "If the universe wanted something," he muttered, "it could've just asked."

A low huff answered him—warm, deep, and impossibly familiar. The kind of sound that lifted the small hairs on the back of his neck a heartbeat before his mind caught up.

Oscar froze.

"...Dug?"

The air changed—pine, wet earth, and the weight of rain-heavy fur. Something vast and kind pushed close without shape, and the bunk dipped beneath a presence too real to doubt.

No words. Just that steady, grounding pressure of comfort.

A paw against his chest that wasn't a paw at all, but felt like one.

Oscar swallowed hard. It hurt. It helped.

"You don't think I was... meant for this either, do you?"

The warmth pressed closer. A breath moved his hair.

Not meant. **Needed.**

Not speech—just certainty.

Then the presence eased, as quietly as it had arrived. The air cooled. The shadows stilled. The ache in Oscar's chest, however, loosened—pain shifting into something steadier. A weight, yes, but the kind that proved you were still standing.

He pushed upright, letting his feet touch the planks. The ship felt awake beneath him—listening, patient.

390

"Alright," he said into the quiet, voice rasped but true. "Message received."

He reached for his boots. As he stood, the lantern above swung on its hook, its flame catching the brass rim of his compass. The needle quivered—once—then settled due east.

Oscar let out a breath, not quite a laugh.

"East it is, then."

Above him, the Skythread gave a soft creak—as if agreeing. Outside, the first bell of morning rang across Soahc: clear, unhurried, full of promise.

Oscar stepped toward the ladder.

For the first time since returning, he breathed without feeling the weight of the wind pressing down.

Only its direction.

Chapter Seven

Lanternlight

"Every voyage begins twice—once in the telling,
and once in the leaving."

— *Dockside Saying of Soahc*

***

The sun had climbed past the towers, spilling long lines
of light through the open hatches of the Skythread. The scent
of fresh pitch and linen drifted along her decks; workers
moved like ghosts through the morning haze, checking ropes,
patching canvas, mending what the journey had worn thin.

Oscar sat on a coil of rope near the aft rail, turning a
brass compass over in his hands. The needle quivered faintly
even though the ship was moored—it always did when the
wind was restless.

Footsteps sounded behind him.

Elenn appeared, sleeves rolled, a length of sailcloth slung
over one shoulder.

"You've been up here since dawn," she said.

"Couldn't sleep," he admitted. "Every time I close my
eyes, I still hear the rigging hum."

She smiled. "That's the Skythread's way of asking what comes next."

Oscar glanced toward the harbor where the *Morning Zephyr* stood on her slipway—half dressed in sunlight, workers fitting her new wings.

"Looks like the city's already answered."

"Maybe for them." Elenn set the folded sailcloth beside him and leaned against the rail. "But for you?"

He flipped the compass shut and slipped it into his vest. "Captain says the Skythread will fly again come spring. Not trade runs—charting. Farther west, maybe beyond the Broken Shoals. They'll need a full crew."

Her eyes lifted toward the horizon where the sky burned pale with promise.

"Then you'll go?"

He hesitated. "If they'll have me. And if… there's reason enough to come back."

Elenn turned toward him, the morning light catching the faint freckles along her cheeks.

"Then give yourself both reasons," she said softly. "Go because the world still needs to be seen. Come back because someone's waiting to hear what you found."

He looked at her—really looked—then down at her hand resting beside his on the rail.

"You'd wait?"

"I've already followed you through one storm," she said with a small, sure smile. "I'm not stopping now. Maybe the Skythread's big enough for two people to chase the same wind."

For a heartbeat, the ship creaked—a low, contented sound, like an old friend clearing her throat.

Oscar let out a quiet laugh. "She agrees."

Elenn squeezed his hand once, steady and warm.

"Then we'll see where she takes us next."

Below, the dock bells tolled—the start of another workday. The wind shifted, tugging gently at the loose ends of sailcloth. The Skythread seemed to breathe, as though already dreaming of flight.

Above the harbor, two gulls wheeled together into the new morning light.

Epilogue

The Passing Light

"The young do not walk in our footsteps. They walk in our light—and carry it farther than we ever dreamed."

— *Attributed to an old griffon-master of Soahc*

***

Below, unaware of the watching heavens, the Skythread sailed on—carrying her small, fragile miracles.

At the bow, Oscar and Elenn stood shoulder to shoulder beneath the new constellations, the wind braiding through their hair, their laughter drift-soft against the hum of the ship's heart.

High on the upper deck, Arrabella and Talon lingered near the rigging, watching them in quiet amusement.

Talon smiled faintly. "Think he knows what he's doing?"

Bella tilted her head. "No. But he's learning."

She watched a moment longer, then lifted a finger as though marking the tip of Oscar's nose through the haze below.

"And if he forgets…"

Her smile sharpened.

"I'll remind him. Kindly, at first."

Talon chuckled. "And after kindly?"

The dangerous curl of her grin returned—the one that made ogres hesitate and scholars rethink their arguments.

"Then I'll make sure the stars remember it too."

Talon exhaled a soft laugh. "Remind me never to get on your bad side again."

"You already did," she said, bumping his shoulder. "You're still here."

Her eyes softened. "So maybe there's hope for him, too."

The Skythread's lanterns dimmed to a warm pulse, matching the rhythm of the sea below. Above them, Faloswansei soared, his shadow slicing the dawn like a quill stroke across parchment.

***

High above the quieting storms of Soahc, the newborn Celestial Dragon watched—her great wings trailing ribbons of dawnlight across the upper currents.
She had only just awakened, still half spirit and half flame, yet already her gaze turned downward toward the fragile blue world below.

In the first hours of her awareness, she sifted through the echo of memories inherited from the Celestials before her—vast, cold recollections of cycles turning, stars forming, worlds drifting through epochs she had never lived. They were the memories of beings who had shaped creation yet never truly touched it. All that eternity, she realized, carried a kind of hollowness: a perfection so absolute it left no room for wonder.

She felt, distantly, the weight her predecessors had borne—duty without curiosity, vigilance without affection.

They guarded worlds, yes, but from the vantage of infinity. They observed lives the way one observed weather patterns or tides: important in their function, but never in their feeling. **No Celestial had ever known the warmth of a single fleeting moment... because nothing fleeting had ever belonged to them.**

Yet below, a mortal ship moved with quiet purpose. She felt the hum of its life: hearts uncertain yet unbroken, minds daring enough to reach beyond what they could hold.

To know a world, she realized, one must first see it through the eyes of those who live in it.

Immortal existence leads, inexorably, to distance—to the long forgetting of everything that breathes and changes.

But mortals—even elves—are not immortal.

They feel their days.

They burn each heartbeat bright.

They give meaning to things that pass.

For three days she lingered near the little ship, drawn not by duty but by wonder. She felt their laughter, their fear, their fierce resolve to keep learning no matter how wide the sky became around them.

And in those fleeting moments, she saw something no Celestial had understood before: **the beauty of limitation.**

Before her ascent was complete, she reached out—not in command, but in kinship.

Her light brushed the Skythread's hull, threading through wood, metal, cloth, and cloud.

A seam of silver appeared in the captain's quarters, where no door had been. Behind it, a small, pale orb floated in still air, glowing like candlelight through mist. It pulsed once—slow, steady—as though remembering the breath it had only just begun to take.

"It's alive," Arrabella whispered.

Corwin knelt beside her, eyes reflecting the soft shimmer. "Alive… or remembering how to be," he murmured.

The light brightened, its rhythm echoing their own.

Someone—no one ever agreed who—breathed the word:

"Cloudheart."

Corwin gave a rueful smile.

"Careful naming things," he said. "Names tend to stick."

The glow pulsed again—gentle, certain—as though in agreement.

Far above, the ascending Celestial lingered one last time, her vast form framed against the birth of dawn.

To know a world, she thought again, one must first see it through mortal eyes.

Then she turned toward Eternity and was gone—leaving behind the ship, the crew, and the newborn heart that would one day help her understand them all.

***

End of Volume IV

Orbus Ignotum

Final Page Bridge

—To the Next Volume—

***

The Skythread did not sleep once she returned home.

In the decades that followed, she sailed light and far—coast to coast, storm to storm, carrying maps, messages, and the quiet courage of those who refused to let the world grow small again. Her Cloudheart learned new winds; her crew changed and changed again. And though only a handful of her journeys were ever written down, those few were enough to kindle a legend.

Oscar remained with Skythread through those years, quill never far from hand, learning the winds as much as the words. Elenn stayed beside him—not as shadow or shield, but as companion—sharing in the long arcs between storms and the quiet wonders no map could hold. Their adventures did not end with this telling; they simply sailed beyond its edge.

The rest of her voyages are stories for another volume, another fire,
another night.

But legends, even beloved ones, do not stop the turning of the ages.

Three centuries passed.

The coastlines shifted. Rivers wandered. Forests reclaimed what wars had stolen. Cities rose where none had stood, and disappeared where many once had. Children who grew up beneath the Skythread's shadow told her name to their grandchildren, and they to theirs, until memory wrapped her like a second hull.

Yet not all stories unfold in the years after glory.

Some wait in silence.

Some wait in shadow.

Some wait for a promise made long before they were born.

And so the tale that comes next begins not with a voyage, but with a reckoning long delayed.

When the years had stretched past four hundred, when even the most ancient trees bowed heavy with time, Arrabella of Lóthanarë felt the last pages of her own life turning.

She had seen peace, loss, rising nations, and the long hum of years—but one truth still unsettled her heart.

One story Talon Silverbow had never told.

Not the battles.

Not the trials.

Not the day he lost an arm, nor the day he gained a world.

She wanted the story *before* all that—before Genni, before Garick, before fate threaded his bow to hers.

So on the final quiet night of her life, she asked him:

"Talon… tell me the truth of you."

And in the silence that followed, the world held its breath.

For the tale she asked for—the tale he had never spoken aloud—is the one that will shape the storm still waiting beyond the horizon.

A storm four centuries in the making.
A shadow that never forgot.
And a final reckoning with a foe who waited just as long.

***

Volume V — The Final Thread
begins centuries later,
where the world is new again…
and one ancient story is finally ready to be told.

Appendix A

It's Late and I Forgot Things

(with notes, pronunciations, and assorted reminders from those who should have written them down sooner)

***

Names & Companions

- Talon Silverbow *(TAL-uhn SIL-ver-boh)*
  Ranger of the Vale of Eagles; apprentice of Garick and wielder of Moonfyre, a bow born of Isa's shard. Calm in storms, lethal in silence, and—though he'd deny it—the steady heart that Skythread sails by.

- Arrabella *(AIR-uh-BEL-uh)*
  Mage of Runedragon's Sapphire Spire; keeper of Isa's memory and voice of the Skythread's conscience. Her bond to Ailinórë deepens as the world grows stranger.

- Oscar *(AHS-kur)*
  Historian, reluctant hero, and officially "twice-returned" (once by mistake, once by miracle). Holder of the Owl Key, recorder of truths others avoid, and future father of legends he cannot yet imagine.

- Elenn *(EH-len)*
  Priestess of Paladin and healer aboard the Skythread. Quiet strength wrapped in dry wit. Partner to Oscar, though neither is brave enough to say it yet.

- Marissa Veyne *(muh-RISS-uh TOLL-und)*
  Captain of the Skythread after Tirpik's fall. Sharp-

eyed, steady-handed, and known for saying, "Wind can't be commanded—only convinced."

- Tirpik Orem *(TIR-pik OR-em)*
  Former captain of the Skythread. Lost with honor in the eastern reaches; his name is etched in brass on the ship's inner bell.

- Greenbough *(GREEN-bow — rhymes with "now")*
  Druid of the Dirgewood. Patient as river-stone, stubborn as oak, fond of teaching lessons the long way around.

- Dug *(D-uh-G)*
  Grizzly of the Elysium Fields; guardian of the Oathbearers. Wise in ways mortals aren't built for. Does not respect doors, propriety, or the boundary between worlds.

- Augustine *(AW-gus-TEEN)*
  Tortosian loremaster whose ears can hear the mathematics in thunder. Often right; always slow; never rushed.

- Faloswansei *(FAH-loh-SWAHN-say)*
  Golden griffon and sometime troublemaker. Loyal to Talon and Arrabella, and occasionally to gravity.

***

Places

- Soahc *(SO-ahk)*
  City of bells and airships. Seat of the Skyguard. Lives, grows, and renovates faster than its maps can keep up.

- The Dirgewood *(DIRJ-wood)*
  A forest where memory pools like water. Home to Greenbough and older things that listen.

- Tortosia *(tor-TOH-see-uh)*
  Cliff-built city of scholars, masons, and impossible staircases. Augustine's home.

- Nandanoléme *(NAHN-dahn-oh-LAY-meh)*
  Elven mountain-top library where stone and living tree share the same breath. Contains more portals than hallways.

- Vale of Eagles *(vayl of EE-guhlz)*
  Talon and Bella's homeland. Windswept ridges, old orchards, and a memory for every stone.

- Ravenglass *(RAY-ven-glas)*
  Western port built on the bones of older empires. Gateway to the unknown.

***

Artifacts & Relics

- Ailinórë *(EYE-lih-NOR-ay)*
  "The Ring of Earth Elemental Command."
  Forged in the Age of Breaking for Isa's shield-bearer. Now bound to Arrabella, awaiting the full price—and gift—of its inheritance.

- Moonfyre *(MOON-fyer)*
  Bow of mithril and silver flame. Forged from Isa's shard, capable of miracles and ruin in equal measure.

- The Owl Key *(owl kee)*
  Fragment of Archeron's judgment. Cold, whispering, honest. Oscar's uneasy companion.
- Cloudheart *(KLOWD-hart)*
  Living soul of the Skythread—gift of the newborn Celestial Dragon. Not quite a spirit; not merely an engine; something between breath and dream.
- Garick's Compass *(GAIR-ik's KUM-pus)*
  A simple relic of guidance, forged by a young Talon long ago. Carried by Garick until his death, returned to Talon by fate, and now an heirloom of two generations.

***

Ships

- Skythread *(SKY-thred)*
  Elder ship of Soahc. Part wood, part cloud, all stubbornness. Has more personality than several members of her crew.
- Morning Zephyr *(MOR-ning ZEF-ur)*
  New courier vessel built in Soahc. Swift, elegant, bright with promise.
- Mistmantle *(MIST-man-tul)*
  Balok Ironforge's earlier vessel. Prototype and inspiration for the Skythread's design.

***

Sayings & Proverbs

- "Roots and wings." Elven reminder to remember one's beginnings without clinging to them.
- "Between storms." Sailors' phrase for peace earned the hard way.
- "The sea remembers." Soahc blessing used at weddings, funerals, and first departures.
- "Every keel carries an echo." Skyguard craftsman's warning that ships learn their crews.

***

Miscellany

- Elysium Fields *(ih-LEE-zee-um feeldz)*
  Realm of peace where noble beasts go when the world grows quiet.
- Archeron *(AR-ker-on)*
  Opposite reflection of Elysium. Plane of shadow, consequence, and truths no one wants.
- Cála-nírë *(KAH-lah NEER-ay)*
  "Sanctuary Flame." Hidden light at the Veil's edge; protects memory, dream, and soul.

***

Final Margin Note

"If you find this, light a lantern.
Someone's still out there, following the wind."
— Scrawled on the last page of Oscar's journal,
Year 350, Second Age

Appendix B

Voyage of the Skythread Timeline

A Chronicle of the Great Voyage
Years 349–350, Second Age

***

1. Departure from Soahc — Spring, 349 SA

- The *Skythread II* launches from the Vale of Eagles under **Captain Tirpik** and **Navigator Marissa**.
- Mission: chart the eastern world and study the Veil's patterns after the age of storms.
- **Oscar**, young archer and aspiring naturalist, joins to learn fieldcraft and basic spellwork.
- Course set eastward into uncharted skies.

***

2. Guardians' Island — Early Summer, 349 SA

- The crew discovers a hidden sanctuary led by a **Brass Dragon Matriarch** and her followers.
- The dragon's accidental revelation of her true form unleashes dragonfear — Oscar famously stands his ground.
- Understanding replaces fear; the Skythread departs peacefully, location unrecorded to preserve its secrecy.

- ***

3. The Tortosian War — Late Summer to Autumn, 349 SA

- The *Skythread* intervenes when **goblin armies** besiege the Tortosian cliffs.
- Tirpik orders the crew to assist from the air, turning the tide but altering the course of local history.
- Victory brings uneasy respect; they remain through winter, helping rebuild the shattered outposts.

***

4. Winter Among the Tortosians — Winter 349 to Spring 350 SA

- The ship winters amid the mountain settlements, trading knowledge of skycraft and cloud-forging.
- Waterfalls return with the thaw — the Season of Voices.
- Oscar studies weather and botany while Bella exchanges knowledge with local scholars.

***

5. Passing the Guardians' Coast — Early Spring, 350 SA

- On the return course eastward, the *Skythread* passes near Guardians' old home.
- The lands once alive are desolate and scorched.

***

6. The Dirgewood and the Sea of Roots — Late Spring to Early Summer, 350 SA

- The ship enters the newly formed **Sea of Roots**, bordered by the ancient Dirgewood.

- For weeks, the crew charts glowing waters, drifting trees, and harmonic echoes from the Veil.
- The **Ancient Elves** are glimpsed among the canopy, watching but unapproachable.
- Bella records the first verified instances of Veil resonance affecting natural ecosystems.

***

7. The Celestial Dragon's Ascension — Summer Solstice, 350 SA

- Over several days, the heavens blaze with silver light.
- A **Celestial Dragon** rises into the sky, ascending to become a new constellation.
- The crew witnesses the event in reverence — a cosmic realignment restoring balance to the Veil.
- Two months of study follow as they catalogue the aftereffects on tide, wind, and dreamflow.

***

8. The Realm of Arden — Late Summer to Autumn, 350 SA

- Arrival at **Arden**, the shining city sustained by the Celestial Dragon's lingering energy.
- The crew discovers a civilization of longevity, mastery, and stillness — the pinnacle and peril of control.
- Six great lessons emerge:
    1. Power without humility becomes dependence.
    2. Longevity without renewal breeds stagnation.
    3. Memory without pain breeds amnesia.
    4. Magic tethered to place becomes a cage.

412

5. Purity pursued too far becomes sterility.

6. Balance requires imperfection.

- Bella's reflection defines the voyage's heart:
  "They live long, but they do not live wide."
- With respect and melancholy, the Skythread departs westward.

***

9. Return to the Vale of Eagles — Late Autumn, 350 SA

- Familiar peaks rise; the *Skythread II* crosses her own wake.
- Lanterns and bells welcome her home to Soahc.
- Her maps, logs, and journals redefine the known world: the continents connected, the skies recorded, the Veil mapped.
- The crew disembarks changed — not by what they conquered, but by what they understood.

Appendix C

The Cloudheart and the Celestial Ascension

"She was born of wood, metal, cloth, and the clouds."
— Traditional shipwright's proverb, Soahc (2nd Age 334)

Origins of the Skythread

The *Skythread* was the first true skysailing vessel crafted by the united races of the Second Age.

- **Humans** envisioned her and shaped her hull from living sky-oak.
- **Dwarves** forged her spine and keels of sky-steel tempered in mountain flame.
- **Elves** wove her cloud-silk sails, light enough to catch sun and starlight alike.
- **Gnomes** laid the harmonics and spell-engines that let her balance between air-current and enchantment.

She was a wonder of cooperation—a mortal dream made manifest, meant to explore the upper winds and reconnect the scattered cities of the world.

The Ascending Celestial

At the turning of the season above Dirgewood, a new **Celestial Dragon** began her rise.
She was young, radiant, and uncertain—ascending to take the place of the elder who had long guarded the Veil.
As she climbed through the thinning clouds, her light brushed the high skies of Soahc.
For three days and nights she drifted near a single mortal craft that held her attention: the *Skythread*.

From that fragile vessel she felt something wholly new— hearts that beat with hope and fear, minds that built not for power but for wonder.
And she thought:

To know a world, one must first see it through the eyes of those who live in it.

Immortal existence, she understood, leads to distance and the soft forgetting of all that breathes and changes.
But the mortal races—even the long-lived elves—are not immortal.
They suffer, rejoice, create, and lose; and in doing so, they give every heartbeat weight.
Through them, the world remembers itself.

The Gift of the Cloudheart

Before her ascent was complete, the Celestial reached out—not in command, but in kinship. Her light threaded through **wood, metal, cloth, and the clouds**, infusing the vessel with a fragment of her living essence. When dawn broke, a seam of silver appeared in the captain's quarters where no door had been.
Behind it hovered a pale orb that pulsed like a slow breath.

415

"It's alive," Arrabella said.

"Alive, or remembering how to be," answered Corwin.

Someone—no one remembered who—breathed the word *Cloudheart*.

Corwin smiled faintly. "Careful naming things," he warned. "Names tend to stick."

Thus the name endured.
The *Cloudheart* was never bright like a sun; its light was the quiet glow of awareness—listening, learning, and dreaming. Through it, the Ascending Celestial could sense the world not as a god above it, but as a traveler within it.

Meaning and Legacy

The *Skythread* did not become divine.
She remained a mortal ship—crewed by mortal souls—but she carried within her the empathy of the heavens.
Every voyage she undertook thereafter was shared by the unseen consciousness of the young Celestial who sought to understand creation through mortal eyes.

Scholars of later years would say that this moment marked the birth of the "Age of Sky," when divine curiosity and mortal craft first met and neither was diminished.
The *Cloudheart* still beats softly in the hull of the *Skythread*, a reminder that even the gods learn best from those who dare to live.

***

From the Codex of the Celestial Weave

Collected by the Chroniclers of Nandanoléme and annotated by the crew of the Skythread

"The stars breathe when balance returns."

— *Inscription upon the High Mirror of the Moonwell*

***

I. The Celestial Dragons

In every age, a **Celestial Dragon** rises to watch over the world.

Their reigns span roughly ten thousand years—ages measured not by crowns, but by breath and balance.

When one's light fades, another awakens—not born in mortal fashion, but stirred from a **seed** of radiance hidden deep within the world's luminous heart.

When the Veil trembles, when shadow and grace draw too close, the Seed stirs.

Its awakening renews the Weave of magic, dream, and divine order.

It is not a creature of conquest, but of **continuity**—a guardian ensuring that time, memory, and light remain in harmony.

The Celestial of this age rose on the summer solstice of Year 350 of the Second Age.

The Skythread's crew recorded the birth while sailing over the northern Dirgewood:

a forested storm that sang in color, a dawn that bled silver through every reflection, and a light that cast no shadow.

From that night onward, tides bent subtly, magic thinned and reformed, and the dreams of mortals began to flow once more into Eternity.

***

II. The Wardens of the Northern Seed

Nearly a thousand years before the recorded First Age— long before kingdoms rose—a reclusive elven enclave found the resting place of the Celestial Seed.

They became its **Wardens,** keeping silent vigil beneath roots and snow.

When the Skythread discovered them, their chronicler, *Elaren the Long-Minded,* revealed that their watch had lasted eleven centuries.

They had seen lesser dragons rise and fall, rifts open and seal, and still the Seed slept—until this age's awakening.

"The Celestial does not choose through love or wrath," Elaren told Oscar and Greenbough.

"It weighs the world and decides if it is worthy of continuity. We are but the ink upon its breath."

These elves, unchanged by time, saw themselves not as priests but as **witnesses**—scribes of a divine rhythm no mortal could command.

***

III. The Thinning of the Veil

The Veil—once a radiant barrier dividing the Prime from the Outer Realms—has grown more porous with each passing age.

In the First Age, it shimmered but held; by the dawn of the Second, it **breathed**.

418

This thinning was not decay but design.

It allowed Elysium's spirits to guide the living and Archeron's whispers to test them, maintaining equilibrium between compassion and resolve.

Even the **Oathbearers**—agents of purpose rather than dominion—were again permitted to walk the mortal world.

The Celestial Dragons govern this ebb and flow.

They tighten the Veil when imbalance festers and loosen it when the world grows forgetful, ensuring that faith, fear, and freedom coexist.

***

IV. The Changing of Magic

Since the First Age, the nature of magic has transformed.

Once it was **commanded**—a force that answered divine words without question.

Now it is **courted**—a living resonance that responds to intent, empathy, and the truth of the caster's spirit.

Healing, once effortless, now demands both skill and sincerity.

Resurrection, once the right of the devoted, is now the gift only of those whose souls are anchored in the **Outer Planes**.

The divine no longer serve mortal summons; they act through the Weave itself, woven by meaning rather than command.

As Anna of Trechellus once told Talon Silverbow:

"In my day, to heal was to ask the Light.

In yours, it is to *earn* it."

***

V. The Renewal of Dreams

When the Veil fractured and the Syk were twisted by the Crimson Arcanum, the dreamstream to Eternity was severed. Prophecy faded, nightmares multiplied, and the sleeping minds of mortals drifted unmoored.

But when the Talon and Arrabella connected the **Cála-nírë** beneath Nandanoléme to Eternity. The conduit opened anew.

The Syk, once perverted into shredders, were freed from their torment.

They remain now as **custodians of the Dreamstream**, guiding dreams through the restored channels to Eternity— not messengers, but keepers of balance.

From that moment forward, the dreams of mortals once again found their rightful home—gathered, renewed, and preserved.

***

VI. The Balance of the Ages

The newborn Celestial, now awakening to full awareness, sees the mingling of the mortal and divine as necessary, not profane.

It deems that enlightenment does not lie in separation from the cosmos, but in **harmony with it**—a recognition that courage, compassion, and curiosity are the truest prayers the living can offer.

The Oathbearers remain the bridge, not between gods and mortals, but between **purpose and choice**.

Through them, the Veil holds steady, neither shutting out the divine nor letting chaos flood in.

So long as mortals strive against shadow and uphold the balance, the Weave will endure, and Eternity will dream.

***

Captain's Log: Addendum

Month 12, Year 349 of the Second Age
— recorded by Marissa Windborne, acting captain of the Skythread.

"Tonight the heavens themselves tore open, not in fury but in revelation.

We saw it — a storm made of song and light, the Celestial Dragon's birth.

The crew knelt without command. Even the wind paused, as if listening.

Since then, our sleep has changed. Dreams come steady, and kind.

I believe Eternity remembers us again.

The stars exhale, and the world dreams with them."

***

—Filed and verified by Corwin of Nandanoléme,
Archivist of the Moonwell, Keeper of the Third Loom.

Acknowledgment

No story is ever written alone.

To my family—thank you for your patience and encouragement through every long night spent shaping this tale. Your love is the light that keeps me steady.

To my friends and fellow adventurers around the table, past and present—these pages are rooted in the stories we built together. Every laugh, every battle, and every journey carried into dawn became part of this world.

To those who read these words—thank you for stepping into the Chronicles of Talon and Arrabella. Stories live only when they are shared, and you keep this one alive.

To Paul Lucas—thank you for lending your vision and talent to the cover of this volume. Your art brought color and form to Talon and Arrabella's world in a way that words alone could not.

And finally, to absent friends whose voices still echo—you remain part of the path, and always will.

**

About the Author

Patrick Dandrea has been building fantasy worlds and telling stories for more than four decades. A lifelong Dungeon Master, he began crafting adventures in the late 1970s and never stopped. His writing blends the sweep of epic fantasy with the intimacy of character-driven tales, shaped by countless hours at the table with friends, family, and fellow travelers.

He lives in the Northeastern United States with his wife and a small menagerie of beloved companions. Many of his characters are inspired by those he has walked beside—people and animals alike—each leaving their mark in memory and myth.

***